THE HERBALIST'S SECRET

ANNABELLE MARX

Storm

Quotes throughout are drawn from the following publications:
Herbal Delights by Mrs C F Leyel (1937)
The Englishman's Doctor by John Harington (1607)
Elixirs of Life by Mrs C F Leyel (1948)
The Complete Herbal by Nicholas Culpeper (1653)
Compassionate Herbs by Mrs C F Leyel (1946)

To request permissions, contact the publisher at rights@stormpublishing.co

Ebook ISBN: 978-1-80508-106-7
Paperback ISBN: 978-1-80508-108-1

Cover design: Beth Free, Studio Nic&Lou
Cover images: Shutterstock

Published by Storm Publishing.
For further information, visit:
www.stormpublishing.co

'A rob of Elderberries will prevent a chill after bathing. Coltsfoot syrup cures a simple cold, and confection of wild roses a sore throat, and who indeed could refuse such herbal delights as a nightcap of syrup of Cowslips, or a conserve of lilies for a tired heart?'

Herbal Delights by Mrs C F Leyel

PROLOGUE

Two small bodies, lifeless and cold. One boy, one girl. Someone has taken the time to present them neatly, arms laid carefully by their sides, hair swept off their faces. The girl's smocked dress is soaking and grass-stained but has been smoothed out to give the impression of modesty, the boy has one shoe missing and his sailor suit is too small, puckered at the top of the arms, a slight rip on the collar. The little girl has the fragment of blue cotton fabric held in her slightly pudgy hand, grains of sand under her fingernails, a tiny silver bracelet on her wrist, a wisp of weed wrapped around it.

They are lying exactly perpendicular to the water, the very slight *slap, slap* of the waves the only sound to be heard. The sand around the bodies has been smoothed over, and there are footprints down to the water. There is a deep groove in the sand, where a small boat must have recently been resting.

The beach is by the side of a large, ribbon loch, stretching away for four miles, the calm water reflecting the purplish-brown hue of the heather-covered hills and the contrasting almost turquoise sky. On the other side of the loch stands an imposing house made from red sandstone with gargoyles and gothic arches, tall chimneys and turreted roofs. There's something in the air that suggests it can see those two small bodies, that suggests its reaction is a silent scream, a silent howl of distress, a cry for help that reverberates over the loch and the hills making the rabbits sit up, the deer turn their heads and the birds turn their gaze down to the beach where those two bodies lie, undisturbed and awaiting discovery.

ONE

GREER

Loch More, 2003

Sage

'Sage strengthens the sinews, feaver's heat doth swage
The palsie helps and rids of mickle woe,
In Latin (salvia) take the name of safety,
In English (sage) is rather wise than craftie;
Sith then the name betokens wise and saving,
We count is Nature's friend and worth the having.'

The Englishman's Doctor *by John Harington*

'Looks like she's here,' Colin calls out from the bedroom, as I finish mopping up the floor in the bathroom. With a sigh, I put the floor cloth into the bucket and make my way into the bedroom and over to the window.

He's right. I can see a grey Ford Mondeo slowing snaking its way along the drive; the drive that runs along the edge of the water. I watch from behind the mullioned bay windows, as the car momentarily disappears at the corner of the loch, behind the row of alder trees that line the loch shore. I step to the side of the window and stand beside the open curtain, watching as the car eventually rolls into the driveway and parks up.

She steps out of the car. She's less corporate than I expected. I thought there'd be a tight-fitting suit, high, impractical heels, red lipstick. But she's in jeans and an ill-fitting jumper, her hair is slightly wild – a dark brown, ringleted bob that may not have seen a hairbrush this morning. Her face is clear, no make-up, just a mass of freckles and deep-set eyes that look up and inspect the outside of the building. She steps back to get a better look and then, suddenly, gives an unexpected laugh that shocks me into action.

I duck away from the window and rush downstairs, hoping I wasn't seen.

The heavy wooden front door is already open to let a breeze run through the corridors on this unexpectedly hot day, and as I walk down the stone steps to the gravel driveway, I see that she's turned around to look over the loch, now only a few metres in front of her, glistening in the noonday sun. I stop to take in the view that she's seeing for the first time. The loch is neatly embraced by hills on either side and the coned peak of Ben Stack is off to the far right. Large regular blocks of pine trees stud the hills, giving an unnatural asymmetry to the otherwise barren landscape. Living here every day it's easy to forget the majesty of this view and the effect it has on those who see it for the first time. The only noise is the breeze in the two rowan trees close to the house. But as I continue to look at her, I notice an almost imperceptible change in her shoulders, as if some long-held tension begins to loosen.

'Miss Black?' I ask.

She turns quickly, almost jumping. She puts her hand on her heart, and there's a look of slight amusement in her eyes.

'Hi, yes, I'm Caitlin Black.'

Another surprise, she's American. Well, her accent is more trans-Atlantic, and I can't quite place it. Awkwardly, I put my hand out and we shake hands.

'I'm Greer. Greer Mackenzie.' Her amused gaze runs down my body, and I remember that my jeans are soaked.

'Would you excuse my appearance? We've been mending a leaking pipe in one of the upstairs bathrooms.' I look down at my greying, white T-shirt, damp and grubby, pulling at the bottom of it to emphasise my point. 'Never quite the cleanest of places.'

It seems my appearance doesn't bother her as she turns her gaze back to the house.

'I've never seen anything so full of humour.'

I turn to look. Normally, I see this building as tired, in need of rescuing, in need of a knight in shining armour, but today, with her unexpected injection of warmth, I'm able to see it from her point of view. Today I can see this house, this lost colossus that's made from crumbling red, Sutherland sandstone, trumpeting its complex stonework of mullioned windows and arched doorways; I can again see the riot of pinnacles and turrets that hide a team of winking and shrieking gargoyles, pitted and weather-beaten. Today's Caribbean blue, cloudless sky sharpens the image and gives it an intensity that even makes me smile. It's been so easy for me to overlook the audacity of the building, an impressively bold statement, almost ridiculous in such harsh and bleak surroundings. I notice her gaze stop at the rampant rose bush, with blood-red blooms, that climbs up beside one of the bay windows, standing out from the exposed stone, a startling contrast to the fading walls and all the other white, less radiant rose bushes that line the front of the building.

She frowns, but before it turns into a question, I say, 'Please, come in. I'm sure you're tired from your journey and could do with some tea.'

Her gaze lingers on the red rose a moment longer before she follows me into the house, up the steps and into the expansive hall. It's an impressive room, the forward to the building, the room that announces what else you might expect from the rest of the house: the sweeping staircase leading down to the black and white tiled floor, grandiose portraits lining the walls and a large, mounted stag's head glaring at the path of any guest, red light bulbs in its eye sockets. She stops and stares at it.

'An old family joke,' I say. 'My father hated that stag, but it wasne his place to get rid of it. When electricity finally arrived here in Achfary in 1955, he wired it up and put in those light bulbs. Will you be wanting to freshen up?'

Pulling herself away from the stag's menacing gaze, she replies in a distracted manner, 'Yes, thank you.'

I point to a door on her left. 'The cloakroom's in there. Take your time; I'll be in the kitchen, just at the end of the corridor.'

I turn and start walking down the dark corridor leading to the green baize door, but as I do this, I begin to feel the cold on the back of my neck and the old, familiar muffling of sounds comes down on me like a heavy fog. The distant ticking of the grandfather clock is muted, and the sound of my footsteps on the tiled floor is stifled. Suddenly, they're running towards me. The girl, four years old, runs ahead of the older boy, holding his hand. Both are pale, their eyes bruised with fatigue, their skin unused to sunshine. Her ringleted, white-blonde curls sit on her shoulders and her pale blue, smocked dress is grass-stained at the hem. The boy is trussed into a dark-blue sailor suit, his brown, wiry hair ruffled and unkempt. I expect them to stop, as usual, and ask the same question, asked with their voices always rising in expectation, always answered with disappointment. But they don't. They don't even notice me. They run past and stop in front of the door to the cloakroom which is now open, the light spilling out into the corridor.

And now the girl asks the question.

'Mama?' Her voice is timid, reedy, she has a sad, slightly anxious look.

When there's no answer, I can see both their shoulders droop, the expectation slipping away and disappointment finally flickers across the girl's face.

I feel as if the floor has given way under my feet, and I have to put my hand out to the wall to steady myself. But before I can begin to make sense of what has just happened, I hear the woman's voice.

'Hello?' she says gently.

The girl doesn't take her eyes from Caitlin Black. She's staring, a fierce, enquiring glare, the dark smudges under her eyes heightening the enquiry.

'Are you looking for someone?'

Caitlin Black's question knocks me out of my reverie, reminds me that I shouldn't be here, that I'm intruding.

Silently I open the green baize door and make my way into the kitchen. I busy myself: filling the kettle, putting it on the stove, finding the tea bags, the mugs and teaspoons, pouring milk into a small jug; doing the mundane things that calm the mind. Monotony always silences the conversation in my head, it quietens the anger, stopping it from becoming fury. There are days when the dialogue is so loud that I have to take a tooth-brush to the grouting in the shower and meticulously scrub. Two hours later, I will feel that I'm able to be civil. On other days, filing does the job: invoices and receipts, utility bills and bank statements. The checking of figures and the smoothing of the paper before I punch the holes and put it in the correct folder. The neatness pleases me as if I've just done the filing in my mind. I always sleep better after I've done the filing.

She appears, her face slightly flushed, a question on her face.

'Tea?' I ask.

'You don't have any coffee, do you?' she asks hopefully.

'Will Nescafé do?'

She grimaces. 'Strong tea will be fine.'

She pulls out a chair and sits at the kitchen table. It's a wide, heavy, well-used wooden slab; knife cuts, candle burns and water rings denoting character, each mark able to tell a tale. Behind her there is a wide, yawning sofa and haphazard piles of papers sitting on a table beside it. I really should have made a greater effort to tidy up.

She seems to hug herself as she looks around the room. 'It smells like you've been baking.' She closes her eyes briefly and takes a deep breath. 'Ginger cake?'

'Aye. An old family recipe. Would you like some?'

'Oh no, thank you. A bit early for me.' She looks around the room again. 'How long have you been here?'

I put a large mug of tea in front of her, and pull up my own chair, taking a sip of tea. 'My family have been housekeeping here since the house was built in the late 1880s.' I throw her a wry smile. 'Somehow we've been unable to stay away, something has always pulled us back, however hard we might have tried.' It's impossible to keep any bitterness out of my voice, I look down at my tea to avoid her gaze.

'But you don't live by yourself. You mentioned that "we" were mending a leaking pipe.'

'Aye, my husband works here too. He's still upstairs, finishing up. He keeps the grounds and does any maintenance jobs that are needed in the house. But we just do whatever is needed to keep the house in good condition.'

'And your children?'

My heart skips a beat, but I try to give her a look of slight amusement, trying to keep her off guard.

'No children I'm afraid, Miss Black.' I blink but keep my gaze on this intruder. I can tell that she's already horrified by her blunder; making assumptions about other people's ability to have children is always a taboo. But I'm happy to let her think that being childless is not my choice. After a pause I, again, look into my tea, holding the cup with both hands. 'Just one of those things that never happened.'

The red on her face deepens. 'But... I thought I saw two children in the corridor just now.' As she says this, her breath seems to become short and she grabs hold of the arms of the kitchen chair.

I'm momentarily disarmed by her reaction. I realise that, perhaps, I've gone too far, so give her a reassuring smile.

'Oh... that'll be our neighbours. Their children are always racing in and out of here.' I give an uneasy laugh, awkwardly running my hand through my hair. 'I asked them to stay away today, but they obviously can't resist the cake.' I stand up. 'Are you sure you wouldn't like some?'

She repeats the rejection without even considering it.

There's something vulnerable about this woman. She seems to have shrunken into her chair and looks almost girl-like: thin and brittle. Ignoring her refusal, I bring the plate over to the table, the dark, sticky ginger cake, heavy and inviting. Experience has shown me that cake, especially this cake, can have a calming effect on even the most highly strung. Its enveloping childhood smell of sweetness and nostalgia can instil some serenity into a worried mind.

It works. She leans forward and inhales the gingery aroma. Her face relaxes and a smile appears in her eyes. She sits up and seems ready to go back to business.

'Thanks for agreeing to see me without the land agent. The woman I spoke to knew very little about the house, she just seemed wary, almost unwilling to help. She didn't even know how long it had been on the market. She was more interested in selling me a two-bed cottage in Lairg.' She seems to scoff at the thought. 'But it looks like, with your family history, you'd be a far better guide.'

She smiles, looking directly at me. I rub at a sore patch on the palm of my hand.

'I'd be happy to show you around the house, I rarely get the opportunity. We're so remote here; we don't even get visitors that are just passing by. You see there's not much to pass by to.' I wonder if she fully appreciates how remote this area is. 'Now, if you've finished your tea, shall we start?'

Standing up, she asks, 'How many people have already been around?'

I try not to snort at the question, try to keep my answer nonchalant. 'Oh, no one this time. Shall we start in the library?' I wave her towards the corridor.

'This time?' She stops as if she's briefly choked on something.

I suppress a sigh of impatience. 'Yes, the house has been on the market, on and off, for the last fifty years. We've had some serious interest over that time, but nobody has ever stood by this old house. Something has always happened to make the buyers pull out.' I walk on down the corridor, not waiting for her.

I can feel that she's staring at me, but since I continue walking without her, she eventually hurries after me.

'The house has been for sale for fifty years?'

As we reach the light of the hall, I turn back to her. Her thoughts are written all over her face, it's obvious she can see the absurdity of the situation; a large, crumbling mansion that nobody wants to buy, more than thirty miles from the nearest train station and at least two hours by car to the closest provincial airport.

'What made the buyers pull out?'

I push down the frustration, the years of disappointment, and start counting the reasons out on my fingers. 'Well, either they suddenly realised they didn't have the money to renovate properly or they decided it was too far from civilisation. One decided there wasn't enough land with the house, another lost all his money in the crash of '87, two weeks before exchanging contracts.' It's hard to keep the bitterness out of my voice. 'Many didn't bother with a reason, just pulled out without a word.' I look at her squarely, the matador assessing the bull, hands on my hips, letting the red lining of my cloak show.

She meets my gaze, keeping her voice low and says, 'You're very honest.'

'Miss Black,' I sneer, 'we've been here before. I'm just a realist. I don't need my time wasted again.'

She almost puffs up her chest, as if she's realised that her part in this scene is that of the bull.

'Well, Mrs Mackenzie, let's deal with those first two points. I may not look the part. Just because I'm not dressed in a suit and carrying a briefcase doesn't mean that I haven't got the money. In fact, I'm a cash buyer. And "too far from civilisation" is what I'm looking for.'

Bravo, Miss Black. I let the matador's cloak drop and step back from the bull.

'If you don't mind me asking, why are you selling? Or rather, why have you been trying to sell for so long?'

Perhaps my assessment of her as a bull is incorrect. She's a terrier. A terrier that's got hold of its catch and doesn't want to let go.

'Why don't I show you the house first and then I can answer your questions afterwards.' My clipped words resonate around the hall. 'Does that sound like a good idea?'

We're standing on the pebbled beach close to the front of the house, both of us watching as the water gently laps the shingles. Without a breeze, the dark loch mirrors the surrounding hills, the complete stillness only broken by the sound of bubbling water running from the burn beside us. I have shown her the magnificent library, each of the twelve bedrooms, I've expounded on the construction of the elaborate fireplaces, we explored the servants' quarters and we marvelled at the grandeur of the stable block. Miss Black admired the intricate carvings, the delicate stonework on the stairs and the inlaid wood on the writing desk. We've discussed the originality of the design, the early central heating system and the unusual investment in speaking tubes instead of servants' bells.

It's so long since I gave a full tour of the house that I'd forgotten how much I love to show it off. It's reminded me how attached I am to this old white elephant and, just because it's had such a profound effect on me, it doesn't mean that it still isn't the most magnificent building I know.

Caitlin Black closes her eyes briefly and breathes in the clear air.

'Days like this are rare and precious up here.'

I turn to my visitor. 'Do you know this area?'

'My father is from Edinburgh. Although I grew up in Manhattan, we used to spend every other summer holiday and some Christmases near Lairg, staying with my aunt. Those summers were a welcome break from doing my very best to be the worst possible teenager for my mother. To be somewhere where nobody cared what clothes you wore, what school you went to or what neighbourhood you lived in; it was a revelation to me.'

So now I understand the accent: Edinburgh and Manhattan. Not a combination you hear too often.

She looks into the distance wistfully, as if she's remembering one of those summer holidays.

'How long has Ardbray been empty?' she suddenly says, pushing the dark curls off her face, seeming to push away that memory, an old-forgotten emotion.

'Well, it's never stood empty; my family have always worked here, maintaining the house. But Mrs Maclean died in 1947, and she'd lived a fairly solitary existence since the death of her husband at the turn of the century. So, I'm afraid this house has seen little of the world since the late 1890s.'

She looks back at the house, her gaze carefully scrutinising every detail.

'How did this house survive?' Her question seems rhetorical. 'So many of these kinds of houses were bulldozed and obliterated, now only ever seen in old catalogues and books. They were too big and too unwieldy, crumbling away, their owners usually too poor or their families too unwilling to take on the titanic task of reviving the great family seat. Why has Ardbray House been mothballed until someone could be found to rescue it?'

I stare at her, unable to answer, even though I'm perfectly capable of giving an explanation. But she misreads my stare.

Smiling, she says, 'I have a long-held fascination for old houses. You see, my father is an architect and we were indoctrinated from an early age.'

'Miss Black, why do you want to buy Ardbray?' I ask.

'I've been looking for somewhere to run a retreat. Somewhere people can get away from the constant noise in their lives. We so rarely get the opportunity to just "be", just listen to our own thoughts, or just do the thing we love to do. I'd like to run a writing retreat, an art retreat, a yoga retreat and even a silent retreat. And, of course, there'll be food. Food is what I'm good at, what I'm passionate about. Whilst the guests are feeding their souls, I will be feeding their bodies with good, locally sourced, vegetarian food.'

I fail to hide my raised eyebrow. 'You'll not be making the most of the local salmon, trout or venison then?'

She smiles. 'No, Mrs Mackenzie, I won't. But rest assured, I will be making the most of the other incredible fresh produce available.'

'Will it not be too remote?'

I can see she's trying to hide her amusement. I need to stop acting as if I'm interviewing her.

'Remote is exactly what our guests will need. They'll be looking for secluded and difficult to reach.'

'When you say "our guests", does that mean that it's not just you who's taking on this venture?'

She cracks her knuckles and waits a beat, a shadow of annoyance flickering through her eyes. 'Mrs Mackenzie, my brother Jim will probably take on most of the financial negotiations, perhaps some of the budget planning, but when I said "we", that was just a turn of phrase. I will be the sole owner and proprietor of the house and business.'

Her candour confounds me, and I suspect she's had this type of question before.

Suddenly distracted, she points to a large, irregular mound on the other side of the burn. 'What's that over there?' Weathered bricks and large boulders are sticking out of the grass at haphazard intervals. It's a stony knoll that screams of neglect and abandonment.

'It was the walled garden, destroyed by a landslip over fifty years ago. I'm afraid there's never been the money to dig it out and restore it.'

'Can we get over there to have a closer look?'

'Aye.' I can feel her excitement, she's keen to get nearer to it, so I begin to walk up the side of the burn. We walk beside the peaty water of the stream that cascades down the hill, neither of us speaking. The water gives off a distinct clean, sweet smell that's all at once refreshing and uplifting. We reach the old wooden bridge that's badly in need of repair. She's as mesmerised by the water as I am. Sometimes, I stand here and am so enthralled by the theatre of rushing water that I forget about time. This cacophony of sound helps drown those angry conversations in my mind, temporarily taking away the disappointment.

'This way,' I call, as we cross the bridge and carry on walking down towards the hilly mound. But she doesn't follow, so I give her some time to enjoy the watery show.

I find the old tree stump that's been my sunset-watching perch for years. I used to come down here as a child, late in the summer evenings when I should have been in bed. I'd watch the clouds as they turned from pink to orange and sometimes to red. It's the remains of an apple tree that used to stand outside the walled garden, destroyed in the landslip. It feels like an old friend.

I look back towards the bridge. That's when I hear the giggle; a happy, unwatched giggle. And then I see them; she's running after her brother. And they're laughing. I don't think I've ever seen them laugh. I feel an odd sensation as if I'm floating. I feel like I'm an outsider, seeing them for the first time. As usual, the sounds are muffled, the din of the water is subdued, the breeze in the trees is silent, but I feel as if a tectonic shift has occurred, I feel superfluous, no longer needed.

They're beginning to fade. I can't see the detail of the smocking on her dress, the lines of his sailor suit are slightly blurred. I feel as if I have lost something.

'Mrs Mackenzie?'

She startles me.

'Are you all right?' she asks, slightly out of breath. There's a colour in her cheeks that wasn't there when she first arrived.

I struggle to answer her, not wanting to open up to this stranger. But I think she recognises that this isn't the moment to pry, so she carries on talking.

'I've always dreamed of a walled kitchen garden. I love the order. I'd far rather go and visit a famous kitchen garden than something more classical or formal. Maybe it's the knowledge that everything in it will be put to good use.' She looks around her, at the higgledy-piggledy mess of stone, bricks, moss, grass and bracken before turning her attention to the loch and the view ahead of her. 'This is a great spot for a garden.'

Finally, I'm on easier ground and can readily respond. 'It was beautiful, one of the most well-known gardens in the Highlands. Apart from the beds in front of the house, there was very little formal planting around the grounds. Mrs Maclean threw all her energies into this one spot.'

'Have you got any pictures of it?'

'Of course, I'll show you when we get back to the house. Unlike most of the Victorian and Edwardian gardeners she didn't try to grow peaches and pineapples in great glass houses, she didn't try to master the garden; she was a more natural gardener, understanding the seasons and flowering periods. But she wasn't just a gardener, she was a herbalist and a midwife. She had an unequalled collection of herbs; people used to come from all over the world to see her.'

I look down at the ground, a sudden emotion swelling in me. I pull up a few blades of grass and start ripping them apart, throwing the remnants into the air. 'I'm only sorry we've never been able to recreate the garden. I would have loved that.'

There's an uncomfortable silence between us. I want her to leave now so that I can stop myself from hoping and then having those hopes dashed all over again. But suddenly, she turns to me.

'Mrs Mackenzie, could we take a break and go find those pictures over another cup of tea and some of that cake?'

The empty mug and crumb-strewn plate lies forgotten as she carefully leafs through the photograph album. The thick, cream-coloured pages, dappled with age, hold the sepia pictures of Ardbray, the garden and long-gone house guests. She's completely absorbed, soaking up every detail; the neatly laid out planting, bountiful harvests of fruit, vegetable and herbs, as well as stiff images of an elderly Kitty Maclean, determined in tweed and thick stockings, sensible brogues and slightly wild hair, leaning on a garden spade. These photographs soothe me; they show what this house used to be; they show its function, its usefulness, but also its soul, its grandiosity and its splendour.

As she goes through the pictures, every now and again she looks up at me, excitement in her eyes. Finally, I realise that I need to give a little, let her understand this house a bit more.

'The reason Ardbray has been empty for so long is that there were no heirs when Mrs Maclean died,' I say, trying to keep the fatigue out of my voice. 'She'd outlived her husband and both her children by many years. There were no siblings or cousins to leave her fortune to. So, she left most of her money to the Society of Herbalists, a society she'd been an ardent member of and had supported until her death. But there was a very particular codicil in her will, stating that the house was to be held in trust and maintained until a buyer could be found. Once the house was sold, only then could the money raised by the sale be given over, along with her papers and herbarium. She specified that a housekeeper and maintenance man should live here and use a set-aside pot of money to ensure the house was kept in good condition.' But now I can no longer keep the sour tone out of my voice. 'And here we are over fifty years later, unchanged and stagnating.'

She stares at me. I can just see the questions brewing: the 'whys' and the 'hows'. But I'll not answer those, I cut them off before they're even articulated.

'Are you still interested in the house, Miss Black?'

'Please, can we possibly drop the formality? Perhaps you can just call me Caitlin.' Again, she looks at me, her gaze now more sympathetic. 'I'm afraid we didn't get off to a good start. Maybe we could begin again?'

I maintain her gaze but know that I'm being stubborn. Colin tells me it's one of my most unattractive qualities. I should be accommodating. After all, it's in my interest for this woman to buy Ardbray and to give me my freedom.

I nod.

'Okay.' She gives me a conciliatory smile. 'So, in answer to your question, yes, I'm interested. How could I not be? There's so much...' She hesitates and I watch her closely as she seems to look around the kitchen for the words. That vulnerability that I saw earlier appears to have shifted away. I can almost feel the excitement welling up inside her; her eyes are bright and there's that gentle flush to her freckled cheeks. She unconsciously pulls at the sleeves of her jumper, trying to make them longer than they already are. But I don't think she can find the words or, maybe, she's unwilling to say them to me.

Suddenly, she snaps the photograph album shut as if she's made a decision and is ready to act.

'But I need to know more: more about this place and more about Kitty Maclean. I want to find the heart of this house and who made it what it was. If I'm going to buy it, I'd like to reclaim some of its original magnificence. But I can't do that without understanding everything about it.'

I blink, caught off guard by her sudden enthusiasm. That isn't an emotion I've encountered much recently. I push my chair back and stand up.

'Aye, I can do that,' I say guardedly, 'but it'll take a while. I think we'll be in need of some more tea.'

TWO

KITTY

Glasgow, 1889

Meadowsweet

*'... it was strewn in churches at weddings and made into garlands
for brides as its old country names still testify; a cordial was
distilled from its flowers and it was gathered on St. John's Day to
reveal a thief.'*

Herbal Delights *by Mrs C F Leyel*

Sitting at her dressing table, Kitty Gray stared at her image in
the mirror, the silence welcome as she anticipated the day
ahead. Her white nightgown caught her unbrushed hair; her
face, puffed from a lack of sleep, had a pink glow as if she had
recently hurried into the room.

She sighed, dissatisfied with her own reflection and looked
behind her, her childhood bedroom which had hardly changed

over the last nineteen years. A cream-painted child's desk covered with unruly piles of correspondence; her books overflowing from a large bookshelf. A tallboy, dark and austere, stood to one side with a deep, enveloping armchair next to it, holding an army of dolls and teddy bears, no longer in commission. Directly behind her was an oversized single bed with a cream-painted, metal frame. It was covered in a thick, paisley-patterned eiderdown, thrown across the bed in a hurry. Lying on top of the covers was an ornate cream dress; high collar and long sleeves with a lace finish and covered buttons, the heavy duchess satin giving a dull but expensive sheen. Kitty's eyes rested on the dress. She blinked and her focus changed to somewhere far beyond as she absently rubbed the diamond and ruby ring on her left hand.

'Good morning, miss.' A happy, lowlands accent crashed into her thoughts. 'Ready to face what the day'll throw at you?'

Kitty refocused and looked around at the smiling, freckled face. 'Almost.' She made herself feed off the girl's enthusiasm, rearranging her face to mirror Martha's. 'How about you?'

'Ach, miss.' Her curly hair jiggled as she shook her head. 'I hardly slept a wink, I couldnae stop thinking about how much I've to do before eleven o'clock, and how I've got to do it just that wee bit better'n usual. I've already had to dress Miss Eva and Mrs Gray a'fore coming to you. Mrs Gray has bin very particular about how she looks today, quite difficult to please.' With a sniff, Martha picked up an ivory-backed hairbrush and began brushing Kitty's hair. 'Did you manage some sleep?'

'No, not really,' Kitty said. 'My mind was spinning all night. I had the strangest dream. I was running up the aisle, my dress all muddy, my hair in a tangle, feet bare, chickens following me, and, of course, I was terrified of what Mother would say.'

Martha stopped brushing, her head on one side. 'You're not one for dreams, miss. What brought that on?'

'I don't know.' Kitty shook her head, the dull look threatening to return. She looked down at her hands, splaying them out on the flat of the dressing table in front of her. 'I suppose I'm just worried about getting it all wrong today. You know me, never very good on a big occasion. Given the choice, I'd far rather be outside walking the hills by myself.'

In two hours' time, Kitty Gray would be marrying Charles Maclean, one of Glasgow's richest and most eligible bachelors.

'You cannae be doing that today, Mrs Gray might have sommit to say if you did.'

'What if I did turn up with a muddy dress and chickens at my heels?' Kitty asked conspiratorially, mischief on her face. 'You can just imagine the scene.'

'Aye, let's not do that,' Martha said, shaking her head and continuing to brush.

'I'm going to miss you, Martha. Who's going to cheer me up when I'm faced with Glasgow's very best society? Who's going to make sure my skirt doesn't have grass stains on it?' For Mrs Gray would not let Martha go with Kitty to her new married life.

'Has Mrs Gray not bin helping you to find a new maid?'

'I couldn't let her do that. She'd only find someone that suited her, someone that would report back to her. I don't need my mother breathing down my neck, I'll just have to find someone myself.' But Kitty had been ignoring the problem, hoping that, perhaps, it would somehow resolve itself.

'Well, maebe you'll find someone up in the Highlands. Someone who'll keep you from the mud and the chickens.' With a smile, she continued brushing. 'You'll have found out more about the house?'

'Well, only what the gossips say. Charles is being very coy as if he's trying to hide some great secret from me. He doesn't seem to realise that everyone is talking of a dining room to seat fifty, a ballroom and twelve bedrooms. I don't believe any of it, the house is just too far away from anyone to be that big. Who'd visit it? I'm hoping it'll be a cosy, country house, just big enough for a brood of children and a few chickens.' Kitty almost sighed, the image of a noisy, haphazard family so far from her own experience.

Martha's brushing got faster and harder.

'Ach, this hair. Maebe some of Mr Maclean's money could find you sommit to sort it out. Some potion to make it sleek an' smooth like Miss Eva's. Tsk, I'm never going to get this wiry mop tamed in time, it's like wild heather.'

'Martha,' Kitty said gently, as she touched her maid's hand. 'We've plenty of time and I'm sure Mother would prefer it if I didn't walk down the aisle with great bald patches.' She smiled as Martha put the brush down with a sigh and started to pin and pacify, curl and straighten.

Watching Martha's freckled face as she worked, Kitty again wondered how she was going to do without the happy face that had woken her up every morning since she could remember. This was the face that had kissed away the tears when her mother was being unreasonable, when she had fallen down and hurt herself and had explained what to do when she first got the curse. This was the face that had helped her grow up. But no more. And, as she considered this, the true impact of the task ahead of her began to dawn on Kitty. A bleak vulnerability started to spread through her, a cold fear that made her say,

'Will you stay with me until we get to the church?' But seeing the confusion on Martha's face, she made herself brush off her insecurity and gave a hollow laugh. 'I need you to make sure I don't get mud on my dress or my hair in a tangle.'

There was a moment's silence before Martha laughed too. 'Oh aye, I'll be there, nae worry. Anyway, wi' that dress what could possibly go wrong? Even the Duchess of Argyll will be wishing she had one of those.' Martha turned around to look at Kitty's dress lying on the bed. She walked over and carefully picked it up. Turning to the full-length mirror, she held the dress in front of her, humming as she admired its cut, the length and the shape.

Kitty got up from her stool and went over to the mirror. 'Why don't you try it on?' With her hands on her hips, she watched her maid's reflection with a broad smile. Martha stared, her mouth open, the dress still hanging in front of her.

'Go on, we've plenty of time before I need to be ready.'

'Nae, I cannae.' She shook her head, her curls jumping as if clamouring to get away. 'What if Mrs Gray came in? She'd dismiss me straight away.'

A playful smile passed across Kitty's face. 'I'm sure Mother is far too busy fussing over the flowers and the endless food to come up here yet.' Carefully, Kitty took the dress from her maid and placed it back on the bed. Martha didn't move, her face pale.

'Here, help me with the buttons, I'm not so used to these as you are.' Kitty beckoned to Martha. 'I need your strong fingers.'

Without a word, she walked over to the bed, and they both began undoing the buttons running down the back of the dress. Then, silently, Kitty helped her maid out of her work dress, and with thoughtful effort, eased her into the wedding dress; her slow attempts at the buttons lulling Martha into a trance as she looked straight ahead of her, out of the window. The silence was strained, the easy air between them destroyed.

'Close your eyes and I'll lead you to the mirror.'

Martha shut her eyes tight while Kitty drew her back over to the mirror.

'Just let me take your cap off.' Having done so, she pulled out Martha's red curls. 'There, you can open your eyes now.' Kitty stood back, eyes gleaming and arms folded.

Martha stared at her reflection. In silence, she turned from side to side, watching her figure in the mirror, enjoying the noise of the heavy silk as it swayed, falling like ribbons of thick cream. Eventually, she stopped, the distant clatter of crockery and voices floating in the background. Soon her eyes began to shine brightly and she looked downwards, blinking.

'Why are you crying?' There was a kind amusement in Kitty's voice, and she caught Martha's hands in her own. Her only reply was a muffled sniff.

'Here, take this.' Kitty handed her maid a handkerchief. 'If you cry on my dress, Mother really will cause a scene.'

Martha smiled through her tears and blew her nose.

'A bride in tears isn't an unusual sight, but I'm confused; the right dress, the wrong girl.'

The unexpected voice caught both of them unawares. They looked at each other for a moment, Kitty blanching at the note of authority. But as she looked towards the door, Kitty's stomach caved inwards with relief.

'Eva, you scared us.' Kitty breathed, her pale face flushing, putting her hand on her heart. 'You sounded just like Mother.'

Eva walked over to Kitty, her eyes teasing. 'I'm not sure whether to be flattered or offended by that remark, sister dear.' She touched Kitty's arm. 'Anyway, I came to warn you that she'll be on her way up to see you shortly.'

It was Martha's turn to blanch.

Eva gave a gentle laugh. 'Don't worry; she's still with Mrs Baker going through every single dish for the wedding breakfast. Poor woman, she's at the wrong end of Mother's particularly sharp eye this morning.'

'Mrs Baker will be hoping you don't get married for some time.' Kitty grinned.

'Oh, my darling sister, you can laugh, but I have it on good authority that our mother is already making plans. Poor Father, any more talk of weddings just sends him straight to his study.' With a playful smile, she took Kitty by the hand. 'Here, you sit down, let me help Martha out of that dress.' She led her sister to the edge of her bed and kissed her forehead as if she were a small child.

Kitty sat and leaned back on her elbows, watching her two best friends, easy in each other's company. Martha, her nurse-maid and confidante, Eva, her bright and beautiful little sister, party to all her childhood ambitions and protector from the worst artifice of their mother. Her mind wandered as she listened to Eva's light-hearted commentary on the general wedding commotion, and her eye was caught by a seagull landing outside the window. She moved to get a closer look, watching it pecking at the wooden frame. She thought of the freedom it had to make its own decisions, to choose its own mate.

Soon Martha was re-dressed in her correct outfit and her hair re-pinned. Both she and Eva turned to Kitty.

'Now, it's the turn of the "soon to be" Mrs Charles Maclean,' Eva announced with a girlish smile, as if she had come to ask Kitty and Martha to go out and play. Kitty pulled her gaze away from the seagull at large and submitted to her friends' attentions.

The door swung open with a flourish and a rustle, followed by a bouffant of silver hair brushed to perfection, a long, pointed nose and an ample bosom dressed in a pale-grey silk dress. Susan Gray, Kitty's mother, swept into the room.

'Darling, let me look at you.' She held her arms out in front of her, framing Kitty and looked her over carefully. She was scrupulous in her inspection, starting at the shoes and finishing with her hair. Kitty held her breath.

'Yes.' She smiled. 'Apart from that hair.' Her voice quivered. 'Martha, I don't know why you can't learn to tame it. But,' she continued, putting one hand to the side of Kitty's head, 'I'm not sure anyone can.' She dropped her hand in a dismissive gesture. 'Your father's hair.' She sniffed. 'Nothing to do with me. But, yes. I'd say you'll do. You look like you'll make a good wife.' She gave Kitty a half smile and patted her arm before drawing herself up. She looked at Eva and Martha. 'Girls, would you leave us a minute?'

Kitty watched her sister and Martha leave the room, wondering what her mother had to say.

'Now that you look the part, I need you to play the part. Today's the day you forget about any ideas you may have had about university, about working in those slum clinics, about any kind of working at all. Today you become a wife. That's the most important job of all. Just make sure you mix with the right people; be aspirational for your husband.' Mrs Gray looked down her nose. 'And don't trust the servants.'

Kitty blinked. Was this the marriage talk she'd been dreading? Be ambitious for your husband and don't trust the servants? No advice about what to expect on her wedding night? Not that she needed it; her anatomy books had given her all the education she needed.

Kitty tried not to smile. 'Of course, Mother.'

'Now, your father needs to see you in his study. Wise words on marriage, I assume.' Susan Gray turned with another sniff and as she left the room, she said, 'And don't let him go on too long. You mustn't keep Charles waiting. It wouldn't do.'

Kitty knocked on the door, a gentle knock, a long-known signal telling the insider who was there. She turned the handle and pushed the door open. As usual, her father was sitting at his desk, glasses perched on his nose, reading. Dr Cameron Gray was framed by a high-backed chair, upholstered in a dark-blue, woollen tartan. The large mahogany desk in front of him was covered in neat piles of paper, journals and letters, a recent photograph of Kitty, her mother and Eva stood imperiously in an ornate silver frame, an empty china teacup and saucer in front of it. On seeing Kitty, his frown disappeared and his worried furrows levelled out; a satisfied glow appeared in his deep-set, brown eyes and he stood up.

'Kitty, my darling, come in,' he said, as he passed a hand over his speckled-grey beard, then pulled each shirt cuff down to ensure they were both showing equally below his morning coat sleeves.

She made her way to her usual corner of his desk and pulled a chair up to it.

'Now, my dear, we're not working or reading today, so come and sit comfortably by the fire, as my most honoured guest.' He gave a small bow and gestured towards one of the two leather armchairs facing the grate. Kitty did as she was told, but stood by the fire, warming her hands.

'I thought you might want a few minutes to catch your breath, before the onslaught, and perhaps have something to calm your nerves.' His eyes flickered as he walked over to the dark mahogany sideboard and pulled the stopper from a large cut-glass decanter. Kitty watched him pour the dark-red port into heavy stemmed glasses, before turning around to face the room.

Dr Cameron's study was like a womb to her; warm and reassuring. The books would always lull her into a feeling of profound security, whatever her mood. His dark wooden desk, so familiar to her, was the place where her father always appeared most at ease; the piles of medical journals, papers and notebooks all in neat and precise piles, his fountain pen, lid back on, placed exactly in line with the letter that he'd been writing. Turning back to the fire, she could see that nothing was out of line except two large, leather-bound books placed hurriedly on the side table beside one of the armchairs, their disorder intruding upon the strict regulation of the room.

Kitty frowned at the books as her father handed a glass of port to her.

'Kitty, you look truly beautiful. I'm so proud of you, so proud to take you down the aisle.'

She noticed that his eyes were glistening as he spoke. She held her breath; her father so rarely showed any kind of emotion.

Holding his glass up, he continued, 'To the future Mrs Charles Maclean.' He took a slow, unhurried sip. Kitty followed his example.

The warm burn of the port on her throat gave her a boldness she might not otherwise have felt. 'Papa, why have you got my anatomy books? I asked Martha to pack them with all my other belongings. I thought they'd already been sent over to Park Street.' She looked directly at her father. He reddened slightly, put his glass on the mantelpiece and, with his hands in his pockets, he looked down into the fire.

'Your mother asked that I take them.'

Kitty's lips tightened.

'She said you would have no need of them anymore and that they were better off here.'

She watched her father as she unconsciously began smoothing down the front of her dress. As always, his attire was immaculate: his tie crisp, trousers appropriately creased, his shoes polished to a high shine. But now, unable to meet her gaze, he appeared uncomfortable, as he often did when he was caught in the web of one of his wife's schemes.

'But I need those books. They're...' Kitty's voice trailed off into a whisper as she turned away and closed her eyes, putting a hand on the mantelpiece as if to steady herself.

'My dear.' Dr Gray sighed. 'I'm sure Charles will have plenty of other books you can read, you don't need those particular ones.' His voice was without depth, his eyes still intent on the fire. He took a handkerchief from his pocket and wiped his face.

Kitty put her glass down and walked over to the window. 'I

know this is the path I've always been destined for. This is what we do, we get married. If we don't, we become inconvenient spinsters, a drain on your finances. But I could have studied; you know there's talk of setting up a medical school at Queen Margaret College. I could have helped you with your surgery. I could even have supported myself in time and, who knows, maybe I could have become a doctor.' Her eyes were focused somewhere far beyond the window.

'Kitty, you know your mother would never have had that.' Her father's voice was muted.

'Yes, that's why she was in such a hurry to marry me off,' she said abstractly, almost to herself.

Her mistake had been in telling her mother her ambitions.

'I'd like to be able to study medicine at Edinburgh University, just like Doctor Sophia Jex-Blake,' she'd said one evening at dinner.

Her mother had bristled at the name. 'That woman has the determination of a mountain goat. I am reliably informed that her jaw is as square as her persistence, and that she is no beauty. No, no daughter of mine is going to be associated with her.'

'But, Mother,' Kitty had realised her mistake and had tried to change tack, 'it's her tenacity that has ensured that women can study medicine now. Her tireless work has meant that people like me can go and get a medical education. Now I can go and do what I'd love to do, what I'm interested in. Wouldn't that be a good thing?'

Her mother had grunted, almost spilling her tea. 'Next you'll be telling me that you've been attending those suffrage meetings. No, darling, nice girls don't do such things.' She had patted Kitty's hand. 'Don't you worry, we'll find you some dashing young man to take your mind off those ridiculous ideas.' And, no sooner had Kitty aired her opinions than the drawing room parades began. Endless teas and morning visits had followed, entertaining some of Glasgow's dullest bachelors in her mother's quest to find her a suitable husband. No longer was she allowed to sit reading with her father in his study or even occasionally help out in his surgery. Her mother had always found something more important for her to do.

Kitty turned back to her father. He began to speak again, but she interrupted.

'Of course, I've known that from the beginning.' A smile had returned to her eyes and she kissed him on the cheek. 'Marriage to Charles must have its benefits. Surely, I can do something useful with all that money?' She halted as she saw her father's eyes drop. With an almost inaudible sigh, she pulled herself upright. 'Perhaps I should finish that drink before the carriage arrives.' She swept back to the fireplace and picked up her glass of port, raising it to the room.

'To the future of the future Mrs Charles Maclean,' Kitty announced triumphantly. Her father joined her and as they drank, there was a sharp knock on the study door.

'Come in.' Dr Gray turned to see Mrs Kennedy, the Grays' housekeeper, walk in with a small bouquet of flowers. A tidy woman, she held the flowers in front of her as if she were the bride walking down the aisle.

'These have been delivered for Miss Gray. I believe they're from Mr Maclean.' There was a childish excitement in her eyes as she passed the flowers to Kitty.

'Thank you, Mrs Kennedy.' She'd been caught off guard and found herself flushing. Having forgotten that there could be any romance on this day, her stomach fluttered just slightly. A small, understated bouquet made from little white flowers and a hint of greenery. She fingered the tiny blooms before taking in the heavy aroma. She smiled. Charles had remembered which flowers she loved; Lily of the valley. That was a good start.

Glasgow Herald, May 4th 1889

The much-anticipated wedding of Mr Charles Maclean, only son of the late Mr and Mrs George Maclean, and Miss Kitty Gray, eldest daughter of Dr and Mrs Cameron Gray of Wood-side Terrace, Glasgow, took place yesterday at Glasgow Cathe-dral. The Minister, the Very Reverend Dr Alexander Macintosh, took the traditional Church of Scotland service which was attended by over one hundred guests. The bride, wearing a sumptuous cream, duchess satin dress, was given away by her father and attended by Miss Evangeline Gray. The best man was Mr Roddy Argyll. A wedding breakfast was held at the home of the bride's parents. Mr and Mrs Maclean will be honeymooning at their Highland residence, Ardbray.

THREE

GREER

Loch More, 2003

Burnet Saxifrage

*'... the juice was used for injuries to the head, and the distilled
water was a cosmetic for removing freckles... Country people
used it sometimes to cure toothache.'*

Herbal Delights *by Mrs C F Leyel*

Yet again, I'm making tea. I'd rather a dram of whisky, but it's
too early and I don't think Robert Urquhart would approve.

Robert Urquhart is the solicitor to Kitty Maclean's estate.
He, his father, grandfather and great-grandfather have all
worked as solicitors, all for the Maclean family since the day
they decided to buy the land from the Westminsters and build
this house. What is it about Ardbray and the Maclean family
that garners so much loyalty from their employees?

Robert Urquhart sits on the kitchen sofa, his legs crossed and his arms resting across the back of the high cushions, surveying the room. He's a man who thrives on company, feeds off the energy of others. In his late-fifties, he's a tall, red-faced, wiry-framed man with expansive gestures and an embracing smile that puts everyone at ease. There's a slight eccentricity to his attire: a well-cut three-piece suit made from pale-green tweed with a faint pink line through the fabric, a watch chain hanging from his waistcoat pocket and a pair of brown brogues with a high shine. His father would dress in a similar manner and wear the same pocket watch. As a child I used to think he was some sort of government official; he was so formal and a little dour. Robert is a more relaxed version of his father, with a greater enthusiasm for life.

He leans forward and rubs his hands together vigorously, almost as if he's trying to produce additional energy with the friction he creates. There's an enormous smile on his face.

'Is there any of that famous ginger cake to be had?'

I can't help but return the smile. He always asks this exact question every time he comes to Ardbray. Without saying anything, I open the tin that's already lying on the table and show the contents to him.

'Excellent!' he says, again rubbing his hands together before getting up from the sofa and sitting at the table.

As he cuts himself a piece of cake, he starts talking.

'I've been doing some research into our prospective buyer. Purely to make sure she's financially viable you see.' He grins at me. 'My wife's accused me of downright nosiness, but I've told her that we need to be sure she's not a time-waster.' He takes his first bite of the cake.

'God, that's good.' He swallows, inspecting the cake before continuing.

'Did you know that Caitlin Black's grandmother is none

other than the famous Maisie McIntyre?' He has a look of triumph on his face.

'I've never heard of Maisie McIntyre. Sounds like some kind of film star.'

'Maisie McIntyre was a well-known couturier, originally from Edinburgh, but set up business in Manhattan, just before the First World War. From what I hear, she was a woman who didn't like to be told what to do.' He suddenly looks wistful. 'My mother had a Maisie McIntyre dress, she looked magnificent in it. It was so vibrant and colourful and had the most lifelike embroidery on it: birds, exotic flowers, and insects. I've never seen anything like it since.' He picks up the mug of tea I've left in front of him and takes a sip. 'Anyhow, she had a daughter, Jessica Smyth and she, in turn, had three daughters and a son: Rebecca, Laura, Jim and, last but not least, Caitlin.'

'Do you mean Rebecca and Laura Black? Those two are impossibly glamorous. They're always on the pages of *Hello!* magazine. Surely, they can't be related to our Caitlin Black?'

Robert looks at me sideways, his eyes brimming with delight. 'Well, well, Greer Mackenzie, I never took you for a subscriber to *Hello!* magazine!'

I roll my eyes. 'I only ever get to read it when I'm at the hairdresser.'

'Thousands wouldn't believe you.' He shakes his head with a mischievous smirk on his face. 'So, contrary to your assumption, Caitlin Black is part of the McIntyre dynasty, and she has plenty of money behind her. But there's little that I can find out about her private life. She ran a successful café in Manhattan, then she seemed to drop off the face of the earth about two years ago, the last snippet I can find is a picture of her at her mother's funeral last year, she looks so out of place alongside her two sisters and brother, all of whom are dressed impeccably, whereas she looks dowdy, thin and miserable.'

'If her mother had just died, I should think she's allowed to look thin and miserable,' I quip back at the solicitor, suddenly feeling a little protective of our wild-haired, prospective buyer.

'I gather she had an aunt who lived in Lairg. Annie Black. Never married, died about ten years ago. But her brother, Miss Black's father, is the much-celebrated architect Finn Black. He won the Stirling Prize for Architecture last year, putting the Grassmarket back on the map with his work. He's designed some outstanding buildings in America. That girl comes from a talented family, but something tells me she's the black sheep of the family. She plays no public part in the running of the family business, if at all, and there's no mention of architecture in her biography. She appears to keep herself to herself and, unlike her sisters, has no desire to see her picture on the pages of *Hello!* magazine and the likes.'

'Do you see her as a suitable candidate for buying Ardbray?' I ask.

He gives a small shrug. 'Difficult to tell. It seems she has the money, but whether she has the business acumen...' He takes another sip of tea. 'But look, we've had millionaire stockbrokers, multi-national corporations, hoteliers and syndicates interested in this place, and look where it's got us. Maybe a young woman with no track record to speak of is just what this house needs. Isn't that what Kitty was when she arrived here?'

Just as I'm about to reply, I hear a voice in the distance that I don't recognise.

'Hello? Is anybody about?'

It's a man's voice, the local accent, but I can't place him. I get up and open the green baize door. 'We're in the kitchen,' I shout.

As the light seeps into the corridor from the kitchen, I see two silhouetted figures, a man and a woman. I can make out Caitlin's shape but not her companion's. I hold the door open, and they walk in a little gingerly, the man holding Caitlin's left elbow.

Robert gets up as he sees the large graze on her face and blood on her hair and shirt collar.

'My dear girl, you look like you've been in the wars.'

Caitlin gives an awkward smile. 'It looks worse than it is.' She's holding her right arm a little delicately. 'I had a minor car accident. Ran into a stag and killed it.'

Robert and I throw a furtive glance at each other.

Caitlin turns to the man who is with her. 'I was rescued by an old friend, Duncan Mackay. We used to know each other as children. He lived next door to my aunt Annie, and we spent our childhood summer holidays together, running amok around the shores of Loch Shin.' She gives Duncan a slightly embarrassed smile. 'It's incredible. I haven't seen him for over ten years, and there he is just when I'm in need of help.'

'Aye. Duncan.' I nod at him warily, trying to keep my composure, and then turn to Robert. 'This is Duncan Mackay, he's one of the maintenance workers on the Reay Forest Estate. And this,' I continue, turning back to Duncan, 'is Robert Urquhart, he's the Maclean family solicitor, here to meet with Caitlin.' But as I speak, I can feel my mouth drying up and my legs giving way on me. I put my hands on the back of the kitchen chair to maintain my balance, not wanting anyone to notice.

The two men shake hands, but Robert hesitates as he faces Caitlin.

'I better not shake your hand, that arm looks like it could be a little sore. But I think we'd better have a look at your head.' He takes her left elbow and steers her towards one of the kitchen chairs. 'Greer, do you have any cotton wool, antiseptic cream or something like that?'

I've been rooted to the spot, my shaking legs making it difficult to move. I feel as if everything has slowed down, the voices are mumbled; the news of Caitlin's crash has taken me by surprise. We've been here before: illness, injury and even death. This can't be happening again.

'Greer?' Robert repeats himself.

I mumble something innocuous and fumble around for the first-aid kit. And then I overcompensate and fuss over Caitlin, cleaning up the graze on her forehead, checking there are no broken bones under the bruise on her cheek. The mundane task begins to calm me, bringing my breathing under control.

'Honestly, it's nothing too dramatic,' says Caitlin. 'It's more of a shock than anything. He just came out of nowhere; I couldn't avoid him. The stag was the only one to come to any real harm. We put him in the back of Duncan's Land Rover, I think there's someone he can give the meat to.'

'Aye, Willie Elliot will take it, I'm sure of that,' Duncan pipes up. 'Can I use your phone? I'll get him to come over and collect it.'

As Duncan goes back to the hall to find the phone, I begin to pull myself together.

'Sweet tea, that's what you need.' And I busy myself with the kettle.

'How's that arm?' asks Robert. 'Should we be getting you to a doctor?'

'No.' Caitlin rubs her shoulder as she talks. 'I've probably pulled a muscle or two and am a bit bruised and battered, but nothing that some painkillers and a hot bath won't cure.'

I pass her a mug of tea, the sugar bowl, the required painkillers and a glass of water.

'Would you like to postpone our meeting?' he asks.

She shakes her head and waves off any hint at delay. 'I know we have a lot to discuss. I'm sure I'll be fine.'

'What about your car?' Robert asks, ignoring her encouragement to get down to work.

'I had to leave it on the road. If I can, I'd like to phone the rental company a bit later so that they can come and pick it up.

To be honest, I hated that car, it made me feel middle-aged. It was just too boring. I'd like to get myself an old Defender, just like Duncan's. He says the garage at Lairg may be able to help me out.'

'Aye, Sandy will find you sommit, no doubt,' I say. Reluctantly, I find myself beginning to like this girl; there doesn't seem to be any pretence about her. She's unlike previous buyers who were all money and fast cars.

'So,' interjects Robert, 'I'm keen to know what your thoughts are about the house and what your plans are. I'm sure you have lots of questions, I expect there's paperwork you'll need us to provide etc. etc. But before we get into all of that, what I'd really like to know is what you thought of Kitty Maclean's herbarium. Is it not the most magnificent room you've ever seen?'

There's confusion on her face. 'I don't think we saw the herbarium,' she says, glancing at me warily as if she's worried she's made some terrible faux pas. 'I'm sure I'd remember if we did.'

My face begins to redden. How is it that Robert is always capable of finding someone's weak point and so amiably needle it? 'Well... we didn't really have the time to see it. We had so much to do and' – I run my hands through my hair, the flush in my cheeks deepening – 'well...' I sigh, unable to say what I should.

But Robert quickly interrupts. 'Greer Mackenzie!' he exclaims. 'You have done Miss Black a great disservice,' he says this with a grin on his face, a twinkle in his eye.

'I absolutely insist that I take you there straight away.' He stands up quickly making a loud scraping noise with the chair. 'But where are my manners? Only if you're up to it.' Concern wipes away the childlike enthusiasm.

Caitlin gives me a secretive smile, amusement spread across

her face. She shrugs at me and gets up. 'Of course, I'd love to see it.'

'But... your tea,' I say rather pathetically.

'Bring the tea with you,' shouts Robert, as he heads down the corridor. 'And you must come, too, Greer; you must show Miss Black your favourite room.'

As the solicitor's shoes click in a military manner on the corridor floor, his footsteps urgent and hurried, I sigh and scramble to catch up with them.

The three of us reach the hall and we bump into Duncan, just finishing up his phone call.

'Is it okay if I wait here for twenty minutes or so until Willie arrives? I can sit in the car.'

Before I can reply, Robert, with increasing gusto, urges Duncan to join us.

I frown. This isn't a party. And then, to my even deeper misgivings, Colin appears from the kitchen with stockinged feet, having come in from working in the garden and Robert eagerly invites him to join the group.

It's almost as if he's a modern-day Pied Piper, nobody questions him, we just follow. A motley troop, traipsing up the stairs in a strangely sombre procession to the first floor and to Kitty Maclean's herbarium.

We reach the landing and too quickly we're in front of a plain wooden door.

'If you ever wanted to learn anything about Kitty Maclean,' Robert announces, 'then this is the room where you will find out almost everything you need to know.' He opens the door with a flourish. 'This room represents the last fifty or so years of her life.' His self-assured manner paired with his soft accent gives him that air of easy confidence that makes him so engaging, that makes his followers take in every word.

Inside it's dark, the familiar, faint waft of furniture polish greeting us. Robert walks over to the window and carefully opens the wooden shutters, exposing three floor-to-ceiling windows. Bright shafts of sunlight light up the room, revealing Kitty's immaculately preserved, early twentieth-century science lab. In front of the windows stands a long wooden bench with an old microscope, several plant presses, a pestle and mortar, and a chipped, china pot, full of paintbrushes. One wall is lined with shelves crowded with old dispensary bottles, each neatly labelled, and a small library of botany books, including two large and well-used books on anatomy. The other walls are occupied by neat, cream-painted cupboards or drawers, a label on each front, the brass label-holders bright and shining. Despite the dust motes hanging in the air, there is not a speck of dirt on the bench or shelves; I've made sure of that.

I don't like sharing this room, especially with so many people, especially with strangers. I've had this room almost to myself for the last fifty-six years. I'd come here as a child and hide on the days I didn't want to go to school, and as a teenager who was raging about living in such an isolated place, away from boys, music, and even a telephone.

If I want to get a sense of my mother, I just need to go to the kitchen where I'll catch the smell of ginger cake, freshly baked bread and raspberry jam. If I'm in need of consolation, the taste of soda bread straight from the oven will bring a smile to my face, however bad the day may be. But if I need to reason with the unreasonable, if I need Kitty Maclean, it's to the herbarium that I come. Here I can work out the unworkable, I can come up with solutions to life's impossible problems. That's because this room was and still is, as Robert said, the essence of Kitty Maclean, even now, fifty-six years later; this is the room where she was at her most prolific, her most energetic, her most engaged, utterly absorbed in her world of herbs and the power of healing. When I'm here, on my own, I can still rekindle that atmosphere of concentration, I can hear the scratch of her pen or the rattle of the paintbrush as she'd wash it in a jar of water.

Here was where I would do my homework or get inspiration whilst studying interior design at university. If I set out to do the work in this room, I'd get it done; if I did it in the kitchen or my bedroom, I'd get distracted, and find something more interesting to do. But here I could, and still can, apply myself when needed.

I take myself into the corner of the room and look out of one of the windows. The elevated view of the loch, looking east towards the boathouse and the now ruined pier is still entrancing. Kitty would work here in the early morning, catching the first rays of sun and jealously watching that now broken pier where she would, without fail, spend at least half an hour every dusk, sitting watching the water, sometimes, it seemed, even talking to it. It's still warm today with little breeze to trouble the water, showing a mirrored reflection of the hills.

I turn so that I can get a good view of everyone in the room, so that I can gauge their reactions. Caitlin wanders over to look at a set of paintings beside the window, neat, botanical drawings of native plants, expertly coloured and annotated. She inspects them intensely as if she's trying to learn something from them.

'Each one produced by Mrs Maclean,' Robert announces, before opening one of the larger cupboards, revealing a bank of paper files and pulling one out at random. I want to stop him, tell him to leave them alone, but I manage to stay silent. He opens the file and lays out several specimen sheets on the bench, showing pressed plants annotated with full botanical descriptions, all written in neat, small, sepia-brown ink handwriting.

'She had this room made in the late 1890s, so some of these specimens are almost one hundred years old. It seems she began with a full discovery of the local flora and fauna before her interests moved to herbs from all over the world. She never travelled, but she had the specimens sent to her. The correspondence she had with some of the world's most eminent botanists, taxonomists and herbalists is exceptional, plus a very lively communication with the medical profession, especially in the last few years of her life. And it's all neatly filed in date order, just waiting for someone to come and search through it. It's this room that typifies what Kitty Maclean became during the last half of her life.'

As I watch Caitlin slowly walk around the room, fingering bottle labels, then picking up a book and leafing through it carefully, I wonder if there is something here that's affecting her. She seems to be in some kind of trance, not hearing Robert's words.

'Did she file all the correspondence?' Caitlin suddenly asks, leaning into the drawer that Robert has opened.

'Yes, as I understand it, Kitty did it all in the last few years of her life. She had become quite arthritic and could no longer paint, but she made sure that she left everything in a logical order for the Herb Society, well that's what they call the Society of Herbalists these days, when they would eventually have ownership of it.'

'Why haven't they already taken it all away?' Caitlin is now looking intently at one of the specimen sheets, handling it carefully.

'Another strange quirk of Kitty Maclean's will. According to my grandfather, she was very insistent that not only did nothing in the house get moved before a buyer had been found and that no money could be given over before the sale was approved, but that they could only know a brief outline of the contents.' He pulled open another cupboard to show deep index card drawers. 'At first I thought that perhaps she'd hidden something of importance in here. But I think that was just my overactive teenage mind hoping for some stark revelation. In the holidays I used to come here, and, I can tell you, I've been through everything. I've read almost every letter and trawled through all the specimens etc. I've studied her paintings and read her journals, and I can't find anything that's unusual.' He shakes his head. 'It's almost as if she knew what was going to happen.'

Caitlin looks up at Robert. 'What do you mean?'

'Well...' he hesitates. 'I mean that it was almost as if she knew that this house wouldn't sell, as if she knew that Greer's family would still be living here fifty years later. I think she wanted to make sure it was preserved correctly until the right person came along.'

FOUR

KITTY

Loch More, 1889

Box

'It has narcotic and sedative properties in full doses and can be used as a vermifuge.
To dream of box portends long life, prosperity and a happy marriage.'

Elixirs of Life *by Mrs C F Leyel*

She stepped out of the carriage and looked out across Loch More.

It had been a grey and blustery day and the ground was still wet from earlier rain. The setting sun had just appeared at the far end of the loch, giving the low, rolling clouds a purple hue. The unexpected sunlight danced on the jittering water giving some cheer to the end of a gloomy day. To the right of the ribbon loch, the hills rose steeply and rocky outcrops were scattered among the bright green of the young bracken and the darker, more solemn spring heather. The cone-topped Ben Stack looked down on them with authority from the west, a diagonal strata of rock etched along its side. The air was clear, almost sharp, and Kitty could hear a burn simmering somewhere beside the house. Her drooping shoulders became more upright, her whole body more alert as if she had been given a sudden boost of energy.

Charles put his hand on the small of Kitty's back.

'This is why my father bought this land.' His voice was almost a whisper as if he didn't want to disturb the scene in front of them. 'The view is never the same. The clouds, the colours on the hills, the patterns on the water; they're always changing. You can see why he fell in love with it.' He paused as he stared, and they both stood silent, mesmerised by the performance playing out before them.

There was an intensity and gentleness that Kitty hadn't seen in Charles until now. Usually serious and focused, he rarely showed emotion. It was his grave countenance which had drawn her to him when they first met, his unwillingness to be pulled into the more frivolous conversations within their social circle. But she'd sometimes wondered if he kept a veil over his emotions, sensing an aversion to displaying any sentiment. Or perhaps it was just his way of somehow ageing his baby-faced looks. At forty-two his fresh, seemingly worry-free features defied his years, a fact which he still found a hindrance during his dealings within his world of business. But, looking at him now, it was as if he was no longer ashamed of his youthful looks; there was an unexpected openness in his whole demeanour.

'It was the one thing we had in common, our love of this place.' He was staring into the distant water, and Kitty, enjoying this new openness, didn't want to quiz him too much, just happy to let him say what he needed to. But the moment passed as he suddenly turned to her with a boyish grin on his face.

'Come, let me show you the house.' Keeping a hand on Kitty's waist, he turned her around to look at the building behind them.

Ardbray House faced the loch, standing close to the water. Looking at it more closely, Kitty was now taken aback by the sheer size and complexity of it. Built from the local sandstone, it stood out from its bleak surroundings. Despite the rumours of a mansion with grand pretensions, this house was far beyond anything she'd been expecting. A sombre and imposing door greeted them, surrounded by a stone archway, carved with criss-crossed vines, which was then topped by a yawning gargoyle. The longer Kitty looked at the front of the house, the more she noted the attention to detail. Each spiralling turret was finished off with a different patterned pinnacle; every roof had its own distinct type of red tile. Elaborately carved gargoyles could be seen on every corner and gable, staring, laughing, winking; each one with a different expression. The windows were latticed, resembling those in a church; always arched and surrounded by vaulted, patterned stone.

The late evening sun shone on the red stone, accentuating the details, but as the dark clouds gathered, the sun threw an unnatural, golden sheen onto the house, inviting those who were outside to come in.

Before Kitty could laugh at the sheer audaciousness of the house, Charles took hold of her hand and pulled her towards it. Approaching the steps leading up to the front door, it opened and they were greeted by the sight of a petite, middle-aged woman, with neat, mouse-brown hair, tucked into a bun.

Walking into the hallway, Kitty could see two wrought-iron candelabra sending an orangey, murky light upwards, revealing a hall that rose up through three storeys to the roofline of the house, with glass panels at the very top letting in a now watery grey light, cold against the warm flames of the enormous hanging lanterns. An expansive staircase swept into the room, with shadows accentuating the intricate stone balustrade. She could see that the walls were lined with a geometric floral pattern but were, so far, empty of any pictures or ornaments, except a large stag's head, mounted onto a wooden panel, staring menacingly at Kitty. Without any decoration or daylight, this room was cavernous and a little intimidating.

'Mrs Lindsay, may I introduce you to my wife, Mrs Maclean.' He waved Kitty into the hall in a grand manner and almost bowed. Kitty suppressed a smile as she turned to the housekeeper.

'It's a pleasure to welcome you to your new home, Mrs Maclean. On behalf of all the staff, we hope you enjoy your visit and many more to come.' Mrs Lindsay's congenial tone poured warmth into the room.

'Thank you. It's a pleasure to meet you too.' She dried up and looked to Charles for help.

'Mrs Lindsay, I'm going to show my wife around, perhaps you could furnish us with a lantern and then arrange for tea to be brought to my study in, say, half an hour?'

Ahead of her lay a pair of imposing oak double doors, again arched, this time the carved panels showing an oak tree which split in two vertically when the door opened. Charles pushed both doors to reveal a spacious room with high ceilings.

The walls were covered with a red and gold brocaded wallpaper, the ceilings decorated with intricate plaster mouldings. Without any furniture, the room seemed vast and hollow, but a grand fireplace dominated the room, the fire blazing and already relishing the task of warming up such a magnificent space. The grey marble surround intrigued with its inlaid pattern of different coloured marble: red, green and white in a symmetrical design.

Kitty was silent as she walked around the room, her hand touching the cool marble, feeling the pattern of the wallpaper. As she stopped at a deep window seat, with a luscious, red velvet cushion to match the curtains and the window overlooking the loch, she could smell the newness of the room, a smell not yet friendly but with promise.. Charles walked over to a large set of French doors, his footsteps booming on the uncarpeted floorboards. A key was already in the lock and he turned it, and there was a crack as he pushed, the doors not yet used to being opened. The evening air was a welcome intrusion, filling the room with a fresh perfume.

'As you can see, there's still an enormous amount of work to be done. Many of the rooms are yet to be furnished, we'll be one of the first to install what's called a central heating system, designed to keep the whole house warm, and we haven't even started on the gardens.' He looked outside and then put his hand out to Kitty. 'Come over here.' His eyes sparkled as he spoke.

At the doorway, Kitty stopped and once again breathed in the clear air.

'Would you help design the gardens? There's so much to do and I don't have the time to be involved with the garden as well as the house. It would mean a lot to me if you could.'

Kitty smiled. A project; something to keep the new bride busy. It wouldn't do to have her bored now, would it? She might stray. Her mother would have approved of the ploy. But there was a childish innocence in his manner, a naivety that could only persuade her to join in.

'Of course.' A stray length of hair blew across her face. 'Have you had any ideas about what you'd like to do?' She surveyed the ground in front of her; a wide flat area of mud and wild grass extending towards the shingled beach. Off to the side, the grass gently sloped down to the mouth of the burn that ran close to the side of the house. She could smell the fresh, tumbling water.

'Fruit and vegetables will have to be our priority as we are so far from the railway and access to fresh food will always be difficult. We must build a walled garden as soon as possible so that we can be self-sufficient. I think the best place is over there.' He turned and pointed across the burn to a further expanse of flat ground. 'I've just employed a gardener, Fraser. He can work out the best aspect and all the other technicalities with you.' He turned back to Kitty, his boyish grin returning. 'After that, the rest is just,' he frowned as he hesitated, 'well, just a few flowers. I'm sure you can manage that.'

He took Kitty's hand again and walked her down to the stony beach. 'We don't have much land here. My father wasn't interested in sheep farming or foresting, and neither of us wanted to get into maintaining a large amount of land. I don't know if you've noticed how people want to own as much land as possible these days; some kind of status symbol. I don't need status symbols.'

Kitty suppressed a smile as she glanced back at the house.

Charles shook his head, his hair falling across his eyes. 'I don't need troublesome crofters or cotters, I have enough of that at the mill.' For a moment, the usual seriousness returned as he seemed to consider his remark. 'So, all the hills you see around you are owned by the Duke of Westminster. My father managed to persuade him to let him buy these one hundred or so acres. But we have a gentleman's agreement that states that he's happy that we walk the hills as much as we want, and I've arranged to be able to take our guests stalking or grouse shooting when I need to.'

Kitty let go of Charles's hand and walked onto the beach, wishing she could take off her shoes. The angular beach stones begged her for adventure. Ignoring the desire to pick up one of the stones and throw it into the water she turned back towards the house. The clarity of air was beginning to sharpen her mind, dulled by the long, jolting carriage journey.

'Why did you build in such a remote place?' Loch More was thirty-three miles from Lairg station, an uncomfortable, four-hour carriage journey along a narrow and twisted road.

Charles looked up at the stone walls as if he was inspecting the workmanship. The evening light was fading and the house had lost its golden gleam, its presence had become almost menacing against the darkening hills.

'Well, my father began the build. It was his dream to have a big country house, somewhere he could show off to all those new friends he'd made, show them how far he'd come, show them how some hard work can go a long way. He wanted to let them see that now you can build in such a remote place, now the railway is close enough, now the road is good enough and now, if you've got the money, then almost anything is possible. He just wanted to show them that it could be done.'

Kitty blinked as she caught the bitterness in his voice. Charles was staring into the loch, his gaze lost into the distance.

'But, as you know, he died last year. When he was ill, he made me promise to finish what he'd begun. He was insistent, told me I wouldn't inherit if I failed in this one quest.' He smiled at Kitty, his voice now wistful. 'But the irony of it all is that I love this place even more than he did. Building Ardbray was the one thing I genuinely wanted to do. Here is where I feel at ease, away from the hustle in Glasgow, away from the mill, away from my—' He stopped abruptly and turned away.

Kitty wondered what he was going to say but still didn't feel able to probe. There was no rush; they had three weeks to look forward to, three weeks without interference when she could get to know this new husband of hers. She looked back across the water and could just make out two small, whitewashed cottages. She'd been assured that at the far end of the five-mile loch, there was the small village of Achfary with its Estate Office, a few estate workers' houses and the Duke of Westminster's Lodge. But on the journey from the station, they had passed only a handful of cottages, a small coaching inn and a couple of fishing lodges. Not many people wanted to live here.

'Come on,' Charles broke into her thoughts, 'I've got something to show you.'

Charles was talking: projects, ideas and the future in their new house. Kitty couldn't listen, the words blurring in her mind. She looked around her, pushing away the desire to let out a childish giggle. A library, the kind of room she had dreamed of, right where she was going to live. Her heart was jumping as she ran her hand across the rows of leather-bound books, feeling the indents of the lettering on the spines. The smell was overpowering her, making her feel almost dizzy.

'Kitty?' Charles stopped his torrent of talk. 'You're very flushed. Are you all right? Here, sit down. Perhaps the long journey has taken its toll on you.' He led her towards a chaise longue that was close to some French doors. 'Let me open the doors and give you some air.'

She sat, the cool air calming her glowing cheeks.

'You rest whilst I check with Mrs Lindsay that tea is ready, and then we can go to my study and sit by the fire.' He'd squatted down in front of her and laid his hand on her shoulder, giving it a gentle squeeze before leaving the room.

The evening air continued to dance on her face, the soothing *slap, slap* of the waves on the loch shore inducing an almost trance-like state. For the first time since she'd left her parents' home, she began to relax, the deep knots in her stomach releasing.

Her eyes skipped from shelf to shelf. Here was an exhilarating room full of books. Every single piece of available wall space had been dedicated to reading and learning. She couldn't stay sitting any longer; like iron filings, she was being magnetically pulled towards the books. As she got closer, she noticed that the wooden vertical struts that divided each set of shelves were individually carved. Every strut was decorated with a wooden image related to the subject of the books on the adjacent shelf. The struts denoting Food and Drink were etched with grape vines, loaves and fruit, the Agriculture section with wheat sheaves and threshers. Religion was decorated with crosses and hands in prayer, whereas Military History had cannons, swords and shields. Kitty walked around the room, finally beginning to cool down, a smile appearing as she examined each surprising detail. It wasn't until she reached the medical section that she let slip a small gasp. Hiding amongst the wooden shelves decorated with the Rod of Asclepius, scissors and needles, were a wide range of medical books, many of which she recognised from her father's study, including exact copies of her recently removed anatomy books.

She leaned in closer and pulled out Nicholas Culpeper's *Complete Herbal* and began flicking through it. Absently turning to the middle of the room, she sank into one of the deep, leather armchairs clustered beside a drinks' cabinet and a small desk. After a couple of minutes of reading, she put the book down and leaned back, closed her eyes, letting a huge grin spread across her face. Someone had spent time considering the people who would use this room and she was looking forward to finding out more. Another knot in her stomach eased. Just maybe this marriage might work, just maybe they had something in common. Perhaps, they could enjoy this room full of books together.

'There you are, looking better already.' Charles walked in. 'Tea's ready, let's go to my study and you can tell me what you think so far.' He put a hand out for Kitty. She pulled herself upright and with a determined glint, tucked a stray hair behind her right ear and took her husband's hand.

Kitty poured the tea into delicate porcelain cups decorated with tiny pink rosebuds. This warm, elegant tea set was in stark contrast to the cold, oppressiveness of the room. A wide, leather-topped desk stood in front of the window, no papers or photographs worrying it, a plain wooden chair beside it. The shelves on either side of the fireplace were empty, no pictures on the walls. The stiff, high-backed chairs they were sitting in seemed formal and uninviting. The ceiling was sectioned into deep squares of intricate plasterwork that bore down on the room's occupants, making the room seem slightly claustrophobic, despite the lack of furniture and the usual country gentleman's accoutrements of guns, bronzes, paintings and hunting trophies. Perhaps Charles had not spent much time here, hadn't yet had time to give the room his attention. She frowned. The room was spotless, weighty and without soul.

As Charles took a sip of his tea, she noticed his fingers, long and elegant, almost like a woman's; manicured and fastidiously kept. He held his cup in a very particular way, just like he held his pen, almost as if he had re-taught himself to hold it differently, wanting to make an effect.

'I see that you were taken aback by the outside of the house. That's exactly the kind of lasting impression my father and I wanted; we wanted people to notice the detail and talk about it. He let the architect have free rein, his only brief being that it make a mark on all those that visit.'

Kitty stared at him, unable to find anything suitable to say.

'And what do you think of the library?' He put his cup and saucer down on the coffee table between them.

'I was... astounded, surprised.' Kitty reddened and looked down, unable to meet his gaze. 'I've never seen a private library like that. So big, so well stocked and so inviting.' The fire cracked and a log fell on the hearth. As Charles got up to deal with it, she continued, 'I didn't think you were that interested in books.'

He sat back down heavily. 'You're right. I don't have time for them. I prefer to learn through life.' His tone was brisk, a little pompous. 'My father had made no plans for a library, but I decided I needed one for our guests. Whenever I've been to any of the great houses, Hopetoun or Culzean, I noticed they always had an impressive library, which never failed to appeal to the male guests. I have every intention of using Ardbray as somewhere to entertain, make our mark in society. And if I'm going to make any impact on these people, I need them to think I'm well-educated and well-read. I'm not; I hated my education and did as little as I could get away with. It doesn't matter that I'm not interested in any of those books, they won't know any better; it's the impression I give that makes the difference.' A note of defensiveness had crept into his voice.

Kitty blinked, her teacup on her knee.

'So, I found an expert in books; a bibliophile, if you will. I asked him to design the room and fill it with the right sort of books.' He stopped and picked up his tea again, drinking until finished. 'So,' he continued, his demeanour suddenly more genial again, 'I think you'll find that this is the finest library north of Glasgow.' There was a hint of glee in his voice as he patted his chest.

Kitty bit her lip, still searching for something appropriate to say. 'Are you still looking for books? I see there were some empty shelves.'

'Yes, I gathered from your father that you enjoy books. So, I left some space for you. I'm sure you could fill it with those penny novels you girls like to read. Besides, they would be good entertainment for the wives when they come to stay, something else for them to do.'

To Kitty, his words dropped like a silent stone to the floor. The fire cracked again and she could just hear the evening wind in the trees outside. She fixed her eyes on her teacup as disappointment filtered through her body. She looked carefully at the pretty rosebuds on the outside of her cup and wondered who had been in charge of choosing this tea set: Charles, the housekeeper, or some faceless expert in home decoration.

Kitty lay in bed, her eyes closed, still half-asleep. She was not quite sure where she was, the unfamiliar smell confusing. Opening her eyes, she smiled, that altogether new smell of course being the new furniture, new bedding, new rugs on the floor. Turning, she found an indent next to her, the covers pulled back. Charles must have already risen. Looking at the slit of light coming through the curtains, she couldn't quite tell what the time was, the light in the Highlands being different to Glasgow; the mornings arriving a little sooner at this time of year. She got out of bed, walked over to the window and drew back the heavy drapes.

It was a dull day; the cloud was low, covering the hills. With the heavy drizzle, the loch appeared to be closing in. The accentuated colours from the evening before had disappeared, and the smudged slopes were beginning to merge into the dark, matt black of the water.

Kitty sat on the window seat, pulling her legs up to her chest and drawing her nightgown around her knees. Her sleeping mind was starting up as she looked over the quiet loch. The last two days had been a whirlwind and she was glad of some time to herself.

It was becoming clear that Charles was made up of a whole set of contradictions. She'd seen so little of him before the wedding that she'd not had the time to get to know him. In their restricted, heavily chaperoned meetings, he'd been more interesting and more serious than any others from the procession of suitors. She'd wanted to ask him so much, but too often her mother would interfere and had never given them the opportunity to discuss anything in detail. It seemed so strange to her that she could enter into a marriage, enter into an intimate relationship with someone she hardly knew.

But last night she'd begun to see several sides of her new husband, sides which didn't seem to match up. There was the playful, excited Charles with a hint of real passion for his country residence, but he'd all too quickly been replaced by an angry and bitter Charles that she didn't recognise. At dinner, after a few glasses of wine, he'd softened into someone more approachable, someone who appeared interested in her. He'd even asked her about the work she'd done in the Saltmarket Clinic, where she sometimes worked as an assistant to the busy doctors, and how she thought she could make use of that experience. And then there was the man who didn't like books, who only wanted to use them to impress. She watched the drizzle as a gust of wind threw it to one side like a sheet of paper.

She'd been used to consistency in her life, people who were predictable: Martha who was always there, smiley and bubbly; Eva, bright and perceptive; her father, kind and thoughtful; and her mother, watchful and interfering. But now she realised that she was going to have to feel her way around this marriage; she was going to have to spend time working out who this man was, this man who only wanted to use the house he professed to love so much to better his position in society, this man who didn't want land as a status symbol but needed as large a house as possible to show off his wealth. She followed the grey landscape outside, realising that she was going to have to learn to see life through a different lens, to live it with someone she didn't understand.

'Treat it as a lifelong adventure,' Eva had declared a few days before the wedding. 'How lucky you are to be on the brink of something new and exciting, whilst the rest of us are still on the marriage merry-go-round.'

She had laughed at Eva's optimism. She couldn't see how her life would change that much. 'I'll still be doing the same round of Glasgow tea parties and dances, it's just that nobody will be watching to see whether I've caught the eye of some bachelor on the hunt.' But today she was happy with Eva's idea of adventure. She could see the possibilities that Ardbray offered and, since Charles appeared more relaxed here, perhaps she could start the conversation about finding something meaningful to occupy her time. Perhaps, now that they were away from the strictures of Glasgow, he might be open to, what her mother described as, some of her more unconventional ideas. Kitty smiled as she thought about Charles's little boy grin that he had kept from her until yesterday and decided that she'd like to see more of it. She anticipated three pleasurable weeks stretching before her. Surely, she'd find plenty of opportunity to coax it out of him again? A feeling of optimism began to needle its way in as she watched drops of drizzle gently slide down the window.

There was a sharp knock at the door.

'Come in.' Kitty turned her head to see Mrs Lindsay walk in, her swift, purposeful manner belying her petite frame. Kitty stood up, smoothing down her hair, pulling at her nightdress, her cheeks still flushed at the thought of Charles.

'Good morning, Mrs Maclean. Have you slept well?'

'Thank you, yes.'

'Aye, well it's a dreich day out there.' Mrs Lindsay walked over to the other window and tucked the curtains behind a large brass hook. 'You'll not be wanting to be outside today.'

'Well, a miserable day in the Highlands has to be better than a miserable day in Glasgow.'

Mrs Lindsay stopped her busying and looked at Kitty, her hands on her hips. A broad smile crossed her face. 'Aye, you'll be right there.' The businesslike demeanour softened. 'Can I bring you your breakfast?'

'Yes, please, but... have you seen Mr Maclean this morning?'

The housekeeper briefly looked down at Kitty's feet. 'Aye well, he's an early riser, you see.' Her right hand was clasping her flattened left hand, almost massaging it with her thumb. 'We had a messenger at about six o'clock and in half an hour, Mr Maclean had left for Glasgae.' She fumbled around with the pocket in her skirt. 'He left a note.' She stiffly handed Kitty a piece of folded paper.

Kitty took the note with a slow, heavy hand. Without thanking Mrs Lindsay, she unfolded it and read:

Kitty, darling,

I have to return to the mill immediately. It seems the union is forcing some kind of strike. Stay here and enjoy Ardbray, get to know it. I will be back in a few days.

Your loving husband,
Charles

She stared at the note, the words slowly becoming a blur as her eyes focused somewhere behind it. She could feel her tongue on the roof of her mouth, dry, almost sticky. Making herself sit up straight, she did her best to show no outward reaction to Mrs Lindsay, trying to keep her shoulders from sloping, as if she was still reading the letter; a long love letter, a letter that should have made her smile and blush. But the paper became taut, her fingers white as she held it too firmly. Her stare continued and she wondered if her adventure had already ended.

No. She inwardly shook herself. Surely, she couldn't fall at the first hurdle? There was more to her than that. She had the house and all the staff to get to know, a garden to construct and miles of hills to discover by herself. She had no mother to chaperone her, and, for the moment, no husband for her to follow. For the first time in her life, she could be her own woman. She had no idea how to run a house or design a garden, but she didn't care; there was definitely some of Eva's adventure to be had. The dull ache of disappointment was slowly replaced by a slight buzz of excitement. Resolutely, she pushed her unbrushed hair off her face and stood up.

'Mrs Lindsay, it seems you are to be my companion for the next few days. Perhaps you could spend some time with me and help me to get to know the house, Achfary and... well, show me what I need to do.' She shrugged her shoulders. 'I'm afraid I come here very unprepared and need some instruction on household management.'

Mrs Lindsay unclasped her hands. 'It'll be my pleasure.' But her smile quickly turned to a question. 'But I hope you don't mind me askin', I noticed that you didn't bring a lady's maid. Were you expectin' one to be here?'

'Oh, no.' Kitty touched the collar of her nightgown. 'I wasn't expecting anything.' She hesitated. 'You see I just thought nobody could replace Martha, my maid in Glasgow.' She watched Mrs Lindsay smile, gentle experience in her eyes.

'Aye, Mrs Maclean, when it's just the two of us, you may not need a maid, but when the house is busy with guests an' you're ensuring they're happy, it'll be vital to have some help.' Mrs Lindsay moved over to the wardrobe and opened its door. 'Don't think she just helps with your dressing, she's responsible for mending an' cleaning every item of your wardrobe,' – she pulled out a skirt, looking at its hem – 'makin' sure you don't wear the same thing twice in front of your guests. Then there's your hair, the hats an' packing when you need to travel. It's a busy job.'

Kitty understood the chastisement but was glad of the

gentle manner it had been said in. She considered how the same conversation would have played out with her mother.

'Of course, you're right. Might you know of someone who would be suitable?' Kitty walked over to her dressing table and sat down, starting to brush her own hair.

'Well, I've bin thinking. There's a girl in Lairg I know of. She's bin working as a dressmaker in Glasgae but had to come home because her grandfather was ill. He's died now, but she doesnae want to go back to the city. I could arrange for her to come here an' meet you.'

Kitty continued to brush, looking in the mirror at the image of the housekeeper. 'Yes, can you do that? But, could you wait a few days? Let me settle in, get to know Ardbray a little?'

The slight movement of Mrs Lindsay's head to one side was almost imperceptible. 'Aye. I'll arrange for her to be here in, shall we say, four days' time?'

Kitty nodded. 'Perfect.'

'Meanwhile, shall I be getting you that breakfast?'

'So, I would expect you to go through the menu with me every day, and when that's done we can talk about anything else that's needed. Maebe problems with the staff, or you could let me know if we've guests expected...'

Mrs Lindsay's voice faded into the background, Kitty's mind full and no longer able to take in what the housekeeper was saying.

They were in Mrs Lindsay's room, neat and spotless, just like its occupier. It was a cosy, cupboard-lined room with two upright armchairs, not too comfy, in front of the fire. The room was dominated by a cloth-covered table acting as a desk, covered in ledgers and papers. Kitty sat at this table, her eyes glazing over the accounts and straying towards the bookshelf in the corner of the room: cookbooks, a battered copy of *Debrett's*

Peerage as well as *Cassell's Household Management*. A plain linen sewing basket sat underneath the shelves with a tidy pile of mending.

Perhaps Kitty should have been angry at her mother for giving her no preparation for household management. Part of her was surprised at her mother's lack of foresight. If she'd been planning a brilliant marriage, surely she'd have looked ahead and given Kitty the ability to plan and deliver triumphant house parties. She was beginning to see that running a smooth household must at least be part of the complicated puzzle that was a successful marital alliance.

She knew she should be more attentive to Mrs Lindsay's patient and painstaking explanations: accounts, linen, winter and summer curtains, spring cleaning, preparing for the winter, bottling, preserving, the hiring of servants, the arrival of new furniture, the planned decoration and the installation of the heating system and bathrooms. The list was endless and Kitty's mind kept wandering back to the library and all the hours of promised pleasure that it held. With difficulty, she pulled her mind back to the figures in front of her. Listening to the kind patience in Mrs Lindsay's voice, she could see that her housekeeper was turning out to be her ally, showing no surprise or irritation at her lack of domestic tuition; she suspected that the woman sitting in front of her had seen it all before.

'You must check my accounts every month, just so that you're absolutely certain of everything that has gone on in the house, and so that you'll be able to report with confidence to Mr Maclean whenever you need to.'

Kitty went to interrupt, but Mrs Lindsay put her hand up to stop her.

'Aye, that maebe. But you and I need to be able to trust each other. You need to understand this if I'm to work for you, I need everything above board.' She held Kitty's eye with a steely glare. 'And, you wouldnae want to be in the position when Mr

Maclean questioned you about some aspect of the household and you couldnae answer.'

Kitty wondered if her mother's housekeeper had ever spoken to her like that. But there didn't seem to be a hint of resentment in Mrs Lindsay's voice and the glare was quickly replaced by a smile as she changed the subject. 'Now, I believe we should be looking for Fraser. I suspect he'll be out front, finding out what he's got to work with.'

The housekeeper stood up. She shut her ledger and laid it on a pile of books and then straightened them. When all her papers were in order, she gave them a quick pat and stepped back to look at her work. With a nod of her head, she turned and indicated to Kitty that they leave the room.

Fraser was pacing outside the front of the house. As Kitty approached, he grabbed his cap from his head and began screwing it up between his hands.

'Ma'am.' He nodded.

'Fraser.' Kitty didn't quite know how to proceed.

'Perhaps you should walk the grounds,' Mrs Lindsay suggested and then turned and left them to it.

The two did as they were told, silence reigning over them until Kitty stopped at the burn.

'Fraser, I can stitch up a gash in your leg, I can help bring a fever down, I can take your blood using a hypodermic syringe if needed, but I don't know the first thing about gardening. I hardly know a buttercup from a thistle.' As she spoke, she could see the gardener's face drop. 'I've lived in Glasgow most of my life. I know that oil made from camomile makes a good antiseptic, but I wouldn't know how to grow it. I have no notion of when the best time to plant a rose is, or how you cultivate a carrot. Form and shape in a garden are not something I'm familiar with. But I'd like to be useful, I'd like to make this a practical and magnificent garden. I know that being surrounded by beauty will make every one of us who live here happier, and if we can make our practical garden beautiful then so much the better.'

Fraser stopped wringing his cap out and the lines on his weather-beaten face disappeared. The hat went back on his head, hands in pockets, and he began pacing up and down as he spoke.

'Well, ma'am, obviously we need a kitchen garden most urgent. If we're tae survive the winter here, we need tae be as self-sufficient as we can. Mrs Lindsay is badgering me tae plant fruit, trees an' bushes, an' some vegetables raeght now. We've missed a fair bit of the season, but we could get by with some planting straight away. We maebe a bit short this winter, but if we get on wi't now, we should be raeght for next winter.'

Kitty was emboldened by his enthusiasm. 'My husband believes that a walled garden just beyond the burn would work. Do you agree?'

'Aye, it's south facing an' it's the place we'll get as much sun as is possible here, and we'll be sheltered from the north by the hills.'

'Well, we should start straight away. Tell me, what do you need me to do?'

There was a smirk threatening to break out on his round, leathery face. What was it that was amusing him, her naivety or her honesty? She guessed he must have been in his early thirties, much older, and surely more knowledgeable than her. She knew she must defer to the experience that had caused those crows' feet around his eyes, that had shaped his lean and wiry frame.

'Drawings. We need to do some drawings. To show the stonemason where to build the greenhouses, to show the planting. Can you do that?' As he looked at Kitty, she felt there was still a hint of mischief, that he was testing her.

Panic began to take over; she had no idea where to start. Fraser laughed.

'That library. There'll be books in there. Why don't you start there?' His voice was light, now there was no trace of mockery.

Kitty looked away at the loch, suppressing a smile. Here was a genuine invitation to go and make use of the library. So far she hadn't dared. Despite wanting to, she'd felt it would have been too much of an indulgence when she'd had so much to learn with Mrs Lindsay. But here was the opportunity to pander to her love of books, learning and the need to be useful.

'Well, yes, of course.' Kitty turned with sudden heat. 'I'll start straight away.' Without thinking, she picked up her skirts and turned to the house, rushing in an ungainly fashion towards the front door. Just as suddenly she remembered herself and stopped, turning back to Fraser.

'Sorry.' She reddened. 'Thank you. Yes... perhaps we can talk again tomorrow when I've had a chance to look up a few things?'

A broad grin had spread across his face. 'Aye, if you'll let me start preparing the ground over across the burn?' It was as if he was making a deal; her indulgence for permission to get started.

'Oh.' Kitty paused, looking at Fraser's feet briefly and then started to walk back towards him. 'I never asked, how did you come to be here, I mean...? She shuffled awkwardly.

Fraser's face darkened with annoyance. 'If you mean what gives me the right tae be here, I've spent the last ten years working with Mr Osgood Mackenzie in his garden at Inverewe. I think you'll be finding that qualification enough. Good day.' He turned abruptly and walked up the hill.

Kitty sighed, brushed her hair off her face and turned to the loch. Not for the first time, she hadn't handled herself well. She had no problem talking to anyone if they were sick or in need of help, but her ability to manage staff was, clearly, woefully lack- ing. Again, she thought of her mother. But she knew that she couldn't lay all the blame at her feet; she'd just never been interested in domestic details and, when in her own small world of medicine or tucked up in her father's study reading, she'd unconsciously hoped that she'd never have to deal with the everyday minutiae of managing a house, servants or their welfare problems.

She walked over to the burn and up the hill until she came to a small wooden bridge. Leaning on the railing, she looked down into the water, mesmerised by the clusters of dancing foam, tumbling into themselves like a bunch of unruly children. Slowly, her disquiet began to dissolve, and soon she began to look forward to the days ahead of her, days which were hers alone, with no one to interfere or meddle with her thoughts and ideas. Suddenly, a delicious feeling of freedom spread over her; despite her shortcomings, she knew that she had four days in which she could make her own decisions and work to her own schedule without a chaperone, mother or husband to hinder her every move.

Kitty sat at the large desk in the library. She was surrounded by open books and had a neat set of papers in front of her with drawings and ideas set out. Fraser had been right; Charles's so-called bibliophile had filled the horticulture section of the library with everything she'd needed. Spread out in front of her were books about the famous gardens at Inverewe, Drummond Castle and Dalkeith Palace. Charles McIntosh's *The Book of the Garden* had given her a good steer in the direction of style, layout, colour and the importance of soil and water. But her head was spinning, she was trying to learn something which, it was becoming obvious, took a lifetime to master.

She'd spent four days holed up in the library, immersing herself in the subject and doing her best to understand what she was supposed to do. The pleasure of being able to sit with books and study had been even greater than she'd expected;

uninterrupted and sustained reading was something she would gladly do for as long as she was allowed. The fact that she'd been able to do it without needing to ask for permission had almost been a thrill. The days passed without her noticing, and only because Mrs Lindsay insisted she eat and take exercise did she remember to tear herself away at regular intervals and take herself into the hills to explore her new surroundings.

'Ma'am?' Fraser stood before her with his cap in his hands.

'Oh, Fraser. I didn't see you there.' She put her hand to her heart, flushing as she stood up. 'Please, sit.'

Awkwardly, Fraser sat in the chair opposite her.

'When I've been out walking, I've seen that the ground preparation is going on apace. Likewise, I've been busy doing as you suggested. I've been reading about garden design and I've managed to come up with some ideas. I know that perhaps they're a bit basic and that my knowledge is lacking, but maybe with all your experience, we might be able to turn them into something useful?'

Fraser was staring at the table, seemingly unmoved by her words.

Haltingly, she picked up the sheets of paper. 'Here... why don't you have a look?' She passed her drawings to him.

He took them, his eyes narrowed and then he sat forward in his chair to inspect her handiwork. After a few minutes of studying the papers, he examined the books on the desk briefly, before putting them back down.

Kitty felt she needed to fill the silence. 'I'm interested in making a herb garden. I'd like to grow some medicinal herbs as well as those for the kitchen. If you look closely, I've made an area in one corner of the garden.' She pointed to the plan. 'I've been reading Mr Culpeper's book and I'm keen to grow herbs that will be useful to all of us here, since we're so far from a doctor.'

As she said this, Fraser frowned. 'Aye, but food is the most important thing...'

'Which will be no good to us if we're all sick,' Kitty quipped back without thinking.

The two stared at each other. Kitty, astounded at her audacity, trying to stand her ground and not give in to her inherent politeness and apologise for her bold interruption.

Eventually, Fraser sat back in his chair, sighed and said, 'Ma'am. You have your corner.' He picked up one of the papers. 'It's a start. To be honest, I didn't think you'd take me seriously.' He shook the paper at Kitty. 'They's some basic errors in here, but we can work around them.' Grinning at her, he continued, 'Aye, we can get moving, I've already got seedlings growing, and we might even be able to get some of Mrs Lindsay's planting sorted.'

Kitty let out a silent sigh of relief. 'So, let me know what you need me to do now, would you?'

'Aye, I'll look these over more carefully an' make a start. We've the stone arriving tomorrow and the men to start building.' He stood up. 'Maebe you could get out there diggin' with me.' He did nothing to hide his amusement as he left the room.

She leaned back in her chair and let out a heavy sigh. She wondered if Fraser would even take a moment's notice of her plans, would already have his own ideas. Perhaps this was just a ruse to keep her out of trouble, make her feel that she was in charge when in reality they would have happily carried on without her. She started closing the books and putting them back on the right shelves. Perhaps one day she'd master the art of reading people.

'Mrs Maclean?'

Kitty's thoughts were interrupted by Mrs Lindsay.

'Eleanor is here.'

She frowned, not knowing whom Mrs Lindsay was referring to.

'The girl from Lairg, she's here to see about the position of lady's maid. Shall I show her in?'

Kitty's heart sank. Another situation that she wasn't qualified for. She pulled herself upright and gritted her teeth. 'Yes, of course. But perhaps, Mrs Lindsay, you could join me so we can both talk to her?'

Yet again, Kitty only just noticed the slight movement of Mrs Lindsay's head, a momentary question that would have passed most people by.

'Of course. I'll be raeght back.'

Kitty finished tidying the desk and sat down in the chair listening out for approaching footsteps. She let her gaze wander to the window, the greying afternoon rendering the hills into a green blur, any definition disappearing as if a painter's brush had just swept across the hillside.

Her few days being alone and unchaperoned were coming to an end. With no parent supervising her, no false task to complete for her mother and no husband to answer to, she'd been able to be her own master. Her nose in a book, walking the hills or even paddling in the loch with her shoes off; she'd tasted a liberty that she'd never expected. Perhaps, one day, she would look back in horror that Charles had abandoned her on their honeymoon, but right now she could only see it as a serendipitous gift that she might never have again. With a new lady's maid and Charles's imminent return, she couldn't see that there'd be much time again for her own company. A small part of her wished that she could stay in the library and not have to worry about navigating a marriage, running a house or returning to Glasgow.

'Mrs Maclean.' Mrs Lindsay hustled a young girl into the room. 'This is Eleanor.'

Kitty watched the girl shuffle towards the chair. Round and fresh-faced, she stood with her hands clasped together rigidly, her face taut and her eyes watching earnestly.

The three women sat.

'Um, well. It's good to meet you, Eleanor,' Kitty stuttered. 'Thank you for coming so far.' She looked down at her hands, struggling to know what to say. 'Um, can you tell me what experience you have working as a lady's maid?'

This time it was the turn of the girl to struggle. Shuffling in her seat, she reddened before replying. 'I've only ever worked in a factory, ma'am.' She looked to Mrs Lindsay who stared back at her as if she was willing her on.

'I worked in a clothes factory, sewing,' Eleanor said, her tone bitter. 'So, I know how to look after your clothes.' Her shoulders were hunched as she held her hands in a prayer position between her knees. 'I could even make them for you if you want. I know how to pin hair an' I'm discreet. I'm not one for talking or gossiping an'...' She looked at Mrs Lindsay again, her voice trailing away.

To Kitty's relief, there was a loud knock and one of the housemaids walked in bringing an envelope to Mrs Lindsay. She gave it a brief look and passed it to Kitty.

As Kitty saw the handwriting, her heart sank, her limbs became heavy. Charles. She carefully opened the envelope, her face blank but her mind racing.

Kitty, my darling,

I am on the verge of securing a financial agreement that could seal our future. I need you in Glasgow. We must entertain my new business partner; I wish to show you off to him.

Be back in Park Street Friday afternoon. Our guest will be arriving for dinner at seven o'clock sharp.

Your husband,
Charles

Yet again she found herself pretending to read a longer and more alluring letter, a letter that was going to entertain her, tell her how much he missed her, wishing for her to return because he couldn't bear to be without her. But as much as she wished for this, she was already mourning her freedom; her permit to do as she pleased had been rescinded and she needed to take up her new life as Mrs Charles Maclean.

'Mrs Lindsay, I have to return to Glasgow.' Her voice faltered. 'I... I have to be there tomorrow evening.' Her thumb played with the edge of the paper.

It was as if her housekeeper had expected this all along. 'Aye, you'd better be getting to Lairg this evening. I can arrange for the carriage so you can stay at the Sutherland Arms tonight and you'll be able to catch the morning train. You'll be in Glasgae by five o'clock.' She turned to the girl. 'Eleanor, maebe you could help Mrs Maclean pack. And, ma'am, if you're happy, she could accompany you to Lairg, pack her things overnight and take the train wi' you in the morning.'

FIVE

KITTY

Glasgow, 1889

Lavender

*'A tisane of Lavender, or even a spray of Lavender worn under a hat,
as the harvesters themselves apply it, will generally get rid of a nervous headache.'*

Herbal Delights *by Mrs C F Leyel*

The train pulled out of Lairg station as Kitty sat in her compartment alone. Facing forward and sitting by the grey, soot-daubed window, she watched the hills roll by, serene and sedate, unaffected by the intrusion of the steam train. Shortly the Dornoch Firth spread out in front of her, the sun catching the water, glistening with a rude cheerfulness that didn't match her mood.

Her hurried departure from Ardbray at the behest of her absent husband had put her in a melancholic temper. Petulantly, she realised that the strictures of Glasgow life were soon to surround her again and now, despite the fact that this was what she was used to, what she had spent the last nineteen years putting up with, she was no longer prepared for it. Just one week of her own freedom, her own company and her own decisions had changed all of that. She pulled off her gloves and removed her hat. Glad to be alone in the compartment, she was not ready to talk to strangers. She kept her eyes on the landscape, allowing her mind to empty and soon the rattling of the train began to entrance her, slowly drawing out the despondency and replacing it with a begrudging optimism. Hopefully, they'd be able to return to Ardbray within the next few days, where she could re-establish her life in the garden, the library and walking the hills, but this time with her husband by her side.

A knock at the compartment door interrupted her sleepy thoughts. The door opened and Eleanor put her head in.

'Excuse me, ma'am. I just wanted to let you know that all the luggage made it onto the train and that we should arrive in Glasgae by a quarter past five this afternoon.' Eleanor's voice brought some unexpected sunshine into the compartment.

'Come and join me.' Kitty pointed to the seat opposite her.

Her new maid frowned before checking the corridor behind her. 'Ma'am?'

'It's all right; I need company to lighten my mood. Come in, please, sit down.' Kitty gestured to the seat in front of her.

Eleanor checked the corridor again as if she was worried someone might catch her, before closing the door behind her.

'So, Eleanor, I do hope you'll be happy coming back to Glasgow. I'm just sorry it's been such a rush.' Kitty smiled at the girl as she sat down in the seat opposite.

'Oh, miss.' Eleanor grimaced. 'I'm sure working in your

house will be better'n where I worked an' lived a'fore.' She looked out of the window as the train slowed to stop at Tain station.

'You said you worked in a clothes factory. What kind of clothes did you make?' Kitty watched her closely, fascinated by the honesty in her face.

'Fine ladies' clothes. The kind of clothes you'd find in a big department store.' She began to hunch, almost shrinking as she continued to speak. 'It was machine sewing for fourteen hours a day. I don't mind working long hours, but it were hard work on the fingers and if they could ha' got away with us working longer hours, they would've done.' She showed Kitty her calloused and toughened fingers. 'They used to find any excuse to keep us working longer than we should. "Oh, today you made a mistake, you need to make up for that." Or, "Today you arrived five minutes late, you'll be doing an extra thirty minutes for that." They were hard on us.'

'How old are you?' Kitty asked.

Eleanor sat up, the change of subject bringing a smile back into her eyes. 'I was seventeen two weeks ago, the twenty-second of April.' A triumphant look on her shiny, apple face.

Just two years younger than Kitty. 'Well, many happy, belated returns of the day to you.' Kitty laughed. 'I hope you had a good birthday.'

'Aye, I did. Although it's bin sad because ma grandfather died recently, but it was the first birthday in years that I'd been able to spend with ma mother.'

'Why have you not been able to celebrate your birthday with her before?' Kitty watched Eleanor blush and she began to fidget.

'Ma mother's al'ays worked away in the big houses, just like Ardbray, since I cannae remember.'

'And your father?'

'Ma father died, I never knew him. Ma grandfather was like

ma real father. I've always lived with ma grandparents. Ma grandma still lives in Lairg.'

'But why did you go to Glasgow to work? Didn't you want to stay at home with your grandparents?'

The guard's whistle blew and the train jerked to a start before its slow, hypnotic rhythm began again, increasing as it left the station. Kitty absently watched the guard at the end of the platform as he leaned on a pile of well-travelled luggage, the leather cases plastered with labels of destinations, times and dates.

'I couldnae, there was nae work for me in Lairg. Even though I could sew, ma grandma taught me you see, there was nothing for me. I wanted just to take in sewing and mend and perhaps make some simple clothes, but there's already a couple o' seamstresses in Lairg and naebody wants a fifteen-year-old girl when you've got experience at hand.' Her face darkened. 'That's why I went to Glasgae.'

As Kitty watched the girl in front of her, she seemed to diminish as she spoke, almost cowering as she mentioned Glasgow. She decided that she shouldn't pursue her questioning. But she'd caught a flicker of something familiar in her manner, her voice, but she couldn't keep hold of it, couldn't work out what it was. She let go of it as she looked out of the window, the sea now yawning in front of her, flat and calm, the train jogging along, comfortable in its even flow.

Like Eleanor, she didn't want to return to Glasgow. She was going back to a husband, a house and a life that she didn't know. And until now she hadn't realised how much she hated Glasgow. But was it Glasgow she hated or the life she had to lead that she no longer wanted to be part of? She could identify with the attitude of her new maid, so perhaps it would help to have this new ally with her.

'It'll be an adventure for both of us.' She looked down at her hands, fingers scrunched up and white. 'A new house and a new husband for me, a new mistress and a new job for you. Between us, we will muddle through and let's hope that we'll be back at Ardbray in no time at all.' She straightened herself up and gave Eleanor her most encouraging smile. Turning back to the window, she noticed that it had begun to rain, diagonal lines of water sleeting across the glass, jiggling in time with the train, picking up grains of soot as they travelled. After a while, she leaned back in her seat and closed her eyes.

'You're late.'

The tone was jovial, but Kitty thought she heard a hint of irritation.

'I'm sorry, the train was delayed. A rock fall near Aviemore. I got here as quickly as I could.'

Charles gave her a quick peck on the cheek. The smell of whisky and cigars overwhelmed her for a moment, almost catching her off balance. As she drew herself away, she noticed his skin was a pasty, grey colour and he had dark circles under his eyes, his hair was dishevelled and his cravat undone. In just a few days, he had aged noticeably.

He took his watch out of his waistcoat pocket and clicked it open. 'There's not a minute to lose. Hardgrave will be here in half an hour. I need you dressed and looking at your finest.' He grabbed her elbow and steered her towards the stairs. 'You see, this partnership could turn out to be the biggest and most successful in the cotton industry's history.' He was sweating, his eyes bloodshot. 'Not even my father would have imagined that I could pull this one off,' he crowed, puffing out like a bird on display.

Kitty couldn't help but stare at this man she didn't recognise.

'There's no time for hanging about.' He shooed her along, but his words lost their urgency as they slurred slightly and he had to put a hand out to the banister to keep his balance. 'Tonight, we need everything to run like clockwork. I want to show Hardgrave that we can celebrate in the very best style.'

She gave him a questioning smile. 'Are we having a party?'

'Well, no. Just you, me and Hardgrave. You see we're in sore need of some female company and poor Hardgrave had to leave his wife at home in Yorkshire. Apparently, she hates to leave their estate and isn't a great one for parties. He would have had us out on the town tonight, a bachelor party indeed! But I felt sorry for him, thought he could use a quiet night in, something a little more homely after our long days of negotiations. I need you to play your part, be the perfect hostess, draw him out and see if you can show us the real John Hardgrave. Besides,' he continued, leaning forward and patting her hand, swaying slightly, 'I need to show my new business partner my beautiful new wife and make sure he lets his hair down a bit.' He checked his watch again. 'Now go, quickly, you must get ready!' Again, he shooed her up the stairs, but Kitty held her ground.

'Charles, you look terrible. Are you feeling quite well?'

'My dear, I haven't slept a wink for three days, just been too busy. You're quite right, I could do with some sleep, but I've committed to this dinner.' He frowned as he looked up the stairs, shuffling his feet. 'Please, would you go and get ready? I need you down here before he arrives.'

Kitty would have laughed if her husband's anguish didn't seem so real. 'Of course, but perhaps you could show me to my room?'

'Oh.' Charles blushed and appeared lost. 'Haven't I shown it to you before?'

Kitty did laugh at this. 'No, Charles, don't you remember? I have only visited for dinner; I have not had the pleasure of seeing the upstairs of your house.' In the hectic excitement of wedding and honeymoon preparations, somehow, the logistical plans for their future life in the Park Street house had been neglected.

'Oh,' Charles repeated and he ran his hands through his hair, looking around him in confusion. 'Fergusson,' he shouted. 'Fergusson!' Even louder. 'I'll get Fergusson to show you. I must finish some letters before John arrives and then I too must dress for dinner.' He started towards his study and then turned back to Kitty and opened his mouth as if about to speak, but Fergusson appeared from the depths of the house. His shadowy figure seeming to glide along the floor, his feet making no sound on the cream tiles.

'Ah, there you are. Would you show Mrs Maclean to her room?'

Fergusson gave a shallow nod and carried on noiselessly towards the stairs, his pale, drawn face blank but his right hand indicating to Kitty the direction she must go.

Kitty started back up the stairs, following the steward, but stopped and looked back down to Charles. He was gone, the door of his study already closing. She stood watching the door and blinked as she pushed an invisible strand of hair from her face.

'Ma'am?' Fergusson's bland voice called from the top of the stairs.

Briefly, she closed her eyes, then catching her skirts, she turned and followed.

The over-furnished dining room was dark and oppressive; the red and black patterned, flock wallpaper causing the walls to enclose. Gas lamps shimmered with a thick haze above their frosted glass, oozing heat and throwing a dull, sticky light over the room. Forbidding red and black draped, velvet curtains dominated one end of the room. Sombre portraits of important men watched everything in front of them, gravity and industry seeping out of their pores. Kitty was sure she had once been told who these men were, most likely Charles's father and other renowned cotton kings, but however hard she tried, she just couldn't remember.

The table in the centre of the room was large and graceless. Thick candelabra, holding fist-sized candles, little helped the gloom. Silver cutlery and ornaments, crystal glasses and gold-leafed china did their best to reflect cheer across the room. Hovering in the shadows stood Fergusson, swaying to and fro, his hands behind his back, face devoid of expression.

Charles sat at the head of the table. His eyes were alight with the tales that he told, his cheeks red and shining. Gone was the tired and pasty look. In that heavy, melancholy room he seemed to glow, his brightness illuminating the oppression. His hand often fell on his wine glass, Fergusson almost as often refilling it. As he addressed his audience, he would pat his stomach or pull down his jacket cuffs, looking from Kitty to John Hardgrave. Occasionally, he would lean back into his chair, his hands grasping the edge of the table, surveying the room. Kitty recognised some of the pomposity he'd revealed in his study at Ardbray. It seemed like he was playing a part, being the person he thought he should be to his new business partner.

To Charles's left sat John Hardgrave, jovial and red in the face. He was a magnetic character, his face full of life, his small brown eyes watching everything with enthusiasm, his shocking mop of blond, floppy hair bringing light to the dark room. Kitty found herself fascinated by the entertainer in front of her; always looking for the opportunity to lighten the conversation, ready to drop in a witty comment to make the room laugh. When she or Charles spoke, he gave them his full attention, as if their opinion was of vital importance to him. At first, she thought that he was the polar opposite of Charles: frivolous to Charles's seriousness, fat to Charles's thin, impetuous to Charles's thoughtful demeanour, a quick wit to her husband's earnestness, but she soon began to find they had more in common. Both were only sons of successful industrialists, both looking to make their mark on the world.

'Charles, perhaps you can help me out. If I'm to be spending much more time in Glasgow, I'm going to need a club. I need somewhere civilised where a gentleman can be his own man.'

'You must join my club, The Western. It's full of business contacts, you'll find plenty of opportunity to meet like-minded people,' said Charles.

'As long as I can get a good meal, somewhere to play cards, have a smoke and a decent glass of port, I'll be happy.' John winked at Kitty. 'Don't want to talk shop all day long, need somewhere to let my hair down.'

'Will your wife not be coming to Glasgow?' Kitty enquired.

'Sadly, Caroline doesn't travel well,' John answered. 'She's a home-bird, far happier in her own little nest, preening her feathers and making herself look more beautiful for my return.' He said this with such humour and light in his eyes that Kitty almost overlooked what he had actually said.

'Would you consider setting up home here?' she pushed.

'My wife has never lived in a city and I don't believe she ever will. She's too set in her ways. Perhaps I could consider renting a bachelor pad for myself, but I'm not sure I see the point, a decent club would do the job. No staff to be concerned about, no worry that any previous conquests might turn up unannounced.' Again, he winked at Kitty before emptying his glass.

The man was full of such bonhomie that Kitty was confused by his words. She couldn't tell whether he was joking or not.

'Why Glasgow then? What brought your attention to our city?'

John Hardgrave leaned back slightly in his chair as

Fergusson filled his glass before moving on to Charles. She noticed her husband grabbing the glass with almost indecent haste and emptying half of it before their guest had taken a breath.

'Why, your husband, of course.' Those dark, deep-set eyes had a fierce intensity that held Kitty's attention, made her feel as if her question had been of paramount importance.

Kitty looked to Charles for help. But it seemed as if he hadn't been listening, just absently watching the interaction between his wife and their guest, and made no answer. She looked down at her napkin considering her next words, but she was rescued.

'My dear Mrs Maclean. Let me explain. My family hail from South Yorkshire. The estate we own sits on a rich seam of coal, meaning that the Hardgrave family lead a very comfortable existence indeed. My father is a coalman through and through. He has lived and breathed coal all his life. But I'm afraid I find coal a little,' he struggled to catch the right word before finally saying, 'grubby. Don't get me wrong, I am grateful for the filthy stuff, I'm grateful for the layer of grime one finds on the table if it's not cleaned twice a day and the slightly acrid smell in the air, but this all came a little too easily. This black money was simply handed to me on a plate – we sell it and we make money from it. And I don't even have to get out of bed.'

Kitty shuffled in her seat, disarmed by the charm by which these strangely honest words were dressed.

'I need more of a purpose to my life. So, I've been looking for somewhere to invest my money, somewhere I can make a difference.'

Kitty leaned forward. 'How will you be investing your money?' She looked at both men as she spoke. 'Will you be upgrading the machinery? I understand that the technology has moved on quite a bit in the last twenty years and that the

Glasgow mills face increased competition from the more efficient Lancashire mills.'

Charles spluttered. 'My dear, what do you know of these things?'

John Hardgrave interrupted before Kitty could reply. 'What we're in need of most urgently is more workers. We'll be expanding the mills, taking on additional premises and more women. Now that we've quashed the unrest within the ranks, we can move forward and meet the increased demand.'

'What caused the unrest?' She turned to Charles as she said this. He smiled, bemusement on his face. Kitty blinked. 'Tell me, I'm interested.'

'Oh, the usual: better conditions, more pay, fewer hours. They want it all and I refuse to provide it for them.' He swatted away the subject with his hand and then picked up his glass. 'More wine, Fergusson.'

'Who was it who wrote extensively on how improving conditions and safety standards, shortening the working day and introducing education, made the workers more productive and more open to changes when they were required? I can't remember his name. Robert... Robert someone.' She looked from their guest to Charles for help.

Whilst Charles stared at his wife, a huge smile spread across Hardgrave's face.

Finally, Charles spoke. 'Surely, you don't mean Robert Owen?'

'Yes, yes, I do.' For a moment, Kitty's eyes lit up and she started to talk faster. 'My father always used to talk about him; he had several of his publications. He believed that it was important to their health and welfare. Where was his cotton mill?'

'New Lanark.' Hardgrave almost laughed. 'Charles, you never told me your wife was so well-versed in social reform.' He turned to Kitty. 'Sadly, Mrs Maclean, I think you will find those ideas rather outdated.'

'Kitty, darling,' Charles exclaimed, 'John is right, that all happened over seventy years ago. Our industry is finding things difficult right now. It's all very well introducing those ideas when there's plenty of money about, but we have to deal with the competition from the Lancashire mills. They're producing cotton more cheaply than we can, more efficiently than we're able to. We can't afford to overindulge our workers.' He leaned across the table and, for the second time that evening, patted her hand. 'My dear, you mustn't get worried about these things. That's what John and I are here for.'

'Mrs Maclean. I admire your interest in your husband's business. My wife couldn't care less about the coal industry. As long as it keeps her in new dresses and a decent carriage, that's all she feels she needs to worry about. I don't believe "social reform" is a phrase she is familiar with. Charles, you've done well.' He raised his glass towards Kitty. Both men took another slug of wine.

'Well,' said Charles, wiping his mouth with his napkin, 'that was a most satisfactory dinner.'

'Yes, Mrs Maclean, you run a good household here. That was a dinner to be savoured.' He again held up his glass towards her and winked. 'I look forward to many more of these ménages à trois.'

Kitty reddened and quickly turned to Charles, but it was as if he hadn't heard John's comment.

'Could I come and see your work? Could I come to the mills?'

Charles, just in the process of putting the scrunched-up napkin on the table, stopped mid-air. 'Why on earth would you want to do that? The mills are no place for a woman.'

'But aren't most of your workers women?'

'Why, yes, but not your sort of woman.'

'And what kind of woman would I be?' Kitty asked playfully.

'Well...' Charles hesitated. 'A woman of fine clothes and a fine mind.' He straightened up, perhaps pleased with his response.

Kitty laughed. 'Well, perhaps this woman with a fine mind could find out what her husband, of a fine mind, does with his days. Perhaps she'd like to see what it is that occupies so much of his time.'

Charles stared at her as if he was misunderstanding her.

'Well, my man, what harm could it do?' John asked.

'Well... none, I suppose.' Charles seemed bewildered and turned to his wife. 'Are you sure you want to go there? It's very noisy, very hot and humid. It really isn't somewhere you want to spend much time.'

'But you spend so much of your time there. Surely, I'm able to withstand it for a morning?'

'But we don't work in the spinning mill or the weaving shed. We have a comfortable suite of offices next to the mill. Somewhere we can concentrate on the business in hand, where we can discuss matters without the noise of the machinery, without the thick dust in the air.' His tone was a little patronising.

Kitty put on her best smile. 'Indulge me. Let me come and see the place that dominates your life. Let me see what it is you really do.'

'I think we should let her have her way,' John said. 'It would be a novelty to show a lady around our venture and show her how we intend to make it a better place.'

Charles looked between Kitty and John. Eventually, he nodded. 'All right. Let's do it.' He smiled. 'Come next week.'

Before Kitty could agree, her husband swiftly changed the subject. 'I believe port and cigars are what's needed. Fergusson!' He leaned backwards on his chair recklessly, almost tipping over. The steward caught the back of the chair and effortlessly pushed it forward.

'Port and cigars for our guest. Kitty, will you?'

'I'm afraid, gentlemen, I've had a very long journey today and I'm beginning to feel the effects of it.' She started to push her chair back. 'I must retire and leave you to your port.' Standing up, she continued, 'Mr Hardgrave.' She bowed her head. 'I'm sure our paths will cross a great deal in the future.' Turning to her husband. 'Charles, I'm sorry to abandon you, but I must sleep.'

Both men stood up as Kitty started to walk across the room to the door behind their guest. But as she walked, she began to feel unsteady, her face was hot and her ears pounding, her breathing laboured. The heat quickly became unbearable and before she could reach the door, she began to stumble, the room disappearing, her eyes blacking out. With nothing nearby to steady herself, she fell. Suddenly, arms were around her, gently catching her, carefully letting her to the floor. As she opened her eyes, she saw John leaning over her, deep concern on his face. He put his palm on her forehead.

'Mrs Maclean, you're too hot.' His voice was gentle, like a father seeing to his sick child. 'I fear you've been overdoing it. You must look after yourself.'

'Kitty!' Reacting too late, Charles stood up too quickly, his empty wine glass falling to the floor as he staggered towards her.

'Get her a drink of water, man,' Hardgrave barked at Charles. Her husband appeared to flinch before lurching back to the table.

As his back was turned, John carefully helped Kitty to a chair. 'Mrs Maclean, I'm afraid you do your sex no credit.' Again, the tone was almost tender. 'Fainting at the dinner table does nothing for the reputation of women to hold their own. I notice you hardly ate a morsel at dinner, didn't touch your wine. As I said, you need to look after yourself.'

'Here you are.' Charles thrust a glass towards her.

As Kitty drank her water, their guest continued, 'I'm guessing that you haven't eaten anything since you left Lairg this morning,' he said, kneeling so his face was level with Kitty's. 'I'm also guessing that since this is the first dinner you've hosted since your marriage that you were more than a little apprehensive.'

Slowly, Kitty nodded, putting her glass on the table beside her.

'My advice, Mrs Maclean, at all times, is that you should always remember to eat. When you eat, you will find that life's travails always become a little easier.' John Hardgrave gave her a sympathetic smile before he squeezed her hand gently and stood up, turning to her husband.

'Sir, your wife.' This time his tone was a little cool. 'I suggest you take better care of her.' He blinked three times in a row, his face impassive. 'Perhaps you should take her to her room whilst her maid is found.'

Charles stumbled towards Kitty, clumsily pulling her up from her chair. 'Of course, would you excuse me?' He took Kitty's arm and guided her out of the room, into the hallway.

As they reached the bottom of the stairs, exhaustion began to overwhelm her again and she held onto the bannister for support. Charles was distracted, looking around him, obviously struggling for words. They both stood awkwardly until relief suddenly flooded his face at the sound of approaching footsteps. 'Ah look, here's your maid.'

Eleanor arrived, out of breath and pinning up her hair.

'Please can you take Mrs Maclean upstairs? She's not well.' He kissed Kitty's hand. 'I'll see you in the morning.' He made a hasty bow before turning away.

Kitty watched her husband almost run to the dining room and say, 'So, John, how about that cigar?' before closing the door.

. . .

Kitty strode along the pavement of Park Street, her head throbbing in time with her steps. She'd needed to get out of the house, away from the left-over cigar smell of the night before, away from the silent disapproval of her husband's steward and away from the empty house. She needed to shed the over-bearing feeling of disappointment and find some energy and vitality. She needed to see Eva.

She reached the corner of the street and stopped by the entrance to the church, her attention caught by the multiple pinnacles on the tower above her. The colour of the stone against a moment of blue sky reminded her of Ardbray. She stopped and revelled in the intricacy of the stonework as the sunlight accentuated the details. For a minute, she could forget her feeling of inquietude and indulge in the beauty before her. But her distracting reverie was abruptly interrupted as a carriage clattered past her, spraying water onto the hem of her dress.

With a sigh she picked up her skirts and rushed on to Woodside Terrace, her thoughts returning to her absent husband.

She had spent most of the night awake, considering her husband's new business partner and his strange naive behaviour. Maybe he was just in a playful mood, maybe he behaved differently around the board table, but she was finding it difficult to see how these two men could benefit each other in the struggling cotton industry. But it wasn't her place to question, it wasn't her place to even notice. She was only the wife, after all; her position was to sit at the dinner table and entertain, put their guests at ease, tell a witty or informative story.

As she'd waited for Charles to join her in the bedroom, she'd longed for the man with the little boy grin and the assertive hand that had guided her around Ardbray, not the drunken, nervous individual she had shared her dinner with. But her husband never appeared. After several hours, she heard him say his goodnights, the front door close and then stumble up the stairs. She listened for his footsteps outside her door, but they didn't even hesitate, just strode directly by. His night was completed with a fumbled door slam.

Kitty lay on her bed looking up at the ceiling arguing with herself about the merits of being visited by a drunken husband, a husband she'd so far only spent two nights with alone. She'd been married for over a week. Was he being a gentleman and leaving his sick wife to sleep? Or had he forgotten all about her? Suddenly, she sat up, lit her candle and went to him.

The landing was dark, but she could see the outline of Charles's door as a faint light percolated through the tiny gaps in the doorway. Her first timid knock produced no response and so, with a sigh, she rapped on the door louder. She listened intently to the silence, eventually broken by a grunt and a muffled bang. She stood back and self-consciously smoothed her hair down. Still, he didn't appear. Finally, she took hold of the door handle, her ear against the door and slowly pushed it inwards. She was greeted by the smell of stale smoke and alcohol, and the sight of Charles lying prostrate on his bed, his arms flung out wide, one leg slipped to the floor, fully dressed. Walking towards him, she could now hear his faint snoring. Putting the candle down on the bedside table, she stood watching him, her hands on her hips, a rueful smile beginning to break across her face. And then carefully she pulled his leg back onto the bed and took both his shoes off, undid his cravat and smoothed down his ruffled hair. Looking around the room, she saw a blanket on a small armchair and used it to cover his almost lifeless body. Picking up her candle, she stood back and regarded her work.

Going back to her room, she still hadn't been able to summon any sleep. She'd tried to read, but restlessness took over and she'd started pacing the room, waiting for tiredness to arrive. Finally, she finished her unpacking and spent more time than she would usually bother with finding a home for all her belongings. Eventually, just as the sky had been awakening, she'd fallen asleep.

Two hours later, she had been at her dressing table, taking care with her toilet and carefully considering the upcoming morning with Charles. In her mind, she had set out a day with her husband, getting to know the house, the staff and making plans for a return to Ardbray.

But the well-laid plan fell apart as soon as she'd descended the stairs, with Fergusson informing her that her husband had departed for his regular monthly board meeting just twenty minutes earlier. With a square jaw, she had put her coat on and left the house, overwhelmed by the oppressive rooms, their fussy decoration intruding on her solitary anger.

'Mrs Maclean! Ma'am.' The kindly welcome of Mrs Kennedy, her parents' housekeeper, enveloped her like an inviting warm blanket. There was no hint of surprise at seeing her so soon, no question in her eyes, just an affection that made Kitty's eyes prick.

She walked into the hallway and felt her anger dissipate. The simplicity of the décor, the lack of showy ornamentation brought relief to her overcrowded mind. The old grandfather clock ticked just as it always had, the sound so reassuring. Kitty felt a weight leave her as if a window had been opened and the irritable parrot on her shoulder had flown away.

She took her hat off and began unbuttoning her coat as she looked at herself in the large hallway mirror. Her careful dressing had done a good job of hiding her wakeful night.

'Mrs Kennedy, is Mother at home?'

'No. She's away at her Ladies Welfare Meeting.'

Relief. There would be no inquisition today.

'And my father?'

'No. He's away on his rounds, visiting patients.'

Disappointment. She could have done with his comforting presence.

Before she could say any more, she heard a trill of the piano; scales being practised albeit in a rather vigorous manner.

'But I can hear that Eva's home.' She handed her hat and coat to the housekeeper.

'I'll let her know you're here.'

'Oh no, let me surprise her.'

As the scales got louder, the hand that played them seemed to get heavier and more bad-tempered. Kitty opened the door of the drawing room and silently walked in behind her sister playing at the piano.

Eva suddenly stopped and then ran her finger down the keys angrily and shut the lid before standing up with an impatient sigh.

Kitty laughed. 'I see that your morning routine hasn't changed since I've been gone.'

Eva swept around, opened her arms with joy and cried, 'Kitty!' She fiercely hugged her sister before holding her out at arm's length and looking her over.

'Well, you look... somehow more grown up. My big sister, a true gentlewoman.'

Kitty blushed.

'Oh, I'm so pleased to see you. Mother was in high dudgeon this morning and nothing would please her. It was one of her ladies' meetings and you know how she is before one of those, all fussy and particular. Father was brooding over another terrible article about public health in the paper this morning.' She sighed. 'He takes it so personally.'

Kitty frowned. 'What was the article?'

'Another exposition about the overcrowding in the tenements, the lack of hygiene, the absence of public concern for the children. I'm afraid Charles wouldn't like it as there's also a lot of blame attributed to the cotton mills for the harsh working conditions contributing to the poor health of women workers.' She waved at the table in the corner of the room. 'The article's over there if you want to read it, but,' – she gave her sister another hug – 'that's for later. Tell me, what are you doing here? You should be enjoying your honeymoon, touring the Highlands, getting to know that elusive husband of yours.'

'Well,' Kitty almost choked, 'Charles was recalled to Glasgow because of his work, so I decided to accompany him.' There, she'd done it. She'd lied to her sister, the one person in the world she had never kept secrets from.

'Oh, how loyal of you.' She giggled. 'I don't think I'd have been quite so understanding. Anyhow, I assume you'll be returning as soon as possible?'

Kitty sat heavily on the piano stool. 'I don't know.' She splayed her hands out on her lap, staring down at them. 'I don't think so.' She looked back up at her sister. 'Charles has just brought in a new partner for the business, and I don't imagine it would be very politic to disappear on his honeymoon.'

'He must have known about this new partner before the wedding?' Eva queried, her head on one side.

Kitty turned to the window. She didn't dare reply.

'Kitty?' Eva asked.

Swiftly, Kitty stood up. 'So, what have I missed whilst I've been away? What parties have you been to? Any new marriages on the horizon? Has there been any fallout from the wedding?'

As if she had completely forgotten any concern for Kitty, Eva's face opened out and she began.

'Well, I heard that there was lots of talk about your dress, how you hadn't used the more accepted soft materials, how bold you were to move away from the fashionable blue-grey colours. Personally, I thought you looked more gorgeous than I've ever seen you. And then there was...'

But all too quickly Kitty found she couldn't concentrate on

her sister's tittle-tattle. A great yawning hole of future boredom was opening out before her. Naively, she'd thought she would be getting away from the everyday inconsequential gossip, from the same old round of parties, the talk of princess dresses with jet and chiffon trims.

'... and of course, our mother has already started the husband hunting for me. She's taken up that baton and she won't be passing it on until she's seen me wedded to the man of her dreams.' Eva's face was flushed, her eyes full of excitement. 'But... it means lots of new dresses, we've been at the haberdasher's three times this week.'

'Eva, do you think it would be seen as respectable for me to go back and help at the Saltmarket Clinic? Just like I used to, perhaps only a couple of mornings a week.'

Eva stared at her sister. 'Why would you want to do that? You'll not have the time anyway. You'll be busy being... well, busy being Mrs Charles Maclean. You won't have a moment to think about that terrible slum. Anyway, do you think Charles would approve? You know what Mother thought of you getting involved with those people, as well-meaning as Doctor Forsyth might be.'

'Well, perhaps he needn't know.'

'Kitty, don't be so naive.' Eva took her sister's hands. 'This is Glasgow, after all; everyone knows everyone else's business. Can you imagine how quickly the news would travel that the new Mrs Charles Maclean would rather be down at the Saltmarket than at home receiving guests? Look, you're the talk of the town, everybody will be wanting to find out what your new home is like, how generous your father was with your trousseau, what kind of glamorous lifestyle you and your husband will be leading. You should be seen out and about in the park, at the theatre and at all the most fashionable parties. Don't let me down, I've been looking forward to your return so that I can hang on the coattails of my newly famous sister. I'm banking on it to help me find that perfect husband and... so is our mother.'

Kitty stared at her sister, her face expressionless and slowly draining of colour.

'And, I don't think anyone would be happy if they knew you were visiting the Saltmarket, even Father; it's a dangerous place.'

She found herself overwhelmed. The noise was deafening, the heat stifling and the added humidity made her feel claustrophobic. Now she wished she'd listened to Charles more carefully as he'd talked her through the spinning and weaving processes in his office. It was so noisy in here that she couldn't ask him a question, she could only look on and walk through where the women were working, taking in the noise and the smells and enduring the heat.

They'd briefly visited the vast engine room before moving on to the opening room, where the large, compacted bales of cotton were opened and thrown into a heap on the floor, before being conveyed into another room where two different machines cleaned and took out all the impurities using a high-speed drum and fan. The dust had been choking, and they'd moved on swiftly. From there, they'd walked through a series of rooms, each with a different purpose; the carding room with large encased rotating drums of wire spikes combing the fibre into untwisted slivers, the draughting room where the slivers were drawn through a series of rollers, the doubling machine which then took the elongated slivers and blended them together for strength. And then they had moved up a floor to where the spinning began in earnest. The symphony of noise was overpowering as the clattering of the wheels, the rollers, the bobbins and the spindles all rose to accompany the movement of the cotton from machine to machine, drawing it out, twisting it, turning it into something refined yet robust. But despite the noise, it was a deft operation, fingers of iron and wood working in harmony to produce delicate threads amongst the hulking machines.

And now they were in the weaving shed, a vast single-storey building housing the looms, all identical, all sitting side by side in long rows, almost as far as she could see. The atmosphere was completely different from the dark spinning mill, the glass roof letting the daylight pour in. The floor was vibrating as the looms worked, the leather belts powering the machines via horizontal line shafts running the length of the room. She watched the women work. Each weaver appeared to be in charge of several looms, spending their time checking each one, sometimes gently touching the fabric, feeling for anomalies in the cloth. If this happened, they would swiftly disable the machine and correct the error by replacing one of the bobbins. The machine would be stalled for less than a minute before it was restarted and able to rejoin the orchestra, its own sound helping create the great noisy concerto. The women were like the players, tweaking and fine-tuning their instruments, ensuring they produced the best possible output. The foreman, the only man in the shed, was the conductor, making sure each instrument was playing the right harmony and kept to the beat.

Sometimes, the women would pass comment on the other's machine, but Kitty couldn't possibly see how they heard each other, the noise being so thunderous. As they talked and gesticulated, she came to the conclusion that they had learned to lip-read.

She found herself captivated by the strange beauty in the movement of metal and wood, the rattle and clatter, the spinning of the bobbins, the flying of the shuttles. This scene was so far from her own quiet existence, but here was a mesmeric reality that she could never have imagined herself part of.

Her thoughts were interrupted by a tap on her shoulder.

Charles indicated for her to follow him and he led her through the side door and along a corridor, finally ending up in his office where John Hardgrave was waiting for them.

The room was large and masculine. Wood-panelled walls encased two wide windows overlooking the River Clyde, Charles's large, leather-topped, mahogany desk sat next to a glass-fronted drinks cabinet, three Chesterfield armchairs were gathered around a vast fireplace, the fire roaring and keeping the room at a pleasant temperature, a relief after the intense heat of the spinning mill.

She sat in one of the armchairs, her ears still ringing with the noise of the looms.

'So, Mrs Maclean, what do you think of our modest enterprise?' John Hardgrave asked, a twinkle in his eye.

'I'd say it was far from modest, Mr Hardgrave. It is an achievement of extraordinary invention.'

Charles coughed as he opened the drinks cabinet and poured three glasses of port. 'My father built the spinning mill when he started the company in '52. It's one of the largest in Glasgow. He added the weaving shed fifteen years later. As you know, we're looking to expand the business. We're considering buying a couple of struggling mills a mile or so along the river and we're also contemplating adding some of the finishing processes to our portfolio.' Charles's voice was self-important, showy as if he was playing to an audience, not chatting to his wife. 'We'd like to introduce bleaching, dying and printing so that we can control every aspect of producing the cotton from receipt of the bales from America and India, to finally selling the finished article to the clothes manufacturers and the companies needing less refined textiles, like sheeting or flannel.' He passed around the port and sat in the remaining free armchair.

'How many people work here?' Kitty asked.

'Across both the spinning and weaving, we employ about

nine hundred, mostly women. The numbers fluctuate through illness and injury.'

Kitty frowned. 'What do you mean?'

'You can imagine that with the kind of machinery we have here, with so many moving parts, that bored or inattentive workers could find themselves with pinched fingers, or worse. The other hazard in the weaving shed is that weavers with long hair can get it tangled in the warp. There have been some nasty injuries where the scalp has actually pulled away from the skull. Unfortunately, because of the nature of the work, it's nearly impossible to hear a person cry for help when entangled.'

Kitty winced as she heard this.

'We also find we lose some of the workers who've been here a long time due to ill health.'

'Would that be caused by the dust?' Kitty leaned forward.

'Well, that can't be proved. The general physicality of the work, especially during the spinning process isn't very conducive to a long working life.'

Kitty stared at her husband. A thousand questions began to bubble up in her mind, but before she could start, there was a sharp knock on the door.

'Come,' Charles shouted.

A weather-beaten man walked into the room, shirtsleeves rolled up, red-faced and harried.

'Mr Maclean, Mr Hardgrave, ma'am.' He nodded in Kitty's direction.

'Yes, Atkins, what can we do for you?' Charles asked, his tone short and impatient.

'Another accident, sir. One of the girls has got her hand crushed. It were her own fault. She weren't concentrating.'

Charles sighed and looked into the fire. Then he glanced at Kitty before asking, 'Have you sent for the doctor?'

Atkins looked confused. 'No, sir, I haven't.'

'Well, you'd better do so. We can't leave her lying around

with no help. Get to it, man.' The colour had risen in Charles's face and he drained his glass.

But before Atkins could leave the room, Kitty rose from her seat. 'Let me see to her. I might be able to help. At least I can be of some comfort until the doctor arrives.' Her voice was urgent, almost pleading.

'Well...' Charles spluttered. 'I'm sure there's no need—'

'But, Mrs Maclean, what a perfect idea,' John Hardgrave interrupted, enthusiasm spilling out of him like a toddler who's just been given a new toy. 'Atkins, take us to her, I'm sure Mrs Maclean will make the ideal nurse.'

Before Charles could protest any further, John Hardgrave took Kitty by the elbow and led her towards the door, a bewildered Atkins showing the way.

Kitty was led into a small, windowless room, with a table, chair and the injured girl.

'You left her by herself?' Kitty asked incredulously.

'Aye, that I did. I needed to find Mr Maclean,' Atkins said, shame spreading across his face.

'But she'll be in shock; surely, one of the other girls could have stayed with her?'

Atkins wouldn't meet her furious, questioning stare.

With an enraged sigh, Kitty hurried to the side of the girl, who was bending over, cradling her left arm.

'Let me take a look,' Kitty said softly.

She gently picked up the girl's arm, a slight moan escaping her lips, she winced and there was the colour of pain in her eyes.

Kitty did her best to keep her face impassive as she carefully put the mangled hand onto the table. Blood, bone chips and already swelling flesh.

'A bowl of cold water and a clean cloth, please,' she barked.

Atkins didn't move.

Kitty stood. 'Do you have any medical supplies somewhere in this factory?'

With a slight shake of his head, he said, 'Aye, a few. But—' His eyes strayed to the girl's hand.

Kitty's lips flattened. 'But you have cold water, a bowl and a clean cloth, surely?'

'Get to it, man!' John Hardgrave ordered from beyond the room. She'd forgotten about his presence and was glad of his mirrored frustration.

As Atkins scurried away, Kitty called after him, 'Just make sure the cloth is clean.'

She returned to the girl and the badly broken hand. She could see that only a superior surgeon would be able to set it properly, and she knew that the girl would be lucky to even get to see a surgeon. This girl would never be working in the factory again, she was certain of that.

'Will you be able to make it better?' the girl whispered.

Kitty put her hand on her shoulder, noting the frayed shirt collar and much-darned skirt. 'We'll do our best,' she said with a sinking heart.

Four days later, Kitty closed the front door of the house in Park Street and looked out at the street ahead. The oppression almost immediately lifted from her shoulders as the sun moved from behind a cloud.

She had changed her impractical dress to something more utilitarian but had covered it with her long winter coat in case she bumped into anyone she knew. As she felt the unfamiliar sun on her face, she thought she'd walk a bit before she found a hansom cab.

'Mrs Maclean. What a pleasure.'

She almost jumped, having been caught up in her own thoughts. Beside her was John Hardgrave.

He grabbed her hand as she brought it up to her chest in shock and raised it to his lips, bowing with his other hand behind his back.

'Mr Hardgrave. You startled me.'

'My apologies.' He looked her up and down. 'Should you not be out in your finest attire? Out meeting the good and the great?' He smiled his disarming smile, a slight question in his eyes. 'But, somehow—'

'Mr Hardgrave,' Kitty interrupted. 'What news of Erin?' Her voice was urgent, hurried.

Hardgrave looked confused. 'Who?'

'Erin, the girl whose hand was crushed at the mill last week?'

'Oh, her. Well,' Hardgrave blustered, 'I have absolutely no idea. I'm sure Atkins could tell you.'

Kitty's stare was blank before a switch flicked inside her, and she suddenly gave him her most winning smile. 'Perhaps you could find out, I'd like to know.' She squeezed the hand that was still holding hers, then whipped it away. He took a breath to speak, but she interrupted. 'I'm sorry, Mr Hardgrave. I'm late for an appointment.' She looked to the road, searching for a cab.

'But since I've been so fortuitous as to bump into you, could I not persuade you to take tea with me? The tea rooms just down the road are quite superior.'

Kitty hesitated, momentarily entranced by the man in front of her; his manner startling, beguiling even.

'Surely, your appointment can wait. Would you not join me?'

With relief, Kitty saw a cab. She stepped to the edge of the pavement and put her finger and thumb in her mouth and blew, releasing a shrill and startling whistle which grabbed the attention of the driver and brought the rest of the street to an astounded standstill.

John Hardgrave's eyes widened with a look of astonished amusement as Kitty quickly grasped the approaching cab. With one swift movement, she managed to pick up her skirts and jump into the carriage, knocking on the trap door in the roof indicating to the driver to move on.

'I'm late, Mr Hardgrave, I mean no discourtesy, but I must dash.' The cab moved on and, when she thought she was out of range of his hearing, she shouted up to the driver.

'The Saltmarket, please.' She leaned back into the carriage and closed her eyes, letting out an audible breath. Why was her heart thumping? Why were her hands shaking? But despite her anxiety, a smile escaped her lips. She would always thank her father for teaching her to hail a cab. He had the enviable ability to summon a hansom cab on the busiest and noisiest of streets. She'd loved how his ear-splitting whistle could be heard above anything else and, aged ten, had asked him to teach her. She so rarely got the opportunity to use it. She didn't care that it was unladylike; it was one of the few practical things that she'd mastered, and it had just got her out of a sticky situation.

As the cab moved from the quiet and airy roads of Kelvinside, Kitty's uneasy mind became mesmerised by the busy shopping streets. Charing Cross was vibrant and alive. She'd always loved gazing at the richness of life walking down the street, the colourful hats, the striking dresses, liveried carriages and festooned shop windows. But soon the affluent, ordered streets disappeared and a different kind of busy took over. The pavements became even more crowded, but the vivid colour had gone, replaced by blank faces, threadbare clothes and grey tones. The contrast was sometimes overwhelming, and Kitty was always surprised that this kind of poverty could exist just a few miles from her home of elegant attire and plump bodies. She would marvel at those who lived close to her and their ability to believe that such hardship couldn't possibly reside on their doorstep, happily ignoring the problems of disease, over-crowding and lack of hygiene.

Her mother had encouraged her to do 'good works' from a young age, but only at arm's length, never with the intention of getting her hands dirty. And when Mrs Gray had finally discovered that Kitty volunteered at the Saltmarket Clinic, she had been wholly banned. Nothing even her father could do or say would change her mother's mind. But eventually, duplicity had got the better of Kitty and she'd found herself sneaking back whenever her mother had visitors or one of her women's meetings. She'd learned to lie deftly with Eva playing the loyal accomplice.

Of course, this sort of dirty work should be given up. It would never do for the wife of a prominent businessman to be seen in such a place. People would talk, her husband would be embarrassed and her mother would, yet again, be horrified. Her father had known about it all along, he was the one who had arranged for her to help out, but he had encouraged her discretion, understanding that there were those in their social circle who would not approve of her behaviour.

And she'd tried to give it up. She'd done her very best to play the part of Mrs Charles Maclean. She'd been 'At Home' for the last three weeks. She'd received guests she'd never imagined would be interested in meeting her. Never before had anyone taken notice of the bookish daughter of the doctor. But now she was the wife of a rich industrialist, it seemed that, overnight, she had become noteworthy, someone who could have their opinion sought. But these people didn't really want to know what she thought, they wanted to know about her lifestyle, and her husband, inspect their house in Park Street and find out more about their mysterious mansion in the Highlands. When would they be seen at the theatre? Would they be attending the ball at

Pollok House next month? Why had they cut their honeymoon short?

The scrutiny disturbed Kitty. It was false and she could no longer maintain her calm, interested exterior. She'd felt suffocated by their fawning and longed for some reality.

Finally, she'd found the courage to change her mind.

The previous night there had been respite from the whirl-wind of social engagements and they'd just had a quiet dinner with Charles's oldest friend and best man, Roddy Argyll. Sweet, kind Roddy, who had known Charles since they were young men, was tall and awkward but the most thoughtful of any of their friends or acquaintances. Unlike the loud and flamboyant John Hardgrave, whose company was enthralling but exhausting, Roddy would give the room an air of calm kindliness, his voice warm and affectionate, his interest sincere and earnest. It was his intense questioning of the work she had previously done at the Saltmarket Clinic and a casual remark he had made that meant she'd finally found the nerve to make this journey.

'You know that when Charles first met you, he could talk of nothing else than the work that you'd carried out at the Salt-market Clinic and your ambitions to study. He'd never met a woman who had such a concern for others. He was tired of the fly-by-night girls who only cared about how much money he had. You were a yellow primrose in the winter compost.'

She'd blushed at his clumsy lyricism, but even in her embarrassment, she'd seen an opportunity. 'It's a shame I've had to give that up.' And gave Charles a look of guileless sincerity.

'No, no, no. You must continue, it would be such a waste,' Roddy, her unwitting partner in her shameless ruse, proclaimed.

'Well...' Charles had mumbled. 'I'm sure we could sort something out.'

So, before he could change his mind, she'd decided to return to what she loved doing and to hell with what the rest of the world might think. But she thought she'd leave it a while before she told her husband what she was up to. Perhaps she wouldn't love it as much as she used to, perhaps the appeal was no longer there. Perhaps she was just putting off a difficult conversation.

At one of the largest tenement blocks, she asked the driver to stop. Stepping out of the cab, she checked up and down the street. The children playing in the road ignored her, but the women, standing in a group beside one of the tenement doors, stopped their conversation and watched her in silence. Sleeves rolled up and with ruddy faces, hair tied back in loose buns, they scrutinised her with a vague possessiveness. For a moment, Kitty hesitated, but, buttoning up the top of her coat, she gave the women a brief smile before turning to the black door ahead of her, paint peeling and mud thrown up from the road. The building was bland; a large stone block of one-room apartments built to help purge the city of its shameful slums. This would have been a pleasant area if it hadn't been filled with over ten times more residents than it was planned to house. It was as if the city felt it had done its job in clearing the slums and had now forgotten those very people they were supposed to be help-ing. One privy for up to one hundred people, two families living in one small room; it was unsurprising then that these tene-ments were squalid, however hard those proud women tried to keep them clean.

Kitty already felt more at ease, she was no longer on show, she was here to do a job. No one would comment on her ability to hold a room, on the brilliance of her costume, or whom she had dinner with last night, here she could push away the disquiet she felt about her encounter with John Hardgrave.

The door opened onto a dark corridor. The smell was stifling, musty and stagnant, her feet cloaked with a cold shadow, the walls damp with mould growing in gloomy swathes.

Undeterred, Kitty headed towards an open door at the end of the passage and walked in.

The room was lit by a single gas lamp, casting a dim lustre across the occupants. Benches ran down each side of the room, all filled with silent, dull-eyed men, women and children, a baby was crying in one corner, the mother holding it against her shoulder, walking up and down, jiggling and singing a quiet ballad. Most of the people turned to look at Kitty in silence, more out of habit than interest. Most immediately withdrew their eyes, looking down, keeping to themselves.

Kitty cast a brief glance around the room and then walked towards a closed door. She gave a sharp knock.

'Come in,' came the muffled voice.

Opening the door, she walked into the windowless room. She was hit by the familiar scrubbed and well-cleaned smell. An ashen-haired, elderly gentleman in small, round glasses looked up from the table he stood behind, but when he saw Kitty, his face lit up.

'Kitty!' he exclaimed, as he walked around the table to greet her. 'Just the person I need. Get your hands washed and help me with these stitches, would you?' His tone was as welcoming as a warm fire in a freezing room.

She smiled, glad of the lack of questioning, her thumping heart calmed by the affability. 'Good morning, Doctor Forsyth. It's good to see you.' She took her coat off and laid it on a small chair with her bag and then walked over to the sink in the corner. An elderly woman was sitting on the top of the scrubbed wooden table; her thick legs straight out in front of her, rough woollen stockings pushed down to her ankles exposing a deep, infected cut on her left shin.

'Mrs Murray here fell over a few days ago and, like most people who live here, had better things to do than get it treated. This morning she couldn't get out of her bed. Both she and I would appreciate your help with cleaning it up and stitching it back together.' He spoke to the patient loudly and a little slow, as if she was foreign, but his eyes twinkled at her and just a hint of relief made it through her tough exterior.

Kitty smiled at the patient before she rolled up the sleeves of her white, high-collared shirt. She washed her hands, took a tunic from her bag and put it on. Dr Forsyth continued to chat, telling his patient what he was about to do. His greying hair was thinning on top, his own shirtsleeves were rolled up to above his elbows and he wore a white apron. His face was round, his cheeks ruddy and his mouth seemed to wear a permanent smile. It was eleven o'clock in the morning and his clinic had been running for almost three hours, but, despite this, he was still jovial, keen and chatty. The room was gloomy, like his waiting room it was lit with only one gas lamp. Kitty glanced at the meticulous row of medical instruments laid out on the table in one corner, bandages in exact rows, a medical bag sat exactly straight against the wall.

'I hadn't expected to see you, Kitty. Should you not be on your honeymoon somewhere?' Without waiting for an answer, Dr Forsyth continued, 'Could you pass me the lint, bandages and that bowl of water?'

Kitty picked up the items needed and passed them over. Without looking at him, she replied, 'Charles had to return home. There was urgent business.' She picked up Mrs Murray's hand as the woman winced. 'So, I decided that since I was back in town, I might as well be useful.'

'Well, it's good to see you. I've been very busy this morning. There's a bad bout of influenza going around and I have to make quite a few visits later.' As he cleaned the wound, Mrs Murray was tensing up, squeezing Kitty's hand. Dr Forsyth looked at his patient and then at his assistant. 'Kitty, I think you have a lighter hand than me, perhaps you can clean up this wound, then I can get my sewing kit ready.' He put the bowl of water down and, looking at the patient, began speaking again in his loud, slow voice. 'Mrs Maclean here will be better at cleaning you up; my old fingers are getting a bit clumsy.' He patted her hand. 'She'll make it less painful for you. I tell you, she'd make a fine doctor.'

He walked over to his medical bag whilst Kitty took over. Intent on her work, she engaged in the task of painlessly cleaning up the wound, taking care with the raw, infected areas. Mrs Murray watched Kitty with interest, the silence only interrupted by the weak cry of the baby in the waiting room and the crash and splash of a bucket of water being kicked over in the distance.

Having finished gathering his instruments, Dr Forsyth moved back to the table. 'To be honest, I thought we'd probably never see you here again. I wasn't sure if you'd have the time, now that you're an important married woman.' His face had a mischievous look on it.

Kitty ignored the remark, continuing to work, and then stopping as the woman groaned and her leg made an involuntary movement. 'It's all right, Mrs Murray, I'm nearly finished. We just have to make sure this doesn't get infected any further.' Her soothing voice seemed to relax the patient a little.

'It seems a waste to forget all that medical knowledge I've gained over the last two years with you. Perhaps I can't go to university, but someone should benefit, shouldn't they?' Kitty's face coloured as she spoke, finishing up her task of cleaning. 'There, I think I've done the best I can.'

The conversation ceased whilst Dr Forsyth stitched up the wound. The patient was watching Dr Forsyth's sewing skills carefully.

'Aye, ay'll be sending mah darning to you; you're better'n mah.' She grinned at him. 'And ay've bin darning a few years now.'

'There, all done, Mrs Murray.' Dr Forsyth cut the final stitch. 'Kitty, can you dress the wound whilst I clear up?' Kitty did as she was asked whilst the doctor continued, 'Now Mrs

Murray,' again in his shouting voice, 'make sure you keep that wound clean and try to rest it.' He put his hand in the air, making a stop sign as Mrs Murray was about to speak. 'I know, I know, that's probably far too much to ask; you ladies are always so busy. But can you not persuade that husband of yours to make you a cup of tea once in a while so you can put your feet up?' He looked at her sternly, as if he was trying to make his words stick in her memory.

Mrs Murray laughed. 'Mah husband hasnae made a cuppa tea for twenty years. He widnae mind how.' She let herself down from the table and limped towards the door. 'But thank you, Doctor.' And then looking at Kitty. 'Ma'am.'

As she walked out of the door, Dr Forsyth called after her.

'And come back next week to have the wound re-dressed.' He shut the door and then looked back at Kitty. 'I doubt we'll see her again,' he paused, 'unless she's dead.' He laughed as Kitty's eyes widened. 'Oh, Kitty, it's a pleasure to see you, I really mean it.' He walked over to the sink to wash his hands. 'But I just assumed that married life would be taking precedence and all that. Well, perhaps I'm just being old-fashioned.'

'I'm sure in between all those "At Homes", dinners and dances I can manage a morning's work.' Kitty threw the dirty lint into a small basket a little harder than she needed to. 'I'd like to help more often but perhaps...' she considered how to continue, 'I'd be missed.'

Dr Forsyth smiled as he dried his hands. 'Well, you know I'm here every Monday and Thursday morning, and we'd always welcome your help at the clinics in the Infirmary.' He put the towel down. 'Although, I'm not sure what Sister would have to say about you turning up. She's a little territorial.' He looked at her over the top of his glasses.

She couldn't hold his gaze. Reddening, she looked down to her hands and began picking at her fingernails. 'Doctor Forsyth, you know I'd help out every day if I could, but I don't think it would be seen as...' she again stumbled, looking for the correct wording, 'the right thing to do.' She spat this last remark out as if it had given her a bad taste and she was eager to be rid of it. Unexpectedly, she found herself having to blink away threatening tears.

She turned away and took a deep breath before, discreetly wiping her eyes, she said, 'But, I have been thinking. I was at Charles's mill last week and I'm worried about the number of accidents and the lack of concern for the women who work there. I'm wondering if there's anything that I can do. Perhaps we could talk to Charles about introducing a fortnightly clinic or...' again she struggled to find the right phrase, 'or just something that might help.' There was a note of exasperation in her voice as she turned back to face Dr Forsyth.

Her father's oldest friend pushed his glasses back up the bridge of his nose before putting both his hands on the table and, leaning forward, stared at her. 'I don't understand you, Kitty.' He'd lowered his voice. 'And I don't think you do either.' He looked down at the scratched table. 'Let me see if I can speak to your husband.' Smiling again, he drew himself up and walked towards the door. With his hand on the door handle, he turned back to Kitty. 'Maybe I can do something to help out.' He gave her a sympathetic look before opening the door.

'Who's next?' His voice had changed, commanding and loud. He pulled himself into a military stance and clicked his heels together.

SIX

GREER

Loch More, 2003

Jacob's Ladder

*'It is an old cure for the vapours and was given as a tonic in
hysterical complaints.
It had a reputation for curing epilepsy and can be used in the
same way as valerian.'*

Elixirs of Life *by Mrs C F Leyel*

I'm sitting at Charles Maclean's desk, surveying his study. In
contrast to Kitty's herbarium, I've never liked this room. Despite
facing south, with a large window overlooking the loch, it's dark
and unwelcoming, a typical Victorian gentleman's refuge, clut-
tered and full of testosterone. The desk is made from a deep-
coloured mahogany with a green leather top, and there's an
upright, uncomfortable-looking armchair facing the desk. There

are game prints on the walls of salmon, pheasant and deer and a small glass-fronted case holding two handguns. Two deep Chesterfield armchairs frame the fireplace with a drinks cabinet, still stocked, to one side. The walls on either side of the large fireplace are filled with books, probably never touched since the day they were placed there. There is a large oil painting of a sleek, chestnut horse above the fireplace, and the heavily patterned plasterwork on the ceiling is beginning to look a little worn, adding to the feeling of oppression.

It's a room that personifies the man who only wanted people to see the image he had conjured up. There's a stuffed porcupine from Africa, a country I know he never travelled to. I loathe it, not because its hideous glass eyes glare at me, but because it's a nightmare to keep clean; its sharp quills gather dust in the most awkward places, requiring me to risk multiple stab wounds whilst wielding the duster. It would have been sensible to have placed it into a glass case, but, in those days, there would never have been consideration for the servants. He never read a book, not unless he needed the knowledge for work or wanted to be seen with one. These books are purely for show. The stuffed pheasant would imply that he was a hunting man, but local gossip has it that he was a poor shot, the Duke of Westminster always reluctant to invite him to his shoot. However, the presence of a drinks cabinet makes sense; he liked a drink and I suspect he would hide in this room, stay away from those intimidating and glamourous guests, nursing a malt whisky rather than attempt witty conversation.

Charles's study is in stark contrast to Kitty Maclean's morning room. It's not pink and feminine, but it's tasteful and restrained with a hint of her humour. That was the room where she ate her breakfast every day, where she'd read her post and respond to household matters. In the morning room she was a mother, a daughter and a wife. In the herbarium she was a midwife and a herbalist.

I'm pulled out of my reverie by the sound of footsteps coming towards the study. I jump out of the chair. I shouldn't be in here; all I came to do was light the fire and open the shutters and now I've been in here for over half an hour, wasting my time by thinking about the past.

'Greer. Good morning,' Robert exclaims, as he comes into the room. Behind him is Caitlin, looking exactly as she was the last time she was here: hair unbrushed, jumper worn at the elbow, jeans slightly baggy and frayed at the ankles. They are an unlikely pair, Robert thoughtfully and fastidiously dressed, Caitlin dressed only because she must, to be comfortable and keep warm.

'I'll bring you some tea shortly,' I say. 'The surveyors are here. They're currently working up at the stables. I assume you'll want to catch up with them at some point. They should be finished up there soon, then they said they'll start work in the main house. Also, I've made lunch for you all. When you're ready, come down to the kitchen and there'll be something warming for you.'

I leave reluctantly. I'd like to stay and hear what they're discussing. I know those two have been in frequent contact. It seems Miss Black is thorough and will not be putting in any kind of offer until she has detailed information on the house: its structure, the programme of maintenance, the landslide and any damage that has been caused over the years. I described her once as a terrier and I'll stick by that portrayal. It appears that if she wants to do a job, she wants to do it well. I don't like to admit it, but I'm happy she's like that. This house needs someone who's committed, who wants to nurture it and bring it back to life. But I still don't trust her. There's a fragility to her that unnerves me, she's too easily spooked, too quickly upset, although she does her best to hide it. Can someone who's so obviously damaged have the strength to renovate and restore Ardbray, can someone who's always lived in a busy metropolis have the resilience to live out here, miles from civilisation and a decent cup of coffee?

I shut the door on them and then stand quietly. It's tempting to put my ear to the door and listen, but it's too much of a cliché, the interfering housekeeper listening in for her own gain. No, I won't stoop that low.

An hour later, I find myself back in the study, clearing away the tea things, tamping down the fire, as Caitlin and Robert go and freshen up before lunch. I don't think this room has seen so much company or heard so much conversation for over one hundred years. It feels a little lighter, a little less oppressive as if human interaction has made it more approachable, more welcoming. Now even the porcupine's stare appears more optimistic.

As I pick up the tea tray, a movement catches my eye. Through the window, I see Caitlin approach her car.

She's proud of her newly acquired, beaten-up old Defender; I can see by the way she smiles as she approaches it. She opens the passenger door and leans in, I assume to get something. I can see that she's dropped her car keys on the drive and as she leans back to pick them up, she suddenly stops, and I notice a shimmering image to the left of the open car door.

It's the children, but I can hardly see them. They flicker in and out of focus, blurry and sometimes disappearing altogether. I don't feel that paralysing cold that usually descends when they appear, the muffling of sounds is only slight. As I notice this, I ache with a loss that I can hardly fathom.

Slowly, Caitlin stands up and faces the shimmering images. She can see them clearly; I have no doubt of that. She's having a conversation with them, but I can't hear through the glass. All too quickly they're gone. And as they're gone, I see a look of desolation on Caitlin's face, as if she has lost something so precious, so irreplaceable, that I want to reach out and console her. She sits down sideways on the passenger seat of the car and puts her head in her hands. I can see that she's struggling to breathe, each attempt at taking a breath becoming more and more difficult.

I recognise the symptoms. Putting the tea tray down, I grab one of the untouched glasses of water and rush out to the front of the house. As I arrive at the car, I can see she's trying to concentrate on her breathing, but it doesn't seem to be working. I put the glass down on the driveway and make her stand up.

'Stamp your feet,' I command, my voice level and reassuring. 'Come on! Do it now. Count to five as you do it. Breathe in, one, two, three, four, five. And out. Count again. Keep breathing and keep counting.' We must look a sight, me holding her shoulders, giving orders, she stamping and counting. But it works, slowly the correct colour returns to her face, her breathing quietens, and she slows her marching pace to a sound-less dawdle until, finally, she stops.

I pick up the glass of water and encourage her to drink.

'How did you know?' she asks.

I shrug. 'It's like riding a bike, you always know what to do once it's happened to you.'

She can see I'm not going to elaborate.

'But how did you see me?' She's looking around.

'I was in the study, clearing up the tea.' I point to the window.

'You must have seen them, the children?' she quickly asks, still a little breathless.

'Who?' I play dumb.

There's a flicker of frustration on her face. 'The boy in the sailor suit and the girl in the smocked dress. You must have seen them. They were right in front of you.'

'No, I didn't see any children.' It's not a complete lie. I

hardly saw them this time, they were like flickering images, fading in and out, almost unrecognisable.

'I've seen them before. On my first day here, I saw them in the cloakroom. They look like brother and sister.'

She eyes me with an enquiring stare, she's testing me, trying to get the measure of me. So, before she can continue her interrogation, I say,

'Lunch is ready. The surveyors are in the kitchen, and I'm sure Robert will have joined them by now. We have soup, bread and cheese waiting for us. Food will help you recover.' I give her an encouraging smile, leaving her with her mouth open, and walk back to the house.

The noise at lunch is unrecognisable. I haven't heard loud conversation like this in years. This is what it must have been like when Kitty was alive; servants' meals would have been lively and full of gossip. There is a clatter of knives on plates, spoons on bowls, the glug of water being poured into glasses. The room is filled with the heady smell of roasted tomato soup and freshly baked soda bread. The welcoming aroma of good food combined with the animated sound of chatter and laughter is an intoxicating combination. I realise how much I've missed friendly company, how satisfying it is to feed a roomful of people.

There are three surveyors at the table, Pete, Alex and Cameron, along with Caitlin, Robert, Colin and me. I've known Pete since we were wee kids; we were at school together. Alex and Cameron are both young boys, distant cousins of friends in Lairg. Everyone is connected around here; everyone knows each other's business, and it's no surprise that they're keen to gain as much information about the house as possible. No doubt they'll be the centre of attention in the pub on Friday night. I try my best to shut down the questions, but Robert is so open-hearted, he can't help but fill them in on the quirks of Kitty Maclean's will and he's already promised a full guided tour of the house before they continue with their survey; I can see he's impatient to show them the herbarium.

Keen to get away from talk of the house, worried it might stray into the danger areas of gossip and ghosts, I change the subject.

'Have you heard the news that Skibo Castle has been sold?'

And now the table is even more alive with discussion. A small consortium has just bought the castle, once the home of Andrew Carnegie, for twenty-three million pounds. It's been an exclusive private members' club for some time, boasting a golf course, indoor swimming pool and peace from prying eyes. Everyone is talking at once about whether the new owners will invest the millions required to restore and refurbish the eight-thousand-acre estate, whether they'll create the much-needed jobs.

'D'you think it'll stay as a private club?' Pete asks. 'We'd all like to use the facilities a bit more, play a bit more golf on that under-used course. It would be nice to see the house in all its glory, not keep it hidden away.'

'But if it was a private residence, never intended for public consumption, why should it be any different now?' Caitlin exclaims. 'Okay, I understand that people might be curious, but it's a business, they're catering for exclusive clients. Those clients would want to know that discretion is going to be a top priority.'

There's an awkward silence around the room. Pete takes a mouthful of soup.

'Would you do the same here?' I ask. 'Would you make sure the house and garden were kept only for your guests?' I struggle to keep the aggressive tone out of my voice.

Caitlin seems confused, her brow furrowed. 'What do you mean? This house has been shut away for over a hundred years.

Almost nobody has seen it in that time. Haven't you seen to that?'

I am bristling all over. 'This house has been preserved. It's been my life's work to ensure it's been kept in as good a condition as possible, getting it ready to hand over to its next owner.' I try to keep my voice measured and calm, despite a wave of irrational anger building inside me. 'If you manage to dig Ardbray out of its mausoleum, then it should be celebrated and enjoyed by all of those whose lives it has touched, not just by those who are willing to pay through the nose to stay here.'

My words have hit their mark. She can't hold my gaze and busies herself by cutting a slice of cheese and breaking a lump of bread from the loaf.

Robert, always the peacekeeper, changes the subject. 'Caitlin. After lunch, I'd like to take you up the path at the back of the house and up the hill. From up there you'll be able to see the house in plan and its extensive layout.'

'Oh, that reminds me,' she says, the tension dissipating. 'I've been wondering whether it's possible to have a look at the original plans for the house as I'd like to show my architect. And if there's any correspondence about the original build, I'm sure that would be useful too.'

'Of course. I don't see any reason why not. I can't remember seeing any plans of the house, but you're welcome to have a look. There are very few papers of Charles's, I've been through everything and there's nothing of significance. It's Kitty's correspondence that we have a lot of, pretty much from the day she first arrived here until she died. You might find something interesting there. It's all in chronological order, so it should be easy to work through. By the way, which architect will you be appointing?'

I realise that Robert and Caitlin are talking as if the sale has been agreed, as if building work is due to start shortly, as if my whole life has already been changed. I'm uncomfortable with this assumption. So much can still go wrong, I don't dare think about life beyond Ardbray, we've been this close so many times. Each time the disappointment drives deeper into me, making me wonder whether I'll ever be able to leave.

Caitlin hesitates. 'Well, I'm not quite sure. I'm considering someone from Edinburgh.'

I can't help myself. 'Will you not be using someone local?' It's a cheap shot and I know it. Colin glares at me, his signal that I should be ashamed of myself. He's right, of course. I'm behaving like some spoilt child who can't get her own way. Only five minutes ago, I was relishing sitting at this table, full of people, feeding them, watching them enjoy good, home-made food. And now I'm ruining the atmosphere for everyone.

Robert, however, looks delighted. 'Do you mean your father, Finn Black? What a perfect choice. We could do with some innovation around here.'

Caitlin gives him an impish grin. 'I might consider a local woman.'

A wry smile crosses Robert's face. 'Ah, I never took you for a diplomat.'

'It's all right. I'm teasing.' Caitlin scrapes the bottom of her soup bowl and swallows the last mouthful. 'I'm just not quite sure whether it's a good idea to work with him.' She pushes her bowl away. 'You see I don't have the closest father and daughter relationship.' She looks at the three surveyors, who start to mumble about the fact that there's still a lot of work to do and perhaps they ought to get on.

As the three men disappear down the corridor, Caitlin turns to Robert.

'Can I ask you a strange question?' She doesn't wait for an answer. 'How often do you come out here? Surely, it's not usual to spend so much time at the house of one of your dead clients?'

'Well spotted, Miss Black.' Robert laughs. 'I come out here every couple of months. I talk through the maintenance plan for the house, we discuss how much money we have for the coming year's work. I like making sure everything is in order.'

'Can't you do most of that over the phone? Driving up here from Inverness every two months must take you away from your other work.'

Robert sighs and leans back in his chair. 'The truth is Ardbray has the pull of a magnet. I find it exceptionally hard to stay away. In fact, I'm a little bit like Kitty in that I certainly wouldn't have minded being banished to live here.'

She almost does a comical double take. 'What do you mean?'

He laughs again. 'Well, perhaps banish is a little strong, but that is the word she used.'

'Who?' Incredulity spreads across Caitlin's face.

'Kitty Maclean.' He runs his index finger around one of the marks on the table as he continues, 'Kitty Maclean was banished to Ardbray by her husband just two months after she was married.'

'How do you know this?'

'It's all in those letters. Kitty's letters will tell you almost everything you want to know about Ardbray.'

SEVEN

KITTY

Loch More, 1889

Raspberries

'*Raspberries almost rival Strawberries in their popularity. They are more refreshing; and Raspberry vinegar is invaluable in domestic medicine, not only for feverish colds and sore throats but for its astringent and stimulating properties.*'

Herbal Delights *by Mrs C F Leyel*

Ardbray
July 5th 1889

My Dearest Eva,

I am back at Ardbray where I can stay out of trouble and not cause my husband any more difficulty. I have been told that I am to stay here until winter draws on. I have been banished. But perhaps it's for the best.

Oh, Eva, he was so angry with me. My friendship with Dr Forsyth and his well-meaning entreaties to Charles have caused him untold anger and humiliation. All I have ever wanted to do is be of use, to help others who need it and to make something of my life. But it appears that my usefulness will not be permitted.

I'm afraid I haven't been truly honest with you over the last couple of months; I have been too ashamed to admit to my failure as a wife. The Charles I thought I had married has gone. The enthusiastic, liberal-minded and interesting man who courted me has disappeared. The man who seemed to truly care that I wanted to study medicine, that I wanted to help others has vanished.

For someone who used to be very casual about his work, he has suddenly become obsessed with it. After we returned from our truncated honeymoon, I rarely saw him. He was either at the mill, dining out late with John Hardgrave, or occasionally he slept at his club. He'd often come home drunk. Usually I'd be in bed, but he'd never knock on my door or wish me goodnight; it was as if he'd forgotten I was there. And then he would forget to turn up at engagements; I'm sure you noticed that I was having to make excuses for him.

And that's why I returned to helping Dr Forsyth at the Salt-market Clinic. I couldn't sit at home pretending my life was fulfilling. You know how much I hate the constant merry-go-round of teas, musical salons etc. etc. A few weeks of talking to the same dull women about the same persistently dull subjects persuaded me that I had other, more important, things to do.

I'd forgotten how much I enjoyed it, what a sense of achieve-ment it gives me. Of course, it meant that I ended up spending much more time at the clinics than I ever intended to. It was simply more interesting than my life at home.

But I should have listened to you when you said I would be

found out. Not only did I make the mistake of not mentioning anything to Charles, but I had discussed an idea I'd had with Dr Forsyth. On my visit to Charles's mills, I noticed that there was a general lack of care for the women who worked there as well as some appalling accidents. I talked of setting up a women-only clinic with Dr Forsyth, not just helping with their health at work but seeing if we could improve their health through what they ate etc. This would mean they wouldn't need to take so much time off work. This would surely be beneficial to Charles and his business. But before I could mention any of this to Charles, Dr Forsyth visited him at his office to present the idea.

That evening he arrived home early from work, a surprise in itself and, perhaps, should have been a warning. He requested I join him in his study. Without a preamble he completely lost his temper, almost roaring at me. How dare I go behind his back and be so underhanded. And to make it worse I had involved a complete stranger. How dare I discuss his business with someone he didn't know. Did I have a better understanding of the cotton industry than him? He was embarrassed, he was humiliated, he felt like he had been made a fool of. What gave me the right to interfere with the status quo at the mill? Where did I get the nerve to believe that I could make his workers' lives better? How could I possibly think that my efforts would make a difference? He would become the laughing stock of the board, being controlled by his wife. Every little thing that was wrong he brought up: my deceit in working at the clinic, my 'infernal desire to read and better myself', my inability to socialise in the right way or mix with the right people, he even brought up how awful Mother was. Finally, he declared he'd had enough of me and wanted me out of Glasgow.

So, I've been sent here to consider my wrongs. The first few days were difficult, and I couldn't settle. I was so angry and bewildered, pacing the house and walking the hills to stop my head from whirring with fury. My life is being controlled by *another. It is no different from my life before marriage where our mother, the conductor of her own family choir, would keep us in time and make sure we created the right kind of familial music. But this time my own personal conductor seems clumsy and ham-fisted and doesn't seem to know which type of music he wishes us to sing.*

But, now that my anger has abated, I can see many advantages to staying. In fact, I can't think of a better place to be exiled to. I've been here three days and, finally, my soul has been lightened by the fresh air, the simplicity of each day has not been clouded by expectation or worried by the restrictions of city society; Charles cannot control me here. Can you imagine being left to your own devices all day, every day? What a freedom Charles has given me, even if he didn't intend it. I spend almost as many hours working in the new walled garden as I do in the library. At least Charles's so-called bibliophile had the good manners to furnish the library with as many books on medicine, horticulture, herbs and herbalism as I could ever imagine existed.

Perhaps my love affair with Charles is already over. But I find consolation in the fact that any pain caused by him is slowly being healed by Ardbray and the unrestricted life I can lead here.

So, given that Charles will be staying in Glasgow for most of the summer, I should enjoy this magical place. It will be no hardship to remain here until September or October. And, surely, I can stay out of trouble.

But please, Eva, do NOT tell Mother why I am here. I will write to her and explain that I have left the city for the summer, that I am supervising the final touches on the inside decoration and making sure that the garden is being laid out as I planned. I will tell her that we'll be ready to receive guests soon and that I'd be very pleased if you all came to visit.

Meanwhile, please send me all your news. Perhaps in a few days' time, I will not be so happy with my own company and will crave news from the outside world.

With all my love,
Kitty

Kitty sat back on her haunches and wiped her soil-covered hands on her apron. She pushed the stray hair off her face and admired her work. For the last few weeks she'd be nurturing her tiny corner of the garden; she knew it was simplistic, a beginner's patch, but she felt a childish satisfaction at her achievement.

A small patch of garden mint, some chives, sage and thyme. Cook would be pleased to have some fresh herbs for the kitchen, but she was more concerned that they'd be medicinally useful as well. Fraser was dubious about planting herbs for purely medicinal reasons so she was taking things slowly and only planting those herbs that Cook would welcome – just for the moment, whilst she and Fraser jostled for control of the herb garden. She didn't want to upset him, but, somehow, she was going to have to persuade him that herbs and botanicals could make up a large part of her walled garden. After all, it was *her* walled garden.

The new garden was coming on. The surrounding walls were completed, the glass houses finished and in full use, the paths laid and the planting well underway. Fraser and his two undergardeners had been hard at it for weeks. There were shoots of green in the beds, garden canes waiting for the young beans and peas, and new fruit trees planted against the walls. Kitty's tiny corner for her herbs was taking time. Fraser had suggested she lay it out like a formal physic garden, everything ordered and divided up in rectangular beds, but she didn't want that, she wanted something more relaxed, something more soothing and inviting.

'You'll need to dig up those mint plants,' Fraser's harsh voice called out from behind her.

Kitty got up from her knees. 'Why? Are they not in the right place?' she asked.

The gardener kicked his own heel in apparent frustration. 'Mint is rampant. It'll take over your whole garden if you don't plant them in pots. You can plunge the pots in the ground, but you'll not want the roots taking hold.'

'It didn't say that in the books I've been reading. Are you sure?'

'Aye. Cannae learn everything from a book. Should've asked me.' He turned. 'I'll get you some pots.'

Kitty scrambled after him. 'I'll come and get them.'

'They'll be too big for you to carry. Mind.' And he pushed past her into the shed beside her patch of garden.

'I wondered if you knew when the lavender and rosemary were arriving?' Kitty was doing her best to hide her annoyance, he kept treating her like a child to be indulged.

'Well, I'm going over to Lochmore Lodge tomorrow, they'd potted up some cuttings a while ago and have some spare, so I'll get them for you.' He picked up three large pots and put them under his arm.

'Could you see if they've got some Lady's Mantle?'

Fraser blinked and put the pots onto the bench. 'We can't treat them like a shop. They're doing this as a favour for me. Anyways, what would you be doing with Lady's Mantle? Cook won't have much use for it.'

She had to stop herself from sighing. 'Well, apart from it being a good plant for treating wounds, I was thinking of planting it along the path, to soften it a bit and stop the garden from looking so formal.' But as soon as she'd said this, she regretted it as Fraser appeared to almost convulse at the suggestion.

'Aye. I'll take these pots over to the mint.' And he left her abruptly.

Kitty shook her head. One day they'd see eye to eye, at least she hoped they would. Every time she got enthusiastic about some new plant or a new way of planting, he would sigh and huff. He was a man of experience who liked to do things the traditional way and didn't seem too pleased with Kitty and her new-found love of gardening and herbs.

"Ma'am?' Eleanor interrupted her thoughts. 'A letter has arrived from Glasgow.'

Glasgow, Charles, and her disastrous marriage. She was so caught up in her life of liberty at Ardbray that she'd almost forgotten what life was like back there, in the world of reality. Eleanor handed her the envelope with Charles's handwriting on it.

None of his letters ever seemed to give her good news.

Kitty,

I will be returning to Ardbray on Tuesday. We are expecting house guests exactly one week later. Please inform Mrs Lindsay that nine guests will be arriving for the inaugural Ardbray shoot and to prepare as required for a four-day house party.

I very much hope you'll be as well prepared as I expect Mrs Lindsay and the house to be.

Your husband,
Charles

All she wanted to do was rip up the letter and throw it onto the compost heap, but that wouldn't do. With control, she folded the paper and put it in her apron pocket. A petulant gardener and a discourteous husband. Couldn't they just leave her to her mistakes and let her get on with it? No, of course not. She must play the dutiful wife.

'Eleanor, we need to go and see Mrs Lindsay. We'll be expecting guests in a few days.' And she took her apron off as she walked back to the house.

EIGHT

GREER

Loch More, 2003

Marjoram

*'Marjoram is one of the old strewing herbs; and the clean, spicy
smell of the juice made it particularly suitable for scouring
furniture.'*

Herbal Delights *by Mrs C F Leyel*

Last night I saw the children again. They were clear and sharp,
and they were looking for me. I'd taken their fading, their disin-
terest in me, to mean that they were becoming reliant on
Caitlin, that the burden was being passed onto her. Although
this should have been a relief, what I've been hoping for since
the day my mother died, I've found it upsetting, desolating even.
Is this what it feels like when your children leave home?

But last night they were, again, in full view, well-defined

and bright. They ran into my little garden, just at the back of the kitchen, whilst I was tending to my small range of herbs: lavender, rosemary, catmint, sage and thyme which give off that evocative smell of my childhood in Kitty's herb garden. I concentrate so hard on making it look beautiful. If I can reproduce just a minuscule piece of what Kitty had, if I can bring back something of the main garden that I have failed to resurrect, then perhaps I can begin to forgive myself for failing in my task.

As I was trimming back the lavender, I realised that the familiar muffling of sounds was occurring: the bees in the flowers, the evening birdsong and the distant rush of the burn. The utter relief that this was happening again was overwhelming and, as I looked up, there they were, running across the lawn, running to me. The boy, dressed as always in his too-tight sailor suit, his thick, wiry hair, thrown back by his speed, his face unsmiling. And behind him she ran her childish, ungainly run, her white, blonde curls bobbing up and down as she followed her brother. Her feet were bare, there was a smudge on her cheek.

Finally, they stopped in front of me. It had been so long since I'd seen them properly that I began to wonder if it was some sort of dream, but her sharp blue eyes had that unmistakable, penetrating quality, that barbed reality that I cannot forget.

'Where is she?' she asked.

I didn't know if she was asking about her mother or whether she was wanting to find Caitlin. Either way, I was unable to help, her question, her clarity of voice producing such a cloud of misery over me that I was struck dumb, the childish honesty in her face hitting me like a physical blow. This question had such an obvious meaning; these children believe Caitlin will not be buying this house and that I am responsible. Their anger at me has made me interrogate my own motivations, made me wonder why I find myself being so belligerent to Caitlin Black when, surely, she's the answer to my dreams and those of the children.

Have I become so institutionalised that I can't imagine a life away from Ardbray? Will I cope without the crutch of these children who have needed me for so long? Who will need me instead? Colin? Maybe, but not in the way a child does, not in the way a...

I want all this to stop. My anger, my unfailing loyalty, my inability to make a decision or to trust anyone. Most of all, I want these angry conversations to leave me, let me lead a quiet and fulfilling life.

Caitlin is here, reading through Kitty's correspondence. She's been here for a few days, filling the house with her enthusiasm and excitement. But she hasn't even put an offer in on the house yet. I find it odd that Robert is so happy for her to be going through Kitty's papers. He's never let any previous prospective buyers do that. But maybe he believes she's different, he believes she's more like Kitty than anyone we've met before; maybe he truly believes that she will buy this house and because of that, he's willing to bend the rules.

While she's here, I find it difficult to settle to any work. I should be embarking on our annual cleaning of the drawing room. It's a massive job that involves rolling up the huge rug, checking for carpet moth and ensuring the viability of the underlay. Whilst the carpet is up, we clean the curtains, upholstery and tapestries with a speciality hand-held vacuum cleaner. Pictures are taken down and checked for damage. We set up a scaffold tower so that we can clean the decorative plasterwork on the ceiling. Windows are cleaned and furniture is moved and given a light wax polish. This is a big job for just the two of us. Usually, I relish it; it's my way of making sure the house is properly preserved, of making sure that I make my own mark on its unlikely survival. It gives me a purpose, a reason for getting up in the morning. But now I can't find the energy that's required to do it. What's the point if it really is going to be sold?

Once I'd called myself an interior designer, I thought my designs would be famous and I'd be in every interiors' magazine. Once I had the optimism of the young and that bulletproof, hard-core belief in myself. But none of those came about and my belief is now generally framed by my ability to dust and polish, clean and scrub.

Instead of beginning the work in the dining room, I find I need to focus on something smaller, so I've retreated to the pantry where I've been checking through the itinerary of crockery, glassware and other items, making sure everything is clean and undamaged. I decide to tackle the picnic basket.

It's a beautiful wicker basket containing a full set of bone china crockery, completely impractical but would delight any antique hunter. The leather straps that hold the crockery in place are a little dry and I have been intending to treat them with saddle soap to ensure they don't crack.

I become so absorbed in my work that I don't hear Caitlin enter the room. Suddenly, there she is, towering over me, as I kneel on the floor.

'Can I interrupt you for a moment?' she asks. There's a boldness in her words that I haven't heard recently; she's been quiet, reticent. I don't answer, just slowly put my cloth down.

'Those children I've been seeing, I don't think they belong to your neighbours. They come and talk to me; I see them in my dreams when I'm here. I think you know who they are. They're wearing strange, old-fashioned clothes. They look as if they haven't been outdoors for weeks, all pale and miserable and they're looking for their mother.'

I lay both my hands on my thighs and look her directly in the eye as I say, 'I'm not quite sure what you're saying.' I try to keep my voice level, without emotion.

She holds my stare, her self-assurance growing. 'I just want to know if there's something you're not telling me, something you're hiding that you're worried will make me pull out, make me not want to buy Ardbray.'

I say nothing.

'Look, I want to buy this house. I'm ready to put my money down. The survey is done and the preliminary report indicates that everything is fine. It suggests you and your family have done a fine job of keeping this house in a good state, keeping it ready for a new owner. But I just get the feeling that there's something you're keeping from me, something important.' Our eyes lock, we can both see that a stalemate is looming, neither of us is willing to give an inch.

But something dislodges in my head. Maybe it's because I saw the children again, maybe I've come to realise that I need to give her something, let her see the real Ardbray, then perhaps she'll let us see the real Caitlin Black. If she pulls out of the purchase, then so be it.

'Yes. There are children. They're Kitty's children. They're the ghosts of Kitty's son and daughter.'

I've blindsided her. She seems to hold her breath and then turns so that her back is to me, her hand running through her hair, and now a long, slow outward breath. Slowly, she starts to pace up and down the room. I can see that there's an internal conversation going on, that she's deciding how best to approach my lies.

'Why didn't you tell me? Why didn't you admit that they existed?' There's exasperation in her voice. I feel as if she'd like to take me by the shoulders and shake me.

How do I say to her that I've protected these children most of my life and that I'd be lost without them? How do I say that I'm jealous of her ability to see them, of their need for her? She'll see this as petty, overprotective and small-minded. I can't admit to that.

'Why would you want to buy a haunted house? Nobody

wants that burden. If you'd known that, you'd have pulled out of the sale and we'd all be back to the way we were in 1947.'

There's a silence between us that's too heavy, neither of us able to break it. Wordless anger is spreading over her face, but it's as if she's rooted to the spot and is unable to move.

Finally, I get up off the floor. 'Colin will be back shortly; I need to make his supper.' I wipe my hands on the cloth and make to go towards the kitchen.

She seems to come out of her reverie. 'Yes, of course.' She looks around her, almost as if she's not sure where she is. 'I should go. I have a phone call to make.'

NINE

KITTY

Loch More, 1889

Sweet Cicely

'It gives back strength and courage to those who have lost both.'

Herbal Delights *by Mrs C F Leyel*

Ardbray
September 11th 1889

My Dearest Eva,

Where shall I begin?
My peaceful, hermit-like existence was shattered two weeks ago when Charles wrote, announcing that we were to expect nine guests for, what he insisted on calling, the inaugural Ardbray Shooting Party.

We had six days to prepare, no easy task when this house had never before seen guests. A daunting list of crockery, cutlery, bedlinen, assigning rooms for our guests and their servants, food to be ordered from Glasgow and temporary staff to be found was dealt with efficiently by Mrs Lindsay. The guest list was glittering: The Marquis of Stafford and his beautiful wife, Lady Millicent, the Duke and Duchess of Argyll, the Duke of Westminster and, of course, Charles's best man, the very affable and amenable Roddy. Making up the numbers were Charles's business partner, John Hardgrave, and another business colleague, Fraser MacDonald, a rather grey man who never seems to say much. Lady Millicent brought a companion, a Miss Lucy Sealy.

Despite my initial misgivings, it all started well and our guests arrived without incident. The weather was glorious, perhaps a little hot for shooting, but for those of us who weren't shooting, it was a wonderful excuse to get out; picnics on the hills and boat trips on the loch. Of course, it was my duty to look after the ladies. They all knew each other very well, so I had some work to do to include myself in their little threesome. Lady Millicent and the Duchess quickly let me in on their clique, but Miss Sealy tended to sulk and avoid eye contact with me, preferring to direct all her conversation at the other two. There's a falsity to Miss Sealy that I can't help but dislike. She wears her loose dresses and turbans and smokes Turkish cigarettes whenever she can. Sometimes, I feel she's doing it just to be different.

On the first day's shoot I took the ladies up the hill and we joined the men for lunch. They'd had a successful day and were pleased with their bag. In the evening we had quite a party. After a dinner with food of the highest order, we had an impromptu dance in the dining room. Did you know the floor is sprung and it's a wonderful room to dance in? I even managed to persuade Charles to dance!

Day two followed along similar lines and I began to feel

confident that we could make a success of our hastily put-together party.

The third day was where it all began to go wrong. As the men left for this hills, in high spirits, John Hardgrave stayed behind to respond to some urgent family business, whilst the ladies sat out on the patio enjoying the continued fine weather. After I had been through the day's arrangements with Mrs Lindsay, I went to join them.

I approached the patio through the drawing room, but as I came to the French doors, I found I couldn't interrupt their conversation; they were talking about Charles and me. I stood beside the curtains that surrounded the French doors, able to hear them but not able to see.

'I don't know how they have the audacity. Pretending they are of importance in our circle when we all know that he's a cotton merchant and she's just the daughter of some social climbing doctor. He only married her because no one else of any standing would have him, no one with any half-decent family would have anything to do with him. Oh, I'm sure there were plenty of lesser girls who'd have had his money, but he wasn't interested; he wanted someone with connections. And that's where Kitty Gray came in. No one cared for her, so plain and bookish, but her father had all the connections Charles could possibly want. Physician to the aristocracy. So, by default, she had the all-important link to the world he so craved to be part of. And her fabulous naivety made sure she had no concerns about his lack of breeding. So, you see, that's why he chose her.'

Miss Sealy's slow, lazy voice made me want to spit. I could hear her inhale on her cigarette, a sharp, dismissive noise. And then she continued as if she'd been strengthened by the smoke.

'And then building this outlandish house, with bathrooms upstairs and running hot water, throwing his money around. I don't know where they get their nerve; Hugh Grosvenor, one of the richest men in this country with an impeccable lineage and Mr Charles Maclean dares to outdo him right on his doorstep.'

Eva, is this true? Would no one else marry Charles? Was I his last resort?

How can that woman accept our hospitality and then so readily damn us? I knew I had to hold my temper before going outside to face her, to show her a defiant exterior that would put her to shame. I leaned against the curtain, trying to calm my breathing and gather my strength, thinking of what to say. But just as I was preparing myself, I turned to find John Hardgrave on my shoulder, almost touching me, also listening to the conversation. The shock caused me to jump to which John caught me, his hands on my arms before putting his finger to his lips, silently gesturing to keep quiet. With a conspiratorial wink, he joined the ladies.

Did he defend us? I'm not sure, his words are so often ambiguous and slanted. He praised the organisation of the party, but he tempered his compliments with a side whisper of my lack of experience and social graces.

Eva, I cannot fathom John Hardgrave. He appears to be a bumbling, mop-haired buffoon, but, at the same time, the perfect house guest. He's always punctual, has impeccable manners and is continually entertaining and attentive to the other guests. He joins in the men's activities with gusto, bagging his fair share of the birds, but not too many, making a good show at the billiard table, winning or losing with good grace.

But there is something that stops me short of trusting him. There is not a woman in this house who has not been flattered by him, Mrs Lindsay and Cook included. But I notice that attention is only produced when he needs something. I cannot fault his behaviour towards me, always polite and always keeping an eye out to make sure that I have kept my head above water. But there is just a hint of something in his manner, his look, that makes me think he is not sincere. I feel that it is all a great façade. But look at me, how can I criticise him for putting up a front? That is what I am doing all day long when I play Mrs Charles Maclean.

But the complexities of our house guests pale into insignificance with the following.

The last day of the shoot went better than expected, but the weather broke early in the afternoon. A great storm had been brewing as a result of the relentless heat. Torrential rain meant the men had to return to the house sooner than hoped. As we were all gathering for tea, I was called away by Mrs Lindsay, explaining that the doctor was here to see me. Puzzled, I followed her to the hallway where a very wet Dr Beattie was standing. Dr Beattie is the Lairg doctor, but he will sometimes see patients in Achfary. I know him as he has treated some of our servants previously. As you can imagine, I was very surprised when he began by asking me for my help with a patient of his in Achfary who was having a particularly difficult birth. I couldn't understand why he would think I could help him. Then he told me that he knew both our father and Dr Forsyth. It seems Dr Forsyth has told him of the work I had done at the Saltmarket Clinic and the Infirmary and he was under the impression that I had enough experience to help him out.

'She needs a woman's touch, Mrs Maclean. She's a little nervous around me and I believe you might be able to help.'

I hesitated, knowing that Charles would not be pleased if I abandoned our guests. But that slight tingling in my stomach started; the same as I used to get whenever I was allowed into Father's surgery. And with that, I went. I thought I could be back by dinner. It was only a few miles away, after all.

Dr Beattie took me to one of the most basic crofts on the edge of the village. Crumpled into the corner of the room was the patient, cowering like a tiny, frightened bird on a heap of sweat-soaked blankets. It was as if her whole, fragile body had been overtaken by a swollen balloon, ready to burst. As I looked at her, the rough, rumpled nightgown, her wild hair, her deathly pale *face, I was frightened for her; I couldn't imagine how this baby would come out. She had been in pain for so long that she would no longer allow Dr Beattie near her. He told me exactly what to do – feeding me instructions from behind a curtain. And we did it. I coaxed her into drinking a little chamomile tea to calm her down, then soothed and talked her through the birth. And finally, a bonnie little boy was born. Oh, Eva, I have never cried such tears of joy! Sarah, the birdlike mother, and I hugged and cried and became the best of friends in that short time. I don't know how to describe to you the feeling of elation I had, the feeling of privilege to have witnessed such a humbling scene. After we had cleaned the baby up and made Sarah comfortable, had a cup of reviving nettle tea and shed more tears, Dr Beattie took me home. It was late, I had no idea how late, and the rain was still pouring.*

I must have looked like some wild animal when I appeared in the hall. I didn't realise what a picture I must have presented until I saw myself in the mirror later. I had left the house without a hat, so my hair had been soaked by the heavy rain. It had frizzed and curled and become matted, sticking to one of my cheeks. My dress and shawl were wet and clung to me. Charles had heard the horses and so had come swiftly to the hallway. I was still euphoric from the success of our evening's work and was blind to any signs of Charles's displeasure. I should have recognised the stiff demeanour, the stony eyes and his clenched fists. Dr Beattie, wishing to ensure my safe return and probably looking for a warming drink, accompanied me into the house. In my naive excitement, I took Charles's hands, introduced him to the kind doctor and then told him all that had happened and how wonderful it had been. As you can imagine, this was received with a black stare and a careful releasing of his cold and granite-like hands. Finally, when I had finished and had begun to realise that all was not well, Charles calmly thanked Dr Beattie and showed him out. After shutting the door, he took me by the hand and silently walked me to his study.

When Charles is angry, he usually shouts, his face turns red and the agitation causes spittle to fly out as he rants. Sometimes, I'm afraid he may even hit me, but this time he was so calm I was more frightened than I've ever been.

In the quietest of voices, he told me of his absolute bewilderment at my abandoning his guests for some irrelevant woman to whom I had no connection. He spoke of shame, embarrassment, disgrace and horror at my disobedience. Hadn't I been told once before not to get involved with the charity of others? Didn't I understand the importance of this shooting party and how much he needed to gain the approval of his aristocratic guests? Did I have any idea how my actions had ruined any chance of gaining long-term favour with our visitors? Eva, he never raised his voice, but he talked and talked in a cold, dead voice until the full impact of his fury took over and I couldn't stop myself from crying. But these weren't just gentle tears; they were full body-wracking sobs. I couldn't help it as all the pent-up emotions from the day crowded around me and threatened to swallow me up.

To my surprise, Charles mistook my tears for remorse. In fact, I think he was so embarrassed by my passionate outpouring that he didn't know what to do with me. How have I never understood the power of tears before now? Without another word, he called for Eleanor and had me taken up to bed.

I don't regret what happened. I still cherish that afternoon helping Sarah bring her little boy into the world. I feel that, finally, I have been useful, that I have made a difference to others.

The next morning our guests were due to leave. I couldn't bring myself to face them despite what they would think of my absence. I had Mrs Lindsay tell Charles that I was ill and unable to bid them farewell. I suspect it suited Charles that I kept out of the way. But just as I'd plucked up the courage to confront Charles, Mrs Lindsay came to tell me that he'd left for Glasgow. Eva, I know that it's wicked of me to think this, but what a sense of relief I felt, even if he had left without saying a word to me.

So here I am again, alone and thankful for it. Having time in the garden gives me the opportunity to consider all that has happened. September seems to be a fine month in the Highlands – the colours heightened, the sun lower, the air sharpening – it feels as if we are eeking out the last of the best of the year. Perhaps you could come and visit? Maybe bring Mother too. Of course, Father is welcome, but I know that he is most likely to be busy with his work.

Write by return to let me know how soon you can come.

With all my love,
Kitty

TEN

GREER

Loch More, 2003

Hornbeam

'In parts of France, near Valenciennes, branches of hornbeam are hung outside the
doors of men's sweethearts as a symbol of their devotion.'

Elixirs of Life *by Mrs C F Leyel*

'I just thought I'd drop by to ask how much venison you'd like this year. Will it be the usual half carcass?'

Duncan has appeared on our doorstep to ask a question he usually asks on the phone. I smile. I suspect he was hoping to see Caitlin. But she's not been here for a few days, and, against my better judgement, I find myself missing her company. He looks so crestfallen when I tell her she isn't here that I've asked him in for a cup of tea. I'm glad of the opportunity to talk.

'We'll have our usual, please. I can't see that we're going anywhere; that'll see us through the winter.'

He's sitting on the sofa, having made himself comfortable with his tea and cake. 'Oh, come on. You think she isn't going to buy?'

I find that I'm squirming in my seat. I don't want to open up to this boy, I hardly know him, but I need to get it off my chest.

'I told her about the ghost children.'

He raises his eyebrows but says nothing. I like Duncan's restraint. Nobody has ever confirmed that there are ghosts at Ardbray until now. So few people have spent time here, I'm certain that no one else has seen them apart from myself, my mother and grandmother before me. He shows no surprise, no glee at being the one to be able to confirm the local gossip.

'I had to tell her. I couldn't lie any longer and besides, I know she's been seeing them. She's the first buyer, that I know of, who's been able to see them.'

He leans forward and speaks almost accusingly. 'Yes, but she's not the first buyer to find herself in trouble. You know that car accident was no accident, that she could have been seriously hurt.'

Of course, his only concern is for Caitlin. That's the only reason he's sitting on this sofa rather than hanging on the end of a phone call.

'Ach, she was fine. Your imagination is putting things out of perspective.'

'I had a drink with her a few days ago. As you can imagine a fair few people in the pub were interested in what she was doing here, and there was some lively discussion about what happened to the previous buyers.'

My heart sinks. I'm already concerned that Caitlin will be put off by my confession about the children. 'And?' I ask quietly.

He gives me a cynical smile. 'Well, Robbie, the landlord,

was happy to tell her how this house is full of tragedy an' misfortune, that once you start looking into its history, you'll find
nothing but unhappiness and loss. He went on to say that you'll
not find a soul 'round here that would buy it, and that anyone
who's tried has been warned off.'

So, it's true. Any chance of a change in my life has been
ruined. I put my elbows on the table and my head in my hands.

'Go on. I know exactly what has happened over the years,
but I'd like to know how bad the gossip has become.'

'Well, he said that there were few workmen who'd be
willing to work at the house, he said that too many tools would
go missing or that there were unexplained voices. But I'm afraid
he really went to town when he listed all the buyers who had
pulled out because of illness or injury.' I still can hear the smile
in his voice, but I daren't look up. Perhaps he's mocking me, but
I jump in anyway.

'Keep going, just tell me what he said.' I close my eyes, not
really wanting to hear what's coming, but knowing I must.

'Well, let me see if I can remember what he said.' There's a
short pause as if he's thinking. I envisage him counting off the
buyers on his fingers. 'The first buyer, this was in the sixties,
once the house had been made fully accessible again following
the landslide, he was up from Glasgae.' He's changed his accent,
it's harsher, I assume mimicking the landlord's speech in the
bar, in front of a semicircle of locals. 'Five days before the sale
went through, he had a heart attack and nearly died. Aye, once
he recovered, he'd supposedly reassessed his life and wanted tae
live more simply. Ardbray, of course, was too much, too complicated. Then there was the millionaire stockbroker, he came in
all gung-ho and ready tae change everything, put in a helipad,
swimming pool and gym. But this was 1987 and just before all
the paperwork was signed, the stock market crashed. He lost his
money and, of course, pulled out. And the most recent one was
in the early nineties.' And now his mimicking voice becomes

conspiratorial. 'He was just on his way from Ardbray tae the solicitors in Inverness tae talk through the final details when he died in a car crash coming into Lairg. Some mechanical fault with the car.'

The trouble is, it's all true. This really can't get any worse. 'What did Caitlin say?' My heart is racing now, I'm even sweating slightly under my arms.

Duncan almost snorts and I look up. There's a big grin on his face. 'She laughed. Said it sounded like some Gothic horror story and then went on to order her dinner.'

'So, she didn't believe it?'

'Honestly, I don't know. We moved on to other things.' He gets up from the sofa and puts his empty plate on the table. 'You know, you shouldn't be so worried about her. She'd never string you along. She may come from a high-profile, high-achieving, demanding family, but she's got her head screwed on. Her heart's in the right place.'

'But there's something about her, something so fragile, so fragmented, that I'm not sure she's able to take on this house with its lost children. Every time she sees them, it's as if she's lost something herself.'

Duncan says nothing, so I ask, 'Tell me about her family and how you know her. She doesn't open up to us.'

'Well, she's a born and bred Manhattan girl, despite all her connections to Scotland. Her parents divorced when she was seven, and I got to know her when she'd spend whole summers here, staying with her aunt. Her sisters hated it; it was far too wet and remote for their liking, but Caitlin and Jim fitted right in. They came from a city life of white carpets, immaculate clothes and restaurant dinners. Annie Black, her aunt, gave her muddy knees, wholesome, home-made food and a love of the countryside. She was taught how to gut a fish, pluck a chicken and shoot a rabbit. She's a better shot than I am.'

'But you said you hadn't seen each other in years. Why did

she stop coming to Scotland, especially if her father had moved back here?'

'Caitlin Black can be contrary and stubborn. Don't ever expect her to do the expected.' I can tell he's enjoying talking about her. There's a slight flush to his cheeks and his eyes are alight. 'She turned into one of those wholly unpredictable teenagers, railing against most of her family, the fashion industry, the money and the lifestyle. The only person whom she didn't punish was her little brother, Jim. There is nothing she wouldn't do for him and, from what she says, he feels the same about her.'

'Well, we were expecting her back today. She told us that she wanted to read through some more of those letters, but she hasn't appeared. Do you know where she is?' I ask.

Duncan frowns. 'No. I dropped by because I wanted to speak to her. She said she'd come by one last time before she flew back to New York.'

A sudden chill runs across my neck. 'She's gone back?'

'Aye. She said she had business to attend to and wasn't sure when she'd return.'

ELEVEN

KITTY

Loch More, 1895

Mint

'It suffers not milk to curdle in the stomach, if the leaves thereof be steeped or boiled in it before you drink it. Briefly it is very profitable to the stomach.'

The Complete Herbal *by Nicholas Culpeper*

The desk in the library had been converted into a makeshift painter's table with paints, brushes, stiff paper, pencils, a pot of water and a vase filled with plant cuttings. Kitty was engrossed in making a watercolour of some wild marjoram. She'd finished the pencil drawing and was now using the paints to give it its colour, but she felt like her sister did after a morning's practice on the piano, wanting to throw the attempt away in a huff of frustration. Her painting was not accomplished. She sighed, leaning back in her chair. As a child, she'd always thought painting was a wistful pastime and not worth pursuing, but now she was wishing she'd been more attentive in those much-maligned painting classes.

'Mrs Maclean?'

'Oh, Eleanor, I'm glad to see you. And look who you've brought, little Miss Flora. That suggests to me that Mrs Mercaut has been having a difficult time.'

Eleanor handed the small bundle over to Kitty who immediately put her on her shoulder and began walking around the room, jiggling her, and humming gently. She put her nose to the clean, thin layer of baby hair and took a deep breath. It was that almost addictive, distracting baby smell that let her momentarily forget her lack of artistic prowess mixed in with the long night and lack of sleep.

'Aye, Mrs Mercaut looked exhausted. I said I'd take her for a while.'

'Yes, I'm afraid she's got colic; we were up half the night. And then, in our exhaustion, Mrs Mercaut and I had a bit of a disagreement. She wanted to give Flora some water with a drop or two of crème de menthe to ease the stomach pains, but I wanted to give her a very weak and cool mint tea. My argument was "surely the less alcohol you give a baby the better". In the end, I won out. I successfully administered the tea and decided it would be easier for Flora to sleep with me. Mrs Mercaut, of course, was very disapproving, but even she was too tired to argue in the end. I think we each managed just a couple of hours' sleep. Remind me, Eleanor, not to have any more children. Two is more than I can manage.' She overdramatically put her hand to her forehead before giving Eleanor a broad grin.

'You'd be bored without them,' Eleanor teased.

'Mmmm, maybe. But I've been working on a more effective tisane for Flora, with some camomile, fennel and lemon balm. We'll try it out tonight.' Kitty suddenly stopped her soft dance around the room, 'I mustn't forget I've promised to help at the school today. It's a lovely day, I think I might walk.'

'It's a way? Would you not like the carriage?'

'No, I don't think so, I feel a bit uncomfortable turning up at that tiny school in my grand carriage. Most of those children have nothing, I'd rather arrive just as they do. Anyway, I'll feel better after a good walk.'

Kitty Maclean, now the mother of two small children, had settled into a double life; frustrating restrictive winters in Glasgow with her anxious and ill-tempered husband, summers at Ardbray free of Charles and at liberty to make a life of her own.

'Now that the school has restarted after the harvest, I think Miss Sutherland would like me to help out a couple of days a week. The trouble is we'll have to return to Glasgow sometime soon before the worst of winter arrives. I hate to let her down, but don't suppose there's any way around it.'

Achfary School was held in the front room of one of the houses in the village. Ten children of varying ages attended, in a haphazard fashion, and no schooling could be contemplated during the harvest as all hands were needed to help on the crofts.

'I'll miss those lessons when we go back to Glasgow. It's been such a pleasure watching those children learn. I wish Callum was old enough to come with me, but I don't think a four-year-old would be welcome.' As she spoke, the baby was starting to wriggle and complain.

'Would Mr Maclean have a few words to say about that?' Eleanor asked.

'Yes. But perhaps he wouldn't need to know.' She smiled at Eleanor as she brought the baby from her shoulder and cradled her in her arms. 'Now, little Miss Flora, it's time for your feed.'

. . .

Kitty walked up the drive to Ardbray in the heat of the late afternoon sun. The five-mile walk back from Achfary had been hot and exhausting. Her face was glowing and her cheeks red. As she came close to the house, she untied her hat and took it off, fanning herself with the brim.

Her visit to the school had given her a sense of achievement and she'd started her walk home full of conviction and confidence, full of energy to get back to her garden. She would need to work with Fraser to get it ready for the winter. But as she thought of this, the realisation that they would have to return to Glasgow within the next few weeks darkened her mood as she anticipated four or five grey and wet months in the city. Callum had never seemed happy in town, always grouchy and badly behaved, and she knew that she became more reserved, unwilling to engage with her family, the servants, well, anyone who crossed her path. Was it only because Charles was present? Or was it because they had all become so used to the freedom of life without him that his unpredictable and overbearing presence caused such a change in their moods? Even Eleanor became more distant; Eleanor who was so outspoken and funny.

As she approached the front door, she could hear footsteps thundering down the main stairs inside, across the hallway and on towards her.

'Mama, Mama! You're home.' Callum came careering towards her, bumping into her with a huge hug.

Kitty laughed. 'Hello. What's this? Missed me?'

'Flora's been yelling all afternoon, it's only now that she's gone to sleep. Mrs Mercaut is quite grumpy, so I've been helping Mrs Lindsay and Cook in the kitchen. We've made cake, and I've been waiting for you to come home so we can eat it.'

'Well, we'd better go and eat it, before someone else does.'

Kitty picked up Callum. 'My, you're getting too heavy to pick up, soon you'll just have to walk the whole way.'

'You'll be having your tea? Shall I bring it up to the terrace?' asked the unusually red-faced Mrs Lindsay as they reached the kitchen, her sleeves rolled up and small wisps of hair frizzing out of her usually neat bun.

'Mrs Lindsay, you look as if you're about to melt. Why don't I help you bring everything up? Perhaps you'd like to join Callum and me, we could do with some company.'

Eleanor, Kitty, Mrs Lindsay and Callum were all sitting out on the terrace, drinking lemonade and finishing their plates of cake. The two servants appeared a little uncomfortable, trying their best to appear at home in their new-found status.

Kitty faced Eleanor. 'I had a letter from Eva today. Can you guess what she said?'

'Something to do with your mother and any suitors. It's the subject she always talks about in her letters.' Eleanor laughed.

'Even better. Finally, she's got engaged.' Kitty couldn't keep the note of triumph out of her voice.

'Aye. That's grand,' said Mrs Lindsay. 'Although, it's taken a while. I thought your mother had been busy arranging her marriage since the day you left home.'

'She has. I think she was beginning to despair. Despite the fact that my sister is far more beautiful than me, far more suited to marriage, somehow those eligible bachelors didn't seem to be forthcoming.' She looked down at her hands.

Eleanor and Mrs Lindsay exchanged glances. 'Aye, that'll mean a good winter wedding,' Mrs Lindsay interjected.

Kitty looked up, distracted. 'Yes, I suppose so.' She watched a bird land on the water. There was an awkward silence whilst the two servants took a sip of their lemonade.

'I saw you had several letters from Glasgae, have you bin

corresponding with those doctors again?' There was a hint of suspicion in Mrs Lindsay's face.

Kitty forgot her distraction, animation lighting up her face. 'Oh yes, although there was also a letter from my father, kindly asking that perhaps I could lessen my ardour for long, probing letters. It seems my enquiring mind is taking up too much of their time. The trouble is there are just so many questions I want to ask, I've been reading up on all these herbal remedies that Nicholas Culpepper recommends, and I wanted to find out how they are regarded today, over two hundred years later.'

'I can see that perhaps they have more pressing matters to deal with.' Mrs Lindsay smirked.

As they were chatting, Mrs Mercaut appeared at the French doors. Unseen by the others, she watched the party for a while, a frown on her face. Eventually, Kitty spotted her.

'Oh, Mrs Mercaut. How's Flora?'

'She's been asleep awhile. I'll have to wake her shortly, she'll be needing another feed.'

'Well, please come and join us whilst you have a moment to yourself.'

The nanny hesitated.

'Please, Mrs Mercaut, you probably could do with some refreshment. I hear from Callum that Flora's been quite vocal this afternoon.'

Mrs Mercaut sniffed. 'Yes, she's been telling me about her colic.' She sat on the bench whilst Kitty poured her a glass of lemonade.

'Well, I'm hopeful that the new tisane I've been making might just help that painful tummy. We'll try it out after tea.'

There was a look on the nanny's face as if she'd just come across a bad smell, but she said nothing, hiding her disapproval whilst sipping her drink.

'Mrs Mercaut, please can we go and look at the burn?' Callum asked politely.

'Callum, poor Mrs Mercaut has only just sat down. She's been on her feet all day. Let her have a minute's peace.' Kitty patted Callum's knee. 'We'll go a bit later.'

'I'll take him,' Eleanor said.

'Oh, would you?'

Callum jumped down from his chair and rushed over to Eleanor. 'Can we throw sticks into the burn and follow them down to the loch?'

'Aye, that we can. Come on then.' Eleanor took the boy's hand and the two of them walked up the hill in the direction of the babbling stream.

Kitty turned to the children's nanny. 'Mrs Mercaut. I fear you do not agree with Callum and me taking tea with Eleanor and Mrs Lindsay.'

Mrs Mercaut nodded. 'Yes, ma'am. It's not right. We have our place in the kitchen or in the nursery with the children. The children should be eating away from the adults.'

Kitty smiled at the hands in her lap before continuing. 'Mrs Mercaut, we live out here in a very remote part of the country, I don't mix much with society. As you've probably noticed, I quite enjoy my own company, but sometimes I need some conversation. Callum is good company, my mornings at the school are precious, but I also need some adult company. Doctor Beattie is kind enough to drop in here whenever he's passing by, but that isn't very often. There are days when, if I didn't have you, Eleanor, Fraser and Mrs Lindsay, I'd have no adult conversation at all. We've been coming here every summer for six years now and, now that I think about it, I'm ashamed that I haven't done this before. When we're here, you're the closest I have to family and, just because convention says so, I can't see why we shouldn't be friends and treat each other as we'd treat our own friends.'

Mrs Mercaut began to shuffle in her seat, looking intently at the terrace stone slabs beneath her feet.

'I'm sorry, Mrs Mercaut, I can see I've embarrassed you. But please, indulge me, and let me invite my friends to join me for tea.'

'Aye, and why can't we invite you for tea in the kitchen some days?' Mrs Lindsay said, as she stood up and began clearing the plates and glasses onto the tray. 'We've all bin too polite, letting you sit by yourself for too long. Mrs Mercaut, there's naebody here who'd tell. Let it be.'

As she spoke, a shout could be heard from up the hill. Kitty stood and walked onto the lawn to get a better view of the bridge where Eleanor and Callum had gone to. Another shout. And now she could see Eleanor kneeling beside Callum, who was lying on the ground.

For a moment, her heart seemed to stop and she was unable to move. 'It's Callum,' she whispered and then more loudly, 'It's Callum.' Kitty gathered her skirts up high and began to run.

She arrived by her son's side out of breath, her hair falling onto her face.

'Ma'am.' Eleanor's frightened eyes searched Kitty's. 'He's having some sort of fit.'

Kitty dropped to the ground, watching her son's jerking body.

'He just fell to the floor for no reason and then he started this shaking, his whole body jolting...'

Kitty stared, her mind was blank, as she watched her son go still. She put a hand to his face. His skin was clammy and his lips showed a tinge of blue. His eyes were closed and his breathing was erratic.

But now her mind began to work, the knowledge she had acquired from her years of reading medical journals and textbooks began to take over.

Eleanor burst into tears, wiping her nose. 'I don't know what happened. I don't know why this happened.' Her voice was desperate, her hand shaking.

Kitty brushed Callum's hair from his face as his breathing began to calm. Picking up his left hand, she noticed the blue colour under his fingernails. She opened his mouth and checked inside. 'We mustn't move him; we must leave him here until he's fully awake.' She was cool and businesslike whilst Eleanor began to hiccup, pushing the unstoppable tears from her cheeks.

'Eleanor, you need to run down to the house and get a blanket and some sort of cushion or pillow.'

Eleanor tried to catch her breath but was unable to speak.

Kitty looked directly at her. 'Eleanor, I need you to do this urgently whilst I make Callum comfortable.' She spoke slowly and clearly. 'Can you do that?'

Nodding and sniffing, Eleanor stood up and ran down the hill.

Kitty kissed her son's forehead and then lay down beside him. She began to hum a nursery rhyme, rhythmic and gentle as she stroked his head again and again, her tune sometimes disappearing before returning loud and melodious. Finally, she stopped and closed her eyes, listening to the now regular rise and fall of her son's chest.

Eventually, Kitty sensed a change in Callum and sat up. He'd opened his eyes and now turned towards his mother.

'Hello, my darling. How are you feeling?' She smiled at him as confusion spread across his face. He tried to sit up but cried out as he put his head into his hands.

'Lie down,' she said gently. 'You must lie down; it'll make you feel better.' She glanced towards the house. 'Look, here's Eleanor with a cushion for your sore head and a blanket to keep you warm.'

Puffing, Eleanor laid the blanket over Callum as Kitty put the cushion underneath his head.

'There, that should make you feel better. Now don't move until you feel you can.' She turned back to Eleanor. 'We need

Doctor Beattie. Could you find Fraser and see if he can ride to Lairg as soon as possible?'

Eleanor didn't stay to be told any more.

'I can't see, Mama,' Callum's tiny voice said. 'Funny spots in my eyes.'

Kitty squeezed her son's hand. 'They should go quite soon. We'll just lie here until they do.' She lay back down beside him and watched the grey clouds moving across the sky at a leisurely pace, in no hurry to reach their far-off destination.

'We should try sleeping out here one night. We could watch the stars and see the moon light up the hills.' Callum gave a small grunt in agreement.

They lay still, Kitty talking and soothing, gladly distracted by the entertainment in the sky, Callum listening intently to his mother's descriptions of the clouds. She heard the clatter of the horse in the courtyard of the stables being hurriedly saddled up and galloping hooves as Fraser departed for Lairg.

Dr Beattie shut his black case and turned to Kitty.

'Let's hope this is the first and only seizure he has. I can't see why it should have happened.' He took off his glasses and used his handkerchief to clean them. 'You say there was no sudden change of light.' Kitty shook her head. 'And he wasn't upset about anything, worried about something.' Again, Kitty shook her head. 'Had he complained of a headache before the seizure?'

'No, nothing. He was having tea with us; he seemed perfectly happy before he walked up to the burn with Eleanor.' Kitty was wringing her hands, unaware of what she was doing. She looked at the sleeping boy beside her, his face peaceful, the colour returned to his cheeks.

'Do you have an idea of what this could be?' Dr Beattie asked.

Kitty sighed, her hands dropping to her sides. 'I have read a few articles recently about epilepsy.' She looked at the doctor, her shoulders slumped. 'But surely he can't be epileptic? He's too young.' She got up and walked to the window, looking out onto the loch. 'You know what they do with children like him. They lock them away,' her voice had turned into an angry whisper, 'hide them and pretend they never existed. He can't have it. I won't let him.' She closed her eyes. Rocking forward on her toes, her forehead hit the glass and she put her hands up beside her head, pushing against the glass.

Dr Beattie appeared silently beside her. 'Don't get ahead of yourself. This could be nothing. One-off seizures can happen, especially to children.' He put his hand on her shoulder. 'But I do need you to keep a sharp eye on that wee boy and send me reports every few days. Can you do that for me?'

Kitty pushed herself away from the window and rubbed her face. 'Yes.' She sighed. 'Yes, of course I can.' She turned and gave him a grateful smile. 'Thank you, Doctor Beattie, thank you for your sensible advice. It's difficult being out here sometimes, so far from help.'

He returned her smile. 'Well, your children and your staff have a better chance than most with you in their company.' He hesitated. 'Look, you may want to think about getting back to Glasgow and arranging for Callum to have some tests. I know a good man who deals with this sort of thing.'

Kitty fought to control tears welling in her eyes, her stomach turning at what she had just heard. She blinked fiercely as the room blurred in front of her.

The doctor coughed awkwardly. 'I'll leave you now and let you have some rest yourself.'

'Doctor Beattie,' Kitty called after him. 'Would you mind... not telling anyone about this for the moment?' She began to wring her hands again. 'It's not that I don't want people talking, it's... I just don't want Charles to know quite yet and I know that somehow the news would get to him. It should be me that tells him, but I'd like to just wait a little... until we know a bit more.' Her eyes were bright as the tears threatened to break out again.

'The boy's father should be informed, but...' He sighed without reproach. 'Why don't I come back in a few days and we can see how he's doing?' He turned and left the room silently.

Kitty leaned against the wooden shutters beside the window, her hair brushing the glass. She wiped her face, closing her eyes, unable to dismiss thoughts of her own stupidity.

This was her punishment for a recent dose of complacency. It had taken a long time, years even, but over the past few weeks, she'd begun to believe that the turmoil that had been her lamentable marriage had been tamed. Though perhaps not conventional, her relationship with Charles had become manageable. He lived in Glasgow, working, whilst she lived in the Highlands during the summer. He would visit occasionally, but would rarely be seen outside his study. They had both learned that they could be civil to each other as long as they stuck to only two subjects, the management of their children or the administration of their household, and found it quite easy never to stray beyond those areas. Kitty's relationship with her children was warm and easily reciprocated and she had congratulated herself on rarely having cause to worry about them. Her walled garden was a place of pride and satisfaction. Finally, she had persuaded Fraser that her herb garden should have equal importance as to the fruit and vegetables, and he'd stopped moaning about her persistent requests to find obscure herbs and botanical plants. She gave him free rein over the rest of the garden, but she'd worked hard with him to make the herb garden tranquil and practical, although there were days when he despaired at her frequent requests to change the design, add a bit of extra space, or move some of the more established herbs. She could never 'sit still' in his eyes. Kitty was also able to revel in Ardbray's library, spending hours reading and researching, too often found fast asleep in her favourite chaise longue by Mrs Lindsay late at night. She had even begun to think that there was, at last, some fulfilment in her life at Ardbray, what with helping at Achfary School and occasional requests for assistance with Dr Beatty's patients. And when she had to return to Glasgow for the winter, she'd found a routine that she could put up with for five months. Visits with the children to her parents, evenings either spent at home whilst Charles dined at his club or occasional evenings with her father, usually at the theatre or attending medical dinners as his chaperone, but every so often holed up in his study just as they used to before her marriage. Her parents appeared to have accepted her unconventional, solo lifestyle.

But the distressing events of the previous day were now casting a harsh light over her self-satisfied bubble and the unwelcome clarity was showing her how she'd been oblivious to her son's health. If he did have epilepsy, was it likely that he'd been having petit mal seizures for some time? She began to look back over the preceding weeks and wondered how often she'd seen him staring off into space and whether this was relevant. Her mind kept turning and revolving, spinning and twisting until it, inevitably, stopped at Charles. If the diagnosis was correct, she knew what her husband would say. He hated anything different, anything that didn't conform. He would want to put the problem where no one could see it or talk about it.

Opening her eyes, she turned away from the window and walked over to Callum's bed, smoothing down the eiderdown before sitting. She caught sight of her reflection in the tall dress mirror; her hair was falling out of its bun and there was a smudge on her cheek. Looking at her wristwatch, she realised how late it was. Flora would need feeding again soon. Absently, she pushed the loose strands of hair from her face as she watched her son sleeping peacefully. His cherubic, round face always reminded her of the Water Babies from the book he loved her to read to him. Usually glowing and healthy with bright eyes full of questions, today she'd seen a different child, pale and confused, only capable of compliance. She stroked his hair, the same wiry, disobedient hair as hers, which, against Mrs Mercaut's pleadings, she'd allowed to grow longer than was perhaps sensible. She smiled at her indulgence, loathe to get rid of the scruffy air of naivety that it gave him.

The light in the room began to flicker, the candle dying down. She sat watching as her eyes grew heavy until her chin fell to her chest. Drowsily, she lay down beside her son, arm around his head, her nose on his cheek and fell asleep.

'Ma'am, wake up.' A hand shook her shoulder gently. 'It's Miss Flora. She needs feeding.' Eleanor stood away from the bed whilst Kitty opened her eyes and stared at her, not sure where she was.

Eleanor hesitated before repeating, 'It's Miss Flora.'

'Yes.' Kitty sighed as she sat up, her eyes bleary and her mouth dry. 'Yes, I'll be there in a minute.' She turned around to see Callum asleep, curled up on one side, sucking his thumb. She swung her legs over the side of the bed but stayed sitting, her hands pushing onto the bed as she stared at the door ahead of her. She could hear Flora bellowing, no longer the bleat of a newborn baby, but the angry blast of a hungry ten-week-old.

Eleanor began to shift about and was ready to speak again when Kitty interrupted.

'It's all right, Eleanor,' she whispered. 'You go on; I'll be there in a minute.'

Eleanor slipped away through the door as Kitty rubbed her eyes with the ball of her hand. Almost groaning, she pushed herself off the bed. Her whole body was stiff; it was as if she was weighed down by an invisible coat of chainmail making her movements slow and deliberate. Across the corridor, Flora's shouts became more insistent. Kitty smoothed her skirt down and hurried across the dim passage.

Kitty was loath to leave the large wooden rocking chair, deep cushions supporting her and a blanket around her shoulders. Flora had fallen asleep whilst suckling and was quietly wriggling and snuffling; the tisane she'd administered seemed to be doing the trick. The nursery was now dark, and Kitty could just hear muffled sounds coming from the kitchen as the staff cleared up after dinner. Eventually, she stood up, put the baby on her shoulder and, swaying gently and patting her daughter's back in soothing circular movements, she walked over to the window. She watched the scene over Loch More – the yellow, full moon hanging above the hills ahead of her with a wisp of cloud running across it, the slightly jaundiced reflection giving the water a soft, ethereal sheen, whilst the winking stars added an air of contentment.

She was grateful for this restorative sight, her own mind in turmoil and unable to make any decision. The luxurious sensation of Flora on her shoulder combined with the serene landscape before her made her feel as if a cool cloth had been placed on her flustered face, finally giving relief to the clatter in her head. Sometimes, she felt like she owned this panorama, she spent so many hours watching it, walking it, taking in every detail. She knew each rise of the hills, understood the sway of the trees, the smell on the wind and the tempo of the clouds. She could sense its mood and gauge its temper far better than any person she knew.

At last, her daughter stopped wriggling, falling into a deep sleep on Kitty's shoulder.

The night sky was so clear she wished she was outside lying

on the grass, just as she'd promised Callum. But she knew that tonight it would envelop her. This massive celestial theatre, full of drama and spectacle, made her commonplace difficulties seem inconsequential. And as the night show played out, the muddy waters in Kitty's head continued to clear. She leaned against the open shutters and closed her eyes, breathing in the heady smell of her sleeping baby.

'Yes.' She sighed. 'That is what I must do.'

Carefully, she put Flora into her cot and tucked her in. Picking up the candle, she tiptoed through the door and stepped into Mrs Mercaut's connecting room.

It was late and Kitty had told their nanny to go to bed ages ago, but there she was, sitting at her writing desk, her pen scratching across the paper. She didn't hear Kitty approach and for a moment she felt a wave of affection for this loyal and faithful woman. This woman whom Kitty hardly knew, who guarded her privacy fiercely, always deflecting any questions about herself. This woman, always dressed in deep mourning, had such an ease about her deportment and her conversation that Kitty was convinced she'd grown up in the highest of society. Her faint French accent only deepened the air of mystery.

Kitty realised that the repercussions of Callum's seizure could put a huge burden on Mrs Mercaut, and she wondered if their nanny would be willing to stay and help confront the unknown.

'Flora's asleep now,' Kitty whispered.

Mrs Mercaut turned towards her. 'And Callum?'

'Yes, he's exhausted. He's slept most of the day.' She gave Mrs Mercaut an unsteady smile before continuing. 'I think we need to ready ourselves to return to Glasgow.'

A flicker of a shadow passed across the nanny's face before she gave a slight nod in agreement.

It occurred to Kitty that Mrs Mercaut found the move back to Glasgow every winter as difficult as she did. Whenever they journeyed back to the city, she would become quieter, less vocal, more introverted.

Mrs Mercaut was spartan and utilitarian in everything she did for herself; her dress of deep mourning, her plain and unfussy food, her bedroom spare of any ornaments, colour or independent character. In Glasgow, despite maintaining an air of professionalism, it was as if an uneasy melancholy descended upon her. But at Ardbray she became animated, almost vibrant in comparison as if a heavy yoke had been lifted from her shoulders. Kitty wondered at what it was that caused her to behave in such a similar manner to herself.

'We should try and leave tomorrow afternoon. I'm sure Mrs Lindsay can help you with the preparations. Now I've had a chance to consider Doctor Beattie's advice, I believe Callum should see a specialist as soon as possible.'

Kitty sat down in the armchair by the fire with a heavy sigh. There was no colour in her face, no powder to hide her drawn exhaustion. She closed her eyes, trying to push away the uproar in her head.

'But he wants Callum to stay at Ardbray all year long. He wants to hide him away, pretend he doesn't exist. I've tried my best to agree with Charles over the upbringing of our children.' She took a deep breath, wiping away a tear. 'I've found myself agreeing to things that I wouldn't normally, but this time I don't think I can, this time I'm going to have to make a stand.' She blinked hard and wiped her cheek again.

Cameron Gray was standing by the window. His hands were clasped behind his back, his eyes focussed on the black railings in front of the house whilst Kitty protested. Hearing the distress in her voice, he finally went and sat beside her.

'Kitty, you're not making sense. What Charles is suggesting may turn out to be the best for Callum.'

Kitty looked up, her eyes wide, her hands balled into fists.

'Please, Kitty, just think about this with some kind of rationality.' His voice was measured. 'Look at it from Callum's point of view.' Kitty opened her mouth, ready to interrupt, but her father continued, 'He has been subjected to test upon test, experimental treatment upon experimental treatment and he's only getting worse. You yourself have said to me several times that Callum is more relaxed at Ardbray and that he's always ill or bad-tempered when you are here in the winter.

'And I know how much you love it there. Perhaps a less stressful life at Ardbray will suit him better. I'm sure it will be very isolated during the winter, but if you plan, you'll find it manageable.' He leaned forward, seeking out Kitty's gaze, his dark eyes suggesting reason and sound wisdom. 'I hate to see you shut away, I hate the idea of seeing even less of you than I do. But I think deep down you know there probably isn't much more that can be done for him. Maybe you should just accept that this is the best for him.'

Kitty stood up. 'I'm always doing what other people think is best.' She turned to the fireplace. Holding onto the mantelpiece, her arms outstretched, she continued, barking the words into the fire. 'What if he gets ill during the winter? We may not be able to get out or get hold of a doctor. What do we do then?' She turned wildly, glaring at her father, strands of hair falling across her face.

Her father stood up. 'Kitty, as good as Doctor Beattie is, he can't do much more for Callum than you can. That son of yours is very lucky, he'll get more medical attention than most of the fat and well-fed can here in Glasgow with some of the best doctors on their doorstep.' He began to pace the room. 'I know you've read everything there is to read on the subject, goodness, we've discussed it enough.' He lowered his voice. 'Look, at least Charles isn't suggesting some kind of asylum. You know that would be the worst possible outcome.'

'Yes... yes.' Kitty sighed. She could feel her whole body on the brink of collapse. 'You're right. I don't think I could cope with that.' Finally, the anger that had kept her together over the last few months was beginning to subside as a deep-seated tiredness began to take over.

'Don't think I haven't noticed that you also are happiest away from Glasgow, away from your meddling mother, away from that self-centred husband of yours and all the malicious gossip.'

Kitty stared at her father who smiled, perhaps amused by her naivety.

'You can't hide much from me, Kitty. I can see what's been going on. I'd rather you managed your lives separately, then at least I'd know you'd have some happiness.' He sat back down beside his daughter. 'Take those two lovely children back to Ardbray and give them the most unrestricted, free life that you can. You keep them away from this filthy, overcrowded city, full of blaggers and thieves, foul air and bad water. You give them fresh air and scabbed knees, laughter and joy. You know you won't get it here.

'Don't surround my grandson with strange, well-meaning but interfering doctors who don't yet understand what they are dealing with. And why don't you make the most of all your herbalist's knowledge? There are old remedies out there. Maybe one of them could be helpful for Callum. If you can't find it, then I don't know who would. Take the opportunity to agree with your husband for once and go back to Ardbray as fast as you can. Callum needs you; he needs some common sense and his mother's love.'

Kitty couldn't help but smile, taken aback by her father's honesty.

'Look, I've made too many mistakes with both you and your sister, too often listening to your mother. Perhaps this advice might go some way towards rectifying things a little.'

Now, for the first time, Kitty noticed an unease in her father. She saw that those dark, twinkling eyes had become dull, his hair was greyer than she remembered and his once confident hands now seemed hesitant. Never before had he referred to her mother in this way. He may have never criticised her publicly or privately for her gossiping, scheming or continual interference, but she now realised that he had also never backed her in anything that she did. His silence had always given authority to her tittle-tattle and plotting.

Kitty suddenly felt ashamed at her outburst. Here she was complaining about the views of a frequently absent husband when her father had lived with a woman who'd never left his side for over twenty-five years and who had so little in common with him. She looked around his study. This had not only been a coveted cocoon for her, but it must be a haven for her father, one of the few places he could be himself, enjoy the things that interested him, live the life that he wanted.

With a quick brightening, she smiled and took her father's hand. 'You're right, of course, I can see your logic. I was just being pig-headed. But, I need you to promise me one thing.'

He cocked his head to one side but didn't speak.

'Please come and visit me more often.' She gave him an impish grin. 'And you know you could even come by yourself, if you tell Mother you'll just be fishing, you just might manage to persuade her to stay in Glasgow.'

Dr Gray chuckled. 'I fear you don't quite have the measure of your mother, especially now that there are grandchildren to lure her into the remotest parts of the Highlands.'

Just as he was speaking, there was a loud but hurried knock at the study door before Eva burst in.

'Kitty! I need you to help me persuade Mother. She won't let me trim my wedding dress with fur, she thinks it's vulgar. How can white fur possibly be vulgar? It's mid-winter! Kitty, please, come with me. Mother's in the drawing room; she's being impossibly stubborn.' She drew breath, but a thought seemed to come to her. 'Oh, and she says that Charles has insisted that Callum will not come to the church. Is that true? Can he really be so unfeeling? I want to show off my one and only nephew to all those high society people she's insisted on inviting, most of whom I've never even heard of, let alone know.'

Eva stood in the middle of Dr Gray's study, oblivious of anything except her own troubles. Glowing in her misfortune, she lit up the room as if she was intoxicated with her own suffering – there was no guile in her rant, no wish to upset or overpower, just an innocent desire for her own justice. But as Kitty watched her sister, she was caught by her last remark. She knew that Charles had never mentioned Callum attending her sister's wedding; either it wouldn't have crossed his mind or he would have assumed that children should not be seen at such events. No, it was her mother who must be insisting that Callum not attend. So, it wasn't only Charles who wanted his son kept out of the public eye, kept away so he couldn't embarrass others, it was her mother too. Susan Gray, worried that her only grandson might cause a scene at her pièce de résistance, her last chance at organising a spectacle, at impressing society.

Kitty felt sick. She looked down at her lap and smoothed out the wrinkles of her skirt, taking a slow and deep breath.

'Kitty? You don't agree with Charles, do you? Surely, you'll bring Callum to the ceremony. I insist.' Eva's voice was rising.

Kitty stood, pushing down the nausea and put on her most serene face.

'I'm afraid Charles is right. Callum is too ill; he'd probably find it all a bit intimidating. I think he'll be happier back here at the house with Mrs Mercaut. I'll make sure she gives him a treat or two, perhaps takes him out for the afternoon. He won't know any better.' She gave Eva her broadest smile. 'And on the day, you won't notice either, you'll be too caught up in the excitement of it all.'

Eva stared at her sister. 'Really? I would have thought you'd have insisted he comes. Important to show a united front, my enlightened sister showing the world that her children can be seen *and* heard all at the same time.' There was no sarcasm, no bitterness in her voice, just wide-eyed misgiving.

There was an embarrassed cough from their father. 'I think you'd better go and sort out the fur situation before it's dealt with by your mother.'

TWELVE

GREER

Loch More, 2003

Rosemary

'It... has been said that Rosemary will only grow well where the house is ruled by a woman.'

Herbal Delights *by Mrs C F Leyel*

Suddenly, she's here, unannounced and unexpected. I heard the Defender before I saw it, scaring the birds off with its noisy exhaust. Once I'd have found that amusing; today I find it offensive.

I can't think why she's here.

She's been away, back in New York, Robert telling us the sale is progressing, but his weekly updates have been too brief. Robert always loves to talk, but in the last few months, he's been short on conversation, on the verge of terse. This is so out of character that I simply don't believe this sale will go through. And to make matters worse, the children have returned to seeking me out several times a day. Their entreaties are becoming urgent, almost desperate. But I can do nothing. I am in no position to help them, and their frequent visitations are causing me sleepless nights as I hear them walking the corridors.

But the worst of it is that Colin and I had our first row in twenty years. We never row, neither of us ever seeing any point in raising our voices. But he said he could no longer put up with watching my childish absurdities, he couldn't watch me put my chances at a new life at risk. And then, when I confessed that I'd told Caitlin about the ghost children, Colin reminded me that this wasn't just about me. Had I remembered that he'd given up everything as well? But since that day of the row, we haven't seen Caitlin for over four months, since that day we've been living in a silent truce, quietly getting on with a life that's become progressively meaningless to both of us.

Now I find myself spying on her again. I don't mean to, but I can't help it. If Colin were here, he'd berate me; he says my behaviour towards Caitlin has been disgraceful, as if I'm some petulant teenager who can't get her own way.

She stops her car about two hundred metres away from the house. She gets out of the old Land Rover and faces the shore, leaning against the bonnet. It looks as if she's closed her eyes as she lets her head fall back, as if she's trying to catch some sun, but there is no sun, the clouds are grey and low. I can see a big smile on her face.

I'm watching from the herbarium window. I've been trying to dust in here and check there's no damp where the books and papers are stored. But apathy has consumed me, and I've been looking for a reason to stop all morning. I move to the side of the window so I can't be seen, but as I move, I hear a slight sigh in the walls. It's almost as if the house is letting go of a long-held tension and is beginning to relax. I look around the room, trying to see if it will continue to talk to me, wondering what it's trying to say.

I walk down the front steps as she is making her way to the house, a spring in her step. She waves at me, that smile still spread across her face. Before I can acknowledge her greeting, she suddenly stops and faces the loch.

I follow her gaze, but the water is glassy.

'Greer, I think someone's in trouble on their boat over there. Can you see?' she shouts. There's a slight look of panic on her face.

I check again. Again, I see nothing but the flat calm of a grey day.

She turns back to me. 'They've gone.' Her brow is creased with confusion. 'I can't see anything now,' she whispers.

I hold my breath. It must have been the children. But they've never been seen on a boat. That would be too... too much.

But I didn't see them.

The realisation hits me with the force of a sudden high wind.

'Greer? Are you all right?' she asks.

I almost laugh. Suddenly, our roles have been reversed. Every time she has seen those children, she has had some sort of panic attack. There is something about the image of the brother and sister that brings back some kind of painful memory. But, today, she seems unaffected, and it's me that's struggling to breathe.

'Yes, of course. I'm fine,' I bluster, embarrassed at my weakness.

She takes me by the top of my arms and looks me straight in the eyes. 'You sure?'

I nod, unable to find the right words.

'Good,' she says with a smile, 'because I came here to tell

you personally that the sale has gone through. Ardbray House, as of five o'clock last night, belongs to me.'

My heart drops into my stomach and my mouth falls open. Eventually, I put my hand up to cover my mouth.

'Surely, you're pleased? Isn't this what you wanted?'

'Yes, yes, I am. I... I'm just...' I look around for the right words. 'It's been so long that I'd got to the point where I never thought it would happen.' Feeling a little shaky, I put my hand to my forehead. 'Well, I don't know what to say.'

Caitlin laughs. 'Whatever it is, I think we should go and tell Colin. Come on.' She takes me by the elbow and leads me towards the house. 'Let's go and celebrate over a cup of tea and some of your ginger cake.'

THIRTEEN

KITTY

Glasgow, 1896

St. John's-Wort

*'The herb used to be hung up over the doors of cottages on the
Eve of St. John to drive away evil spirits,
and there are many legends associated with it.
In the Isle of Man there is a saying that whoever treads on it at
night
will be carried about on a fairy horse and not allowed to rest till
sunrise.'*

Elixirs of Life *by Mrs C F Leyel*

The noise of the wedding party was beginning to grate on
Kitty's nerves. Her parents' house wasn't quite big enough for
so many people, the guests squeezed into every conceivable
corner of the three reception rooms, conversations were held at

top volume, people were having to bend towards each other just to be heard. The best china, the three tiers of wedding cake, so much silk and lace and streams of winter greenery, even some mistletoe had been placed in her sister's hair so that her new husband could make the excuse of kissing her whenever he felt like it. The gaiety, laughter, and her mother's too eager introductions, all were giving her a headache. And she needed to get away from John Hardgrave. Previously she'd been able to accept his careful attentions, always ready to have a friendly conversation with her, never failing to ask after the children, her father, even Eva. She put up with his mischievous jokes often at the expense of Charles. But today he was being just a little too personal; standing just a mite too close, his hand lingering on her arm, his eyes seeming to have some hidden meaning that she couldn't interpret.

She left the drawing room and went to her father's study, a place of refuge where she hoped to enjoy a few moments of peace. She shut the door behind her and almost fell into one of the armchairs by the fire. Leaning back and closing her eyes, she considered John Hardgrave. He and her husband appeared to have become inseparable, spending every working hour together and then sloping off to their club, The Western. Charles would return in the early hours, always drunk, always staggering into his bedroom and falling asleep fully dressed on top of his bed. They never quite behaved like the men of industry she expected them to be, meetings in Charles's study never appeared to be serious or businesslike, just loud and raucous. Was John Hardgrave a fool, a man who wasn't that invested in his work, was he a man who would rather spend his days drinking and entertaining?

There was a loud knock at the door. With a sigh, she got up from the chair and opened the door.

'Kitty, how ravishing you look.' John Hardgrave pushed into the room, shutting the door behind him. He held her in front of him, his eyes roaming over the whole of her body. 'I never got to tell you that earlier. Motherhood has somehow made you more alluring.' His voice was tender and affectionate. 'I do love that about women. It seems the process of reproduction only makes us men want to impregnate you even more. Maybe it's something to do with the survival of the human race.' He pushed his great mop of blond hair off his face.

His words made Kitty cringe. She wriggled out of his hold, muttering, 'I must see to the children.' But he caught her wrist.

'No, no, no. Not so fast.' He pulled her towards him. They were so close, she could smell the alcohol on his breath. 'We have things to discuss,' he whispered.

'I have been thinking about us. We need to spend more time together. But,' – he looked around the room – 'I fully understand the need for discretion. I know that you do not want to be seen with another man, that, outwardly, you will want to keep your integrity. But I have a solution. I have made enquiries about taking rooms. Rooms where we can be together without prying eyes, where we can be discreet but unabandoned at the same time.'

She tried to pull back, but his grip was too strong.

'I have found rooms just off Buchanan Street. There is an entrance at the back, so no one need see you arrive or depart. There is a large reception room. I know we will not be entertaining, but we will need somewhere to entertain ourselves, I have bought one of those wind-up gramophones so we can dance or listen to opera. There are three bedrooms: a large one for the two of us and a dressing room each. I will kit out your dressing room with everything you could possibly desire so that you can drop in at a moment's notice and not be in want of anything.

'I know you won't be able to visit every day, but I would have thought you'd be able to get away a couple of days a week. No one would notice; Charles would be at work and Mrs

Mercaut would be with the children. The world would think you were out visiting.'

Kitty watched the dimple in his cheeks that seemed to get deeper as he talked through his plan, as his face eased with satisfaction. She found herself mesmerised by this animated, portly man, who seemed to have some kind of magnetic hold over her. His words were said with such conviction and tender enthusiasm that, despite the suggestion of adultery, Kitty almost found herself considering the idea. He made it sound like some great adventure, an expedition that would lead to uncharted lands, not some sordid adulterer's affair.

'You see, Mrs Maclean, we can have our cake and eat it. I can continue my bachelor life, I can visit the gambling tables without fear of you waiting up for me and you can continue your married life. But, to bring some joy into your life, you can forget that useless husband of yours, forget your domesticity and for just a few days a week, we can lead a secret life of overindulgence and selfishness.'

Again, she tried to pull away, again he held her. 'Mr Hardgrave, I don't think it would be sensible.' She hated her prim words, her inability to be uncivil in the face of his unwelcome suggestions.

'Oh, who needs sensible! Just think of the benefits, think how much happier you'd be, free from your husband, free from the man who is not capable of looking after you in the same way that I can.'

'No, sir. I cannot agree with you. I will not deceive my husband.'

'But you are already well versed in deception. Don't you remember? You would go off and work at your clinic, discuss the fate of your husband's workers behind his back. You're quite used to dishonesty; this is no different,' he whispered, as he ran a finger along her jawline and down towards the neckline of her dress.

Shuddering, she finally found the strength to wriggle free and staggered over to the fireplace, rubbing her wrists. 'I would ask you to leave. This is my father's study; he may be along any minute. Please,' – by now she'd begun to shake – 'would you go.'

'Mrs Maclean... Kitty.' John Hardgrave moved towards her as she backed off. 'Don't be so ridiculous.' Now his voice was supercilious and patronising.

'No, Mr Hardgrave. It is you who is being ridiculous. Now, please leave.'

'No, Mrs Maclean.' Gone were the dimples, the sparkling eyes, the gentle speech. His pudgy face began to colour and his eyes became stony. He grabbed her wrists again and yanked her to him, the action causing her hair to fall out of its bun and the Wedgwood cameo broach she was wearing to fall to the stone hearth and break.

For a moment, Kitty was overwhelmed by fear, realising that she wasn't strong enough to retaliate and, with all the noise of the wedding, no one would hear her shouts for help.

But no sooner had she thought this than the door to the study flew open and in walked Kitty's father.

'Kitty?' Dr Gray had a puzzled frown on his face, a confused weariness.

Kitty blanched as John Hardgrave dropped her arms. She hid her mortification by trying to pick up the pieces of her broach, the cameo of herself as a five-year-old, given to her by her father.

'I have been trying to persuade your daughter to organise a surprise party for her husband,' Hardgrave blustered, easily pushing away any possible embarrassment. 'He's been working so hard recently that I thought it would be a good distraction. We were trying to thrash out the details whilst we were amongst the party, but it's such a roaring success out there, so loud, we had to come in here just to hear ourselves think.'

'Well...' Cameron Gray said slowly, his voice unconvinced,

his manner wary, 'that's a very laudable idea.' He went over to his desk and sat down, leaning back into his chair, clasping his hands together a little too tightly. 'What were you thinking?'

'I have to go and see to the children,' said Kitty re-tying her hair. 'They will be wondering what's happened to me.' She held the pieces of her precious broach in one hand and was trying to keep away the unasked-for tears. She recognised that look on her father's face. Disappointment. He'd seen everything and interpreted it as the worst. Her father, the one man whose approval she craved, the one person on this earth she wanted to please. She left John Hardgrave crowing with his usual boyish bravado and ran upstairs to her bedroom.

Once inside her room, she poured water into the wash bowl and began to clean her hands, slowly at first, and then with rough insistence, trying to get rid of the stench of Hardgrave, the stench of lust and privilege, bombast and prurience. She felt as if he had permeated her skin, that his blind belief in himself had somehow become part of her. Finally, she stopped and looked at herself in the mirror. All she wanted to do was pick up her children and get on the train to go back to Ardbray.

FOURTEEN

GREER

Loch More, 2003

Ginger

'Ginger is one of the best stimulants that we have in domestic medicine.
It is safe to use, pleasant to eat, warming and comforting to the digestion
and helps a sluggish circulation.'

Herbal Delights *by Mrs C F Leyel*

I'm sitting at the table with Colin, and she's making the tea. This feels a bit odd. It's always me that makes the tea, and looks after the guests, that makes sure everyone is feeling comfortable or has what they need. But Caitlin now owns this house, she's in charge. I'm just a bystander who is about to be out of a job and I'm at a loss for what to do with myself.

Caitlin is talking. I think she's realised that I'm in shock and is trying to put me at ease, filling me in on the details that Robert's been unable to provide me with.

'The last few weeks have been a real whirlwind. Once the details of the purchase had been fully agreed, I had to fly back to New York and pack up my life.' She shakes her head at the memories. 'Long meetings with lawyers to wrap up my commitments so that I could transfer as much as possible to the UK. I had to close my bank accounts, clear out my apartment and put it on the market, say goodbye to my old business partner and, lastly, say goodbye to my sisters and little brother Jim. Then I flew to Glasgow, where I spent a week holed up in the City Archives in the Mitchell Library, researching the cotton industry and Maclean and Son, trying to understand what had happened to Charles Maclean and the industry that had provided him with so much. Long hours with old newspapers and microfiche, in characterless and windowless rooms. But helpful librarians and a new pair of glasses have given me the opportunity to really start to understand the man behind this house. He was flawed and elusive, building a colossus that was supposed to show the world that technology and transport had moved on, that transport could finally facilitate the new technology even in such a remote place. Somehow it's become a forgotten relic, hidden away and ignored by the rest of the world.'

Colin and I are speechless at this woman's ability to talk; it's as if she's just downloading. We both sit, holding our mugs of tea, warming our hands and trying not to stare at this oddity in front of us.

'And then I spent a week in Edinburgh, finally spending time with my father.' Suddenly, she's changed. The fire, passion, and confidence have gone, that vulnerability has reappeared. 'You know, it's the first time I've spent more than a few hours with him since I was a sullen sixteen-year-old. Neither of us quite knew what to do. So, we did the only thing we both understood, we discussed the renovations needed here at Ardbray. He's insisting that he be my architect, won't hear of anyone else working on it. Hours were spent pouring over ideas, rough drawings and previous developments until we were able to come up with some kind of plan. I'm not going to lie to you, I've found the enormity of this project completely overwhelming, but thank God for my dad. He chunked it down into a series of smaller tasks and has turned it into something I can finally see is achievable.' She opens her eyes wide and blows out of her mouth. 'Man, it was hard work, though. I had no idea how much detail would be required.'

Having finished, she looks at us with a radiant smile. 'But here I am, ready and raring to go.' Picking up her mug of tea, she continues.

'I'd like to make a toast. Here's to the future of Ardbray.' She holds her mug out so that we can clink our cups together and takes her own celebratory sip of tea.

I'm still in a hazy fog. I feel like too much information has been thrown at me and I can't comprehend what is going on. I need time to process it all, time to understand what is really happening to me.

Caitlin puts her cup down carefully and leans forward against the side of the table, towards Colin and me.

'So,' she says hesitantly, 'I wondered if you've given any thought to what you're going to do now?'

Stupidly, I am blindsided by this question. For Caitlin, it must be the most obvious request to make of us. For me, I only have a blank space, a void with nothing to fill it.

What will I do without Ardbray? Who will I be without this house? I have lived here nearly all my life, I have never owned my own property, have never been able to put my mark on another home. How will I manage without the life I have always lived, without the house, the children and my vocation to preserve this place, how will I continue without the daily quest to make amends? Ardbray is my glue, without it, surely, I will fall apart.

Colin can see that I'm not going to answer, he can see the internal conflict. So, he answers for us both.

'Well, to be honest, neither of us thought this day would come, so this has come as a bit of a shock. We've done our best not to discuss it, just in case we're jinxed.' He pauses. 'Again. But, in the days when we used to get excited about a prospective buyer showing interest in the house, we used to dream about owning our own nursery. I'm a plantsman, as you know, and my skills are not put to their best use here. Of course, if there'd been the money to restore the walled garden, I'd have happily done that.

'Greer has the brains; she'd run the business, be the face of the nursery. I'd do the behind-the-scenes work, sourcing, growing and nurturing the plants and making sure we're able to meet the demand. We'd have a shop, maybe even a small café.' My husband looks into his tea mug. 'But I wonder if it's too late for that, if we're just a bit too old to start something from scratch.'

Caitlin looks at us, back and forth, her head moving side to side as if she's watching some sort of mini tennis match. As she does this, an easy look of surety comes over her.

'I wonder if I have a solution for you. As you know, your contract with the Maclean Estate has come to an end and you only have a month's notice to leave.'

I didn't know that. I should have, but I've been burying my head in the sand. Panic hits me. A month will go by too quickly. We can't sort our lives out in just four weeks.

'I've been thinking this over for a while now,' Caitlin continues. 'You two know everything there is to know about this house. You also know everyone locally, you know all the tradesmen, you know the back doors that might be useful. So, I have a proposal for you. What if I asked you to stay until The Retreat at Ardbray opens to guests in September next year? That's eleven months. There's a lot to do, but I think it's doable. But I need you, I need your expertise, your knowledge and your local insight. Colin, would you be willing to work with me to rebuild and restore the garden? I'd give you both a salary that's twice what you earn now, you can stay living here until we're ready to open and then... well, you'll have almost a year to decide what you want to do.' She has her hands splayed out on the table in front of her as if she's baring her soul. 'And did I say I don't think I could do it without you?' she says this with a final grin.

Colin and I look at each other. I'm willing him to say yes. This seems like the perfect solution so that I can stay here and get used to the idea of a new life, but will Colin be happy to stay here for almost another year? Ardbray doesn't pull on him as it does on me; I know he's desperate to go, desperate to live his own life. He has given up so much for me. Is it fair to ask him to stay so much longer?

We're both staring at her, unable to speak. I so badly want to say 'Yes' but think I should discuss it with Colin. It feels selfish. Everything about our lives has been for me, or rather, for Ardbray, Kitty and the children. It's never been about Colin. But as I'm thinking this, Colin nudges me and says, 'Go on, Greer, you say.'

I search his face, but he's not giving me an answer.

I take a deep breath, finally realising that I need to be selfish just once more. 'Okay, since we've made no plans, and since we've nowhere to go, and since this is the place I love, despite its foibles,' – I daren't glance at Colin, otherwise I'll lose my nerve – 'I've had enough of keeping this place in mothballs. I'd love to see it come to life again, I'd love to help make that happen and...' Now I can't stop the words from tumbling out, 'I'd love to leave next September and start a new life somewhere else and do some of the things we've always dreamed of doing.'

'Good decision.' Caitlin held up her cup and the three of us put our cups together. Finally, I look at Colin. Thank goodness, he's beaming.

'To the future of Mr and Mrs Mackenzie!' says Caitlin triumphantly.

After a quick drink, she faces me. 'Greer, Robert mentioned that you have a background in interior design. Is that true?'

I bristle. I'm not comfortable with being discussed by others. 'Yes.' I nod curtly.

'Well,' she continues with a glint in her eye, 'since you're going to be here for the next year and since you know this house inside out, then I wondered if you'd be interested in helping with the interiors? Of course, I'll need to brief you on what I'd like, and maybe we'll have differing views. Maybe it won't work out, but maybe you'd like to give it a try?'

Is this an olive branch? If so, why is she trying to be so nice to me? I haven't seriously thought about interior design in almost forty years.

I glance at Colin again. He gives me the look that says *don't you dare say no*. I have to smile at him. Caitlin was responsible for our first row, but now she's responsible for the reconciliation.

'I'll think about it,' I say.

But Colin shakes his head. 'No,' he says. 'She won't think about it. She'll do it. She'll not pass up this opportunity if I have anything to do with it.' His words are firm and decisive, and I know he's right.

'Good,' says Caitlin quickly, before I can interject, then picks up her half-eaten piece of ginger cake and continues. 'Greer, this cake is delicious. Do you think you'd let me have your recipe? I already can't imagine Ardbray without it. When I walk into the kitchen, there's always a waft of it in the background; it's almost part of the house and it gives it such a welcoming atmosphere. I would love to be able to serve this to my guests when they first arrive, on a big comfy sofa with a large mug of coffee. I know that nothing would make them want to leave once they'd tasted your cake.'

And now, Colin is smiling stupidly at me. The man who just overruled his wife appears to be brimming with pride. Over the last few months we've hardly talked and now, so much has been said with just a few words and a beaming smile. The relief is overwhelming. That ginger cake is working its magic on both of us.

'The original recipe was my great-grandmother's. Edith Lindsay was the first housekeeper at Ardbray. My grandmother and my mother tweaked it over the years, adding Golden Syrup when it became widely available and then, when it became my responsibility, I changed it by adding a little fresh ginger, now that it's easier to get hold of. It adds a softer depth.' Talking about my family, about that recipe, fills me with a strange satisfaction.

'Perhaps you could show me how to make it, and if I do a good enough job, then, maybe, you could consider letting me use it at the retreat.'

I nod slowly, realising that I don't have it written down anywhere, the recipe is just part of me.

'When I was in Glasgow, I spent some time researching Charles Maclean and his company, Maclean and Son. I wonder, how much do you already know about the money that built this house?'

I swallow, a little caught out by the change of subject. 'I know this house was built with cotton spinning money, but we never talked about it. It was a bit of a taboo subject. I know that the industry grew as fast as it then declined.'

She nods. 'You're right. Cotton spinning was made for the west coast of Scotland. Damp and wet weather created the perfect conditions for spinning and storing. There was plenty of coal and water for energy and the port facilities in Glasgow were ideal for trade routes to America. George Maclean,

Charles's father, founded Maclean and Son. He was one of those great entrepreneurial characters that were the driving force behind the growth of the cotton industry. A working-class man that made good; a driven man who wasn't afraid of hard work. But, it seems his son, like so many sons of successful industrialists, wasn't interested in his father's work, the cotton spinning industry or Maclean and Son.'

'The man who hid behind the façade of a workaholic.' I nod, having learned this by spending time in his study. 'The man who liked people to think he loved his work.'

'Yes!' Caitlin says enthusiastically. 'After George Maclean died Maclean and Son almost immediately began going downhill. Now you could argue that this was going to happen anyway. Out of all the cotton spinning companies in Scotland almost none survived beyond 1900.'

Colin leans forward. 'Not enough investment in new technology, a failure to establish a coherent system of industrial relations and too much reliance on a cheap workforce. It was as if the rich industrialists just wanted to take their money and run.'

Caitlin grins whilst Colin reddens slightly. 'My wife may not be interested in the Industrial Revolution, but I'm fascinated by it.'

I hide my discomfort by laughing. 'He's right. You should see the piles of books on the subject that sit beside the bed. But why are you so interested in Charles Maclean? Kitty's the one everyone's curious about, she's the person that piques everyone's interest because this house really belonged to her. She made this house what it is today.' I'm still finding myself loyal to Kitty, wondering why Caitlin hasn't focussed on her.

Caitlin shakes her head, picking at a corner of her slice of ginger cake. 'No, I don't agree with you. Maybe the garden was all about Kitty Maclean, but George Maclean, and then his son, made this house what it is today. From what I can see, Kitty made no changes whatsoever to the house she moved into the day after she married.'

I shrug my shoulders, a little unwilling to concede this point. 'Mmmm, I suppose so,' I say slowly. 'But it's her character that's all over the house.'

'Really? The herbarium maybe, and her bedroom and the morning room, but most of the house was fitted out and decorated before she arrived. Those gothic fireplaces, cheeky gargoyles and ornate staircases, they were brought about by George and Charles Maclean. They wanted to put their mark down, they wanted to show the world how much money they had. By building the most ostentatious house with all the latest gadgets in one of the most remote parts of the country, they were making a statement to their aristocratic neighbours.' Her face has lit up, her gestures become more expansive as she warms to her subject. 'But so many of those big, show-off houses have been demolished: Castle Wemyss, Stichill House. How does this house remain standing when it's had no owner for so long?'

We've become unused to this kind of genuine excitement. Occasionally, Robert's largesse would put a spring in my step for a few days, but his visits have become infrequent and with Colin and I not speaking to each other, well, this sudden injection of enthusiasm is downright disconcerting.

She blushes. 'Sorry. You probably think I'm getting a bit carried away.' She puts her hands, palm down, on the bench, considering what to say next. 'There are almost no papers belonging to Charles here, so whilst I had the time I went to Glasgow to find out more. You see it's here where I can find out about Kitty, she's left so much of herself, in the herbarium, in her letters, her morning room. So, now I'm moving in, I can spend some time with Kitty, get to know her too.'

'You're moving in?' I ask, thinking *where the hell is she going to sleep?* Every bedroom has covers over the furniture, no bed has been made up, there are probably dead flies sitting at the bottom of the windows.

'Yes! My bags are in the car. There's a crate on its way from New York with all my worldly goods, but meantime I have two suitcases in the Land Rover, my wellies, and a new waterproof coat.' She's like an overexcited puppy just waiting to be taken out for a walk, unable to keep still. 'I've spoken to Robert Urquhart. He's happy that I continue to go through Kitty's papers; it's going to take a few months before the Herb Society is able to come up here and take them away.'

Suddenly, she can't wait any longer, heading for the door. 'In fact, I'm going to start now. I'll just get my bags. And, Greer, would it be okay if I stayed in the yellow room at the front of the house?'

The whirlwind leaves before I can answer, leaving Colin and me staring at each other in bewilderment.

FIFTEEN

KITTY

Loch More, 1896

Paeony

*'Children in the country sometimes wear a necklace made from
the root to cure epilepsy
and also St. Vitus's Dance. At one time it was popular for
lunacy.'*

Compassionate Herbs *by Mrs C F Leyel*

*Ardbray
March 15th 1896*

My Dearest Eva,

*I am sorry to have missed you on your return from your
honeymoon. I had so wanted to hear of your travels in France*

and Italy. I take your lack of correspondence as a sign that you have been busy doing all the things you love, happy with the man you have chosen to do them with. But since you haven't written I'm hoping that you'll grace us with a much-desired visit very soon.

What I didn't tell you before your departure was that I would be returning to Ardbray for good. Charles has decided that he does not want his epileptic son to embarrass him and he wishes him shut away, away from gossip and prying eyes. So, I have decided to stay with him. I couldn't bear to be in Glasgow knowing that he was here without either of his parents.

And now I'm here I'm glad of it. Apart from your wedding, the winter in Glasgow was tortuous. Callum was so ill and Charles so aloof, hiding at the mill or in his study, or out with his business partner, drinking too much and I don't know what else. But now that we are here, I am immediately soothed by the sheer clarity of the air and the comforting silence. Happily, this place has the same effect on Callum; his colour is returning, and he is finally sleeping well at night.

I have been working on trying to alleviate Callum's seizures, but frustration is setting in. I have read every possible paper written by every eminent doctor on the subject of epilepsy, but they all seem to contradict themselves and none of them come to any sensible conclusion. So, I have reverted to ancient herbal medicine which has been used for centuries. Mugwort is a well-known anti-epileptic and mistletoe is also known to help lessen the effects of seizures. There is much to read on the subject, but as soon as I can get my hands on these herbs, I will start a testing regime for Callum.

Now we are away from the probing hands of the doctors and the soot-filled city air, now that there are no appearances to be kept up, I hope that we can revert to a quieter life. Flora, of course, doesn't know whether she's in Glasgow or the Highlands.

She is still the same sweet-faced, hungry, bellowing baby that she's always been, keeping me and Mrs Mercaut quite busy.

I, of course, am doubly relieved to be back at Ardbray. I am away from the city that I have come to hate, and I do not have to deal with the unwelcome attentions of John Hardgrave or my husband's inability to be a father. There is respite in being somewhere that is not demanding, where there are no complexities to our life. When we arrived, the house greeted us with its usual sigh of approval. I could almost believe it has wrapped us in some kind of enchanted cloak, as none of us can imagine ever wanting to leave despite the continual icy rain and sharp north wind.

Being in the garden helps me the most. Even though the ground is still too hard to dig, Fraser and I have been nurturing our seedlings in the glasshouses and making our planting plans for the year. I fear that Fraser finds my childish wonder at being able to grow something from seed rather trying; to me each seedling is a tiny miracle, to him it's an everyday necessity that he can't afford to get wrong. I tell Fraser that I'm growing bay from seed because it keeps evil spirits away but, in reality, it's a good medicinal herb with multiple uses, most especially for childbirth. He thinks I grow hyssop because it's a good for attracting bees and makes delicious honey, but truthfully, I'm nurturing it so that I can make an ointment for treating adder bites and a cordial that will help Cook with her shortness of breath. Our relationship is founded on half-truths, but we seem to muddle along in a strange fashion.

I look forward to hearing all about your travels and the colour and intrigue of Europe.

Write soon.

With all my love, your sister,
Kitty

SIXTEEN

GREER

Loch More, 2003

Lemon Balm

*'In earlier days it was infused in canary wine
and was drunk as a cordial
and for its balsamic effect on the heart.'*

Herbal Delights *by Mrs C F Leyel*

Today I have a day off, a day off from Colin and Caitlin and a day off from Ardbray. Since the builders arrive tomorrow, we have packed up the house, taken down the pictures, moved furniture and dismantled the chandeliers. Everything is now in storage and there's nothing for me to do. I'm completely alone in the house as Caitlin and Colin are away, spending the day discussing plants, flowers and herbs at Munroe's nursery near Inverness.

Colin is a changed man. All he and Caitlin do is talk about planting, growing seasons, soil type and garden design. I haven't seen him this animated in years. In the morning, he leaps out of bed, instead of the usual groan and turning over for another fifteen minutes of groggy sleep. And he's smiling. That smile disappeared so gradually that I hadn't noticed until the day it reappeared, that day when Caitlin asked us to stay. Being a maintenance man and a lawn boy hasn't suited him; I see that now. Much like being a housekeeper hasn't suited me, it just fitted because it had to.

Seeing Colin so happy has made me look back at my younger self. She's been locked away; I didn't want to revisit disappointment. But Caitlin's request that I help with the interiors has let me hope that I can get back a little bit of the twenty-something Greer, has let me remember some of the ambition, some of the thrill. To be creative again, to be given opportunity, to go back to design and see if I can stretch my world again.

I'm sitting in our rooms, a set of rooms for just Colin and me. A bedroom, bathroom and living room, but, unlike the rest of the house, these rooms are light and airy, these are the rooms that I love to spend time in. Ardbray was decorated in that typical Victorian heavy design: dark reds and greens, brocaded material, flocked wallpaper and intricate plasterwork on the ceilings. Here I have been allowed to move out the dark rugs and bring in my own furniture. It's all white and cream, but I don't have children or dogs, so I can indulge my need for pale colours and light furnishings to get away from the oppressiveness of the rest of the house. I have a framed set of Kitty's botanical drawings which line one wall and I have vases of dried grasses and seedheads that give some form and structure. These light colours helped dissipate the angry voices that used to inhabit my head.

I've decided that I ought to find out more about Kitty; if I'm going to help bring this house back to life, I should better understand the woman who lived here. So, I'm indulging myself, with a glass of wine and a stack of Kitty's letters, knowing that I will not be interrupted.

Both Caitlin and Robert insist that Kitty's letters should only be read in the herbarium, but, to hell with it, I'm here on my own, I would like to sit in comfort and read them at my leisure.

I feel a little frisson of excitement as I pick up the first letter. I've never wanted to read these before because, I realise now, I've wanted to hang on to my vision of the kindly, old, and eccentric Kitty Maclean, my idea of the woman whose fate was thrust upon her, who didn't have the strength to push against it.

But as I read, I can see that she was stronger than I thought, I can see that she made something of the situation she found herself in. This woman I have revered for so long but thought was like me, stuck and unable to move, was so much better. Have I made something of myself, have I overcome my difficulties and disappointments? No, of course, I haven't. I've spent the last forty years seething over my fate, convinced there was nothing I could do to change my position.

When Caitlin reads the letters, she seems to become invigorated, filled with even more energy to reinstate the garden and bring back some of Kitty's strength. When I read them, I feel the weight of my failure but, at the same time, I feel even more bound to her story and the need to finish it.

10 Fitzroy Place
March 31st 1896

My Dearest Kitty,

I was so looking forward to seeing you. It was to be one of the highlights of my return. My disappointment at learning of your early departure from Glasgow was profound. I've missed my level-headed sister, the voice of reason in what has become an uncertain life.

What is the reason for this dramatic start to my letter? Put simply, my husband is not what he appeared.

Perhaps you'll think me naive but the attentive, gentle Alisdair Brodie that courted me has disappeared, replaced by a belligerent, bawdy, drunken oaf. It seems that history has repeated itself with the Gray sisters. Both of us have managed to marry someone who misrepresented themselves. Is it just the men who do this? I don't think so, I suspect our father would never have married our mother if he'd known her liking for gossip and keeping women in their place.

Our tour of the Riviera should have been a delight. We went to Cannes, Nice and Monte Carlo. We took in the sights, the gardens and the scenery. We attended concerts and reviews. I don't have the heart to give you the full details as my husband spent so much time abusing the locals and doing his best to push his way into the highest social crowd. I feel he would have been better married to our mother, then perhaps they would have had some success. I tried to be the most sparkling I could, trying to ignore the brutish behaviour of my husband. But in the end, I was so exhausted by the effort, I joined the hordes of sick and infirm in Menton and spent the last three weeks of our trip recuperating. This meant our travels were cut short and we never ventured into Italy.

But we are home now and I am happy to stay here for a while; it is easier not to put a step wrong when in familiar surroundings.

Father seems shrunken, saddened by your permanent departure to the Highlands. I have done my very best to keep any hint of discord between Alisdair and me away from him, but I imagine Mother has her ear to the ground and is keeping him well-informed.

I miss you dearly, but you are better off away from the city. I *am sure the clean air and lack of gossip create a healthier atmosphere to live in, away from this city of imposters and fraudsters.*

I hope to visit soon if my husband will let me out of his sight. He is of a very jealous nature and finds it difficult to even let me visit our parents by myself.

With love, your sister,
Eva

10 Fitzroy Place
January 15th 1898

My Dearest Kitty,

Thank you for your recent package. I know you are concerned for me and I am touched by the efforts you go to try and make me feel better. The tisane of herbs you sent does help me sleep a little better at night, although, I'm sorry to say, it tastes disgusting. But I'm not sure that herbs will help my current predicament.

I have tried to write this letter so many times. It becomes harder and harder to write to you without me simply moaning about a life that I have come to detest, a husband I have come to hate.

But I know that I can no longer ignore your many letters and thoughtful packages. You are my closest ally, the only one of my friends who has stood by me since my marriage. Everyone else seems to have vanished. I rarely receive visitors and now, when I am out, I am no longer in receipt of the friendly smiles, welcome greetings, and invitations to come and visit. Now I have to endure stares of pity, whispers and turned backs.

I can only wonder at what I have done. I have married a

brute who is a chameleon. But I cannot see his reasoning in billing me as a pathetic, useless wife. Does he not want to be seen to have made a successful marriage? Surely, that's what he was looking for? He cannot have married me for my money – we have none, or very little. He can only have married me for my looks and my ability to charm a room. Those were my two assets – I am no fool. I could use those to get me what I wanted. I didn't have your brains, we didn't have money and we only had a tentative hold on our place in society. The only way I could keep that place in society was to marry. I was charmed by a bully and sly beast who, I will admit, shares my own ability to steal the lime-light. Perhaps that's why, ultimately, we don't work – we compete with each other in company, he doesn't like it if I outshine him, and, to be truthful, I'm not happy if I'm in the shade. I only thrive if I am the centre of attention.

But I have other troubling news. Alisdair, in one of his drunken rages, let slip that he had heard that Charles and John Hardgrave were frequenting the gambling clubs in Glasgow. He says they've been seen in the high stakes poker games, with some big wins but some equally big losses. He said that nobody knew what they were losing more money on, the gambling or their drinking. He said this to me with a kind of glee, as if he had stabbed me and was now taking pleasure in twisting the knife to cause more pain.

Kitty, my apologies; this letter is full of nothing but sadness and pain. But you are the only person I am able to confide in. Both our parents know that I am not happy, but they don't know to what extent. I wish I could write to you with all the gossip and trivia that I used to – I simply don't have the heart.

I can no longer trust that these letters will reach you, as Alisdair will not let me post them myself. I have asked my maid to send it for me, and I believe she will do so as she is as distrustful of my husband as I am.

With love, your sister,
Eva

SEVENTEEN

KITTY

Loch More, 1898

Moonwort

'The old superstition was that it had the magical power to open locks and unshoe horses.'

Compassionate Herbs *by Mrs C F Leyel*

Kitty dropped the letter on her desk; another miserable exposition. For the two years since her sister's marriage, Eva's sporadic letters had described a husband who had increasingly become a domineering tyrant, who would demean her in public and humiliate her in private. Kitty felt helpless. She had done what she could, travelling to Glasgow to persuade Eva to leave her husband, but it had caused more trouble than either of them could have expected. Both husbands had been incensed at Kitty's perceived interference: Alisdair taking it out on his wife,

Charles sending Kitty back to Ardbray, avowing that she never return to Glasgow.

Keeping herself busy with her herbalism and her precious garden meant nothing if she couldn't do anything to help her sibling. Eva had been right when she had once said that history repeated itself with the Gray sisters. Both of them now power-less; her sister, once the sparkling debutante, now a wraith, living a life of pretence and her own high ambitions quashed and buried, hidden away in the Highlands.

This was the first letter of any kind that she had received in several weeks. The snows had made reaching Loch More diffi-cult and there had been no contact with any friends or family. Today's post had been a welcome relief from the monotony of their stranded existence until she had read her sister's letter.

She stood up quickly, stuffing the letter back in its envelope, shoving it in her desk drawer and slamming it shut. She began to pace the room, up and down, wringing her hands, her jaw square, frustration beginning to surge through her like the slow build of a tidal wave. Finally, she stopped pacing and rushed out of the morning room. She ran upstairs to the nursery to find it empty. She had forgotten, Mrs Mercaut had taken the chil-dren out for a walk on the first fine day in weeks and Kitty had decided to stay at home to read her precious letters. Just as quickly she turned around and went downstairs, along the corridor and into the kitchen.

As she walked into the large kitchen, she could hear happy chatter, smell the inviting cake, feel the warmth and homeliness that she rarely felt elsewhere in the house. Sitting at the large kitchen table were Cook, Mrs Lindsay, Fraser, Eleanor and two of the maids. They were preparing to play a game of cards.

Fraser, always polite and a little reticent with her, was sitting sprawled across his chair, an easy smile across his face, Eleanor was perched on the table edge facing the two maids laughing with them at some joke, Mrs Lindsay was shuffling a pack of cards, Cook sat quietly sipping her tea, reading an old newspaper. Kitty stopped herself from interrupting and watched. There was an easy camaraderie that she found herself envying. The only person she'd ever had that kind of relationship with was Eva, and that had now shattered; her friendship needed to be a support rather than companionship. And as she watched the happy troupe joke and cajole each other, it dawned on her how isolated she had become and how she had allowed herself to retreat into her books, her library and her children. She realised that her closest friend was Eleanor, now that she so rarely saw her sister, but try as she might she could not call their friendship close, it was still one of mistress and servant.

'Right, I think we'll start with a game of Loo. Everyone happy with that?' Mrs Lindsay began dealing the cards before anyone could answer.

Kitty stepped forward. 'Can I join in?'

Everyone in the room turned to face her. Mouths open, jaws silently dropping, eyes widening. As the silence continued, it began to bear down on Kitty.

'Well... if...' Kitty stuttered.

'Aye, come on in, come an' join us. The game's best played with seven. Here, take a seat next to me.' Mrs Lindsay was effusive, even if the lie was obvious, pulling a chair out before gathering in all the cards and re-dealing. 'Have you played Loo before? You see that Fraser here thinks he's the champion, whereas Molly, our newest addition, we think has actually been playing it since she was a wee bairn. I'm not sure what that says about her family. You'd think age and experience would help in this game, but somehow, in Molly's case, it's trick-taking beauty that wins it every time.'

Molly, fresh-faced and shy, blushed profusely as the others moved to their seats, shuffled and coughed, not talking, but readying themselves for a game of cards with their mistress. Fraser, no longer slouching, sat upright, scowling. Eleanor smiled at Kitty and sat beside her. Cook pushed her teacup away and sniffed, crossing her arms, staring at the table.

Mrs Lindsay dealt three cards to each of them and a spare hand before sitting down. She placed the remaining cards face down on the table before turning the top one over and placing it on the table.

'Spades is trumps.'

The silence continued.

'You've played before?' Mrs Lindsay leaned sideways to pass Kitty a pile of matchsticks.

Without speaking, Kitty moved her cards away from the housekeeper and pulled them close to her chest as she looked around at her opponents. Fraser hunched over the table studying his cards closely, hands cupped around them, Molly, the newest housemaid, sat rigid and silent, occasionally glancing at Kitty, her eyes darting around the room, before returning to check her hand again. Eleanor continually shifted her cards into some kind of order, humming quietly to herself.

'I have, Mrs Lindsay. Eva and I used to play with our maid Martha and Cook. I'm in for this one.'

'Fraser, are you in too?' enquired Mrs Lindsay.

Fraser flushed, dropping his head. 'Aye, I'm in.' He alternated his cards around from back to front and then again, tapping his foot on the table leg.

'Molly, you're to go first,' the housekeeper gently reminded the housemaid.

Silently, Molly laid a card in the middle of the table before retreating to her chair and continuing to check her cards, tightly held in front of her.

Kitty took a deep breath, knowing she was intruding, understanding she was somewhere she shouldn't be.

. . .

Four games later, four wins later, the room had become even more silent. Kitty was ashamed of herself. She'd got carried away, her competitive spirit taking over, forgetting where she was and too easily taking command. Pushing back her chair, she stood up.

'Who'd like a cup of tea?'

The silence appeared to become even deeper. The staff all looked down at their cards.

'I'm making...'

Eventually, Mrs Lindsay looked around the table and then stood up.

'Ma'am, let me make it with you.' She bustled towards the range and picked up the kettle.

'No, surely I can do it? You've been busy all day. Let me.' Kitty tried to take the kettle from the housekeeper.

Gently, Mrs Lindsay took Kitty's hand off the kettle. 'Aye, ma'am, let me show you where the tea is kept.' She put the kettle down and ushered Kitty towards the pantry.

Once inside the pantry, she shut the door and turned towards Kitty.

'Ma'am, there's an order of things. The mistress does not come below stairs, she does not play cards with the staff and she certainly doesnae make them tea.' Her soft Highland accent made the reproach seem like a simple statement, but Kitty wasn't able to control her response.

'But I always used to play cards with the staff in Glasgow. Why can't I do it here too?'

'Ma'am,' Mrs Lindsay's voice sharpened a touch, 'you were a bairn, I imagine it was rainy days when you needed entertaining and your mother was out of the house. There's a difference between the bairns playing with the maids and the mistress wanting to socialise with the staff.'

'Mrs Lindsay. It has been weeks since I have spoken to anyone outside this house, anyone who isn't my child or works for the Maclean family. I have received little correspondence. I have done my best to keep myself busy with my research and my reading. But I dine alone every night in that cavernous and cold dining room. I sit in the library in silence for hours. I would simply like some adult company with people who are friendly and kind. I know you and everyone out there are such people. If we are stuck here, in the snow, why can I not join you for a cup of tea and a game of cards? Why can't I laugh with you? Why can't I be a normal person who looks for normal company?'

Her voice had risen and she'd begun to shake. Her eyes began to prick and she stopped herself by putting her hand over her mouth before she made an even greater fool of herself.

The silence in the pantry was thick as Mrs Lindsay stared at her. The women assessed each other. Eventually, she laid a hand on Kitty's arm.

'Aye, hen,' she said softly, 'the tea's in that brown caddy.' She pointed to a shelf beside Kitty. 'You bring that along, I'll get the kettle going and we'll make a'reaght cuppa tea. But,' – she fixed a beady eye on the woman opposite her – 'hold your game back, less of the winning. Give them something to play for.'

Standing in front of the long wooden bench in her new herbarium, Kitty surveyed the series of watercolours in front of her. These were her own neat, botanical paintings of the herbs she'd managed to grow in her garden; after eight years of constant practice she was now happy with the quality. She was sorting through them to decide which to frame and hang on the walls and which to file away in alphabetical order.

Fraser had spent the best part of the winter transforming this room from a small bedroom into a workroom for Kitty. Finally, she had a space where she could make her tisanes, ointments or cordials without getting under Cook's feet and causing upset with the smell of her so-called 'concoctions' in the kitchen. Here she could spread out and never worry that her infusions could be confused with Cook's cordials, here she could read, paint and study away from the main heart of the house, away from any chance of noise and distraction. She had filled the room with everything she would need: dispensary bottles, pestle and mortar, funnels and bowls of all sizes, her paints and brushes, fountain pens and pencils, tiny envelopes for keeping the seeds she'd harvested and a few of her favourite indoor plants. There were drawers for filing away all her notes, bookshelves waiting to be filled, and a comfortable armchair by one of the windows for her to read in.

A loud knock almost made her jump. Fraser opened the door and shuffled into the room.

'Ma'am. I've finished what you asked me to make. I thought maebe the bairns might like to try it out today, seeing as the snow has taken a hold again.'

Kitty jumped up from her chair. 'You've made it!' Clapping her hands together, she declared, 'We must find Flora and Callum.' Heading towards the door, she suddenly stopped. Flushed and eyes shining, she grabbed Fraser's arm. 'No wait, let's make sure it works first. Where is it?'

'I've left it by the main stairs as you said.'

'Come on then. I think we should try it out.' She ushered Fraser into the corridor and marched towards the hall.

'Did I tell you we used to have one of these at my aunt's house? It was the best holiday entertainment we ever had. But my aunt learned that we could only do it whenever my mother was out of the house, too much fun, too unladylike. The first and only time she found us using it, she became almost apoplectic, I don't think I've ever seen her so angry – well, perhaps after I fell in the river... Oh my, look at that!'

They had reached the hall, and Kitty came to a halt in front of a long piece of varnished wood propped up against the stairs. About fifteen feet long and three-foot wide, it was varnished to a high sheen with hooked wires on both sides at the top, bottom and middle. Kitty stood and admired it for a moment before bending down and stroking the wood.

'Oh, Fraser, you've done a magnificent job. This is perfect.' She gave him a conspiratorial smile.

Fraser heaved the piece of wood up the stairs and laid it over the steps, turning the stairs into a smooth surface, leaving a gap of a foot either side.

'I've made some fastenings so it will clip securely to the stair risers,' Fraser said, as he clipped the wires in place.

After a few minutes of clipping, checking and making sure the piece of wood was held solidly in place, Fraser put his tools down, and they both stood at the bottom of the stairs, looking at his workmanship.

'Well, we'd better check it works,' Kitty breathed.

He grinned, amusement flickering across his face. 'Ma'am, I think you should try first.'

She needed no second asking. Hitching her skirts, she ran up the sliver of stairs beside the varnished wood. At the top she picked up a waiting cushion, put it on the smooth wooden surface, sat down and shuffled around to make herself comfortable, tucking her skirts in between her thighs.

'Ready? Here we go!' She pushed herself off and slid down the stairs, one arm in the air, keeping her balance, the other arm holding onto her skirts. As she accelerated down the slide, her face lit up and her smile widened. The whole slide perhaps only took about two seconds, but to Kitty, it was two delicious seconds, two seconds of complete abandonment. Childhood memories of summer holidays in Aberdeenshire came flooding through, carefree days without her mother, days without censure, days without disapproval. At the bottom, she continued sliding across the floor until she bumped into Fraser.

'What a slide! That's just how I remember it, maybe even better. I think the stairs are longer here. The children are going to love that. So, it's your turn now. I want your opinion.' She hustled Fraser up the stairs.

Stumbling at the top, Fraser's height became a hindrance as he folded himself up to sit at the top of the slide. He hesitated.

'Just push off, it's just like any other slide.'

Fraser looked down. He held tightly to the sides of the slide. 'I've never bin on a slide before.'

Kitty stared momentarily before she produced an encouraging smile. 'It's easy. Did you ever slide on the ice before? It's just like that, only downhill. Just tuck your legs in and make sure your jacket won't get caught on the sides and push off. It's easy, it's not as steep as it looks. I promise when you've done it once, you'll be wanting to do it again.'

So, with a deep breath, Fraser pushed himself down the slide. Quickly, the tension left his face. The deep furrows and the habitual dark moodiness vanished as a childish liberty took hold.

'Aye! That's pure barry!' he shouted, as he slid across the floor and jumped up. 'I'll be doing that again.' He ran up the side of the slide and straight to the top. 'Ma'am,' he said, as he sat down, a huge smile across his face, 'we should get the bairns, they'll love this.' And then he gave himself a push and hurled himself down the slide, all hesitation vanished.

Kitty put her hand to her mouth and suppressed a giggle.

'*Mon Dieu!* Such noise. One would think that...' Mrs Mercaut stopped mid-sentence as she reached the hall.

This kind of noise had never been heard before at Ardbray: shrieking, yelling, clapping, foot stamping and raucous belly laughs. By the look on Mrs Mercaut's face, she was watching a scene she could never have imagined.

Cook was sitting at the top of the slide, face feverish, hair falling out of her cap. As she braced herself to go down the slide, everyone else was at the bottom of the stairs, goading her: Kitty and the children, the whole household staff. Everyone had a flushed look, all had bright eyes and appeared almost out of breath as they shouted, jeered and egged Mrs Archer on. Mrs Archer, cook at Ardbray for nearly a decade and approaching sixty years, had her eyes focussed on the bottom of the slide, all thoughts of breathlessness vanished, and began pushing herself back and forth, gearing herself up for the final thrust. The crowd grew louder and as she finally pushed off, the noise came to a deafening crescendo.

They roared as she reached the bottom and landed in a heap. Kitty stooped to help Mrs Archer to her feet. Callum took her hand, beaming at her dishevelled appearance and said something to her, unintelligible in the pandemonium.

Kitty turned and noticed Mrs Mercaut standing in the corner and walked over to her. She took her hand and urged her to join the party.

'Mrs Mercaut,' she said gently, 'we've been wondering where you were. We thought you'd enjoy this.' Kitty watched the nanny's face as she continued to survey the scene. 'Fraser has made us a slide, and since it was so snowy outside and we've all been stuck indoors for days, it seemed the perfect antidote to snakes and ladders, which I think the children are a bit fed up with.'

Mrs Mercaut stared at Kitty. 'Ma'am... your dress.' She pointed at a rip in the sleeve of her mistress's blue gown and then back at Kitty, her hair frizzed, cheeks glowing and her hair at full length, its tortoiseshell clip hanging down one side.

'Yes.' Kitty picked at the tear. 'Eleanor ran into me on her way down the slide, I'm afraid her sense of direction is not very good.' She delved into Mrs Mercaut's pupils, looking for some kind of approval. As the two stared at each other, no words passing between them, there was another roar and they turned to see Callum hurtle down the slide and then continue along the hall floor on the cushion. Legs everywhere, his too-long mop of wiry brown hair flopping across his face, he eventually stood up, a triumphant smile lighting up his usually serious face.

Mrs Mercaut blinked quickly, her eyes filming as a slight look of amusement crossed her face. 'One would think,' she whispered, 'that the world had forgotten us.' She looked about her, almost in a daze.

Kitty let out a breath, relief softening her features. 'Yes, one would,' she said very seriously, almost like a drunk who's trying to appear more sober than he really is. 'One of the many benefits of living out here, in the middle of nowhere, nobody need know what goes on.' Her voice grew bolder. 'Nobody needs to know that I couldn't live without all my friends here, nobody can get upset that "the Laird's wife" is kicking up her heels with the staff. Nobody needs to know that the children are happiest sliding down the main stairs at Ardbray and yelling at the tops of their voices.' Her voice grew louder as she spoke, almost at a shout, and she began to spin around and around, her arms out wide, her head turned towards the ceiling.

Mrs Mercaut drew herself up, momentary disapproval flickering across her face. But she couldn't keep it up and, suddenly, her whole countenance changed. Her usual austere demeanour loosened, the stiffness in her face eased like a blancmange being let out of its mould. Her mouth twitched and mischief sparkled in her eyes. Finally, a chuckle slipped out before she could stop it with her hand.

'Let's hope we can keep it that way,' she whispered to herself.

EIGHTEEN
GREER

Loch More, 2004

Nutmeg

'The silver graters our grandmothers carried on their chatelaines were to make Nutmeg tea,
which they gave as much for a languid digestion as for a restless night.'

Herbal Delights *by Mrs C F Leyel*

Today we start work on the interiors in earnest. I've been researching and gathering ideas. I've cut out pictures from magazines, found samples of fabrics and paint colours and have spent many happy hours making up mood boards to show Caitlin this morning.

I feel like it's my first day at a new job. My stomach is a jitter, and I haven't been able to eat a thing for the last twenty-four hours. Colin was the same when he showed Caitlin his designs for the walled garden: excited, anxious, nervous and nauseous. When you're in your sixties, you've already begun to wonder if you'll ever be excited by anything again. It's as if we've been thrown a reverse lifeline; we've been rescued from our steady, safe, grey life and thrown into the broiling sea of the unexpected.

I've discovered that Caitlin doesn't like anything that's new, not when it comes to furniture and design. She wants everything to be second-hand, she doesn't like the modern, minimalist hotel look. She wants a riot of colour, painted furniture, bright-coloured throws and shocking pink cushions. It's a little bohemian for my taste, but I'm willing to go along with it. I even think Kitty would approve; she liked things that were out of the ordinary. I've set up a workshop in the stables for restoring and painting furniture. Colin and I are planning a little tour of Scotland, scouring second-hand shops and auction rooms for suitable furnishings and items to decorate the house.

I walk into the morning room, transformed from an Edwardian lady's writing room into Caitlin Black's office. Gone is the mahogany roll-top desk, the matching upright chair and the ornate mirror above the fireplace. In its place is a large wooden-topped trestle table with a computer monitor and keyboard to one side, neat piles of paper to the other. The stiff, brocade-covered armchairs have been replaced by something more comfortable, more inviting; chairs made for moments of relaxation. The original damask wallpaper has gone, now there are clean yellow-painted walls, giving the room a brighter outlook. Half-full bookshelves frame the fireplace, an abstract oil painting hangs above the fire.

Caitlin sits at her desk, staring at the computer screen. She's wrapped in a pale-blue blanket as she blows on her hands covered in fingerless woollen gloves. Her nose is red and there are dark rings under her eyes. She looks up.

'Oh, Greer, you're just what I need. Please come and save me from a slow death by finances, come and sit by the fire.' She gets up from her desk and moves to one of the comfy armchairs. 'I am so cold; my feet feel like icicles.'

I put the tray of coffee down on the small table in front of her. When Caitlin moved in, she brought a cafetière and a large box of her favourite ground coffee, no other food or drink, and proceeded to teach me the art of making coffee. She's very insistent that we make it correctly.

'You look terrible,' I say.

'I haven't slept a wink for the past couple of days. Too many things running around in my head. There is so much to do, deliveries, paperwork, interviews, food suppliers to find, decisions to make on types of roof tile, finials, new gargoyles, replacement windows, three-phase power. Oh, the list is endless, and I don't seem to be able to get a hold of it. Also, I've been trying to do the month-end finances, and I've just been staring at the same spreadsheet for the last twenty minutes and getting nowhere.' She runs her hands through her hair. 'And my head aches.' She flops back into the armchair, closing her eyes.

'What if I made you an infusion of elderflower and catmint? It's a special Kitty Maclean remedy for feverish colds and lack of sleep. A cup of that and a good long sleep will make you feel worlds better.'

She groans. 'I'll take the tea, any help gratefully received, but not the sleep, I can't, Dad will be here any minute.'

'Finn Black is coming here?' Why didn't she tell me?

'Yes, when I spoke to him last week, he said it sounded like I needed an assistant, so he's coming up to help me clear the backlog. Imagine Finn Black being my assistant. That's just not going to work. He's going to drive me mad.' She let out a heavy sigh.

'Why?'

She leans forward and pours two cups of coffee, passing one

over to me. 'The thing is, my father and I don't get on. We haven't got on since he left my mother.' She takes a sip of her coffee. 'And we had a huge row when I went to visit him in Edinburgh.' She lies back in her chair and closes her eyes again. 'I'm not sure I'm up to dealing with him.'

'Didn't you tell me you spent long hours working on a plan to restore the house?' I ask.

She nods. 'Long hours for certain, but they weren't particularly happy hours. I left before I said something I was going to regret.'

I say nothing. Usually saying nothing helps people to say what they really want to say. Perhaps by being silent, they think that I'll be discreet, so they feel it's okay to open up and tell all.

'You see, I've been angry with my father since the day he left my mother and moved back to Edinburgh, abandoning his four children.'

I can't help but laugh. 'That sounds very melodramatic. Didn't you grow up in a large Fifth Avenue apartment with your mother and many servants? That doesn't sound like abandonment.'

She rolls her eyes. 'Oh, don't you start. That's exactly what Duncan said.'

'How old were you when your father left?'

Caitlin has been living at Ardbray for five months now. We're getting used to having her around. She's just been away to Glasgow for a few days and it felt very odd her not being here. It's like when you're used to having a dog in the house, the soft padding of feet and occasional nudge against the back of your knees reminds you that you have company. But when that presence is gone, however much you didn't think you relied on it, you feel a little bereft. Perhaps she feels a little of the same emotion because she's starting to let us into her damaged world.

'I was seven, but Jim was only four. It might have been okay if Dad had stayed in New York, but he moved across the

Atlantic. It wasn't as if we could just drop in and see him. We had to book flights, make arrangements, pack bags.' There's teenage petulance on her face as if the memory has transformed her back to the sullen thirteen-year-old I can imagine she was.

'How did your mother react to his move?'

She rolls her eyes again. 'She couldn't have been happier. The further away he was, the more delighted she was.'

'Sounds like you're pretty angry at your parents,' I say quietly.

Shame on you Greer Mackenzie. Taking advantage of the girl when she's feeling vulnerable; prying into her life as if you're some kind of therapist when all you want to do is find out more about her.

Caitlin takes a sip of her drink, looking into the distance at nothing in particular. 'You're right, I've been pissed at my parents since I was a teenager.

'I was such a cliché. The classic wild child behaving badly to get at my mother. Furious at my sisters for being so clever and so beautiful. Sullen with my father for running away and leaving me with all those high-achieving women who seemed to consider success to only be about what clothes you wore and where you lived.' She seems to stop herself abruptly and sits up, pulling the blue blanket more tightly around her. 'I don't think you want me spilling my guts at you.' And now she runs her hands through her hair, sighing. 'We're here to work, not get bogged down with the trials of a spoilt girl from Manhattan.'

'So did you make it up with him before you left Edinburgh, or will it be awkward when he gets here?'

She breathes out heavily. 'Sort of. It was a kind of silent truce. You see, he began telling me why he left New York. He was sick of being Mr Jessica Smyth, he needed to be his own man, New York was suffocating both personally and professionally, blah, blah, blah.' She closes her eyes and runs her hand through her hair.

'And then he said, "Sometimes you have tae think about yourself. I couldn't stay for your sakes. I would never have been happy, and I truly believed that if I couldn't be happy, then neither could you. It was better to leave you in the hands of your mother than try tae be something that I wasn't." And just when I thought he couldn't say anything worse, he then likened leaving his four children to experiencing the death of a child.' Her eyes are wide open now, incredulity across her face, and she leans forwards as she continues. 'Can you believe it? Leaving your own children, of your own free will feels like dealing with the death of your child. As you can imagine, I saw red. I told him that he had no idea what he was talking about and how dare he use that analogy with me.'

There's a strange silence between us, I feel that she's let something slip through her armour.

But just as she takes a breath to speak, there is a knock on the door and Finn Black walks in.

'Dad.' Caitlin gets up and gives her father a hug.

The two appear on opposite ends of the scale; the father immaculately turned out in a brilliant-white collared shirt, tweed waistcoat, chinos and highly polished brown brogues, the daughter huddled in her blanket, thick polo-neck jumper with a hot-water bottle clasped to her stomach and her face puffy with dark circles under those rheumy eyes. I can still see the vulnerability, in her body language, in the way she clings on to her dad just a little bit too long.

Finn Black holds his daughter out in front of him.

'Hey, you okay? You look like hell. You been sleeping, eating properly? I don't want you getting sick again.' He shakes his head at her, wagging an invisible index finger at her.

She gives me a sideways look as if her father has already said too much. But she covers it with, 'Greer has been feeding me, don't you worry about that. She makes the heartiest of soups and the best of cakes, it's a miracle that I didn't roll in here today.'

He turns to me. 'The famous Greer Mackenzie! Well, I couldn't be happier tae meet you.' He steps forward and we shake hands. 'Caitlin has told me nothing but great stories of you and your husband. You are a great asset tae Ardbray, and I know Caitlin appreciates it that you and your husband have stayed on tae help with restoring this house.'

His enthusiasm is a little unnerving and I'm not quite sure what to say. Thankfully, Caitlin saves me.

'Dad, come and have a coffee. Greer and I were just about to sit down and look through her ideas for the interiors. Would you like to join us?'

I try not to frown. I'm not prepared for a bigger audience, let alone award-winning architect Finn Black; I was only expecting to run through my thoughts with Caitlin. I'm not used to corporate presentations, PowerPoint slides or overhead projectors. We were just going to sit down over a cup of coffee, with a few mood boards.

Finn Black sits on the bentwood chair in front of the desk. 'No, I'll let you get on whilst I unpack my bags and make myself at home. I'm sure you wouldn't want me poking around your plans. I'm a bricks and mortar man, not textiles and fabrics.'

My relief is mixed in with thoughts about where he's going to sleep, but I quickly push them aside. Not my problem if they don't give me due warning. We'll sort that out later.

'By the way,' he says, 'I wanted to find out how you were getting on with finding an assistant. Have you found anybody suitable?'

'Yes!' she crows triumphantly. 'It turns out Greer knows just the person. She's coming in a little later, so you'll get to meet her.'

'Great news.' But then he frowns. 'You really don't look well.'

Caitlin shakes her head. 'Oh I'm fine, just tired after my trip to Glasgow. Anyhow, Greer says she has some herbal tea that's a miracle cure for the common cold.' She smiles at me, leaning back in her chair and pulling the blanket around her more tightly. But as she does this, she narrows her eyes and leans her head on one side.

'Can you hear that?'

Both Finn and I look at her with puzzlement.

'Sometimes, when I'm sitting here, I can hear the house. It's as if there's a settling in the rafters, a relaxation in the walls. Every now and again I hear this noise that I can only interpret as the house breathing a sigh of relief. It's as if I can hear its inner workings, hear it revel in its renovation and renewal.'

Caitlin Black's audience stares at her with amused disbelief.

'Well, as a man who has spent his life trying to build or renovate beautiful buildings that fit in with the environment and suit their owners, that makes me happy to hear. A house that appreciates its owner, with an owner who can read the house.' Finn Black says this with a slight fatherly pride.

There's an awkward silence in the room. I feel like I have intruded on an important moment of reconciliation. I concentrate on the background noise of the builders, a hammer, an electric drill, the clatter of metal on the ground, the occasional shout up to the roof.

Suddenly, Caitlin throws off her blanket and stands up.

'I have something to show you. When I was in Glasgow last week, I spent more days holed up in the Mitchell Library. It's one of those places that sucks you in, takes you down these rabbit holes of intrigue.'

Her face is transformed. Gone are the tears and the weary eyes, the scowl and resentment. In its place is a kind of fevered excitement.

'Anyhow, yet again, I was researching the Maclean family. I found that I was spending a lot of time wondering what had happened to them, why this house had been left empty for so long and what had happened to the once flourishing Maclean and Son and all that money.' She begins rifling through the papers on her desk until, eventually, she finds a Manila envelope.

'Here, look at this.' She pulls a photocopy of an old newspaper article out of the envelope. A large and grainy photograph of Charles's father standing in front of Ardbray, smiling with his hand on his son's shoulder. Charles looking unsure, unpolished and almost embarrassed. George Maclean, in contrast, stares at the camera defiantly, his full beard covering his jutting chin, his certain eyes, challenging the photographer. All that's missing is a speech bubble in bold, upper-case letters shouting, "COME SEE WHAT I'VE DONE."

Finn takes the paper and begins to read.

Glasgow Herald, September 12th 1888

Industrialist dies unexpectedly before he can enjoy his new home.

George Maclean, founder of Maclean and Son, has died suddenly at his home in Glasgow from a heart attack. It was only last week that this publication was invited into his new home, Ardbray, near Achfary, Sutherland. The industrialist opened up his latest personal venture to let the world see his ambitious building project.

George Maclean, born in Glasgow 1819, started his own business in 1847, after spending three years in South Georgia, America, learning the cotton trade. Mr Maclean quickly understood the growing demands of a changing and burgeoning fashion market and built a business to meet these needs. Maclean and Son has become one of the mainstays of Glasgow's cotton spinning industry, defying the decline in demand for Glasgow cotton over the last decade and maintaining a profitable business in the face of competition from the mills in Lancashire.

George Maclean has been overseeing the building of his new country home for the last two years. The house is still incomplete, but, only last week, he invited a select group of journalists to get a glimpse of what he hopes future homes will be like. He took us on a tour of the main reception rooms, showing us the intended new central heating system, bathrooms upstairs with running hot water and is talking of bringing in a generator for electric lights. He has most certainly been ambitious, many of these amenities are hardly available in the richest parts of Edinburgh and Glasgow, let alone in one of the bleakest and most difficult-to-reach parts of the Highlands. The house is not complete yet, with much of the interior still in need of finishing and further building work in the pipeline.

George Maclean is succeeded by his only son, Charles, who is already a board member of Maclean and Son and is widely expected to succeed his father as managing director and be given overall control of the business.

'Ambition, innovation and death; all the makings of a good story. We just need a bit of greed and love, then you'll have it all,' Finn Black says this with a gleeful tone. Just as he's about to continue, there's an urgent shout outside.

We all look in the direction of the window as we hear another, louder cry. Caitlin heads towards the door. 'Something's wrong.' And both Finn and I follow her.

There's a group of workmen standing, peering into a large hole in front of the drawing room bay window. A big pile of earth stands to one side, the old rose bushes torn out and strewn in a thorny heap on the lawn; a few red straggling roses amongst the white.

'What is it?' Caitlin asks, slightly breathless from running all the way.

All the men turn and then the group parts in silence to let Caitlin in. Their faces are sombre, no longer the joking, cocky colleagues. Their arms hang down by their sides, their eyes are wide and curious. She halts beside them and looks down into the hole, bending down to have a closer look. I lean in beside her and crouch down, my knees cracking as I do so.

The unmistakable sunken eye sockets, horse-like teeth and smooth crown of a human skull.

NINETEEN
KITTY

Loch More, 1899

Lupins

'Lupins have an ancient reputation for increasing courage, and sharpening vision.'

Elixirs of Life *by Mrs C F Leyel*

'Jack, queen, king an' ace o' hearts. An' I'm out,' Mrs Lindsay's voice was triumphant as she put the last of her cards down. She looked at the others around the table, her chin up and her eyes half-shut. A grin spread across her face as she leaned back in her chair and crossed her arms.

There was a roar from the others.

Fraser slapped his cards down and shouted, 'Nae. That's the second time you've done that, Mrs Lindsay!' His eyes twinkled and a wide smile creased his face. 'If I didnae know you so well, I'd say you'd bin cheatin'.' He began to pick up the other cards that had been thrown down in disgust by the rest of the players.

Kitty leaned forward, Mrs Lindsay directly opposite her, the large wooden chair swallowing her petite frame. 'Fraser's right, Mrs Lindsay, it all seems a little suspicious.' She twisted her mouth to one side and wagged her finger at her opponent. She held Mrs Lindsay's stare before she shook her head and began counting out five matchsticks.

'Auch, she couldnae cheat if she had tae. She's too honest,' Eleanor spoke as she counted out her own matchsticks and passed them over to the winner. 'She's just one of those people, al'ays wins tha dae.' She smiled at Mrs Lindsay as she shrank back into her chair.

Kitty and all the Ardbray staff were sat around the kitchen table. A heavy blue cotton and velvet embroidered cloth lay across the wooden surface. Cards and matchsticks were strewn across it. Half-drunk cups of tea lay beside it, plates with dark crumbs dotted across them. The kitchen radiated an all-embracing warmth with the satisfying smell of recent baking which could lure in any passer-by. The window over the large porcelain sink emitted the twilight gloom, laying a murky film over the room. The candles hadn't yet been lit, so intense had been the concentration on the game of Hearts.

Tea in the kitchen, followed by a card game was now a regular event, despite the long-gone snow. Kitty had learned not to be so competitive and the staff had soon got used to her company. She knew not to join them on a Saturday evening, giving them some freedom and herself a night alone with the children. She'd taught them Hearts, they'd taught her poker. There was an unwritten rule that this rendezvous was off whenever they had visitors or Charles was in residence. But Charles so rarely returned to Ardbray and now their only occasional visitor was Dr Beattie, who frequently joined in the card game, with a wink at Kitty and a finger to the side of his nose, so that they almost never had to break their daily ritual.

Kitty picked up the last of her matchsticks. 'I received a letter from my mother this morning.'

The habitual noises of the room fell away, everyone became still and looked at Kitty.

'I'm afraid she's threatening to come and stay for at least three weeks.' She scraped one of the matchsticks along the table and it caught alight. 'Three whole weeks.' She held the match up to her face, watching the flame intently before she suddenly blew it out.

With a scrape of her chair, Mrs Lindsay stood up. 'That'll be formal dinners and the children seen and not heard. We'll need to clean doubly hard before she gets here so that when she gives the windowsills the white glove treatment, she isnae given any satisfaction. And we'll need to get the temporary footmen back in, clear out the spare rooms above the stables for them. Will your father be coming?'

'No, I don't think so. Although I know he'd love to see the children. Sometimes, I think he stays behind so he can have a break from my mother.' She picked up another match and absently lit it, again staring at its flame until it almost reached her fingers and then shaking her hand to extinguish the flame. 'I'm not sure I'll manage to keep up the mother and daughter, master and servant façade this time. It's been too long since I last had to do that. You know I'm not even sure this house can do it.'

Fraser frowned and looked at Eleanor.

'The last time she left I could swear the whole house almost sat down with relief. It was as if the front door commanded the rest of the house to come off the parade ground and stand at ease.'

The comradery of the room had dissipated and Eleanor pushed her chair back noisily and started clearing the plates. 'It won't be just the house; it'll be all of us. It's like doing a double shift at the dress factory. I don't know how her maid Martha puts up with it. Does she ever get any time off?'

'Not to play cards at any rate,' Kitty said. The room fell silent, eyes down on the table, fingers picking at the embroidered cloth. Regretting that she'd dampened the mood, Kitty suddenly piped up.

'Do you remember last time she stayed she found the poker chips in the children's nursery?'

'Oh, and how,' giggled Mrs Lindsay. 'Mrs Mercaut persuaded her that they were giant tiddlywinks! Aye, the look of innocence on her face as she showed Mrs Gray how far she could tiddlywink with those chips. I thought Mrs Gray was going to expire, her face was puce!'

The room exploded into raucous laughter as the stories then began flooding in; close shaves in the cloakroom, mishaps in the kitchen. Kitty relaxed again as she watched her friends. Eleanor had returned to the table and, having shuffled the cards, was now dealing to everyone. The chatter continued as they leaned forward to pick up their cards and continue the game. But as they did so, hurried footsteps could be heard running down the corridor towards them. Kitty looked up, her cards held in front of her.

Callum charged into the room and skidded to a halt.

'Mama, Mama! Father's here. He's just arrived.' Out of breath, he couldn't speak any more.

Kitty pushed her chair back, scraping it along the stone floor and stood up in slow motion, confusion strewn across her face. She dropped her cards on the table, hesitation and bewilderment frustrating her ability to speak.

Callum looked at his mother, simple exasperation clouding his eyes. 'He's here, Mama, come quickly, he wants to see you.'

She looked at the window ahead of her and, seeing her reflection, quickly rearranged her hair. Smoothing her skirt down and tightening the belt of her cardigan, she turned towards her son.

The others in the room hadn't moved; wide-eyed and silent, they watched their mistress. But just as Kitty seemed to have gathered her wits and begun to approach Callum, a sharp click-clack of shoe heels could be heard, and Charles Maclean walked into the kitchen.

For a moment, the room became like the much-read-about displays at Madame Tussauds. Everyone was stock-still, all looking at the same point: their master, husband, father.

Charles appeared with that youthful look that Kitty had almost forgotten. His broad smile and boyish expression of enthusiasm jarred with the awkward silence that now covered the kitchen.

'Charles, wh-what a surprise.' As Kitty spoke, she wrung her hands, her face blank and pale as she began a hesitant walk towards him.

Silently, Mrs Lindsay leaned forward on the table and slowly picked up the cards as if she was hoping no one would notice her actions. Fraser, seeing her stealth, began to pick up the piles of matchsticks. But his efforts at furtiveness were ruined as he tipped the matchsticks into an old tobacco box, the noise so exaggerated it sounded more like marbles clattering onto an old tin tray.

'Well.' Charles clapped his hands together. 'It looks like you've all been having a great game. Please,' he said, as he walked towards the table, his eyes alight, 'don't finish on my account. I can see it's been a successful afternoon.' His childlike grin pushed Mrs Lindsay into the back of her chair, her eyes wide, her hands hiding the cards under her skirts. Fraser stood up but then seemed unsure what to do and sat back down again.

It suddenly seemed easier for everyone to turn their atten-tion to Callum who was eagerly watching his father, his face beaming with expectation, his hands in tight fists hanging down by his sides. Kitty leaned towards him, bent down and took his hand.

'Callum, could you go and find Flora and Mrs Mercaut?' She turned his head towards her own with a gentle hand. 'Tell them your father has arrived, Mrs Mercaut will know what to do.'

The expectation left Callum's face as he turned first to his father and then back to his mother. Searching her face, he whispered, 'Yes, of course, Mama.' And then ran out of the room.

Kitty stood up, the rustle of her skirts cutting into the heavy silence that wouldn't shift. She took hold of Charles's elbow and eased him towards the door.

'The game was finished.' She spoke quietly as if she was talking to a child. 'Why don't we go up to the library? The fire's been on for a while, waiting for me to return. It'll be warm and then you can tell me about your surprise visit.'

Before leaving the room, she turned briefly back to look at Mrs Lindsay, her eyes wide, her mouth in a comical downturn. 'Mrs Lindsay, would you bring us tea?' Without waiting for an answer, she turned back and continued down the corridor, still guiding her husband. 'I'm sure we weren't expecting you for another five weeks.'

Charles couldn't keep still. He sat down, stood up, walked to the fire and threw on a log. He stoked the fire, put on some coal, turned to face Kitty and then walked to the window. He was like an expectant father, waiting for news of the birth of his first child, hesitant to ask in case something had gone wrong.

Kitty made herself lean back into her armchair, doing her best to appear relaxed. She could see that he was trying to say something, but it was as if the words simply wouldn't come out. He would take a breath, ready to talk and then continue with his silence, a frown deepening, his eyes darting around him, unable to settle on any one point. But there was something about him that was fascinating her, a tiny spark of interest stirred in her stomach. He wasn't behaving like the husband she had come to know, the man who kept himself away from her, ignored her wishes and retreated into his study amidst a fog of cigar smoke to nurse a bottle of whisky. She knew nothing of him. Ashamed of herself, she realised she didn't even know what his favourite meal was or whether he preferred jam or marmalade on his morning toast. They had spent so little time together since she had been encouraged to stay at Ardbray indefinitely. Over the last ten years, his always slightly flushed, boyish face had become grey and ashen, worry lines were now a permanent feature on his forehead and his dark thatch of hair was speckled white. A general lethargy had fallen over him, a lack of interest in anything, even his all-consuming work. Occasionally, she had seen a spark of the old Charles when there had been discussions about fishing or shooting the stag, but since he no longer got invited to do either sport the faint light seemed to have been extinguished completely.

But, looking at him now, she could see a glimmer of the man she'd discovered on their first night at Ardbray, like those penny films she'd heard about, images flickering in and out, not quite solid. The salt and pepper hair had fallen across his face, no longer slicked back in his city style, his cheeks were glowing red as if he'd been outdoors all day and there was an excited glow in his eyes. But part of her was wary at seeing this man, she could hardly remember him, could hardly remember if she even liked him, let alone loved him.

She began to pour the tea, hoping this might help ease the conversation, lubricate the words that appeared to be stuck in his throat. And it worked.

'I've left Maclean and Son, and I've left Glasgow,' he blurted out. And as he did so, he sat down heavily in the armchair opposite Kitty.

Kitty stopped pouring and stared at him.

'Yes,' he said hurriedly as if to fill the awkward silence. 'I thought I'd stay here for the rest of the summer and then we'd see whether we'd all like to stay on for the winter or whether we'd like to travel, perhaps go to Europe, do the tour, see the sights...' His voice trailed off as he watched his wife.

It was Kitty's turn for the words to stick in her throat.

'I thought I could teach Callum to row. There's that old boat I found when we originally bought the land, it's sitting in one of the stables, waiting to be repaired. Callum and I could do it together.' He was speaking too quickly now. 'And I could teach him archery. We could get a bow and a set of arrows sent over from Lairg. We could make our own target.' Running his hand through his hair, he looked to Kitty for approval. His voice trailed off as he finished, 'I'm sure there's plenty more we could do.'

Kitty laughed. 'You've never even tried to mend a broken shelf, let alone restore an old boat. When did you learn to do that?' She was trying to keep the bitterness out of her voice.

'Well...' he hesitated, 'well, I'm sure Fraser could help us. It's never too late to learn, is it?' The innocent query on his face made Kitty flush.

She looked down at her fingernails, noticing how rough her hands had become from the gardening that she now did most days. She couldn't decide how to respond. Should she laugh at his childish naivety? Laugh at the fact that he seemed to have forgotten everything that had gone before; the tempers, the embarrassment, the lack of interest, the opting out of his parental responsibilities. Or should she be angry at his lack of compassion, his blindness, his blundering efforts? Should she shout at his years of indifference and his risible fatherly duties?

With visible effort, she pushed down all of these thoughts and drew out a smile from the depths of her body.

'Yes, I'm sure Callum would love that.' But she couldn't

help herself from taking an arrow from her quiver and putting it into her bow. 'But you must remember, you need to be careful only to take him out on cloudy days. The bright sun tends to bring on a seizure.'

The arrow had its intended effect. He blinked, a sudden bleakness taking over his face. 'Yes... Yes, of course.' His voice trailed off into silence as he watched the flames licking the back of the hearth. And then suddenly, he stood up and walked towards the French doors. In the final throws of the evening twilight, he peered towards the outline of the walled garden.

Kitty stood up too, unable to stay still any longer. 'When you say you've left Maclean and Son, what do you mean? That's your life, you've been part of that company since you were a boy. Surely, they need you?'

Charles gave a quiet snort. 'No. No, they don't need me.' There was an enmity in his voice that Kitty had never heard. As he spoke, the grey pallor returned, a cloak of indifference seemed to smother him. He shrank into the wall, a minor player, no longer the supposed cotton king he had once played the part of.

Kitty watched her husband revert from one kind of Charles to another. A feeling of panic began to rise up in her. She didn't know this man in front of her, he was like some kind of shapeshifter, she couldn't get a hold of him.

'No, I've had enough of Glasgow, it's too full of people I don't want anything to do with.' He hesitated, as if he wanted to go on but was afraid of what he might say.

Kitty scrutinised her husband. He was fidgeting again, but unable to meet her eye, looking down at his feet, hands, anywhere but her. She could see that he was full with words, she could almost see them spinning around in his head as if he had thrown them up in the air and was waiting for them to land in the correct order. Except they wouldn't land, they were just continuing to spin, jump and muddle. She knew she would have to be patient and wait for those words to fall into place.

Charles coughed and straightened up. 'You see,' – again he seemed to stumble, the words still settling into position – 'the truth is I'm ruined. My reputation is shredded and it is by my own hand, my own stupid fault.'

Kitty held her breath, knowing what was coming next.

'I've gambled my money and my reputation away. I need to tell you now before the news follows me, which it surely will.' He couldn't look at her.

She wanted to ask how, but it seemed futile. She knew how. She knew that he had spent long evenings gambling and drinking without a thought for what might happen. She knew that he wasn't a natural risk-taker and wasn't gambling all about taking risks?

'But why?'

Charles winced at her directness. 'My own weakness, my ability to be persuaded it was a good thing. My misjudged friendship with John Hardgrave.'

And there it was, the nub of the problem.

'We were two hapless sons of successful men, two disinterested offspring with no talent for running a successful business. But, of course, I didn't see that, I just saw someone who made me look good, made me feel better about myself.'

Kitty frowned, confused, not understanding what her husband was saying.

'You see, Kitty...' He stopped, flashing an abashed smile at her, that rare, boyish look returning for a moment. 'I'm embarrassed we've never had this conversation before. It...' The words were halting as if they were an impossibly heavy weight which he was doing his best to drag across a rutted floor. 'It seems so stupid... we've never talked... there just never seemed to be the right time.' He ran his hand through his hair, pulled himself upright and straightened his waistcoat. 'I need to tell you about me and then you might understand what's happened.' And now the words were tumbling out as if the weight had been pushed into an unexpected breach in the floor.

Kitty stared at her husband, just as ashamed. How was it that they'd never had this conversation? How had they become dolls playing at husband and wife?

'I was born into the cotton industry. I lived cotton from the day I was born. My father brought me to the mill when I was just a few weeks old, showing me my destiny, making sure I started as I was meant to go on.' Abruptly, he walked over to the window and stared into the distance as he continued his story.

'My father founded Maclean and Son. He made his fortune... and much more. He was a good businessman with a flair for making the right decision, but he was also in the right place at the right time. The boy from the Glasgow slums who made it to the top. He was proud of his success and never wanted to be reminded of his old life, of the poverty he crawled his way out of.

'I was sent to boarding school in England, just to make sure there wasn't a hint of a Scottish accent, to make sure I didn't mix with the wrong people. But, when at home, instead of giving me a childhood, he'd take me to work. Let me sit in his office or show me the mill floor, introducing me to the workers, letting them know that I'd be in charge all too soon.' Charles breathed out heavily. 'But he couldn't see that the mills filled me with terror. The terrible noise, the rough and suggestive women who worked there, hardly wearing anything because of the heat, laughing at me in my tight, velvet suits.' He gave out a bitter laugh. 'Can you imagine what they thought of this straight-laced, overindulged child being exhibited in front of them, a picture of wealth and an undeserved life of leisure?

'I wanted to go to university to read law, but Father insisted I work in the family business.' There was a weariness to his voice. 'Believe it or not, I agreed with the kind of social reform that Robert Owen advocated, but my father didn't, the board didn't and still doesn't. I learned to keep those opinions to myself and I had to learn a very different way of running a business, one that involved doing the minimum but taking the maximum profit.'

Kitty walked over to the window and stood beside her husband. 'Why did you agree to work there if you hated it all so much? Couldn't someone else more suited take over the business?' She sat in the window seat encouraging her husband to join her.

'No, Father wouldn't have it,' he said, sitting. 'He couldn't see it any other way. He insisted that his son take over. Of course, it was Maclean and Son, who else should take over? And, unsurprisingly, I was too weak to stand up to him. But the year before we were married, I realised he was dying, a frail heart. How ironic for a man who was so strong-minded.' He shook his head, almost wringing his hands. 'He made me promise that I would never abandon the business. He was so proud of what he'd done, of the empire he'd built up, he just refused to see that I wasn't suited to it, would never be any good at keeping it going.

'When he died, I thought that, after a decent amount of time, I could sell up, be rid of the business and get on with the life I wanted to lead. But my mother was so upset at the thought of selling my father's life's work that I felt I owed it to her to give it a go. So, I began looking for a business partner, someone who'd have the vision to grow the business. But no one was interested, everyone wanted the land, to pull down the mill and redevelop. The board was divided, some wanted to sell up, but I had the deciding vote and, can you believe, I spent my time persuading them to hold on, I couldn't let down the workers, the suppliers, the customers, my mother and, ultimately, my father. I remember feeling like I was in some great vat of sticky treacle, every movement I made was slow and difficult, obstacles always in my way, no possibility of free movement or freedom to think.' He leaned forward, his elbows on his knees and his head in his hands. 'Only the treacle wasn't sweet, it was sour and bitter, like some medicine your nanny would make you take when she thought you were pretending to be ill.

'But then I found John Hardgrave.' He sat up and spoke to the room. 'Suddenly, here was this man who seemed to understand me. He had the money we so desperately needed and he had the enthusiasm. Yes, he had a background in coal, but I thought he had the experience to help run a business, but it turns out he just knew how to talk a good game, how to sweet-talk the board. They loved his energy, his eagerness to make changes. And so did I. But the board were just playing us; they let us make small changes, titivations, just to keep us quiet – they used the money to prop up the company. I didn't know that at the time, I was flattered and thought people were taking notice of me for my opinions, not just my money. John and I both invested large amounts of our personal wealth.'

He became silent, looking at his hands splayed out on his thighs. 'And all they were doing was waiting for the fall, knowing that we would ruin ourselves. And then, of course, we went about making it worse. Put simply, I have frittered away my fortune, squandered everything my father left me and thrown my reputation into the gutter with it too.'

'What about John?'

'John may not be a man for business, but he is a man for the tables. He has the poker face, the cunning, and the wit. He also has the money; John Hardgrave could lose a fortune and still remain a rich man, still be able to pump money into Maclean and Son. He has the family coal business to hold him up.'

Kitty was now sitting bolt upright, her brain in a whirl. 'And Maclean and Son? What's happened to the company?'

'It's still standing, just. I have been voted off the board, thrown out in disgrace.'

'And us? How are we going to live? Can we stay here? Do we need to sell Ardbray, move somewhere where we can live more economically? Are we destitute?' She flushed and looked down at her hands, embarrassed at her barrage of questions.

'There is one thing I did that was sensible. Several years ago, I transferred the ownership of this house along with enough money to keep it up and live a frugal life. Nobody can touch Ardbray, I wouldn't do that to you and the children.'

'What made you do that? Who did you transfer it to?' She was worried now, worried he'd made another serious lapse of judgement.

Charles almost laughed. 'Kitty, I transferred the ownership of this house to you.'

Kitty looked at him sharply. 'What do you mean?'

'I mean that Ardbray belongs to you. Don't you remember? The law changed.' He watched his wife's bewilderment. 'Oh, Kitty Maclean! I thought you were the one who championed women's rights.'

Kitty blushed again, but the realisation of what he was saying began to dawn on her. 'Yes, I know what you mean.' And as she remembered, she recovered her composure, tapping her fingers on the windowsill. 'The Married Women's Act was finally passed in eighty-two, meaning that married women could inherit or be given property or money which wouldn't be immediately passed onto their husbands.'

'Exactly. Which meant I could sign Ardbray over to you and enough money for you to live off and maintain the house without you ever having to worry about me.' Charles was beaming as if he were a little boy who had just come up with a very clever idea all by himself.

Kitty frowned. 'But I don't understand. Why would you want to do that?' She spoke cautiously.

Charles avoided Kitty's searching gaze. 'I did it so that my erroneous life couldn't ruin yours. So that however badly things went for me, no one could ever get hold of the one thing that we both loved.'

Kitty stood up, scratching her head. 'But, I still don't understand. If you love Ardbray so much, why have you stayed away from it for so long? It's as if you've purposefully been avoiding it, or us, or both.'

He sighed so heavily Kitty wondered if he would answer. But she waited as she watched him formulate his words.

'I'd built this façade. The hard-working man, the man who lives for his work. I'd built this suit of armour that, after a while, I couldn't get out of. It had grown too small for me; my character had fleshed out. The real me was lost inside and it was too much hard work to find him again. I was frightened that if I admitted to you that I was a fraud, you'd laugh at me, mock me, or worse, hate me for all that wasted time.'

'What changed your mind?'

'I just became too tired, too tired of the whole game, too tired of trying to be someone that I wasn't.'

Eventually, Charles stood up and walked towards a small sofa table close to one of the windows. He picked up a heavy glass ashtray and weighed it in his hands. He held it up to the light of the fire and watched the orange light dance inside, the sharp splinters exploding like mini fireworks.

'Where did this come from?'

Kitty sat up. 'I'm fairly sure we were given it as a housewarming present, from the Sutherlands when they came to stay.'

'It's hideous.' He continued to inspect it.

Kitty smiled. 'Yes, it is. I've always hated it.'

Charles finally looked at her, that little boy grin returning. 'Well, we can agree on something,' he said softly, putting the ashtray down. 'There's so much here that I don't like, so much that I did to make sure others would be impressed. Take the library; you know I only ever put it together so I could better those great old houses, Culzean, Hopetown. I did it for all the wrong reasons. We made the ridiculous gargoyles and decoration on the outside of the house as outrageous as we thought we could get away with, just so people would talk, so people would write about the house, write about my father and his ambitions. He wanted people to take notice of us and our actions.' He began pacing the room, talking to the ceiling, occasionally looking at Kitty. 'We loved this area. This loch is where my heart is, but we built this big, ugly, ostentatious house because we wanted the world to notice, not because we wanted to live here, not because we wanted to make the most of everything the Highlands has to offer.'

Kitty was becoming alarmed. Her husband was now ranting. Quickly, she stood up and walked over to him.

'What are you trying to say?'

Charles pushed his jacket back and put his hands on his hips. 'I'm not sure I like being here anymore. It isn't the sanctuary I always hoped it would be.'

'Well, it's funny how, if you spend some time here, you'll begin to love it. I've been here so long that I can't imagine anywhere else that I'd rather be.'

Her husband gave a slight shrug of dejection.

'I mean,' Kitty said hurriedly, 'that if you stay here for the rest of the summer, I can guarantee that you'll fall back in love with it.' She searched his despondent face. 'And... and we can get rid of all the things you hate, that ashtray, and some truly terrible ornaments I'd be glad to see the back of. But don't get rid of the gargoyles, not at least until you've spent the summer with them. I think you'll find they'll become your friends. They keep the children company when they're playing in the garden and they watch over the maids when they're laying out the linen to dry or the gardeners when they're working on the flower beds beside the house.'

Slowly, a smile spread across Charles's face. 'All right, all right. But it can only be the four of us. Just you, me, Callum and Flora. No one else to interfere. No shooting parties, no visits, no family.' He took her hand and searched her eyes. 'Yes, can we do that?'

'Yes... yes, of course.'

Without warning, he leaned forward and kissed Kitty on the cheek before walking over to the fire. Putting her hand to her cheek, Kitty watched the stranger before her, lost for words.

'So, Mrs Maclean,' Charles said, childish enthusiasm suddenly exuding from him, 'we've got three months to do whatever we like, let's make a plan.'

'All right, Mr Maclean...' Kitty said coyly. 'But we'll have to consider how we put off my mother...'

Kitty leaned back on the bench and closed her eyes. It was a hot but cloudy day; an oppressive heat had been building over the last few days. The unusual sultriness had made everyone lethargic and a little irritable, so she'd left the house for some peace away from the noise of Charles and the children playing. The wooden bench sat amongst the herbs, in a position so that she could see over the wall and across the loch. The walled garden, her walled garden, had become her own sanctuary, a place where she came to think, a place where problems could be solved, solutions found. She'd planted sage beside the bench because the aroma always seemed to help clear her head, let the fog subside.

Today she was reading a precious and longed-for letter from her sister. She looked down at the sheaf of thin paper, covered in tiny handwriting and couldn't help but smile. It had been over six months since she'd heard anything from Eva, but her news, perhaps along with the sage, was making her feel surprisingly bold.

There was barely a breeze and Kitty thought she could

smell rain in the air. The heavy clouds seemed to be pushing downwards, suggesting a storm was brewing. She folded the letter carefully and put it in her apron pocket as she heard childish shrieking and heavy footsteps running towards her. She smoothed her hair down and sat upright, the grin widening.

'No, no, that's not fair. You can't attack me, not yet, anyway.' Charles's mock, childlike squeal came from behind the wall and she could hear him running towards the garden door, giggles and lighter footsteps scampering after him. She turned to see him dashing through the doorway and up the grassy path towards her. His cheeks were red and his eyes alive, a great smirk spread across his face. His detachable shirt collar had come undone on one side and was sticking out at a right angle. His shirt tails were untucked and his sleeves rolled up. Tousled hair fell across his forehead and disturbed the tiny beads of sweat that clung to his skin.

'Kitty, you need to save me from the pirates, they aren't giving me a chance.' He ran around the back of the bench and slid onto the grass, hiding amidst the lavender bushes just as Callum ran into the garden with Flora following closely behind.

'I am the fearsome Blackbeard and I wish to know where the captain of the Golden Rose is.'

She loved the innocent pleasure radiating from her son, the outdoor happiness that she rarely saw, as he stood brandishing a wooden sword, a red neckerchief falling loosely around his neck. The unusually hot summer had meant long stays indoors, so the overcast day was a treat to be relished. And now he had the added bonus of a seldom-seen father who'd suddenly discovered the art of play. She leaned forward and tucked Callum's shirt back into his trousers.

'If, by captain, you mean that scruffy father of yours, you might find him in Fraser's shed. I'd go and have a look over there. See if he's amongst the pots.' She pointed in the direction of the potting shed. 'But mind you don't disturb any of Fraser's work and make sure you don't break anything,' she called after Callum as he ran up the garden, Flora doing her best to keep up with him.

She dropped her arm over the back of the bench and tapped Charles on the back.

'You can come out now, Captain.'

Charles stood up slowly, dusting himself down, lavender seeds in his messed-up hair. Kitty patted the space on the bench beside her and moved over.

'When was the last time you played like that?' Kitty asked, as he sat down.

Charles brushed his trousers down with his hand. 'Um...' He hesitated, looking at his dusty hands. 'Never.'

Kitty held her breath, considering the dishevelled man beside her, the contrast from the tight-lipped, monosyllabic man she'd become used to over the last ten years, now almost unimaginable. Every day a layer of armour fell away, every day he'd let something else go.

'Can you believe I've never kicked a ball, swung a tennis racket or rowed a boat.' There was a slight note of hysteria in his voice. 'How ridiculous.'

'So how were you intending to teach Callum to row?' Kitty asked, gentle mocking in her voice.

The confessional moment passed and Charles laughed. 'Well, I was just going to see how it went. Try it out when no one was looking. How difficult can rowing be? The boat will be ready within the next few days, so I'm going to have to find out soon.'

'There you are!' Callum came running towards them. 'Hand over the treasure or I'll run you through.' He pointed his wooden sword at his father's chest and stood stock-still, his other hand on his hip, eyes gleaming and his jaw square.

There was a discreet cough from behind them and they all

turned towards the noise. Eleanor was standing on the path, her hands clasped in front of her.

'There's a Mrs Mackay here for you. She's waiting in front of the house, along with all the staff, as you requested.' She gave a tiny bow of her head and then almost ran out of the garden.

The easiness had left them, Kitty clenching her fists by her side.

'Callum, would you please take Flora and go and find Mrs Mercaut? I need to have a word with your father.'

Charles frowned as the children ran off.

'Mrs Mackay.' Kitty's voice was like steel, flat and rigid. 'Remind me who she is.'

'Kitty, don't do this.' Charles sighed.

'Remind me.'

'She's here to help Callum. She's...' He began to falter under Kitty's intense stare. 'She's a healer. She has a reputation for being able to cure epilepsy.'

'How?' Her voice was sharp.

Charles proceeded cautiously, talking slowly as if he was feeling his way forward. 'She uses this ritual where she takes a cockerel and buries it alive in the presence of the afflicted person and their family and friends. And, well... it's proven to work.'

Kitty tried to push down the rising indignance. 'Do you have any idea how ludicrous that sounds? How could it work? How could it possibly?' She began to walk up and down the path as if the only way to get rid of her anger was to exercise it.

Charles pulled himself upright. 'I don't know.' His tone hardened. 'But it has. Talk to anyone from Achfary, talk to Fraser. Talk to Doctor Beattie. She's been doing this for years.'

Kitty continued to pace, she stayed silent as she tried to find the right words. She looked at the gravel path underneath her marching feet and subconsciously rubbed the muscle between her right-hand thumb and forefinger, until, suddenly, she stopped and looked directly at her husband.

'No.' The word hung in the air as she held his stare. 'No. You're not doing this. I will no longer be pushed into doing something I don't want to. I've spent my life pleasing others. My mother pushed aside all my desires so that I could fulfil hers. But when I married you, I hoped things would change. But, no. I've let you quash any hopes that I had of being useful and then I also let you hide me away from the rest of the world. But now, the one thing I have left, the one thing I think I've been allowed to be good at, you're trying to overrule.'

Charles looked like he'd been slapped. 'What do you mean?'

'I've given up everything I ever wanted to do because you insisted: university, helping Doctor Forsyth at the Saltmarket Clinic, helping Doctor Beattie. And, by sending us away, by rarely visiting, you gave up the shared responsibility of bringing up our children. You left that to me, and, I think, I've been doing quite a good job.' Beads of sweat were beginning to appear on Kitty's upper lip as her temper grew.

'And then you swan in, having had no active part in your children's upbringing for years, thinking you know it all. From a conversation with Fraser and a quick chat with some people in the village, you've decided what's best for our son.

'It's nearly four years since Callum's first seizure. In that time have you read any of the medical papers written about epilepsy? Since those first, painful meetings with the doctors in Glasgow, have you spoken to any doctors about the prognosis?' She didn't let him reply. 'Have you read about the long-held medieval remedy of mistletoe that lessens the effects of seizures or that the dried root of the peony has been used in ancient Chinese medicine to treat seizures for centuries?'

Charles took a breath to reply, but Kitty would have none of it.

'No, of course you haven't. So, I won't have you interfering. This is it.' She stamped her foot. 'This is where I stop being the placid, quiet, submissive wife. I will not have that woman anywhere near Callum. You need to go and tell her to leave right now or I will cause a scene in front of her and all the servants.'

Her heart was racing and her face red, her breath coming in great gulps as if she'd just run along the drive.

Charles looked at her, confusion on his face. 'Where's this coming from, Kitty? Why this reaction?'

Kitty put her hand to the letter in her pocket and took a deep breath to calm herself.

'Eva,' she said blankly. 'She has taught me that I shouldn't be strong-armed into doing what I don't believe in, she has taught me that I should fight for my position.' She sat back down on the bench carefully as if she was sitting on a bed of broken glass.

'I don't understand.' Charles stayed standing.

'I received a letter from her this morning. Do you remember that she and her bullying husband moved to America, to Boston? Well, it seems she could stand him no longer. She had enough of his violence and intimidation, of being pushed around and doing exactly as she was told. So, she ran away. She jumped on a train and fled to Los Angeles where she fell on her feet by finding a job as a governess to four children.

'She's taught me that I should stand up for what's important, she's shown me that I shouldn't be compliant when it really matters.' Suddenly, she found herself blinking away tears, the thought of never seeing her sister again suddenly overwhelming her.

A look of panic spread across Charles's face.

'My sister, the life and soul of any party, who thought that her destiny was in a well-connected marriage and being a successful hostess was beaten into submission at every corner.

But, somehow, she found the strength to leave. She found the courage to completely change her life so that she could become an independent woman, fending for herself and creating her own life, not a life that had been constructed by others.' She looked down at her hands, clasped together in her lap. 'If she can do it, so can I. I will not have that woman anywhere near Callum. Please, go and tell her to leave.'

Charles stepped towards her, his hands flat in front of his thighs, palms outward in a gesture of capitulation. 'Kitty, please, calm down. Don't dismiss her so readily. Why not give it a go? What harm can it do?'

Kitty's eyes flashed and she stood, facing up to her husband. 'How... How could you think that?' Her voice was suddenly very quiet. 'How could you think that by subjecting our seven-year-old son to the sadistic ritual of burying a healthy cockerel alive, in front of all the servants, for his sake, will make him better, will "cure" his seizures?' Her voice was mocking. She pushed her fugitive hair from her face. 'How naive can you be? This is our son; our son who helps feed the chickens every day, who's nurtured the chicks from the day they hatched. Our sweet, sweet son who wouldn't hurt a fly.'

Charles's face fell. 'I had no idea.' It was as if Kitty's words had used him as a punchbag causing him to stagger and sag, knocking the breath out of him.

'No, how could you know? You're never here, you've never been here. Do you think that by spending a few weeks with your family, after years of neglect, that you already know what's best for us, that you can take control of our lives?'

Kitty paused for breath. She scrunched both her hands into fists. Quietly, she continued, 'I need you to send that woman away immediately and I don't want to hear any more about her.'

Charles looked down at his feet. 'Yes, yes, of course.' He turned and walked towards the house.

Kitty watched him leave and once he was out of sight, she

started to look around her, up at the sky, down at the herbs in front of her as if she didn't know where she was. Finally, she found the bench and sat down heavily. Hands shaking, she pulled the letter from her apron pocket. Leaning forward, with her elbows on her knees, she placed the folded paper on her forehead and her head in her hands and let the dam of suppression break down, let the flood of tears that she had held back for years finally gush out.

TWENTY

GREER

Loch More, 2004

Bay

*'... resists witchcraft very potently, as also all the evils old Saturn
can do to the body of man,
and they are not a few; for it is the speech of one, and I am
mistaken if it were not Mizaldus,
that neither witch nor devil, thunder nor lightning, will hurt a
man in the place where a Bay-tree is.'*

The Complete Herbal *by Nicholas Culpeper*

Caitlin puts her hand out and touches the collarbone which is just peeking out of the soil.

'I wonder how long that's been there?' she says, as she rubs soil between her fingers. Standing up, she steps away from the group, biting her lip, her hands on her hips. She considers the pile of discarded roses in front of her, shabby and awkward.

'Was that where the single red rose bush was planted?' Caitlin turns to me.

I stand up, the sun glinting on the drawing room windows causing me to squint and put my hand up to shade my eyes.

'Aye.'

Caitlin pulls me back towards the hole. 'Did you know about this?' she whispers.

We both kneel, both staring at the empty eye sockets. 'No, of course not.' But my voice is a little too sharp.

She sighs. 'I'd better go and call the police.'

Just as she says this, a familiar voice says, 'Excuse me, is Caitlin Black here? I've come for an interview.'

The group of workmen surrounding us parts and a young woman greets us with a look of amusement on her face. Eileen Murray, appearing very short beside the builders, steps forward. Both Caitlin and I hurriedly stand up and Caitlin apologises.

'I'm afraid you've arrived at a pretty bad time. We've just discovered a dead body.'

This revelation doesn't seem to faze Eileen. 'Anything I can do to help?'

Her words puncture the atmosphere and Caitlin laughs. 'I don't think so, but if you don't mind waiting for a bit, I'm happy to interview anyone who isn't intimidated by dead bodies.' She turns to me and says, 'Would you take Eileen to the dining room and I'll join you as soon as I've made the call. The rest of you,' she addresses the workmen, 'you probably ought to back off and leave your tools as they are, don't pick up a thing, just in case.'

I've just spent an awkward half an hour waiting with Eileen in the dining room, but Caitlin still hasn't returned. Finally, I suggest we go directly to Caitlin's office.

I knock on her door, louder than I mean to and walk in without waiting for an answer.

'I didna think we could wait much longer,' I say, handing her Eileen's CV. 'Should we start the interview, or would you like to postpone to another day?' I'm struggling to keep the annoyance out of my voice. I shouldn't be so impatient; we've just found a dead body in the garden.

Caitlin halts her pacing up and down of the room. 'I'm so sorry, Eileen.' She runs her hand through her hair. 'I got completely distracted. No, we should do this now. I don't want to waste your time.' She points Eileen to one of the chairs by the fire. 'Have a seat. The police won't be here for a couple of hours.' She sits opposite Eileen as I perch on the edge of the desk.

'Well, I'm betting this is the most unexpected interview you've ever attended.'

'Aye, dead bodies aren't the usual. I'm more used to how many words I can type a minute or whether I'm any good at research.'

Caitlin smiles. 'Let me tell you a bit about what I'm going to need. I'm looking for someone to help me organise the restoration of the house and the set-up of the retreat. You'll need to be resourceful and a self-starter, someone who can put their hand to anything. It's not just about paperwork. I'll need you to organise anything from setting up a proper office, making coffee for the builders, photocopying, booking the course leaders and dealing with their travel, caring for the books in the library and liaising with the Reay Forest Estate Office in Achfary when needed. There is no real job description, no job will be too big or too small. And I may well be asking you to help out with some historical research on the house.'

Eileen nods. 'Aye...' but as she speaks, Caitlin's eyes widen.

'Of course! It's in the research.' She jumps up and runs around to the filing cabinet in the corner. 'I knew something was bothering me, I knew there was an answer to the dead body.' She's pulling a hanging file out of the drawer and now spreading it across her already messy desk. 'I know it's in here.' She flicks through a pile of papers, photocopied news articles, printed emails and scrappy handwritten notes.

Eileen glances at me. I don't know what to say, I would like Caitlin to focus on the job in hand. I shrug my shoulders, the only thing I'm capable of doing without voicing my frustration.

Eventually, I can't wait on Caitlin any longer. 'Shall we rearrange for another day? I'm sure Eileen has had enough mystery for one day.'

'No, she should stay.' She speaks slowly, distracted, scanning each document quickly, before dropping it and picking up the next. The colour is rising in her face. 'Yes, here it is.' Her voice is triumphant, as she holds the paper in the air. 'You see Eileen, the Maclean family history has become a bit of an obsession of mine. I've spent hours in the Mitchell Library in Glasgow, and I received an email from them a few days ago. I only had time to scan it and didn't really take in what it meant. But,' she says, as she walks back to her chair, 'I think we might be able to solve the mystery before the police even get here.'

She hands a piece of paper to Eileen. 'Would you read this? I'm sure Greer would like to hear it too.'

Eileen clears her throat and begins.

Glasgow Herald, October 18th 1899

Former board director at Maclean and Son disappears.

Mr John Hardgrave, partner in the ill-fated firm, Maclean and Son, has officially been declared as missing by Glasgow police. Mr Hardgrave was last seen in the Highlands on his way to visit his former business partner, the disgraced Managing

Director, Charles Maclean. No report has been made of Mr
Hardgrave since he left the hotel, The Sutherland Arms, at
Lairg on 13th August, over two months ago.

Maclean and Son had been in financial difficulties for at
least two years and it has been widely reported that large sums
of invested capital had gone missing. Rumours had been rife
amongst the Glasgow business community of financial
mismanagement and embezzlement. With the unexplained
resignation of Charles Maclean in May, the collapse of
Maclean and Son shortly after, quickly followed by the death
of its managing director and now the disappearance of one of
the more influential members of the company board, this has
become a mystery that will keep even the most tight-lipped
tongues wagging and the column inches of the Scottish news-
papers full for some time to come.

This newspaper asked the remaining board members of the
now defunct Maclean and Son for any comment, but none
were available to give a statement.

And just as Eileen finishes speaking and without a moment
to digest what we've just heard, we hear heavy footsteps coming
from the corridor and a sharp knock at the door. In walks
Robbie, the builder, red-cheeked and covered in stone dust
along with Caitlin's father.

'Caitlin. Greer. Aye, Eileen.' Robbie nods at Eileen. 'Glad
I've caught you. I need a word.'

'Pull up a chair.' Caitlin indicates to a chair sat against the
wall. 'What do you need?'

Robbie dusts down the back of his trousers before he sits.
He looks around the room as if he's unsure of where to start.

Finally, he breathes out heavily before blurting out, 'I've
just been discussing this with your father, and he suggested I
speak to you right away. You see, I'm struggling to hold on to my
good men. They say this house is nothing but trouble, only

brings bad luck. And then this happens, then there's a dead body.' The words are hurried, almost as if he's embarrassed by them.

Caitlin frowns. 'What do you mean?'

Robbie looks down at his feet. If he'd had a cap in his hands, he'd have been wringing it. 'There's bin just a few too many accidents. Nothing too serious, but nothing that should've happened.' He looks back up at Caitlin. 'I run a tight ship, I never have accidents on my team. They're a good bunch, safety first and all that. But in the last week, we've had scaffolding poles fall from the roof, tools drop from the top of ladders and narrowly miss my plasterer, bricks have ended up in dangerous places causing one of my men to trip up and cut his upper arms so badly he had to go to the hospital at Golspie and have stitches. A live electric cable came loose, flapping around in the wind close to where the men were working. Okay, nothing major, but these things never happen with my team. I care about my men, and they know it.'

It's true. In the last week I've begun to feel that there's a layer of fear amongst the men working here. There isn't the laughter and joking I would expect on a building site, none of the whistling or singing I heard two weeks ago. There's been an atmosphere of something sinister, an ugly feeling that I cannot get a hold of. Until now I've dismissed it as my overactive imagination.

Caitlin sighs and sits behind her desk. 'I'd like to help, but I'm not sure what I can do. I mean, obviously, the police will take the body away, so that might help, but apart from that...'

'It's simple, I think you just need to stay here. Last week, whilst you were in Glasgow, that's when all this happened.' Robbie whistles through his teeth. 'It sounds stupid I know, but I've spent so much time in this house now, perhaps more time than you have, but whenever you're here, something shifts, something lets go and' – he looks around him as if he's searching for the missing 'something' – 'something here likes you, thinks that you're okay, believes that you're a good thing.' Robbie's face has now become slightly flushed and he looks down at his feet again, the invisible cap wrung to a twisted knot. 'I know what I'm about to say is ridiculous, but I'm going to say it anyway. This house needs you and wants you to be here.'

The father looks at his daughter and smiles. 'A house that needs you. Robbie, you're not the first person to say something like that today.'

Robbie throws Finn Black an irritated glance.

'Robbie Ross, I'd never have taken you for the kind of man who could read a house.' Caitlin smiles as she pushes her hair back off her face and leans towards the fire. 'So, this house has got to you as well.' Her voice is low, kind even, as if she is talking to a patient receiving the all-clear after a long illness.

We all sit silently watching the flames, the mesmerising dancing orange easing the awkwardness in the room.

Absently, Caitlin continues, her eyes stuck on a point in the fire. 'I'm sorry about the accidents, but I'm relieved to hear that no serious harm was done. And you've no need to worry. I'm back for good now.'

TWENTY-ONE

KITTY

Loch More, 1899

Marsh Marigold

'It is good for anaemia and also for epilepsy.
A tincture of the whole plant when administered has proved
successful in cases of epilepsy,
and cures have also resulted when a vase of the flowers has been
placed in the bedroom of the patient.'

Compassionate Herbs *by Mrs C F Leyel*

Kitty shaded her eyes with her hand as she looked across the water. She had a little more time – the boat was still in the distance. Her basket was full and she'd be able to take it to the kitchen before she needed to get down to the jetty.

She walked through the walled garden, quickly picked a few bergamot flowers, ran her hands along the lavender blooms, the smell always making her feel better, and made her way through the gate and down to the house. In the kitchen she found Mrs Lindsay laying out the sandwiches, biscuits and cake. She looked up as she heard Kitty.

'There's a lot of flowers for the cake, you can't possibly be thinking we'll use all of those for decoration,' she said with a smile of amusement.

'No, just a few for the cake. I'm going to make an oil with the rest of them. You were telling me that you had some pain in your thumb joint. If you massage chamomile oil into it, it might help.'

Absently, Mrs Lindsay rubbed her left thumb. 'Aye, I could do with some of that today.' She picked up the cake. 'Would you like to do the decoration?'

'The boat's on its way in. I promised to be down on the jetty when they arrived, so I'd better go. We'll all come and help bring the food and crockery up when we're back.'

Today was the inaugural Ardbray fishing trip.

It was one of those summer days which you want to hold onto for as long as possible, the slight breeze keeping any intense heat at bay, the flawless blue sky seeming to have become more concentrated as if heat evaporation had caused the heightened density of colour. The intensified blue contrasted with the purple hue of the heather and the sporadic alder trees dotted along the loch shores.

But Kitty's appreciation of the perfection of the day was tempered with a nagging and persistent anxiety. As she walked towards the jetty, she could just make out the small boat with three figures on board. Charles, at the stern, appeared to be in charge, guiding Callum whilst he rowed. Flora sat up front, her tiny body tucked into the bow; just her head showing with her white blonde curls blowing across her face.

It was Callum's eighth birthday and he was doing exactly what he'd been asking to do for months; learn to row. But Kitty couldn't help her worries about his epilepsy, the sunny day and his exposure to bright sunlight. She found herself constantly watching the distant boat to make sure nothing untoward was happening, praying nothing would burst their bubble of happiness.

And Charles had done what he said he would. He'd built a boat, he'd spent the time with his son, learning how to restore the old wooden rowing boat that had been rotting away in the stables. Fraser had been requisitioned to supervise; overseeing the planing, sanding, dovetailing, painting and varnishing. And somehow a small miracle had occurred. Over the last three months, Callum's seizures had lessened dramatically. And he'd changed, he'd become a different child. He'd transformed from a moody, sullen, diffident, pale boy, to someone who laughed, ran, played games and whose complexion had a pinkish glow as though there was some inner fire now keeping him warm. The boy who'd been wrapped up in cotton wool had discarded his enforced bindings and been set free, leaping like a young bullock that had suddenly been released after its long winter confinement.

Maybe she could put some of his improved health down to her continual work on his herbal treatments, but she thought there was more to it than that. As Kitty followed the path of the boat, she wondered at the transformation that had occurred in the household, her marriage and her family.

Since her outburst with Charles, there had been a change in his whole demeanour, in the way he approached his wife and his children. He sought her opinion, he insisted that the children eat with them, he no longer disappeared into his study for long periods with the whisky bottle. It was as if he had sloughed off a skin that had never really belonged on him, cast away a decaying, irrelevant layer that had covered the years of inexperience and the need to meet convention. For the first time in her ten-year marriage, she was beginning to think that she could make something of it, perhaps they could become a normal family. Perhaps she could redeem herself, turn her failure into something that could begin to do some good.

Now she admired the boat shimmering in the sunlight, flaunting its meticulous restoration, the new coat of varnish so dazzling she had to shade her eyes with her hand. The grand unveiling had been earlier that afternoon in honour of Callum's birthday. Callum, now relishing his new-found outdoors life, had been forced to wait for the launch and rowing lesson all morning, whilst Charles held a meeting with his solicitor. Throughout the morning her son had had to sit on his hands, stay focussed on his classroom studies and not jump around with excitement under the stern eye of Mrs Mercaut, whilst the door of his father's study remained firmly closed. He was scolded for shovelling his shepherd's pie down during lunch as he watched the nursery door until, finally, his father arrived, full of enthusiasm and ready to teach his son to row.

Fascinated by this new father/son relationship, Kitty had watched as Callum took his father's hand and they'd walked towards the boat house, continual chatter keeping them close, excitement bubbling through his eager face. Previously, Callum had been wary of his father, standing back, keeping silent, waiting for him to speak, shout, perhaps even bellow. Now he had the confidence to initiate a conversation, ask questions, sometimes even tease. Charles had also begun with caution, unsure of how to approach his son, treating him as if he was seriously ill and finding it easier not to get involved, letting his wife take on that responsibility. But she'd seen a shift in his attitude and this morning she'd had to laugh as she'd watched her husband take on the role of teacher in the boat.

'You've caught a crab.'

Callum frowned and looked at the end of one of the oars. 'Where?'

'Your oar.' Charles grinned.

''No, I haven't.'

'Yes, you have.'

'You're silly, we don't get crabs in the loch.'

'We do.' Charles's mock serious face had caught Kitty's eye on the jetty. 'They're special crabs, ones that only come out when you row.'

Callum searched the water again. 'Are they invisible crabs?'

Charles could no longer keep a straight face. 'I'm just teasing.' He laughed. 'Catching a crab means when your oar catches in the water when it shouldn't. It's a mistake every rower makes. Sometimes, it can be so bad you fall in the water. So, you're doing pretty well, by only catching a tiny crab.'

'Did you catch a big crab then when you learned how to row?'

Charles laughed. 'Yes, sometimes the bigger you are, the bigger the crab you catch. I nearly fell in and it was only because Fraser caught me, that I didn't.'

'When did you learn to row? Wasn't it when you were my age?'

'No, I only learned last week, when you were having your lessons with Mrs Mercaut, when you weren't looking.'

Sitting on the bench in the middle of the boat, leaning on both oars, Callum had exclaimed with amazement, 'How did you learn so quickly?'

'You'll see. By the end of the day, you'll be rowing as if you'd been doing it all summer.'

And he'd been right. In the distance, Callum was in charge, gently rowing his father and sister, no crabs in sight.

The boat approached slowly, Callum straining on the oars, concentration spread across his face as he watched each oar in turn, making sure his technique was correct. Flora was leaning over the side of the bow, fascinated by the wake of the boat, her hand trailing the water. Kitty's gaze moved to Charles, leaning back languorously on his elbows, keeping an eye on his son. By his manner she thought Charles relaxed and happy, but as the boat came closer, she noticed how bleak his face was, how drained and haggard he suddenly appeared. He'd lost the pasty, paunchy look he'd developed in the smoke-filled, dark offices of Maclean and Son; three months of stalking, fishing and walking had given him a workman's tan and he was fitter and slimmer than she'd ever seen him. But the stray strands of grey in his once black hair married with the desolate expression gave him a gaunt, aged look that hit Kitty in the throat.

'Mama! Catch the rope.' Flora's shrill voice cut through Kitty's reveries and caught her unawares. Flora threw the painter to her mother. The rope fell short of its mark and fell in to the water as the boat continued to drift towards the jetty. Kitty dropped to her knees and put her hand out to stop the boat.

Charles sat up quickly. 'Well done, you'll be Ship's Mate yet.'

His face was transformed, the change almost as dramatic as that of a chameleon. The old youthful grin had reappeared, and he pushed his ruffled hair aside, a father inordinately proud of his son.

Kitty retrieved the rope from the water and tied it to the jetty. The three sailors climbed out of the boat.

'Compliments to Able Seaman Maclean on his faultless rowing,' Kitty announced.

Callum's whole face beamed and an unadulterated happiness radiated from his enormous smile. Standing beside his father, Kitty was struck by their likeness; youthful enthusiasm spilling out, the hair falling across their faces, determination steeling through their eyes.

'Who wants birthday cake?' Kitty asked.

'Me! Me! Me!' Callum jumped up and down, his hand in the air, shouting as loud as he could. Charles laughed and grabbed his wife around the waist. Before Kitty could acknowledge the fact, he kissed her, kissed her with a lover's gentleness that made her gasp.

'Father, come on.' Callum pulled at his shirtsleeves. 'We want our tea.' Pulling his father away, he put an end to the intimacy of the moment. Both children took a hand each and flanked their father as they walked back down the jetty towards the house.

Charles looked back at his wife, playing the prisoner being dragged off to an unknown fate.

She laughed and felt her eyes prick. Blinking, she wiped her eyes and gave Charles a twisted smile. She looked around her, as if a veil had suddenly been lifted, pulled her shoulders back and followed her family.

The fire flickered, it's deep mound of red ash intense and glowing, keeping the slight cool of the evening at bay. It threw out an orange tint and gave the cavernous drawing room a friendly shimmer, pulling it in a little closer, hinting at cosiness.

Kitty had brought her chaise longue near to the fire and was sitting upright with a heavy book on her lap. Her concentration was so intense she did not notice a spark crack out of the fire and land on the end of the seat, quietly burning a small hole into the fabric. Beside her was a notebook. Occasionally, she would write down a query which she'd later put to her father in a letter. And then she'd stop and look up at Charles, lost in his newspaper, enjoying the silent companionship that had fallen over them like a deep winter blanket of snow. This was her favourite part of the day; a time when the children were in bed and any daily chores were completed, when she could relish the peace and give her attention to reading and studying her own interests.

When she'd first discovered the library at Ardbray and understood how much time she was to spend alone there, she'd quickly created her own ritual of evening solitude, book in hand, mind lost into a world that was ordinarily barred to her. And for ten years of marriage, her husband had kept away from her and the precious library. But now, Charles having returned to live with his family, he wanted to spend the evenings with Kitty. At first she'd been irritated, finding his presence intrusive and she'd been unable to concentrate. She'd felt silly, her reading useless, her medical inquests a folly. But he'd never once raised an eyebrow at her earnest enquiries and kept his thoughts to himself, reading the newspaper and making use of the library for the first time since he'd created it, enjoying his own research into boat building, fishing, shooting, the law. And finally, she realised, their evenings had become comfortably companionable and she hardly noticed he was there.

But tonight, she was distracted and kept studying his face, a question running across her brow. As she watched, he looked up and caught her eye.

'What?' He laughed.

She shook her head. 'Nothing. Just watching you,' she hesitated a moment before continuing, 'and wondering why you stayed away for so long?'

A cloud passed across Charles's face, a glimmer of the despair she'd seen that afternoon reappearing. He folded his newspaper and put it on the table beside him. 'What are you reading?'

Kitty smiled at the change of subject before shutting her book and showing him the spine. 'More anatomy. Still my faithful old book that I've had for years.' She looked at Charles. 'Father said he would try and get hold of an old university entrance exam and let me have a look; perhaps I could even sit the exam.'

There, she'd said it. Suddenly, her heart was beating too fast and her face was burning. Laughing it off, she continued, 'I know you might find it ridiculous, me trying to emulate some sort of medical student.' She put the book on top of her note-book. 'It'll be difficult. I don't have a lot of practical experience.'

She waited for him to laugh, to explode, to say nothing. She had no idea what he would say, except that he would disapprove.

'Why don't you apply to Glasgow Medical School?'

Kitty wanted to laugh. He had to be teasing her.

'You could go. Now that women are already attending; it won't be quite so difficult.'

Part of her wanted to slap him for being so cruel, dangling this carrot in front of her, saying the words she'd wanted to hear for so many years. But she searched his face and could see no malice, no flippancy, only a strange sincerity. She shook her head, a twisted smile on her face.

'Why not? Isn't that what you've always wanted to do?' Embarrassment spread across Charles's face before he contin-ued, 'You could spend the semesters in Glasgow and always return here whenever you needed. I can stay here with the children...'

She stood up and walked over to the fire to warm herself. Looking into the flames, she shook her head again as she spoke. 'If you thought I brought shame on you before, think of the shame of a married woman attending university. They would think I'd disobeyed my husband, I'd be an outcast. There'd be a lot of talk.'

Charles opened his mouth, about to speak, a sheepish reddening spreading over him, but Kitty put her hand up, indi-cating him to stay quiet.

'It's always been a means of escape. You know that. I needed to escape my mother and her marriage plans, and then I wanted to escape our marriage, and your...' She looked down, pulling at the cuff of her cardigan. 'But as soon as the children arrived, I knew that I didn't need to go to university. Studying was my way of proving myself, showing the world that I could achieve something. But now I have achieved something. I have two beautiful children and I think I do a good job at being their mother. I have my garden and my herbarium. I don't need to go to Glasgow, I'm very happy here with you and Callum and Flora. I'd just like to take the exam, just to see if I'd be any good. Just to see if I could have done it.'

Charles leaned forward, elbows on his knees, looking down at his feet.

'Shouldn't we talk about Maclean and Son?'

He said nothing, chewing his bottom lip.

'Charles,' Kitty took a softer tone, 'you've been here for three months, avoiding any conversation about Glasgow, about the business, about what you're going to do. We've been leading the charmed life of a wealthy family, but perhaps it's time to get back to some kind of reality?' She continued riding roughshod over the eggshells she'd avoided for so long. 'Perhaps it's time to look at what our new life should be like, how we're going to fend for ourselves, and be useful.'

It was as if Charles, a large, proud hot air balloon which had been flying through the air at great speed, had suddenly been halted by a vast stake, piercing his outer fabric, causing him to deflate in an instant. He shrivelled and his eyes sunk back into his face, the look of despair Kitty had seen earlier returning.

'I can't go back to Glasgow. There's nothing for me there anymore. Maclean and Son has collapsed and the mills have closed.' He was now staring at the fire, his hair dishevelled and his flickering gaze far beyond the flames.

The stark words hung in the air. The fire spat out embers as the reflection of the flames on his face gave him an unsettling luminosity, orange and ghostly.

'Mr Urquhart gave me the news this morning. The company has failed and with the fraud, they just couldn't survive.' He closed his eyes. 'My father's life's work has gone.' Suddenly, he stood up and started pacing the room.

'What fraud? What do you mean?'

'Thousands missing over the last five to six years. Of course, they assumed it was me. I'd gambled my own fortune away. I was the obvious candidate; I'd lost my money and I was still living the life of a wealthy man. But the information I received this morning, via Urquhart, informed me that the board now believe it's John. There was no apology, no regret for treating me as they did."

Kitty's mouth opened, alarm lighting up her eyes. 'You've been living here for the last three months knowing that the board considered you a thief and a fraudster. Why didn't you tell me?' She had that frantic look of someone who's just uncovered a terrible secret.

Charles shrugged. 'What was the point? How could I win you back if you also thought I was a cheat and a swindler?

'Today's news was such a relief. I feel twenty years younger, as if I've had some debilitating disease that has finally been cured. I feel as if I can move on now, as if we can start our lives again.'

He was back standing beside her at the fire and picked up the fire poker, prodding at the embers. 'I have been so naive. Three months away from it all and I can see it now. I put my wholehearted trust into one of the richest men in Yorkshire, who has done nothing but bleed the business dry.

'And,' – Charles gave Kitty a wry smile – 'just to make this whole sorry scenario worse, the board are letting him get away with it. He's bought their silence. He's paid them off and is now going to make the most of the valuable land. He'll come out of this better than all of us, his reputation intact and he can slope off back to Yorkshire and get on with his own life and forget about his ten-year aberration in Glasgow.'

Kitty's hands were clasped in a tight knot; her bone-white fingers twisting. 'Are you going to let him get away with it? Surely, there's something you can do? Have you confronted him?' The questions came like bullets from a gun, staccato and sharp.

Charles shook his head. 'No, Kitty, I can't bring myself to do that. I'd rather just move on. I've lived in a fantasy world for the past ten years; our marriage has been a sham and my so-called career in industry has been a farce. We've got the opportunity to start again, let's take it.'

Kitty considered her husband. He was right in his self-assessment, but she was complicit too, her naivety matched his, her own lack of action perhaps even outstripped his. She began to let go of some of her indignation.

'When I married you, I had such high hopes of being able to make a difference. I knew that by marrying you, I could never fulfil my dreams of going to university, but I hoped that with my drive and your money, we could do some good.' She looked at her hands. 'Once you'd made your views clear on my helping at the Saltmarket Clinic, I suppose I thought you'd never agree to such things. So,' she said walking away, restlessness and anger beginning to bubble up, 'I didn't dare approach the subject.' She sat down heavily on the window seat cushion.

Charles followed her. 'When I married you, it never occurred to me to tell you how I really felt, I'd become so caught up in the idea of making a good impression with the people around us, I'd forgotten who I was by then, where I'd come from. I had such high hopes of all those connections you had, I simply wanted to be accepted into the world of theatre, parties and ballrooms that I thought you belonged to. But, of course, it didn't take me long to realise you despised that kind of society, that you were more in touch with reality. I quickly understood the real Kitty Gray, the driven idealist who wanted to change the world. And that's whom I fell in love with. Ironically, I thought it was too late to admit to you who I really was.'

He picked up Kitty's hand, cradling it in his own. She could see he was struggling to find any more words, perhaps spent by his confessional, no longer able to express his anguish. She bent her head and tried to catch his eye, but he wouldn't meet her gaze, wiping his face and straightening up, looking out of the window.

'It seems,' she said with a sigh, 'that we're as bad as each other, that we've spent the last ten years misreading each other, misinterpreting each other's signals and have squandered every opportunity we had.'

'Mama! Mama! Please can we take the boat out?' Callum was jumping up and down, unable to contain his excitement. 'I could take Flora out by myself, I know how to row now. And there's no wind, the water's quiet.'

Kitty looked at her son. 'No, you need to wait for your father. He's visiting this morning.' Her husband was on a rare visit to their occasional neighbour, the Duke of Westminster. As far as she was aware, the two hadn't met since the disastrous shooting party ten years previously. They'd heard that he was in Achfary for his annual stag shoot and Charles had felt it was necessary and polite for him to pay a visit to the man who had helped make Ardbray a reality.

Callum's shoulders dropped. 'Please, Mother?' Eyes pleading, body twisting as if this was too important to be so trivially brushed aside.

'No, you mustn't go out on the loch by yourself. It's too dangerous. Why don't you go and see if Fraser needs any help in the walled garden? Have you been to see how your carrots have grown? Perhaps you could pick some for your lunch.' She watched Callum's face fall. 'What about the raspberries? I know you'd like those, could you go and get some for our lunch today?'

Kitty could see that faint interest had begun to needle its way through the excitement of rowing.

'Maybe, if you picked enough, Cook might make some raspberry jam, and then she could use it in a sponge cake. Would you like that?'

She could see that the mention of cake began to push away all thoughts of boats, water and rowing. The wrinkled brow smoothed out, and he turned to look out the window. But Kitty needed to keep up the momentum.

'The thing to do would be to go and find Flora and then both go down to the kitchen and ask Cook for two bowls. See if you can fill the bowls right to the top. You see how quickly you can do that. Then, as soon as you've done that, I'm sure your father will have returned from his visit and then you can go rowing. Does that sound like a good idea?'

Callum didn't stop to agree with his mother. As he ran out the door, she noticed that the dark-blue sailor suit he was wearing was becoming too tight across his shoulders. He was growing so fast with his new-found, outdoor freedom. She made a mental note to speak to Mrs Mercaut as she heard his thundering footsteps disappear up the stairs, shouting for his sister.

Smiling, she returned to her books. She was in the herbarium working on a new design for the herb garden. She'd been having her regular tussle with Fraser over whether she could take over a little more of his vegetable garden, but this time he'd been adamant she could have no more, otherwise they'd be going hungry. So she'd decided to take over other parts of the main garden and was working on ideas for the areas in front of the house, looking at introducing more planting beds and mixing the herbs with some of the flowers. Fraser was already planting roses, just like the monks used to do in their physic gardens, but she was still trying to work out what herbs she wanted to plant up. The white roses would look striking with lavender underpinning them, perhaps some borage, maybe the blue flowers of lungwort. She loved this part; sometimes, the design was more enjoyable than the actual setting out and planting up; she could hole herself up in her favourite room and surround herself with her most precious books, play with designs, draw up ideas, always learning about new plants and new remedies.

A shaft of light fell across the bench and the designs she'd been drawing. Looking out of the window, Kitty watched the shadow of a cloud run up the hill, leaving the grass brightened by the new sun, as if an old skin had been peeled away to leave a shiny new layer.

There was a knock at her door and Kitty looked up to see Eleanor walk in.

'Mr John Hardgrave is here to see you.' Her voice was quiet and uncertain. 'He wanted to see Mr Maclean, but when I told him he was out visiting, he insisted on seeing you.'

Kitty's heart began to beat wildly. 'He's here at Ardbray?' Confusion surged through her as Eleanor nodded.

'I've shown him through to the drawing room.'

Kitty looked around the room, her safe, all enveloping herbarium. This room was like a cocoon to her, this was the room that always made her feel secure, nothing could go wrong here. She wanted to stay and not have to confront Mr Hardgrave. If she'd been in Glasgow, she could have sent him away, telling Eleanor to convey to him that she was not 'at home' or perhaps unwell. But Ardbray was too remote and he'd only wait until Charles's return. She stood up, her body rigid and clasped her hands in front of her to stop the shaking.

In a solemn procession, Kitty followed Eleanor down the stairs and along the corridor towards the drawing room. She felt like a prisoner being escorted to her cell for the first time as if she was only just noticing her surroundings: the Prussian blue carpet, the engravings of hunting scenes on the walls or the light that was approaching them at the end of the corridor. The air seemed to push down on her, stifling and smothering.

They arrived at the door to the drawing room. Kitty looked at Eleanor and took a deep breath. But just as Eleanor was putting her hand on the doorknob to open it, they heard a clattering of footsteps behind them. She turned to see Callum and Flora running at full speed towards them.

'Mama, Mama! We've picked loads of raspberries. Cook's very happy with us. Is Father home? Can we please go out in the boat now?'

Kitty knelt beside her son, her fingers to her lips. 'Your father isn't back yet. I'm afraid you're going to have to wait.'

'Can't you come instead? Please?'

'I have a visitor; I must see to him. But I won't be long, I'm sure.'

'Is it that fat man with messy yellow hair?'

Kitty had to suppress a smile as she pushed her son's hair off his face. 'Yes, that's him, but I'll make sure he goes as soon as possible. Why don't you wait for your father by the boat house? Then you'll be able to see him riding back home along the drive. You could run out and meet him as soon as he arrives.' Kitty quickly looked at the watch pinned to her chest. Surely, Charles was almost home?

Callum could see his prize was getting closer. He grabbed his sister's hand before turning back to his mother and giving her a dazzling smile. 'Come and watch us on the water, will you?'

Standing, Kitty answered, 'Of course.'

And they were gone. Kitty reached out to the door frame for support, bracing herself for the ordeal ahead.

'Mrs Maclean?' Eleanor asked.

Kitty drew her shoulders back and faced the dark wooden door. She glanced at Eleanor and nodded. Watching her maid turn the handle and the double door split in two, walking in and announcing her mistress's arrival, she felt like she was breathing in a tiny enclosed space, her breaths exaggerated, all other noises slightly muffled.

Eleanor defied their guest, omitting her usual bob curtsey and kept her eyes on Kitty as she entered the room. Kitty held herself upright and stiff, her hands clasped in front of her, her eyes darkening as they fell across their guest, a man she hadn't seen in over three years. Eleanor left the room, shutting the door.

'Mr Hardgrave.' Kitty's voice was stilted and cold.

John Hardgrave was admiring the view through the French doors, but turned on hearing her voice, his mop of blond hair flopping over his eyes, a huge, boisterous grin on his face.

'Mrs Maclean!' he exclaimed. 'What an unexpected pleasure.' He picked up her hand and kissed it.

'What a surprise.' Her voice was reedy. 'You have travelled such a long way. We so rarely receive guests at Ardbray.' It was as if she was an automaton, the cordial words appearing as a matter of course.

'To what do we owe this unannounced visit?' She gestured to the chair by the fire, her voice emotionless.

'Of course, of course.' John Hardgrave rubbed his hands together vigorously. 'I've come to see your husband. We have business that we must discuss.' His voice boomed and there was a gloss of excitement in his eyes.

Kitty stared at the eagerness on his face. 'I'm afraid my husband is out visiting this morning. Perhaps I can help. Please, take a seat.' Again, she waved her guest towards the chair. 'But I understood that your business dealings with my husband are over. What could you possibly want from him?' She sat down on the piano stool, upright and alert.

'Perhaps there's been a bit of a misunderstanding. You're absolutely right that the world of Maclean and Son is over, for which I am truly sorry. It must be heartbreaking to see your own father's business ruined, to see everything you have worked for, all your life, come to a graceless end.'

Kitty watched her guest as he spoke. He exuded a deep sincerity that, had she not known him better, she would have been fooled by. His voice was kind and understanding, his small, brown eyes looking at her with an intensity that was disarming. Here was a man who knew how to sell himself and, as he continued to speak, she could see why so many people liked him. He was a master at telling them what they wanted to hear, and she knew how easy it would be to fall under his spell, believe everything that he told her.

'But I've come here with a proposition, an exciting offer. Your husband and I could join forces again, take up the reins of industry and be a force to be reckoned with.'

Kitty frowned; the spell broken. 'Mr Hardgrave. How do you propose my husband could do that? He lost his fortune at the roulette table under your tutelage, his reputation has been ruined by false claims of fraud and you, the man who was responsible for that fraud, now wish to embroil him further in your shady business dealings.'

He blinked, but held her gaze.

Kitty continued, 'You didn't think word of your crimes would reach us out here in our barren wilderness? You don't think that my husband and I share our innermost thoughts?' Her words were barbed and acidic.

For a moment, her unwelcome guest seemed taken aback. 'You don't mince your words, Mrs Maclean.' But, quickly recovering his composure, he stood up and walked over to the window, putting his hands in his trouser pockets, taking his time. 'Perhaps I should wait and talk to your husband. I can see you've only been given one side of the story.'

'My husband received news from the board two days ago informing him that they had hard proof that you are behind the fraud. He has been fully exonerated. It is you, sir, they wish to speak to.' Her jaw was set square.

'They don't need to speak to me, I've dealt with them, it's I who needs to speak to your husband.' His words were patronising, dismissive of the female presence in the room.

'Mr Maclean will not be returning for some time. So, since we have time to kill, perhaps you can fill me in.' She stood, needing to be on the same level as her guest.

He suddenly smiled that charming, disarming smile. 'Why not? I need a distraction. God knows there's been little to keep me amused over the last few months, waiting for something of interest to happen.' The voice had changed. Again, he was the great storyteller, the centre of attention at a party, his eyes sparkling, his chest puffed out, ready to entertain.

'I'm not sure whether I've told you this before. Perhaps there are parts of my story you are already aware of.'

Kitty looked down at her hands, impatience bubbling inside her. But she kept quiet whilst Hardgrave warmed to his subject.

'You see, I was born into industry. My whole upbringing has been about achieving in the family firm. I am the only son, the heir apparent. My life is mapped out before me; I will have it all handed to me on a plate. But, in truth Mrs Maclean, it bores me. I am not interested in running the firm my father founded, when my father will insist on overseeing every minute detail until the day he dies. I wanted to do something for myself, achieve something on my own terms, be a knight in shining armour and save an ailing firm. You see, Mrs Maclean, I am a very wealthy man. I've always thought I should put that money to good use, make the world a better place with it.'

Kitty frowned.

'I can see you're confused. Put simply, I wanted to invest in a failing company and bring it back to its former glory.'

'How does saving a cotton-spinning firm make the world a better place?'

'I've saved hundreds of jobs. I've stopped families from falling into extreme poverty.'

Kitty blinked. 'But you haven't.'

'Ah, but I had. When I joined, I helped shore up the firm. My investment prevented Maclean and Son from going under. We expanded, we were able to employ more people.'

'What changed?'

'You did.'

The atmosphere in the room became thick as Kitty watched her guest change from the witty storyteller to a moody child.

'Women don't reject me, Mrs Maclean.' His chin began to wobble, his face darken. 'You were lucky that I chose you. I only pick the cream of the crop. You should have been flattered that I deemed to come down to your level. I can have anyone, any woman I want. But I wanted you, and you ignored me. I did my best to be nice to you, woo you, make you see my best side. I made sure you and your husband were invited to the best of the parties, the greatest balls, had the best seats at the theatre. I even looked after that dullard whilst you were up here, at Ardbray, just so that he would give you a good account of me. And then that day at your sister's wedding, when you so rudely put me down, you snubbed me, you denied me my carnal rights.' He paused, still pouting like a spoilt child who has had his pudding taken away. 'Nobody does that to John Hardgrave.'

'You mean you set out to ruin my husband because I wouldn't accept your advances. I wouldn't become another notch on your bedpost.' She almost wanted to spit. 'How self-indulgent.'

'Yes,' he said thoughtfully, 'you're right. I indulged myself in a little game of retribution. Since you and your so-called sick child had been sent away to hide from the rest of the world, I wasn't able to exact my revenge on you. Well, not directly anyway. You'd hurt my pride and I needed to do something to restore it. The next best thing was to take it out on your husband. You see, I was in need of some entertainment.'

'No,' Kitty interrupted, squaring up to her adversary. 'You can't possibly have wreaked that kind of havoc just because I rejected your advances. Just because I wouldn't be taken to your bed. No, there has to be more to it than that.' The colour was running high in her cheeks and her heart was racing again.

A maddeningly supercilious smile appeared. 'Well, well. It's true. Your intelligence outstrips that of the majority of your sex.'

'Don't patronise me, Mr Hardgrave.' She clenched her fists as she felt the anger rising in her like a pan of water boiling over.

He looked at her, amusement spreading across his whole demeanour. Turning to the window, with his hands behind his back, he began.

'The truth is, your husband and I should never have gone into business together. This is something I only realised after several years of working with him. Neither of us completely understood what we were doing, neither of us was cut out for the world of industry.

'Of course, at the start, I had great admiration for him. Your husband was of high standing and he had a long-held reputation for getting business done. I was flattered to be brought in. But the board never warmed to me, never quite trusted me. Your husband, on the other hand, trusted me as a child would.

'What a boost to my ego! We went on a spending spree, buying up failing mills at cheap prices; we bought finishing companies so that we could control the whole process from bale to bolt. We had this magnificent portfolio of companies. It was exciting and terrifying all at the same time.'

He sighed heavily, rocking back and forth on the balls of his feet, his eyes fixed on a point far in the distance.

'We treated it like a game, and for a while, it seemed that we could play that game well; we were getting away with it.

'But, of course, several years in it became clear to me that we were going to trip up or, more likely, completely fail. It had become a precarious game that we were losing, and we were not going to come out of it well.

'Then you rejected me at your sister's wedding. You insulted me by failing to understand my needs. That was when I began to reassess my reasons for being in Glasgow, my reasons for being at Maclean and Son.

'I was there to make money, to do well, to gain a good reputation in business, show my father that I could win. But I was no longer doing any of these things and if I wasn't careful, I, along with your husband, was going to look a fool. Of course, I realised that I had no allegiance to your husband. I didn't need to save him. But I wasn't going to go down with him; I didn't want to lose face. I wasn't going to let the last seven years of my life seem like a waste. It was down to the survival of the fittest and I was determined to be the fittest.

'And that's when I realised how simple it would be. Running a business is boring, it's not something that I do instinctively, but ruining a business, slowly and carefully, I've discovered that's something I rather enjoy doing.

'It's taken a long time, but it gave me exactly the focus I needed. The board couldn't see it coming and, of course, Charles doesn't have the intelligence, he's just happy to do as he's told. It was like pulling a bull along by its nose ring. It was almost too easy.' He gave a snort of a laugh, looking back at Kitty. 'Firstly, I led your husband to the gambling tables. That was the most fun part. Watching someone lose virtually every penny they have, helping them on their way. I found it fascinating, seeing the effect it had, how far he went to keep it a secret. It was almost like an anthropological study of how humans behave in difficult circumstances; I should write a book about it.'

There was an unnatural silence in the house. Kitty couldn't hear the usual distant noises from the kitchen or the children running in the garden. It was as though all movement had been suspended.

'And then, when I could see that your husband was on the path of no return, I began the fraud. Again, that was just too easy. What you need to understand is that gentlemen work on a high degree of trust, they rarely believe you're going to steal, not when you're dressed in a hand-made suit and shoes imported from Italy. Slowly, as your husband sank deeper and deeper into debt, I siphoned larger and larger sums of money from the company. Eventually, the board had to do something and naturally they put the two together; blaming Charles was the inevitable assumption.'

'Let me get this straight. You ruined my husband because you didn't want to look like a failure to your father?' Kitty was seething inside.

'Well,' – John Hardgrave rubbed his chin – 'I've never quite looked at it like that...'

'Why have you come here today?' she interrupted, unable to listen to anymore. 'Surely, you've done your damage, surely, there's nothing left to achieve? You've made sure my husband has lost all his money, you've ruined his reputation. What else is there to take?'

John Hardgrave smiled and looked around the room. 'This is what I came for. This house.' He turned back to her. 'Did you know that this house has a bit of a reputation? It seems there's a mystery about it that's making it famous. The enigmatic house hidden away in the Highlands and the family who've been entombed in it: the lunatic child secreted away from the world, the wife exiled for bad behaviour, the husband who lost all his money. You can imagine the women gossiping, it's a dream for them. And in the men's clubs, they talk of nothing else.'

Carefully, he pushed his coattails back and put his hands back in his pockets. Standing squarely, he continued, 'I got bored of the gossip and decided to come and find out for myself.' His blond hair had flopped across his face, taking the sting out of his snide tone.

'How is it that you still manage to afford to live here? Surely, you've needed to sell this to fund your lifestyle? You have no money; this house must be mortgaged down to the very last penny.'

'Mr Hardgrave, you aren't as clever as you think.' A smile began to spread across Kitty's face and, unexpectedly, she had to suppress a nervous snigger. 'Blinded by your own greed, Mr Hardgrave. Ardbray does not belong to my husband.'

'That cannot be true.' A shadow crossed his face, his voice high and rigid. 'Your husband built Ardbray. Who else could possibly own it? The bank?'

'I do.' Kitty couldn't help the triumphant tone in her voice.

A snarl emitted from across the room. 'How can that be? You're the wife. Everything you own belongs to your husband. That's the law.' His voice grew louder as he coughed out the words.

Kitty clasped her hands in front of her. 'Oh dear, Mr Hardgrave. You're very badly informed. You should know that the law changed some time ago and that anything a woman owns is her own, even when she marries.'

'But... you didn't own Ardbray when you married,' he spluttered, moving towards her, his movements unsure.

'My husband gave it to me. If you look at the deeds, they're in my name.' Kitty's eyes brightened, confidence beginning to creep in. She watched his confusion as he took a handkerchief from his pocket and wiped his sweating forehead. But suddenly his expression changed, an unnerving smile exploding across his face.

'But, no matter. Ardbray would just be another financial possession. I've just thought of something far better.'

To Kitty, everything seemed to slow down, but the clarity was immediate. She understood what he intended to do. The leer on his face, the smirk made it all too clear. But she was riveted to the spot, unable to move; her limbs were leaden, her voice silent. She felt as if she was watching from above when he took her. Surprisingly, he took her gently, his arm around her waist, pressing himself into her.

'This time I think I have the right to take what should be mine. You know I spent so much time courting you, looking out for you, saving you when others were ready to dismiss you. But I've never had my reward.' He looked over every inch of her face. 'You see you don't sully a woman, it isn't the done thing. You need to persuade them, you need to make sure they want you too.' He hesitated, considering his words as if he was worried someone was listening to his confession. 'Take the women in the mills.'

Kitty said nothing, trying to control her breathing.

'You'll remember from your visit, the mills are not a place for a lady; filthy, hot, unbearable places, especially in the summer. You see we have to maintain a high heat when we are spinning the yarn, especially the fine yarn.' He loosened his grip a little on Kitty as he warmed to his story, satisfaction flooding his face. 'And we always employ young women because we can pay them less. These are the women I like to watch. To ensure the heat doesn't escape, there is no ventilation in the mill. It's so hot they have to strip to their underwear.' He lingered over the last word as if it was some delicious morsel to be savoured. 'And if they're piecing, then... well, let's just say they don't like the men watching. It's rather...' he searched for the correct expression '... suggestive.

'But I was a good boy. I was restrained and held myself back. It would have been too easy to have had one of them, as many of them as I wanted. But it would have been too demeaning. And it's been the same with you. I held back, I played the gentleman. I tried to pursue you by playing the hero in your story, show you that Charles was the villain. And all that time I waited for you to change your mind. But,' – he tightened his grasp on her – 'it's evident that my powers of persuasion were not enough. So perhaps I should just let my instinct take over, do the thing I've been wanting to do for years.'

Adrenaline finally began to kick in, frantically Kitty began her fight back.

'What makes you think you'll be able to do it? What makes you think you have the strength, the ability even?' she taunted and as she spoke, she thrashed against him, using all her strength and managed to loosen his grip, giving her the opportunity she'd been looking for. Ripping herself away from his hold, she ran across the room, heading for the door. But Hardgrave was quicker than his stout body would suggest and he immediately caught her, snatching her towards him, pulling her close again.

'Let's not be difficult, Mrs Maclean.' His voice was dark, his eyes resolute.

They were standing by the sofa table. The table where Charles had stood a few weeks earlier, on the first day of his return to Ardbray, telling Kitty that he didn't need the ashtray anymore; the big, glass, ugly ashtray that had sat on the sofa table for years, a symbol of all he hated in his life. And then he'd put it down, perhaps intending to take it to Mrs Lindsay the next day for storage. But for some reason, it had never been moved, even when the room had been cleaned. Most likely he'd forgotten to tell their housekeeper. Kitty could now feel the ashtray digging into her thigh as Hardgrave pushed her against the table. With her free hand, she felt for it. She could feel its jagged edges, the pointed tips of sharp glass. She hated how ostentatious it was and how its hard features reminded her of the male-dominated world that she belonged to. All at once her rage erupted like a volcano. Loathing and disgust spewed out as Hardgrave began to pull at her blouse, ripping the buttons with one hand and plunging his face into her chest. As the clammy rolls of skin under his chin wobbled against her breast, repugnance threatened to overwhelm her, but just as she'd got a hold of the ashtray, her hand was knocked away and he picked her up.

Holding her in his arms, his leering face studied her. 'Let's do this a little more comfortably, shall we?'

He almost threw her onto the sofa and began pulling her skirts up, ripping her underwear. Kitty yelled; a strangled, anguished cry. His anger sprang back and he slapped her across the cheek.

'Let's not disturb the servants, shall we? We have important business to do.' He slapped her again and with sudden impatience, he forced himself on top of her.

She could feel his fat stomach pressing into her and the weight of his body bearing down. His thrusting hips and his cold hardness were pushing against her as he grabbed her face and kissed her, jamming his tongue into her mouth.

The taste of cigars and a greasy hotel breakfast triggered a wave of nauseous fury as she renewed her fight, trying to roll from side to side to loosen his grip. But he was too strong, too heavy; he had her pinned to the sofa.

Sweat had gathered on his forehead and the foppish blond hair fell across his eyes, he suddenly stopped and sat up, starting to undo his trouser buttons with one hand. With the other he held Kitty's shoulder down. With a fascinated horror, she found herself watching the hand trying to undo his trouser buttons. The small, fat, sausage-like fingers struggling with the fastenings, the perfectly groomed fingernails, the soft flesh getting caught in the bindings. For years after, the sight of anyone, man or woman, with pudgy hands would make her feel queasy. This was the moment, the detail, she wouldn't be able to forget.

Eventually, she closed her eyes, no longer able to fight his overwhelming force and turned her face away, her strength diminishing as the realisation that she was going to lose this fight hit her.

But without warning, there was a dull thud, like the sound of the children's football landing on the leather armchair, and Hardgrave collapsed forward onto her, heavy and lifeless. Kitty drew a sharp intake of breath as his face landed straight onto her own, his eyes staring, no longer menacing, just hollow and surprised. His weight was suffocating, but, within a moment, his grasp on her loosened and, without emitting a sound, not even a final breath, he fell in an awkward and ungainly manner to the floor.

Kitty looked up to see Eleanor holding the glass ashtray in one hand, the bottom of it covered with a smear of blood and a single, long, blond hair.

She sat up hurriedly, looking back down at the body in front of her. A large pool of dark blood had begun to spread across the floor, seeping into the cracks between the floorboards. Bile began to rise up, nausea flooding her body, and Kitty dropped to her knees, coughing and retching, her whole body convulsing.

Eleanor dropped the ashtray, the solid glass giving an impressive smack as it hit the floor.

'Ya git all ya deserve, ya big scunner.' Vitriol exploded from Eleanor, her unexpected heavy accent difficult to understand.

Hurried footsteps could be heard coming towards the room and both women looked in the direction of the door. Charles rushed through the doorway and skidded to a halt just in front of the pool of blood.

'What...?' He was out of breath. Bending down, he looked closer at the body. 'Hardgrave?' And then he turned to Kitty with questioning eyes and then towards Eleanor.

Kitty got up off her knees with slow, deliberate movements. She wiped her face, sniffing away tears. 'He attacked me.' She hesitated, trying to find the right words. 'I...' She closed her eyes, doing her best to control her breathing. 'I had to stop him,' she finally whispered.

Eleanor gave her a sharp look.

'He came here to see you. He wanted the house, he wanted me, he...' she took a deep breath, panic beginning to rise '... he just wanted what he couldn't have.' She turned away as she began gulping for air.

Charles turned to Eleanor.

'Sir, it's...' She closed her eyes. 'I was bringing the tea when I heard Mrs Maclean cry out so I came to see what had happened.' Her voice was flat with no emotion.

Again, they could hear footsteps coming towards them, the slower, more deliberate steps of Mrs Lindsay. Kitty felt an assured calm at the familiar sounds of the composed house-keeper. All three turned towards the door as Mrs Lindsay entered the room. She stared at the body and then, in turn, at each one of them.

It was as though Mrs Lindsay understood the situation immediately. She took in the dishevelled and half-dressed state of Kitty and then her eyes moved to the hardened face of Eleanor. She took a step towards the body of John Hardgrave, legs awkwardly splayed, trousers undone, blood still seeping from the gash in his head. Her eyes moved towards the glass ashtray and then to Charles, useless in his paralysis, only able to stand on the sidelines and watch. A few days later, after all the drama and horror had begun to subside, as Kitty, inevitably, ran through the events to see if she could have done anything differently, she would remember the tiniest flicker of contempt passing across Mrs Lindsay's face.

'Eleanor, would you find Fraser?' Mrs Lindsay moved into gear. 'He's digging the rose beds out the front. And then get Stuart from the stables, Fraser will need his help. Mrs Maclean, we'll need some old sheets to wrap the body in. Bring them to the kitchen and we'll meet Fraser and Stuart there. Mr

Maclean, you'll need to find the children and keep them occupied whilst we remove the body and clear up in here.'

It was as though she was briefing the staff to prepare for a house party. Only a slight quiver in her voice gave a clue to the type of situation she was organising.

She continued, 'I'll deal with the coachman, he's from Lairg. There's nothing a few guineas won't do to keep him quiet. Once I've finished wi' him, I'll come back and help move the body.' She started to chivvy them along. 'Let's get this done quickly so the children will nae ken and before anyone comes looking for him.'

Kitty, like a wind-up toy, unable to think for herself, went to the laundry room and looked for the oldest sheets she could find. Carefully, she took them to the kitchen, the swish of her skirts, as she walked along the corridors, bringing her a surprising calm.

As she put the sheets onto the kitchen table, Fraser walked in with Stuart, the stable boy. At seventeen, he was stocky, with a rugged face and enormous hands. He loved the horses and was rarely outside of the stables, preferring the horses to human company. He tipped his cap at Kitty, his eyes wide and seemed unable to speak. Kitty couldn't tell whether he was terrified of her or whether he already fully understood the job he was about to take part in.

Fraser grabbed the sheets, but just as he was about to leave the room, he hesitated and looked about him. Shuffling his feet, he stuttered, 'Ma'am, will you be—?'

Kitty interrupted him with her smile. 'It's all right, Fraser. I'll be fine here. I'm sure Mrs Lindsay will be along in a moment.'

As they left, Kitty absently sat down on the chair at the head of the kitchen table, usually Mrs Lindsay's chair, never used by anyone else. She began to feel cold. As she rubbed her arms, images of John Hardgrave on top of her, ripping her clothes, forcing himself onto her, began to pierce her thoughts. Flashes of his dark eyes and the way those small, fleshy hands struggled with his trouser buttons rushed at her. Revulsion coursed through her and she began to shake violently. She closed her eyes and could only see the bottom of the ashtray and the long, blond hair clinging to it.

'Sweet tea. Tha's what you need.' Mrs Lindsay bustled up to the range and put the kettle on. 'It'll be the shock. Tha's what does it. Your body's grinding to a halt. But hear me. You know this already.'

She pulled a small tin teapot from the dresser and dropped in two spoonfuls of tea leaves. 'Strong and sweet tea will help. And cake.'

Without hesitation, she brought ginger cake to the table and in one swift move cut a slice and placed it on the plate in front of Kitty.

'Eat up, hen.' She placed a hand on Kitty's arm. 'You're going tae need your strength over the next few days. There'll be questions and maybe even the police. I'll see to it that the place is spotless, Fraser's seeing to the body and we'll not have any trouble from that coachman. I know too many of his own misdemeanours.' She sniffed at the last word.

Kitty bit into Mrs Lindsay's sticky ginger cake. This was, to Kitty, the definition of home and security. As she swallowed, it was as though a soothing medicine was surging through her veins.

'He tried to...' She took a deep breath, gathering her strength. 'He tried to...' She couldn't say the word. '...punish me because I wouldn't become his mistress,' she said, pushing cake around the plate. 'He's a man who likes to get his own way, and since I wasn't going to give him what he wanted, he decided to take matters into his own hands.' She put her elbows on the table and her head in her hands.

Mrs Lindsay brought the teapot and cups to the table. She sat down next to Kitty.

'Aye. The man was arrogant, thought the world would come to his beck an' call.' She leaned across the table and pulled the sugar bowl towards her. She put three spoons of sugar into Kitty's cup before pouring the tea. 'The world will be a better place without him. He cannae harm you anymore. You're free of him and of Maclean and Son. Now you can enjoy your husband and the children and Ardbray.'

Suddenly, Kitty sat up. 'The children!'

'Ah hen, don't fuss. Mr Maclean will be keeping them busy, keeping them away from the house. Let him do his job, let him play his part in this sorry mess.'

Kitty picked up her tea. The trauma of the morning's events, the warming effect of the sweet tea and the slight acerbic nature of Mrs Lindsay's words suddenly opened a steel door and she found herself letting go of all her ten years of upset, mistrust and angst, ten years of frustration and anxiety, insecurity and failure. For half an hour, Kitty disgorged the rot. Mrs Lindsay let her keep going, perhaps realising that this was what she needed, perhaps understanding that these thoughts had been kept caged up for too long.

'Oh, but listen to me,' Kitty finally said, rolling her eyes and crossing her arms as if she was cold. 'At least my husband isn't a bully or a manipulator. My sister has put up with much worse than me, Don't let me moan about my lack of independence or fulfilment ever again, Mrs Lindsay. I may never see Eva again, but maybe I can learn from her, make myself as strong as she is.'

Mrs Lindsay didn't blink, didn't shift in her chair, just kept her gaze on Kitty, her face encouraging her to continue. It was as if the Upstairs had merged with the Downstairs and the two had, somehow, met in the middle.

Suddenly, Kitty shuddered, a flash of the image of John Hardgrave collapsed on the drawing room floor. With a laboured sigh, she rubbed her hands over her face and pulled herself upright.

'I should see to the children.' She stood up, breathing in deeply. 'I can't think where Charles has got to with them. I'll go and find them.'

'Aye, you go, I'll be looking to see how Fraser's doing.'

But as Mrs Lindsay stood up, there was a shout from the front of the house. Kitty gave the housekeeper a sharp look and turned to follow the sound.

As Kitty hurried through the front door onto the main steps, she could see a horse and rider skidding to a halt on the main drive. Fraser caught the reins and helped to steady the horse. The animal was blowing heavily through its nostrils as the man began to speak.

'It's Miss Flora and Master Callum. They're on the beach across the loch. You must come.'

A chill spread across Kitty. The sounds around her began to dampen and every movement slowed down. She could see Fraser turn and look at her. He let go of the horse and walked over. He was talking to her, but she couldn't understand. She felt as if there was a waterfall in her head, the water rushing over her, cold and stifling. She felt Fraser take her arm and move her towards the horse, now standing by the mounting block. Fraser helped her onto the block and steadied the horse showing her that she needed to get behind the rider. Kitty looked at Fraser unable to comprehend. She began to shiver involuntarily. Fraser shook her, shouting at her, but she still couldn't understand. Eventually, Fraser picked her up and put her onto the back of the horse. He took her hands and made her put them around the waist of the rider. She could feel the warmth of the man permeate through her dress, but it did nothing to control the shivering.

As they began to ride away, Kitty saw Stuart bring two horses from the stable and both he and Fraser jumped on to follow them. They quickly overtook the more tired horse and Kitty's rider gave hurried instructions. Her head felt like wool, all sounds muted. She tightened her grip, struggling not to slip off. At the head of the loch, they turned to ride down the other side. Realisation dawned on her, of course, the small beach halfway down the loch. A favourite stop on their boat trips, a good place for sandwiches and cake before heading back home. They'd even been swimming there a few days earlier.

Her foggy head began to clear. She looked over the rider's shoulder where she could see the stark yellow patch of sand in the distance. There were two black dots on the beach, but she couldn't see the boat, and where was the third person?

As the horse drew nearer, the dots became bodies, laid out on the sand. Neatly laid, hands by their sides, hair brushed on their faces. Her two children, blue lips, porcelain skin, soaked and still. The breath left her. She couldn't hold on to the rider and horse any longer as it began to slow down. She slid off, falling over and rolling onto the grass. Quickly, she picked herself up and ran over to the children. Fraser was already there, checking their pulses.

Kitty skidded to a halt and slid down beside Callum. She felt his skin, cold and clammy, checking his pulse also. Quickly, she sat him up and started rubbing his back.

'Do what I'm doing. Warming them up might help.' Vigorously she continued the rubbing. 'We need to try and get any water out of their lungs. I've read that if you get their head below their feet that might help.' She looked at Callum and started rubbing his chest and then his arms. 'Come on, Callum.'

Fraser watched Kitty.

'Please, Fraser, keep her warm. Why don't you try and pick her up? Maybe hang her over her feet?' Her voice was rising, the panic taking over. 'Come on, Callum.' She tried to pick him up and bend him double, starting to whack him on the back. She struggled with the weight. 'Where is Charles? I need his help.'

She looked around frantically, still rubbing Callum's back. 'You,' she said, pointing to the man who had ridden her to the beach, 'help me. Take my son and hold him upside down.'

The man looked at Fraser and then stumbled towards Kitty.

'Here, take his feet and hold him up in the air.' She held up her son. 'Now, we have to do this fast.'

The man did as he was told, bewilderment on his face.

'Fraser, do the same for Flora.' She clapped Callum on the back as he swung upside down. 'Come on, Callum, cough up the water.' She continued slapping him on the back and then turned to Flora and did the same for her.

Nothing happened. No cough, no splutter. Eventually, Kitty stopped and sank to the ground. Fraser and the horse rider carefully put their charges down on the sand. Respectfully, they laid them on their backs and put their arms by their sides.

Kitty's face was covered in streaming tears. Her breaths became coughs and sobs rolled together. She looked about her, seeing nothing, wiping the tears from her cheeks, her nose. 'Where's Charles? Where's the boat?'

TWENTY-TWO

GREER

Loch More, 2004

Camomile

*'The flowers make a lovely golden dye for the hair and the oil is
much used in hair lotions of all kinds.
It has a comforting effect on the head and on the brain.'*

Herbal Delights *by Mrs C F Leyel*

On the coffee table in front of us is a large tray holding three
steaming cups of coffee, a plate of bagels, cream cheese, lemon
wedges, three small stacks of smoked salmon and a hefty pepper
grinder. They're all laid out as if ready to be photographed.

It's our usual Monday morning meeting. Ever since Eileen
joined us six weeks ago, the three of us go over what's needed
for the coming week. Every time we do this, Caitlin makes us
eat: pancakes, breakfast muffins, banana bread, croque

monsieur and even her own granola. We're her breakfast guinea pigs and she's building her breakfast menu around our level of approval. Of course, we always approve. I have yet to come across a bad dish of food made by Caitlin Black.

Caitlin is sitting across from me. She's full of Monday morning energy, the exhaustion has abated and she can hardly sit still, her foot jiggling and she's fiddling with the button on her cardigan.

'We can start with some good news,' she says. 'The police have wound up their investigation. They've hit a brick wall and don't have the manpower to continue looking into the death of a one-hundred-year-old body. Inspector Falkirk says he's fairly certain it's John Hardgrave, but they haven't been able to find any living relative to confirm the DNA.'

Work on the house had to come to a halt for a few days whilst the police trawled through the house, looking for evidence. They found traces of blood in the drawing room, but they were too deterioriated to be of any use. I breathe an inward sigh of relief. Kitty and Eleanor's secret can stay that way. I remain quiet whilst Eileen whistles through her teeth.

'To celebrate we're sampling local suppliers of smoked salmon, and I thought I'd make some bagels to go with it,' Caitlin announces proudly.

I can feel a food lecture coming on. She has such a passion for her food that she can't help herself. Frankly, I'm not in the mood. I know the smoked salmon will be delicious, and I'm sure the bagels will be fine, but I had a cooked breakfast at six o'clock this morning and I've got too much work to do to hang around chatting about the nuances of smoked salmon.

'I thought you were a vegetarian,' I declare, peering at the piles of fish in front of me.

'I'm afraid I just can't resist it,' she says, giving me a sheepish grin. 'Most vegetarians struggle with not eating bacon. But I'm a veggie because I don't like the smell or the texture of meat. It makes me retch, but fish is a different thing, especially smoked salmon. I just crave that smoky taste. I have no ability to say no if it's on offer.' She hands us each a plate. 'Please, help yourself.'

She proceeds to slather a half-bagel with cream cheese, carefully placing a few strips of smoked salmon over the top before squeezing some lemon and cracking black pepper over the top. The colours are mesmerising: the pinkie-orange of the salmon, so bright against the stark white of the cream cheese, liberally covered with the black dots of the freshly milled pepper, the picture framed by the dark tan of the outside crust of the bagel.

She brings the bagel up to her nose and breathes in deeply.

'What I love about this salmon is the smokiness. I could bore you about the differences between smoked salmon and the lox you get in New York, about the religion of Sunday brunch in Manhattan, but I'm just going to take a bite instead, I'm afraid I can't wait any longer.'

As she takes a bite, she closes her eyes and chews slowly. Eileen and I look at each other, I raise my eyebrow.

'Oh, I've missed that.' She opens her eyes and puts the bagel down on the plate. 'I don't remember enjoying a bagel that much since...' She stops and looks back at us. There are tears in her eyes.

Eileen leans towards her. 'Are you all right?'

Caitlin just nods, wiping the tears from her eyes. Finally, she gives us a crooked smile.

'I'm sorry if I haven't been quite honest with you. I've realised that it's about time I told you the truth, the reason that I'm here.' She looks at the two of us and sighs. 'When I first came here, I was still a bit of a mess. There was a lot I still didn't want to face up to; I just wanted to bury myself away from my old life. I wanted to forget about what had happened, about the happy life I'd led, about the prescription drugs I'd taken, the alcohol I'd drunk, the people I'd upset.' She hesitates. 'I didn't want to talk about my old life and my beautiful daughter who'd died.'

A thick silence descends on the room. I'm holding my breath, waiting for her story to unfold.

Suddenly, Caitlin breaks the heavy quietness with a nervous laugh. 'I'm sorry. I don't mean to sound so dramatic.' She runs her hand through her wild, dark curls and takes a deep breath, as if she's about to dive into a cold sea from a high cliff. 'Food always has the same effect on me that alcohol does on others; it loosens my tongue.' She puts a hand, splayed out, on her chest. 'I apologise, I've kept myself to myself and you both have been so patient. I've never told you about everything that happened before my life at Ardbray. Let me start from the beginning, then, perhaps, you'll understand me a bit better.' She takes a long sip of coffee to ready herself.

'I come from a very high-achieving family, but I'm the black sheep, the odd one out. It took me years to find what it was that I wanted to do, I struggled in school, I dropped out of college and, to my mother's fury, I went travelling.

'Two years away from the hard and fast commercialism of New York and that constant familial pressure, helped me realise what I'm good at. I wanted to make people's day just that little bit better and what better way to do it than to feed them? So, I started up The Bagel Bar. Front of house was tiny, there was only room for a counter, where I'd serve from, and a high bar with two stools at the window, but we had a big kitchen out the back where Nathan Cohen, my chef, baked the best bagels in New York. It wasn't long before we had lines out the shop and along the street, especially at the weekend. Soon we had to move premises, finding a place just around the corner, big enough to seat thirty people and, of course, a bigger kitchen so Nathan could expand his repertoire. It turns out he's almost as good at baking sourdough as he is at making bagels. We opened at seven in the morning and closed at three in the afternoon. It was my dream come true. Everything I loved all in one place: great food, great people to work with, wonderful customers and we were making money.

'And then I got pregnant. I had a holiday fling with someone who was so incompatible with me it's hard to imagine what I was thinking.' She shrugs her shoulders. 'It was fun for a week or two and then I callously flew home and never contacted him again, not even when I discovered I was pregnant. I've never told him that he had a daughter. Rosie Grace Black, born on June second, 1996.'

I feel a little sick as I look into my coffee.

'Why didn't you tell him?' Eileen asks gently.

Caitlin bites the inside of her cheek. 'We were so unsuited, I just thought it would be easier for both of us if he didn't know. I didn't need any maintenance money; I could easily afford to have a child.' She picks a piece of fluff off the sleeve of her jumper. 'I know it was selfish.'

'Not even after...?' Eileen cannot say the words.

'What would have been the point? There was no reason to destroy someone else's life too.'

Caitlin has been living at Ardbray for over nine months and it's taken her this long to let us in, to trust us enough to know her worst secret. I never wanted my own children; how can I possibly imagine what it's like to lose one? I live in a house where children died, and we let Caitlin move here and be surrounded by those children. The nausea rises again and I have to put my coffee on the table.

'So, what happened?' Eileen asks what I am incapable of asking.

'Rosie became the centre of my life. She slotted straight into my world at The Bagel Bar. At first, she lived in a papoose on my front, then she moved into a backpack. The customers loved her, Nathan loved her and she loved her mollycoddled little world of happy, well-fed customers. When she got a bit bigger, we put a playpen in the shop. She was a very content little child, happy with her toys and happy to talk to the customers.' She pauses. 'And then, suddenly, she was old enough to go to school. I found that hard. She'd been with me virtually twenty-four hours a day for the last five years, and overnight, there was something missing in the restaurant; her happy face was only there at weekends.'

She takes a deep breath. 'Three months into school Rosie got the flu. She was off school for a couple of days. The day she went back I was in a rush; I had an early meeting and I dropped her at Breakfast Club. She'd been a bit quiet, said she had a bit of a headache. But I dismissed it, thought she was playing up. I ran off to my meeting. An hour later, I got a call from the school. I needed to come and get Rosie; she wasn't very well. She had a very high temperature, and she said her head hurt. When I got to school, I was greeted by an agitated secretary. She told me to take her to the hospital straight away; she was worried it was meningitis.'

She closes her eyes and bites her lip. 'She was right. It was meningitis. But I didn't believe her. I thought she was overreacting. It was just the tail end of her flu. I took Rosie home, but by the time I'd got her out of the elevator, she'd developed a rash and said her neck hurt. I quickly realised my mistake and turned right around. I bundled her in the car. I drove like someone possessed. But I was too late. I didn't drive fast enough, I didn't get there in time. They tried, oh those doctors tried. But she died. November twenty-fifth, 2001, my little Rosie died.'

She looks at us, her eyes are bright and she gives us a flat-lipped smile, then gets up and walks over to the window. 'If I'd listened to the school secretary, Rosie just might still be alive.'

Both Eileen and I shift uncomfortably in our seats.

'That was it. My world fell apart. Nothing was ever going to be the same again. I fell off a cliff. Alcohol and prescription drugs became my food. I stayed away from The Bagel Bar; I couldn't stand to be there any more, it reminded me too much of what I'd lost. For five months, I couldn't get out of this high-sided pit of despair; I didn't wash, I didn't leave my apartment, I didn't eat.

'Eventually, Jim rescued me. He arrived at my apartment, threw me into the shower, packed my bags and drove me to a rehab centre in Connecticut. A month there brought me to my senses and I began to climb out of the pit. My brother was clever, though. Our mother had been ill for some time and it was clear she was probably going to die within a few months. He picked me up from the rehab centre and took me to my mother's house in the Hamptons, he fired the carer and took my car keys away. I was under house-arrest and I was to care for our mother.'

Her gaze is fixed on the loch, her back to us as she continues. 'You have to know that my mother and I had never seen eye-to-eye. She was a smart, skinny, beautiful, canny, non-stop, successful businesswoman who rarely smiled and thought I'd been wasting my time on making sandwiches for office workers. But even she knew that I was too fragile and that she should rein in her sharp comments and criticisms. We spent seven months getting to know each other. We went through old photo albums, I cooked her my favourite dishes, I showed her how to do yoga and finally, we re-taught each other how to laugh. Eventually, I understood that I loved my mother and that, perhaps, she even loved me. My brother couldn't have been more perceptive if he'd tried. By abandoning me with my mother, we'd healed our rift and I'd begun to see that there was a life to be had without Rosie.

'My mother died that October. In the end, I felt proud to have had such a strong woman for a mother and understood that maybe some of that had rubbed off on me. Much to my surprise, and my sisters' shock, my mother left me a quarter of the family business and five million dollars. "Go make the world a better place," her will said.'

Caitlin wipes her eyes and turns back to us. 'And that's why I'm here. Suddenly, I had all this money and I could find somewhere to go about nurturing people, just like I love to do.'

But suddenly her shoulders drop and she looks towards the fire. Quietly, she continues. 'Today would have been her eighth birthday. I sometimes wonder if she would have been a country girl or a city girl, into horses or high fashion. There are so many things I will never know.' Her voice trails off into silence.

'Do you have a picture of her?' Eileen asks boldly. I feel both uncomfortable and intrigued at this question. I shouldn't pry, but, of course, I want to. Thankfully, Eileen has saved me the awkwardness of having to ask it myself.

Caitlin seems caught off guard by this request. 'Um, yes.' She hesitates. "I do. Let me see.' She walks over to her desk.

I feel my heartbeat rising. Today we've almost finished the complicated five-thousand-piece puzzle that is Caitlin Black. But we've been waiting for the last, central bit, and something tells me that this is going to be it.

"Here it is.' She grabs a pack of photos and pulls out the top one.

'There are many things that keep me at Ardbray,' Caitlin says, 'but when you see this image, Greer, I think you'll understand one of the big reasons why I stay. Why I bought Ardbray and why I wanted to help restore it and why I wanted to turn it into a place that heals people again.'

She walks around her desk and hands the photograph to me.

It's a close up of her daughter's face; clear, glowing pale skin marked by piercing, ice-blue eyes looking directly at the camera, brimming with laughter and a wide, happy-go-lucky smile, all framed by a mass of white, blonde corkscrew curls.

I stare at the picture and the nausea again rises. I can barely breathe, but I have to say what I'm thinking. 'She looks exactly like...'

'... Flora.' Caitlin finishes my sentence. There's a soft, maternal pitch to her words. 'She looks exactly like the little girl I see almost every day around the grounds, with her older brother, looking for their mother.'

TWENTY-THREE

KITTY

Loch More, 1899

Dill

'In witchcraft, Dill "hindered witches of their will".'

Herbal Delights *by Mrs C F Leyel*

Kitty was sitting on the bench next to the graves of her husband and children. From here, she could see across the walled garden and over the loch towards Achfary. Here she could watch the mood of the water, the wind on the heather and the clouds playing with the sun. Here she could watch over her garden, watch over her wards, protect her young.

The walled garden had always been her domain, Kitty Maclean's province. When Charles first asked her to design the garden, she had thought it would be a distraction, something to keep a young wife busy, but as she'd spent more time with it, she had come to understand that it would define her. It had changed her from the malleable girl who was unable to stand up to others, to someone who was stronger, bolder, more capable of creating her own path.

Herbs were known for their soothing properties; tisanes and cordials could comfort the heart, soothe the nerves and take away melancholy. But nobody had told her that the act of growing the herbs would give her a calm determination she never thought she would have. The planning, the planting, the nurturing all contributed to a composed resoluteness that had never originally been part of her make-up. If it wasn't snowing, freezing or pouring with rain, she would be found in her walled garden, potting, digging, weeding, feeding, pruning or harvesting. Here her mind would clear, however muddied it had become. Here the noise would abate, here the turmoil would cease.

Here she had hidden from her husband's worst tempers; here she had cleared the chatter in her head when Callum had had another seizure. This was the outdoor equivalent of her father's study, somewhere to cocoon herself away from the world's difficulties and complexities.

And now this was where she was starting to learn to live her life without her family. Here she could almost forget the horror that had happened a few weeks earlier, here she could sometimes find moments of peace in the cavern of loneliness. And, of course, here she could be with her children.

The graves were still just mounds of earth, with simple wooden markers. They'd need to wait for the ground to settle before they could put up headstones. As she sat, she planned the planting: sage, thyme and rosemary to ward off the evil spirits, a hedge of lavender for love and devotion, perhaps a couple of bay trees for fidelity.

She looked down at the fob watch pinned to her chest. With a sigh, she stood up and slowly made her way towards the house. At the gate to the garden she picked up a basket of freshly picked herbs. Dropping these by the back door, she slipped into her morning room via the French windows in the drawing room. Shutting the door behind her, she looked at herself in the mirror on the back of the door. She tucked her unruly hair behind her ears and re-pinned what she could. She pinched her cheeks to ensure a faint pinkness, smoothed her dress down and re-tied the belt of her long cardigan. Quickly, she swept up some stray papers and shoved them in a drawer of her desk. Satisfied that the room wasn't too much of a disgrace, she sat down.

When she wasn't working in the garden or her herbarium, this was her room of choice. This warm but light-filled womb was where she kept her favourite novels, which she read and re-read when in need of comfort. Everything in this room was her friend and companion, always able to bring solace when needed. The photographs and likenesses of Callum and Flora on her desk by the window, on the mantelpiece above the fire, even the picture of herself and Charles, so stiff and uncomfortable, on their wedding day, still brought her some degree of peace. That was a day of hope and optimism she still wished she could reproduce. And her few precious ornaments, mainly from her childhood: a music box given to her by her grandmother, a painted egg sent by her friend, Mary, from China where she now lived and a carved wooden dog, lying on its stomach quietly, dutifully, looking at her with his doleful eyes. Its left paw had broken off during a lively game of cards with Eva. Her mother's severe telling off had been tempered by watching her father lovingly repair the ornament, gluing it back together, acting with the precision and care of a surgeon, treating the wooden creature as if it was a live animal. Although dusty and the colours faded, she couldn't get rid of this tired old St Bernard. She picked it up and saw where she had written in pencil on the bottom 'Kitty

Gray' in childish hand, along with 'Berny' in bolder, capital letters.

She looked up as she heard the carriage arrive. She couldn't see it through the window, but she could just imagine the steps being pulled down, the coachman opening the door, the horses puffing and sweating after the journey from Lairg. Closing her eyes, she savoured the last few moments of solitude. She knew she should rush to meet her mother, but she couldn't. She'd asked Mrs Lindsay to bring her to the morning room. She didn't need the formality of the drawing room; she needed this benevolent space to help gather her wits, help her prepare for the battle ahead.

Eventually, there was a rustle of black silk and a slight intake of breath as an aura of disapproval entered the room.

'Darling, I'm here to take you back to Glasgow. You're needed at home,' Susan Gray announced with a sniff and her usual air of authority.

Kitty let the statement go. It was only a surprise that it had taken her mother so long to intervene. Perhaps it was a sign of her declining influence.

Susan Gray walked over to her daughter and waited for the obligatory kiss. 'You look pale. Is Mrs Lindsay feeding you? You must eat. Are you getting outdoors? You must walk to keep up your strength. And there are dark circles under your eyes. That won't do, you know. You must talk to Eleanor about your daily make-up. You mustn't let the world see that you aren't sleeping. You need to keep up appearances. When we get back to Glasgow, I'll make sure Martha sorts you out. She's a wonder at keeping me looking young. And look at your cardigan, you can't wear that old thing, there's a hole in the elbow and the belt is ripped on one edge. Oh, and that dress, you must take the beads off. What will people think? There mustn't be anything but black, it's only been six weeks! My darling Kitty, you're obviously not coping. I knew it, of course, that would happen to anyone who'd lost their husband and children. That's why I'm here. You need bolstering. You need strength. That's what I do best. Let me organise the household, let me arrange the packing up of the house, letting the staff go. I can give them a good reference...'

Kitty let her mother go on, fascinated by her self-belief, the assurance that she was always in the right. But it was true what she had said about Martha; she did do a great job of keeping her mother looking young. She had hardly changed since the day of Kitty's wedding. The same silver, bouffant hairstyle, her dress an austere black with tiny embellishments of dark lace on the collar. Her face, although heavily made-up, had a luminous clarity that Kitty had always envied. It didn't matter whether she was in a ballroom in Glasgow or her breakfast room at home, she was always impeccably turned out. The only concession to age was a slight thickening at the waist and an increase in her already impressive bust.

'I'm not leaving,' Kitty interrupted gently. 'You won't be needing to get rid of the staff.'

Susan Gray continued without drawing breath as if she hadn't heard. 'There's so much to organise, I'm sure Mrs Lindsay will be good at finding other posts for the staff. Perhaps I could have a word with the Sutherlands, I'm sure they could take on a few and they'd surely know others in need of servants.'

'I said I'm not leaving,' Kitty growled.

'Don't be ridiculous, my darling. You can't live here in this backwater with no gas lighting, no telephone, where no one visits. You can't even go to the theatre and there's no one to entertain. Perhaps it felt romantic when you were newly married. You might have been busy when you had the children, but what could there possibly be for you here now? With no husband and no children, nobody will want to visit you in this vast mausoleum. What will you do all day? Sit and read in that

silly oversized library? No, don't be ridiculous. You're coming
back to Glasgow with me.'

Kitty let the tirade wash over her. The years had taught her
that this was the only way her mother could deal with a difficult
situation. She studied her face. A lifetime of total belief in her
powers of persuasion gave her the demeanour of upright confidence. Kitty wished she'd had that certainty, that poise. But,
looking at her mother, she suddenly felt she was looking in a
mirror; the more her mother talked, the more it seemed that an
unexpected audacity was filling her own veins, like the effect of
warm brandy on a cold day.

'Have you brought Father with you?' Kitty asked.

'Oh, of course not. He's busy.' Mrs Gray swatted the question away.

Kitty knew that her father had been left behind on purpose,
always the weak link in their marital chain.

'Mother, I am twenty-nine. I am a woman of means who no
longer needs to live under the protection of her parents or a
husband. I am in the position where I am capable of making my
own decisions, where I can live with the consequences of those
decisions and I can do what I like with my time, my money, my
house and my life.'

'But, darling, I need you. We need you, your father and I...'

'No, Mother, you do not need me. You showed no sign of
needing me whilst Charles and the children were alive. In fact,
I believe you were happy to have your sick grandchild and
embarrassment of a daughter tucked away in the Highlands
where no one could gossip about them. Don't you think I'd still
be the brunt of Glasgow gossip? Can you imagine the whispers
behind hands? "There's Mrs Maclean, didn't you know her
husband killed himself because he couldn't look after his children?" "There's Kitty Maclean; not just the one, but both of her
children drowned. Left alone on the loch. And she's the one
who insists on proving she's a good as the men, she's the one

who believes she's cleverer than the rest of us, she's the pushy one.'''

Susan Gray's mouth opened, but Kitty continued.

'I will stay living here. Here, in the place that I love. I will make a life for myself. I will keep my staff on and make sure that they are all provided for. They have looked after me over the last ten years, it's my turn to ensure they have everything they need. We'll protect this house and everything that lives in it. I will devote myself to my studies. It turns out women do have brains and are capable of contributing to the medical world. And, believe it or not, there are some women whose research has led to important findings, new inventions, medical break-throughs. Maybe you think I need to live in a city to do this? Well, there's a chance that's true, but I'd like to do my best to find out whether I can make a difference, whether I really do have the kind of brain that can be useful, and whether I can do it here.'

The two women glared at each other, Kitty's words hanging in the air.

Susan Gray shuffled slightly, unable to keep Kitty's stare. Perhaps she was weighing up her options. But that short moment to think must have given her the fuel she needed.

'No, your father needs you. He's quite distraught without you. He understood that he could do nothing whilst you were a married woman, but now you're on your own, he's desperate to have you back at home. Without either of his daughters, he's a broken man. He shuts himself away in that study of his, I never see him. Occasionally, he emerges for meals. We never enter-tain any more, he simply won't have it. He's lost without you, Kitty. We need you home.' Mrs Gray pulled a handkerchief from the sleeve of dress and dabbed at her eyes.

Kitty almost admired her mother for her change in tactics, her performance and powers of persuasion. She had to flatten her lips together to stop herself smiling.

'Mother,' she said softly, 'I understand that you've both been through a difficult time. One daughter lost to America, the other buried in the Highlands. But it's not that difficult to come and see me. The trains are good. You are both welcome here any time. This house is more than big enough. But you have to understand that my life is here, everything I love is here and I won't leave it.'

'What is here for you now? Everything that you love here has gone? And what about your father and me?' Mrs Gray sniffed again, the offence obvious.

Kitty sighed. 'My children are here. My husband is here.'

Susan Gray walked over to her daughter, sudden concern on her face, and tucked a stray piece of hair behind Kitty's ear. 'My darling. They are not here. They're in heaven where they are being well looked after. Please come home and look after your father. You can't imagine how much it would mean to him.'

'But what would it mean to you, Mother?'

Susan Gray faltered. 'Well...' She fiddled with her handkerchief. 'It would mean... well, it would mean we'd be a family again.' There was relief in her voice, as if she was thankful she'd managed to say the right thing.

'No, I have to make sure the children have everything they need and they must see me every morning.'

Her mother cocked her head on one side as she studied her daughter. 'You don't mean that,' she said carefully.

Kitty clasped her hands in front of her and, looking at them, she took a deep breath. 'I do mean that. I mean that the ghosts of my children visit me, in the walled garden, every morning. Every morning we sit and talk. We laugh, we tell jokes, we cry over Charles, I tell them stories of Eleanor, Fraser and Mrs Lindsay. I tell them how the chickens are faring, of the jam Cook has made, of how we had to send Mrs Mercaut away. And then in the evening I meet them down on the jetty, the place they loved to be. We sit and dangle our feet in the water, we watch the fish, the sunset. They are lost, Mother, they are not in heaven. They are here. They never left. Charles has gone. I don't know why he's gone and they haven't, but that's what's happened. My children are here and I will not leave them.'

Susan Gray made a visible effort to stop herself from gaping at her daughter. 'Darling, you're talking nonsense. Maybe you think you're seeing them. It's a wonder what grief can do to one's mind. Perhaps you need a bit of time, perhaps I came too soon. What's needed is your father. He'll talk some sense in to you. What I haven't told you is that he's pulled some mighty strings. Against my will, he's talked the medical school at Glasgow University into giving you a place to read Medicine, just like you always wanted to. He's even found you a small cottage to live in, so you won't have to put up with your inter-fering mother. You'll be able to afford to live in relative comfort. You can even bring Eleanor, perhaps Mrs Lindsay too.'

It was her trump card, Kitty could see it in her mother's face. She had come armed with an array of weapons, ready to use them all, prepared to fight for her daughter. And finally, she'd resorted to the heavy guns, every new thought coming at her like a cannonball, hard and fast.

To Kitty it felt like a large jar of sweets had been placed in front of her, the glass lid removed and that she'd been told that every one of them was for her, every one of the coloured jewels was an unfulfilled dream ready to be grabbed, enjoyed and swallowed. She looked at her mother and felt that triumph was beginning to seep out of her. Adversely, annoyance coursed through Kitty; feeling like the truculent teenager she had once been, she straightened her skirt, pushing down the rising tide of irrational indignation. It was a constant wonder to her how her father could still manage to live under the same roof as her mother. Her underhanded meddling, interference and gossip such a contrast to her father's thoughtful, measured and consid-erate way of life.

'Mother, why is it that you've only come now? It's six weeks since...' she stumbled over her words, not yet having had to say them out loud '... since they died.' She clasped her hands gently, feigning a calm façade. 'You haven't even asked what happened.' As she said this, something cracked inside her and the dam began to crumble.

'Shall I tell you?' And before her mother could object, the dam broke and Kitty's story poured out.

'My children drowned. They believe that Callum had an epileptic fit and fell overboard. Flora must have jumped in after him, thinking she could help. What help could a four-year-old give? They both drowned,' she repeated. 'What Charles was doing, where he was when this happened, nobody knows. Perhaps he was on the beach supervising them, but they went too far out.'

Kitty's voice was rising, the pitch frantic. But she couldn't stop; it was almost as if she wanted to punish her mother for her lack of compassion by giving her as much detail as she could.

'Well, Charles must have swum out and brought them back to the beach. That's why they were laid out so carefully when we found them. But he was gone and the boat was gone.

'It was two days before they discovered his body. There's no doubt he killed himself. Stones were found in his pockets. I am under no illusion that he couldn't cope with what had happened. He was ruined, his reputation in tatters and his children were dead, most probably because he hadn't been with them in the boat.' Tears were now streaming down her face.

Kitty wanted to continue, to tell her mother about the visit by the Glasgow police a week after the funeral, just as she was trying to put some order into her life. The police came asking difficult questions about John Hardgrave, interrogating the household staff, searching the house and grounds, quizzing Kitty and delving into her husband's financial affairs. Reluctantly, they had left, frustrated and, she was sure, convinced of some kind of collusion. But Kitty knew better than to bring her mother into that story. She was too indiscreet, too curious. Better to keep silent and never discuss John Hardgrave ever again.

'My children died because my husband wasn't vigilant. My husband died because he couldn't bear the shame. My family died because I was too busy having a cup of tea with Mrs Lindsay. And my mother decided to stay away until six weeks after the event.'

Mrs Gray reddened slightly under her heavy layer of powder and looked away from Kitty's penetrating stare. 'I didn't want to crowd you. The first few weeks after a death are full of well-meaning friends and family. It's once the funeral's over and the hysteria has died down that people begin to forget and think you'll be fine to get on with life. I didn't want you to be on your own now.'

Kitty shook her head as she wiped her face. 'Mother, you know you're the only family I have. There's been no crowding. Of course, there's been no crowding, there's been no hysteria. No one's made the effort to come out here. And once they've left it a few weeks, it becomes too embarrassing to make an excuse that's plausible in the face of a triple death.'

Susan Gray flinched slightly.

'So, no, there have been no crowds of mourners. I could have done with your support. I'd say it's a bit late now; Mrs Lindsay has been very helpful and we're coping as best we can. To be frank, I'm not sure I want to pick up my life with you, as much as I'd love to study, as much as I would like my independence in a little cottage in Glasgow, with Eleanor and Mrs Lindsay. But if I did do it, I'd need your full support, not just your nominal encouragement. I need your patronage, the kind where you'd champion my work, rally support, be proud of me. And I know you wouldn't, perhaps couldn't, do that. We'd constantly be at odds; I'd be working whilst you'd be looking for a replacement husband, trawling the open market, looking for a decent widower or the last bachelor on the shelf, setting up those endless dinners or teas where you can parade me in front of the nearest unmarried man with a little bit of money.

'No, Mother. I won't be your next project. I'm grateful to Father for arranging a place at Medical College, I truly am.' Her eyes filled with tears again, emotion running away with her. She sniffed and pulled herself upright.

'Whenever, or if ever, I go to Medical School, I'll do it on my own terms, in my own time, under my own conditions. I want to earn that place.' Her voice broke slightly.

'Darling,' Mrs Gray drew out the word leisurely, seemingly unflustered by Kitty's outburst, 'you don't need to give me your decision yet. I can wait.' She smiled the smile Kitty remembered, the scheming, knowing smile that too often had driven her to her father's study. 'I can stay for as long as it takes.' She sighed as she spoke, looking around the room, taking her long, black gloves off, pulling at each finger, one at time with great, ordered precision.

'Why don't I get us some tea?' Kitty couldn't listen any longer and headed for the door.

'What a good idea. But why don't you call for the maid? Don't make the effort to find the staff, let them come to you. That's what those ridiculous speaking tubes Charles put in are for.'

Stony-faced, Kitty muttered, 'No, I'll go.' It was as if a storm was raging in her ears, high seas and winds roaring. She rushed out the door, almost ran down the corridor, flung open the green baize door and stumbled into the kitchen.

Mrs Lindsay was standing at the table, glasses on, swiftly rolling out a thick dough. The room was filled with a warm, sweet citrus smell, uplifting and comforting, all at the same time.

'Aw, hen. What's the rush?' She put down the rolling pin and picked up a round, fluted cutter. 'Come, sit by me.'

Kitty sat on the bench beside her housekeeper with an unceremonious thud. She sighed heavily, put her head in her hands and both elbows on the table.

'She's been here ten minutes and already I cannot bear to be in the same room as her. I shouldn't feel like this about my mother,' she wailed.

'Aye, sometimes us parents have a way of annoying our children. It's all done with good intent, though. Sometimes, we're not so good at saying what we really mean.' She swiftly cut out ten circles, gently thrusting the cutter down into the pillowy dough, making a slight twist and pulling it out again. 'Give her a chance.'

Kitty sat up slightly, clasping her hands together and leaning her chin on them, elbows still on the table. 'I'm not sure I can. I spent the first nineteen years of my life giving her all the chances I could. I think maybe it's time to take my own chances.'

Mrs Lindsay looked at Kitty, a slight smile on her face. Nodding slowly, she placed the scones on a darkened baking tray and picked up the scraps. Absently, she rolled the scraps into a ball, threw a cloud of flour on the table and began rolling the remaining dough out again. 'Aye, maybe you're right.'

Kitty stared into the distance, nodding too, until she suddenly stopped.

'Why are you cooking? Shouldn't Cook being doing that?'

'I gave her the afternoon off. She's not been to see her family in Achfary for weeks. She's been cooking for days in preparation for your mother's visit. There's a stew for your dinna, and I told her I'd be glad of the excuse to cook. I never get the opportunity anymore and I love to bake. Your mother sent ahead some Sicilian lemons, so I've bin making lemon curd.' She used her head to indicate to Kitty three jars filled with the bright yellow curd. 'I thought I'd make you some scones to go with it.' As she said this, she scooped the final scones onto the tray and turned towards the range. Opening the top oven door, she slid the tray inside and carefully shut it again. 'I'll make some dumplings to go with your stew and, if I get the time, I'll make a lemon cake too. I'd like to make the most of those lemons.'

But Kitty wasn't listening. Her mind was turning, trying to catch hold of a thought that had passed her by.

'Mrs Lindsay.' She spoke carefully, a frown on her face, as if trying to work out a difficult puzzle. 'Just now, you talked about "us parents".' She paused. 'Are you telling me you're a mother? That you have children?' Her eyes were wide with questions.

Mrs Lindsay sat down gently on the bench beside Kitty. 'Aye, I have a daughter.'

Kitty stared. 'But... I've known you for ten years. Why have you never talked about her...?' Her voice trailed off, but she continued to search Mrs Lindsay's face. But all too suddenly she didn't need to search any more. It was like the curtains had been drawn on a dark room and great shafts of light were streaming over her. She said softly, 'Eleanor.'

Mrs Lindsay nodded. 'Aye.'

Kitty looked down at her hands. Unaccountable tears filled her eyes. She blinked them away as hard as she could. The anger at her mother was forgotten. 'I've been so blind, so caught up in my own petty hardships. Of course, it's Eleanor. Of course, deep down I've always known. She has your eyes, she has your slightly twisted smile.' She looked directly at her housekeeper. 'What a secret to keep.'

The older woman nodded. 'Aye,' she said quietly. They both sat silently, both considering the revelation.

Eventually, Mrs Lindsay turned to Kitty with a wry smile. 'I was twenty-five and headstrong. I was convinced I'd found the man I'd marry, but the truth was I was too easily impressed by a man in uniform.' As she spoke, she looked out of the window, her eyes focussing on some far-off point. 'There's a thousand girls out there with the same story.

'I left my job at Dunrobin Castle before I showed. Pretended I had to go and help my aunt who lived in the Borders. I did go and live wi' my aunt, but we changed my name from Edith Crawford to Edith Lindsay, telling everyone that my husband had just been killed in active duty, part of the 93rd Sutherland Highlanders. It were a uniform that got me in the family way, but it were a Sutherland Rifle Volunteer. You see they were based in Golspie. They were just a volunteer regiment, but they still looked good in that Sutherland tartan and belted plaid.' She smiled at Kitty. 'I made a fool of myself, but, in the end, I was determined to keep my bairn and make sommit of my life too.'

Kitty frowned, a question on her face.

'Once I'd weaned Eleanor, I took her back to Lairg. I was lucky, my parents were able to take her. There we gave the story that she was my aunt's grandchild, they being too poor to look after her. Naebody was fooled, but everybody knew how important it was to have a solid story if you wanted to work in the big houses. They would nae have you if you had a loose reputation. I got a job up at Bighouse Lodge; you wouldne believe how much more seriously people take you when you're a "Mrs". It was my first job as a housekeeper and I loved it. But I would've loved it more if I had been closer to Eleanor. I visited when I could, mind, but that was only once or twice a year. I sent money regularly and with my mother's wages as a seamstress, there was just enough to look after Eleanor. She learned how to sew and at sixteen she decided to give life a go in Glasgow in one of the new clothes factories. It wasne nice. She was home all too soon, homesick and exhausted. That was about the time I began working here. And that's when she came to see you for the job as lady's maid.'

'Why did you never say anything?' Kitty asked gently.

'I couldne say with Mr Maclean, he'd nae approved. We'd both have lost our jobs. And then, well, as time went on, it was just easier to keep the lie going. I didne ken when to say it. There's never a raeght time.'

Kitty felt deflated, as if all the fight had gone out of her. Would it have made any difference if she'd known? Of course, it would. Society didn't let you be a single, unmarried mother, didn't let you defy the rules.

'Why tell me now?'

Mrs Lindsay sighed. 'I know you and your mother fight. Sometimes, you should listen to her. She's your mother, she loves you, even if you don't think it.'

Kitty let the words sink in. 'It must have been difficult for you.'

'True. But you make your own destiny. I al'ays wanted to have my bairn, al'ays wanted to give her the best life I could, even if it meant I had to spend years apart from her. But I did everything I could to keep her, risking my aunt's and my parents' reputation. In my eyes it was the raeght thing to do.'

Mrs Lindsay's words silenced Kitty. She splayed her hands out on her lap, absently inspecting her finger nails.

Eventually, she spoke. 'And I need to do everything to keep my sweet bairns.'

Mrs Lindsay frowned.

Kitty looked at her housekeeper before opening her arms out wide, out towards the window. 'They're still here.' She turned to the daylight. 'I don't think they could leave. It seems that even they knew they weren't meant to have left when they did.'

Mrs Lindsay swallowed and searched Kitty's face, her eyes narrowing.

'I expect you think I'm senseless with grief, perhaps insane; I can see that my mother does. But I'm sure I'm not. They're here. Maybe you can't see them, but I've seen them every day for the last week. They come to me in my herb garden. I've been going there because it's the only place where I can find any peace. My head's been so full of noise, full of what I should do, what I shouldn't do. It's the only place where my anger begins to subside, and I've been so, so angry at Charles, so angry at myself for sitting here crying about my petty marriage troubles when I should have been outside looking for them.' She screwed up her hands as she said this. 'The only place where the clamouring fury seems to abate is right there. When I sit there, I can begin to feel some kind of calm, some kind of clarity.

'And then, one day, they just came and sat down beside me, talking to me about nothing; the chickens, the grouse, the hedgehog they'd found in the compost heap. They were so matter of fact, it was as if nothing had happened. It was as if it was just another ordinary day.'

'Do you call for them? How d'you know they're going to come?'

'No, they just appear. Whenever I visit the garden, I only have to wait a minute or two. I could be collecting seeds or clipping back the box hedge. It's as if they've been on the lookout for me. One minute I'm without company, the next they're sitting down beside me. Flora has a grass stain on her blue smocked dress, Callum's hair is still too long and his sailor suit is too tight. He looks a little anxious, there are dark smudges under his eyes, as if he hasn't slept, and he's so pale. I've asked them where they go, but they don't answer, always coming up with some counter question.'

Slowly, Mrs Lindsay rose from the bench. She put on a pair of oven gloves and opened the oven, pulling out the tray, inspecting the golden scones, pressing them carefully and putting the tray on top of the stove. Shutting the oven door, she hastily picked up a wire tray and transferred the scones to it before bringing it to the table and placing them in front of Kitty.

Kitty was quickly enveloped by the reassuring, clean cake-like smell. She closed her eyes, inhaling deeply. 'Afternoon tea with the children. Piles of Cook's raspberry jam on top of freshly made butter. Callum couldn't get enough of Cook's scones.' Her slight smile disappeared and she pressed her lips together tightly, trying not to show her emotion.

'And don't you ever forget that.' Mrs Lindsay swiftly found the butter, a knife and a plate. She picked up a scone, cut it in two and put it on the plate. She grabbed a jar of lemon curd from the dresser and put it on the table. 'Whenever you taste those scones, make the most of the memory. Remember the joy it brought, remember the smile it invoked. I used to do that when I missed my Eleanor. I'd cook her favourite cake, ginger cake. And that would make me feel better, for days. Just eating it would bring back her smile, the dimples in her rosy cheeks.'

She picked up the knife and dug into the butter pat and slathered both sides of the scone with the butter. Picking up a spoon, she opened the jar of lemon curd and dipped it in, pulling out a bright yellow bulb of dripping nectar. She dolloped some on the scone and put the plate in front of Kitty.

Kitty looked at the food in front of her. The butter was melting down the sides, the scones still warm from the oven. The curd began to spread gently across the rough surface, mingling with the butter. Picking up one half, she slowly bit into it, the citrus, summer flavour, blending with the bread like texture and slight cakey taste. The memory of a sunny afternoon on the terrace hit her like the cold glass of lemonade she'd been drinking that day, cool and refreshing, taking her away from the jagged heat of grief, pulling her into a suspended moment of happiness. She held the soft crumbs in her mouth, savouring the sharp sweetness of the curd that evoked her children's laughter, their happy smiles, their untidy hair.

She closed her eyes, the smell, taste and texture of the curd overwhelming her. Mrs Lindsay was right, this was how she should be remembering the good things, enjoying what had been. It was no good being angry at Charles, angry at herself, angry at her mother. Nothing good would ever come of that. She took another bite of the scone. She felt as if something was pulling a veil away, giving her a clarity that she hadn't felt in weeks.

Opening her eyes, she stood up. 'Thank you,' she said simply. It was as if she had just come out of a hazy trance and now she felt a satisfied calm.

'My mother requires tea.' She picked up the teapot from the dresser and Mrs Lindsay put the already hot kettle back on the stove. They worked as a team, Kitty finding the cups and saucers, Mrs Lindsay warming the pot, swirling the water around. Pouring the water down the sink, she put two spoons of tea leaves into the pot just as the kettle began to whistle. Kitty put the tray on the table and the two of them came together gathering teapot, crockery and cutlery.

'Shall the mether be wanting scones?' Mrs Lindsay asked, a glint in her eye.

Kitty hesitated. 'Yes.' She smiled. 'I think so. I think she needs some of that clarity too and perhaps these might help her along the way.'

TWENTY-FOUR

GREER

Loch More, 2004

Horsetail

'They contain so much silica that they are often used by country people to clean their saucepans.'

...

'It is a good wound herb, and it gives strength to the weak in the same way that silica does in a flower border when plants become limp and unable to hold up their heads.'

Elixirs of Life *by Mrs C F Leyel*

I'm bringing the tea to Caitlin and Colin in the walled garden. They've been up since six o'clock, eager to get some of the planting completed before the forecast rain comes in. Their work, like everyone else's around here is becoming urgent. We have six weeks until opening day. There seem to be decorators in every room of the house, the smell of paint, varnish or floor wax is all pervading. Electricians and plumbers are finishing off the last of their jobs, a chef has been appointed and kitchen staff hired, cleaners and front of house staff have all been employed. The place is like a beehive, teaming with busyness; I hardly recognise it.

I'm standing at the entrance, the new wrought-iron gate pushed open, and I can see the bare bones of the garden layout. The walls have been completely rebuilt on the same footprint as the original garden, using as much reclaimed stone as possible. The cobblestone paths have recently been laid, neat wooden edging running around the planting beds, each one dug over and ready for planting. The south-facing wall has already been planted with young fruit trees, horizontal wires fixed along the walls to encourage the adolescent branches along them. Several large terracotta pots stand eager to be filled, bamboo canes lean against the door to the potting shed, a great array of plants are lined up, anticipating their new homes.

There's a benevolence here that I never felt when I used to sit beside the wrecked garden. There used to be a feeling of injustice, indignation at its unfortunate ending, at its devastation. But now, when I walk in, I feel a wave of good-natured approval break over me, perhaps a gratefulness at the loving revitalisation that's taking place. No wonder Colin spends such long hours here, this is again a happy place to be.

I used to play in this garden, used to wander the paths. I invented fairies and chased imaginary pixies; I had a shelter to hide in. Singular games for an only child. I had my own little herb and vegetable garden, which I nurtured and fussed over. This was my playground, my schoolyard, this garden became part of the seven-year-old me.

As I walk in, although it's just a structure, just a basic layout, I can feel flickerings of the excitement I felt as that innocent seven-year-old who knew nothing of disappointment or regret. I'd like to run around and invent my own stories again, talk to those fairies I used to know, as if the life I've led hadn't happened, as if I had it all ahead of me.

There's a bench in the far corner of the garden, just where Kitty used to sit. It has the advantage of overseeing the whole garden and has a view over the loch. Every morning, come rain, snow or shine, she'd be here chatting away with her ghost children about God knows what. I think it was like a drug to her, she couldn't live without them, couldn't live without that daily fix. Some days I would watch her from my secret shelter. I would sit absolutely still, afraid to move, almost afraid to breathe. I was jealous of the friendship she had with the invisible children. I wanted to be their friends, to play with them, run around the garden with them. All I wanted was to be able to see them, to know them.

Today Caitlin is sitting on that bench and it's clear to me that she too is talking to the children that I can no longer see. I am stabbed by that same infantile jealousy to see them again, even though I've had that privilege, I've had that burden and I'm happy to be free of it. The feeling of déjà vu is so strong, evoking a nostalgia for my childhood that I've never had before. Caitlin could almost be Kitty – that unruly hair, the hole in her jumper, that air of greediness as if she's feeding off them, as if she cannot do without this daily encounter. The longer I watch her, the more I want to tell her to stop, that she shouldn't be saddled with this daily necessity, that she needs to lead a life that doesn't constrain her, doesn't tie her down. I suddenly feel cold, despite the warmth of the August morning sunshine.

I shake off the heaviness and approach Caitlin. As she sees me, I can tell that the children have left her; there's a look of emptiness on her face.

I sit beside her. 'Were they with you?' I ask.

She nods. 'Still looking for their mother. Still asking for me to bring her to them.' She looks off into the distance and we sit silently for a while.

'Now that the police have left and we know they won't be pursuing the case, tell me, do you think that was John Hardgrave's body we discovered?' she asks suddenly.

I nod, looking into my lap. It's time to let go of another of Ardbray's secrets.

'When I finally moved back here, when I had agreed to stay and look after the house and I'd begun to see the children, my mother told me about the single bush of red roses at the front of the house, why it was there. A warning symbol to all who passed through the front door, of what can happen if you cross the women of this house.

'John Hardgrave was last seen at Lairg station enquiring about a carriage to Ardbray. Nobody ever owned up to taking him to the house or even seeing a carriage take him to Loch More. The Glasgow detective who was assigned to the case was frustrated by the locals' lack of co-operation and the complete ignorance of the staff at Ardbray. Kitty was deemed too distraught following the death of her husband and children and incapable of giving the police any sensible information. It seems he just vanished into thin air. Everyone who was left at Ardbray closed ranks and wiped away any suggestion that John Hardgrave had been anywhere near Loch More.

'My grandfather, Fraser, planted that rose. He had little patience with men of the law, little belief in their abilities. He was willing the police to find that body, to understand that blood red symbol that was right in front of their noses.'

She smiles. 'Buried in plain sight.' Then she turns to look at me.

'But why is it that the women of Ardbray never left, never went out into the world and made something of themselves? Kitty, your mother, you. You're all strong, intelligent, clever women. Why did you stay here? Why did you hide your talents and choose to stay?'

'Isn't that obvious?' I feel some of that old bitterness returning. I fail to keep it out of my voice.

She looks at me with slight amusement in her eyes and shakes her head.

'The children. We couldn't leave because of the children. They wouldn't let us. However hard we tried, we were pulled back. You remember when Robbie said that things started to go wrong when you visited Glasgow? When workmen got injured, tiles fell off the roof, unexpected mistakes occurred. You remember that he said this place was happier when you were here? That's exactly what happened to us. If we tried to leave, something went wrong. Kitty never tried to leave; she was too attached, but when my mother was due to go and visit an old friend in Edinburgh, my father, James Munroe, stood on a rusty nail. My dog was killed in a freak accident as I was leaving to go and stay with Colin a few weeks before we married. And a few months later, Colin, who never gets ill, came down with a debilitating flu when I tried to go and stay with an old university friend.'

The scepticism is still there. I can tell she feels these are all petty examples. Maybe she doesn't need to know the full story yet. So, I pick her up on something she said earlier.

'How can you say Kitty never made anything of herself?' I feel a fierce protectiveness over the woman who has influenced my whole life. 'How can you say that about the woman who produced all those detailed, accurate botanical paintings, who catalogued every herb and their healing properties and culinary uses? How can you think that the woman who was midwife to every child born in Achfary from 1889 to 1947 didn't make a difference? That woman who had more medical knowledge than most doctors in the whole of the Highlands. She made something of herself, she just chose to keep it here. You've seen all the evidence of it, in her papers, her paintings, her garden. You even want to copy her garden.'

I'm suddenly so unaccountable angry that I'm balling my fists, knuckles white and the skin tight.

'Look at yourself,' I say in a more measured tone. 'You didn't run a multinational company or become a wealthy investment banker. But you ran a successful café. You fed people, made them happy. You made something of yourself in a way that satisfied you. You might not have brokered world peace or discovered a life-changing medicine, but you made people's lives just that little bit better every day.'

She nods her head slowly. Quietly, she says, 'Perhaps you're right.'

There is an awkward silence between us, so I pass out the tea, forgotten beside me. We both take a sip; I'm wondering how to continue this conversation, but she suddenly leaps into a speech about Kitty.

'I found her original plans for the walled garden, the plans from 1890 and then I found more, spanning the next forty years, much more detailed and informed, mainly plans for sections of the garden. It seems she would overhaul about a third of it at a time. Each time she'd become more experimental with the types of herbs she was growing, more ambitious. She's covered these drawings with later annotations. One says "Failed, won't grow in our climate." Or somewhere else she had the opposite problem. "Too prolific, need to re-plant into large pots." Using the photographs she took in situ, Colin and I have been able to see exactly what each herb looks like and how it will sit. Her notes have given us precise information about size, smell, when each herb flowers, etc. And her detailed paintings have given us a perfect idea of the colours. She's given us everything we need to recreate the garden as she left it. The main part of the garden will be turned to vegetables, but about a third of it will be a near copy of Kitty's herb garden.'

I've found myself feeling a little jealous of the working relationship she has with Colin. They spend hours together pouring over those drawings, discussing planting plans and other things I can't even begin to understand. He's re-becoming the man I met in my early twenties; those deep blue eyes glow again, and there's an energy in his movement that I'd forgotten he once had. I should be happy at this re-emergence, but instead I seem to be saddened at the revelation that I've kept this person living under a stone for over forty years.

But right now, I can't stop Caitlin from talking.

'In the evenings I find myself reading one of Hilda Leyel's books or Kitty's notebooks. I think I'll just spend half an hour in Kitty's herbarium, on my way to bed, but suddenly it's three in the morning. There's so much to discover, an almost infinite number of herbs: pot herbs, culinary herbs, cooling herbs, healing herbs, poisonous herbs. Herbs that have been used throughout history in the name of love, religion, medicine and mysticism. There are the herbs you hear about every day: mint, basil, lavender and camomile. But then there are the ones you've probably never heard of. There's viper's bugloss, which would look lovely dropped into your Pimm's but will also help cure your chesty cough. Then there's adder's-tongue, once renowned for helping with the healing of wounds, but now used in an ointment to ease mastitis in cows' udders.'

Here we go again; Caitlin caught up in another of her passions.

'I'd like to pass on some of Kitty's knowledge. Maybe we'll run herbal workshops at the retreat. I've just got to find the right person to do it.' As she says this, she seems distracted, as if she's thinking of something completely different as she speaks.

'Where is Kitty buried?' she asks suddenly, looking at me. 'I need to find out where in the walled garden she was buried. Charles's and the children's graves are marked on some of the plans, but, of course, her grave is not marked. I assume she was buried right next to them. You've seen the area we've pegged out where their three graves are, but I can't find out where Kitty's is. I want to put up new headstones and put in some special planting for them.'

I sigh. This is the sadness my grandmother carried. This is the reason my family are still here.

'She's not here.'

Caitlin's mouth opens. 'What do you mean? Wasn't she buried with Charles and the children, here, in the garden? Just as she'd requested?'

Looking down at my hands, I slowly shake my head. 'Kitty isn't buried here. It was impossible to bury her here. She's buried in the cemetery at Lairg.'

TWENTY-FIVE

KITTY

Loch More, 1947

Thyme

*'In the Middle Ages a sprig of Thyme was given to knights by
their ladies to keep up their courage,
and even scarves embroidered with a bee alighting on a sprig of
Thyme
were supposed to produce the same effect.'*

Herbal Delights *by Mrs C F Leyel*

She was on the bench beside the graves of her husband and
children. She'd had her daily conversation with Callum and
Flora and should have felt revitalised, should have been ready to
turn her energies to her garden. But, too often now, she was
drained by their exchanges, just wanting to lie down, close her
eyes and wake up beside them. And she was tired, oh, so tired.

Increasingly, she had no strength to get up and out of her chair, get up off the bench, too often her heart physically hurt, and she'd have to sit and wait for the pain to pass.

As she waited, she surveyed her garden. Despite enjoying the order of a well-organised vegetable garden, she still missed her prized herb garden. For the last eight years, the garden had been turned over to vegetables, chickens and pigs to help with the war effort and contribute to the village kitchens. But rationing was just beginning to ease and Kitty wondered if this was the last year they'd need to commit the whole garden to feeding Achfary. She knew she was luckier than most, having the ability to grow more than they needed to eat, being able to share their plentiful harvests with the families in the village, but her heart was in her herbs and her heart had been broken when they'd had to destroy over forty years of hard work, research and plant love when rationing had been introduced eight years previously.

Following the death of Charles and the children, her garden had become her third child, the child that had survived. So, of course, she'd poured all her energy into nurturing it, cultivating it. With herbalism, she'd found a subject she could throw herself into, combining her knowledge of medicine and her innate curiosity. She'd used her father's medical contacts and her ability to grow and research and turned her walled garden into a place of serious study and application for herbalism. Her friendship with Hilda Leyel had widened her horizons, leading to opening her own small practice. She'd hosted intimate conferences with Hilda and others, including Eva Napier of D Napier and Sons, Edinburgh, spending hours ceaselessly looking for ways to use herbalism to improve people's lives.

Every now and again Kitty had wondered whether she'd made the right decision to stay hidden away at Ardbray. Should she have taken the opportunity her parents had offered her to go back to Glasgow and join the small, but growing, band of women who'd been allowed to study medicine at university? Perhaps. But she'd also wondered whether she would ever have been tough enough to deal with the prejudice and daily abuse that they'd put up with over the years. When she was being truly honest with herself, she knew that she would never have been able to withstand the male-dominated world of medicine. She'd rarely been able to stand up to her mother, let alone eminent and outspoken male doctors and professors.

Now, aged seventy-six, she had a reputation for being the eccentric herb lady, the old hermit who talks to her plants in her walled garden. She liked that reputation; it made her smile. But, still, something would needle at her, something would tell her it didn't do her justice, didn't recognise everything she'd done. Yes, just occasionally she wondered if she should have returned to Glasgow.

No, on a day like this, with cloudless blue skies, the garden full of colour and late summer produce, she was glad she hadn't returned to the city. The now infrequent letters from old friends always portrayed Glasgow as grey – its food, weather and attitude – war having drained it of any colour and vibrancy. She wouldn't have fitted in, she was too unconventional for that life. She valued her freedom too much.

But as she contemplated whether she'd have the energy to bring her garden back to its former glory, she heard young footsteps coming towards her.

Greer Munroe, Eleanor's granddaughter, casually sat beside her on the bench. Seven years old, she was a precocious only child, a child who'd only grown up with adults, who spoke as if she was forty but who still had no filter, didn't worry about what she might be saying.

'Were you talking to your bairns?' she asked, her legs swinging below the bench, her feet unable to reach the floor.

'Yes, I was.' Kitty smiled. She loved the honesty of this child.

'I wish I could see them. I wish I could talk to them.' She looked at Kitty. 'I'd like to play with them in the garden.'

Kitty gave her a distracted smile. She had a fierce and protective love for this girl. She felt responsible for her fate. She wanted her to have all the opportunities she'd never had, she wanted to make sure she grew into a self-assured and independent woman.

Looking at her, she said carefully, 'Will you make me a promise?'

Greer nodded seriously.

'Will you promise me that when you're older, you'll leave Ardbray? Promise me you'll do the thing you love and do it away from this house.' Kitty tried to keep her voice level, keep it light, as if they were discussing the need to put on clean socks every day.

Greer stared at her, no surprise on her face, no confusion, just a stare that seemed to look inside Kitty.

'But I'd like to live here, live in the garden,' she said, pointing to the far corner. 'I'd build a little house over there and I'd live in it and look after your garden. And the children.'

Kitty shook her head. 'No, you won't need to do that. There'll be others to do that. Promise me you'll leave Ardbray. Leave and find your own life.' She wanted to pick up the girl and shake her, make this promise become part of her, but she kept her hands in her lap. 'This garden will look after itself, and I wouldn't worry about the children because when I leave, they'll follow me.'

Kitty watched for a reaction, for her to say something, but Greer stayed still, her eyes glued to Kitty. She couldn't tell what was going through her mind. She wanted to drive her point home, make her understand, make sure she never forgot this conversation. But she let it go, let the already said words sink in.

They stayed on the bench, Greer swinging her feet, Kitty

watching the beetroot tops swaying in the breeze, the autumn sun slowly dissipating the intensity between them.

Eventually, Kitty got up. 'Come on, come with me.' She put out her hand with a smile. 'Help me pick some raspberries.'

The back door from the garden to the kitchen was already open and Kitty walked in, a slight limp impeding her, lugging the heaped basket with the precious raspberries.

Substantial maroon-coloured tweed skirt, pale-yellow brushed-cotton collared shirt, thick skin-coloured stockings and dark-brown lace-up brogues, Kitty's daily gardening uniform gave her the air of brusque determination, but her face softened the indomitability, glowing from her afternoon's work in the warm day, her always wild hair was, as usual, escaping from her loose bun, now grey with only a very few streaks of her old wiry brown left.

She put her booty on the table, girlish pride exuding from her face.

'That granddaughter of yours knows how to pick raspberries, and she knows how to eat them too. I do hope she's not sick.' She picked up a raspberry and put it in her mouth. 'We can't eat all of these,' she said, mouth full, her words muffled. 'We'll have to make raspberry jam. Luckily, I've been saving some of our sugar ration just for this very moment.'

Eleanor, who was sitting at the kitchen table shucking peas, her gnarled, arthritic knuckles causing her obvious difficulties, grunted slightly.

'Would you like some help?' Kitty asked.

'Och, no. I'll get there.'

Kitty knew better than to interfere, so set to work. After washing her hands in the large Belfast sink, she poured the raspberries into a big tin colander and ran cold water over them. Weighing out five pounds of the fruit, she then tipped them into a large, battered jam kettle and put it on the stove. Disappearing into the pantry, she reappeared with a large enamel, lidded tin.

'Have you been hiding that?' Eleanor smirked.

There was a thud as Kitty dropped the tin on the table. 'I saw that there was going to be a bumper crop and I've been craving jam. We haven't had it for such a long time and if we don't have it now, it might be too late.'

Eleanor raised her eyebrows.

'I'm an old woman.' Kitty's eyes flickered. 'This might be my last chance, and I'm not going to die without tasting raspberry jam again.'

'Tsk, you're so dramatic. There's a few years left in you.'

Kitty didn't respond as she measured out the sugar. Both women watched the crystals piling up as if it was the first time they had seen the sparkling granules, creating a hypnotic pull over each of them, just as it had to countless others over hundreds of years. Eventually, they were pulled out of their mesmeric reverie by the sweet, warm smell of the raspberries beginning to cook on the stove. Kitty put down the sugar tin and moved back to the pan to carefully stir the fruit. She put her head directly over the berries, deeply inhaling the sweet aroma.

'That's the smell of pure luxury.' She inhaled again. 'Something we haven't experienced for a while.'

Kitty continued to stir absently. 'I'm looking forward to being able to turn the walled garden back to my herbs. I feel as if I've been in limbo for years and growing veg is such back-breaking work.'

'Listen to you. One minute you say this is your last chance for jam, and the next you're planning to replant the garden. Make up your mind,' Eleanor teased.

Kitty put down her wooden spoon and sat down opposite Eleanor, clasping her hands in front of her and then looking down at them. She opened her mouth to say something and then halted, tried again and failed.

Eleanor smiled. 'Out w' it.'

With a deep breath, she began, 'Last week you asked what's going to happen to the house, ummm... after I die.' She twisted her hands, pulling at her fingers. 'As you know, the solicitor was here and we've been updating my will.'

Eleanor frowned, flushing. 'You don't need to tell me, you know. I was just—'

Kitty cut in. 'It's all right, Eleanor. You need to know. I'm sorry, I should have said something before now.'

Kitty had no heirs, no family to leave Ardbray to or anything else she might own. As she had grown older, it had begun to bother her about what to do with the house that she loved, the herb collection and all the research that she had spent almost fifty years putting together, and, of course, any money that she might have. She couldn't bear the thought that it would all go to waste.

'After I die, you, Bridget and Greer can stay in the house until your death. I'll be leaving both of you more than enough to live off; you'll be comfortable and won't need to worry about anything. And Greer. I want to make sure she has every chance to make the most of her life, that she's not left languishing in this remote world. I've left her some money that she will only get if she does something that takes her away. Maybe studying or travelling or working in Edinburgh. Anything to make sure she widens her horizons.'

Eleanor dropped her peas and looked up. 'You have not?'

'I have,' said Kitty. 'I don't want her to be caught up here like you and I have been, like Bridget has been.'

Eleanor gave her a steely gaze. 'Trying to make up for the life you didn't have?'

'Why not? I've got the money, why shouldn't I?' Before Eleanor could interrupt, she continued, 'The house will be held in trust and the money to pay for the upkeep of it and the garden will come out of my estate. But when you die, the house and any money left will go to the Society of Herbalists.'

Eleanor continued shelling peas, the process slow and deliberate, pain etched on her face. 'Hilda Leyel and her lot?'

'Yes. But they don't want the house.'

Eleanor frowned at her peas.

'They won't be able to manage it; it's too far from anywhere. So, I've agreed that once the house is sold to a suitable person, they can have my herb collection, all my research and the money to fund their continued research and work.'

'A suitable person? Who might that be?'

Kitty looked down at her hands. 'Someone who'd look after my herb garden, someone who'd preserve this house, someone who'd make sure it's somewhere myself and my family would like to be buried.'

Eleanor put down the pea pod she was holding. 'That could be difficult. All those big houses being destroyed or decaying away 'cos nobody can afford to run them. Nobody's gonna want to be out here, w'out electricity, w'out the telephone, a bad road to Lairg and ghosts in the house.'

Kitty almost flinched at her friend's harsh words. She got up and went back to her jam pan, stirring thoughtfully. With her back to Eleanor, she spoke into the pan. 'It would break my heart if this place was abandoned. I've put my whole life into Ardbray; I've nurtured it and let it mature. When I first came here, it was just a child, an unformed character. Now it's fully grown, it belongs here, it has roots, a history, a meaning. It can't be left to rot, I'll make sure of that.' Determination coursed through her voice like sandpaper on metal.

Kitty continued to stir as Eleanor dropped the last pea into the bowl, before clasping her hands together and closing her eyes as she sank back into her kitchen chair.

'I know it'll take a while to find a buyer. But now the war's over, things must get better; the economy has to improve and there must be buyers out there. There's enough money to keep the house well cared for, enough for a housekeeper and a gardener, money for essential repairs.' There was a forced jollity in Kitty's voice. 'And those ghosts, my children, well, once we're reunited, they'll leave the house, they won't bother you anymore. They just want to be with me. Once we're buried together, there'll be no need for those daily visits, those everyday updates. I'll be with them and we'll go to wherever it is we're supposed to go.'

Eleanor, hunched and arthritic, leaned on the windowsill, watching the carnage outside as the wind raged and the rain pelted the window.

Behind her lay Kitty's body, in her bed; peaceful and no longer heeding the storm. Two hours earlier, after five days of unexpected but rampant illness and five days of torrential rain, Kitty Maclean had died. During those days Eleanor had sat beside her friend and employer, her vigil constant, her attention slow but complete. It had all been as it should, little pain, no fuss, a time when the two friends could talk when needed and sit in silence when not. They had talked of old times and old friends, and Kitty had passed on what she needed to. She had been ready for her end, almost willing it to come. Those five days had been without the ghosts of her children, unable to go down to the garden to find them, but she had known that she would be with them soon enough.

Eleanor felt that her friend had had a good and fitting death; no hospital, no upset. All her affairs had been put in order so that she could finally be at peace and with her children once she had died.

But now, as Eleanor looked at the destroyed garden below her, she could see no way of carrying out Kitty's wishes.

'A burst 'o the hills,' she whispered.

As if the Gods had been furious at the loss of a much-loved companion, the garden had been obliterated by a titanic landslide. At the emergence of dawn, the hillside had no longer been able to hold on to its lifetime possessions. Five days of rain had culminated in a terrifying rumbling, disgorging a wave of silt and boulders on top of the walled garden. Now nothing was left of Kitty's life's work; nothing existed but a mountain of mayhem and disorder that Eleanor could see no way out of.

She could think of nothing except that it would be impossible to bury Kitty anywhere near her children or husband, impossible to carry out her friend's final request. The landslide had spread its deposit over an enormous area, redirecting the burn and destroying the wooden bridge. All Kitty's hard work had been wiped out in a minute of rumbling rocks, mud and silt, almost surrounding the house and eradicating any semblance of order and regulation.

Two hours previously, Eleanor, resigned and awaiting her friend's death, had been happy that everything was ready, everything was exactly as Kitty had wanted it. Now nothing was as it should be, nothing could be reversed, nothing could be made right.

She began making a mental note of all that needed doing; send for the doctor and the minister, send a message to Kitty's lawyer, begin the merry-go-round of death rituals. She rubbed her stiff hands, struggling with the constant dampness and humidity. But she couldn't stir herself and only stayed looking at the destruction outside, too tired to face the upheaval ahead. Kitty had just wanted to be buried, quietly and with dignity, beside her children. But now there would be fuss, people would have opinions, they'd know best. The special application for burial Kitty had received meant she could only be buried directly next to her children. This was now impossible. Eleanor would need to see if she could apply for further permission for her to be buried just outside the area destroyed by the landslip.

She sighed at the thought of the paperwork, red tape, solicitors and council officials. She knew how curious people were about Kitty and the life she'd led. She knew about the rumours of ghosts, how they talked of the woman who would never leave her house, how they believed the house had some sort of curse on it. Now that talk would be amplified, now they had new fuel to fan the gossip flames. She pulled her shawl more tightly around her shoulders and slowly turned to leave the room.

TWENTY-SIX

GREER

Loch More, 2004

Rue

'*The Greeks venerated the plant and thought it had magical powers because it antidoted the indigestion that they suffered from when they had to eat before strangers.*'

...

'*There is an old tradition that rue grows best when it has been "stolen" from another garden.*'

Elixirs of Life *by Mrs C F Leyel*

This morning, when I walked into the house, I realised that the smell had changed. It used to be woodsmoke, wellies and waxed jackets, baking, and sweet raspberry jam. But today I recognised a subtle adjustment, a movement away from the old guard and towards the new. Today I still smell woodsmoke, but it's caught up with paprika, freshly ground coffee and just baked bread.

It's a smell that suits Caitlin. But it happened so slowly that I hadn't noticed it; somehow, I hadn't noticed that Ardbray has become Caitlin's house. It no longer belongs to Kitty Maclean and I'm no longer its guardian. Caitlin Black, the passionate cook, the part-time vegetarian and lover of the outdoors, believer in nurturing souls, has become its custodian and, finally, I've become reconciled to it and am ready to leave.

This realisation, that I no longer need to stay here, that I'm no longer needed, should terrify me. Once I wondered what I would be without Ardbray, once I thought that Ardbray was the glue that kept me together and that I would fall apart without it. But here I am, feeling like I've shed an overly heavy suit of armour. I'm no longer going to be protected by the cover of this old house, but I feel as if I've been rehabilitated and am ready to go back into the world. I'm going to be open to the elements, but I'll be able to feel the air on my face and the rain on my back.

I've discarded my daily uniform of greying white T-shirt and stained jeans and I'm wearing a bold floral, mid-length dress with a bright turquoise cardigan. I'm wearing jewellery and long boots with a slight heel. Today I am Greer Mackenzie, interior designer for the Retreat at Ardbray. I am no longer the housekeeper.

Today the rest of the world gets to see Ardbray, others get to see my work, both my preservation work and my interior design. I'm nervous. Actually, I'm terrified. Few people have been in a position to scrutinise what I do: Robert, the builders, Caitlin. Tonight, everyone who has been involved in the restoration of Ardbray, anyone who lives in Achfary and some others from Lairg are coming to a party to celebrate the revival of this old house and garden. Colin is just as nervous as I am. His work in the garden is as important to him as my work in the house is to me. Neither of us slept last night.

So, both of us got up early and, as Colin went to the garden, I took myself through the house, just to check everything was as it should be and make a small snagging list of forgotten jobs.

Caitlin briefed me very clearly that we should be careful not to make it seem like some expensive country house hotel. She wants it to feel like a home, somewhere her guests will be comfortable and not feel that they must talk in whispers or be on their best behaviour. This is a place where she wants people to relax, find themselves, abandon their daily anxieties, and learn new skills. In the large drawing room we have replaced the formal furniture with big comfy second-hand sofas and armchairs and covered them with a multitude of colourful cushions and throws. It seemed wrong to remove the old, brocaded wallpaper, it was in such good condition, but I changed the curtains to something plainer but still full of colour. I can't stand it when there are busy patterns confusing the eye. All the original paintings have been cleaned and re-hung in their usual places. We took away some of the old Victorian paraphernalia, especially that ugly glass ashtray. I can't imagine who thought that was a pretty ornament that warranted keeping.

Every bedroom is festooned with haphazard colour, 'eccentric themed' in Eileen's words. I've had fun trawling car boot sales for textiles: wall hangings, curtain fabrics and even using dress fabrics to make cushion covers. We've put vintage Roberts radios in each room and freestanding baths wherever possible. Any flowers, dried or fresh, will only come from the walled garden. Each room has its own recycled old desk, there are no televisions, and the internet is restricted to a few study rooms, but guests have unfettered access to the library and Kitty's herbarium. There's no mobile phone signal here so that easily filters out the kind of guests who are wedded to their phones.

In the dining room, we have two long wooden tables with benches to ensure guests mix during meals. Caitlin has found a chef who understands her need for relaxed and rustic food, packed with flavour and innovative ideas, but who also understands the importance of brunch; if the meals are like those I've sampled recently, the table will be groaning with dishes that will delight even the most seasoned foodie. She will be joining her guests for dinner every night, hosting and encouraging them to make the most of the area, pointing them towards her favourite pubs, restaurants, walks and beaches when they aren't taking part in any of the courses.

Both Colin and I feel a lightness that we're struggling to acknowledge. Years of familial duty had made us tired, leaden and bored. The rehabilitation of Ardbray hasn't just been about the house and garden, it's also been about Colin and me. Eleven months of intense therapy in the form of hard work and unexpected achievement have made sure that we're not ready to retire, but that we're ready to rejoin society.

The headstones are simple: granite to withstand the weather with just the names and dates inscribed in clear lettering.

Caitlin has made the creation of the tiny graveyard at the northeast end of the walled garden her own personal project. Colin has kept away from it, perhaps recognising that this was a cathartic venture that she needed to do alone. She's framed the row of headstones with a background of Korean angelica, a tall ornamental plant with umbelliferous flowerheads, now turning to delicate seed pods. She's been telling us of the thyme walk she's planning around the graves, of how the scent of thyme becomes even stronger when it is trodden on and how she's going to plant it up with varieties with differing scents and coloured leaves, how the plant is said to make you more courageous, how its medicinal characteristics made thyme a herb for everyone. Her enthusiasm occasionally makes me feel very tired.

'Tea anyone?' Caitlin asks.

We're standing facing the graves following a short, non-denominational service, led by Robert, for the re-burial of Kitty in the walled garden, the reunion with her family and the unveiling of the new headstones. It turns out to have been more emotional than any of us could have expected.

Robert Urquhart, Colin, Eileen and Caitlin all look like they could really do with a stiff drink. I wouldn't protest at the offer of a wee dram.

'We have Greer's famous ginger cake and scones and some freshly made raspberry jam,' announces Caitlin.

'How could we possibly refuse?' Robert enthuses. 'I think we probably need some bolstering after that ceremony. Although I suspect we could all do with something a bit stronger.' The solicitor gives Caitlin a paternal wink.

'Don't worry, Robert. There's a bottle of Balblair sitting right next to the teapot, just in case...'

Relief shoots across the solicitor's face. Robert, as usual, is immaculately turned out. He wears a green-yellow tweed suit, bright shiny brown brogues, a checked shirt with discreet knotted cufflinks and a tiny point of yellow handkerchief peeping out of his jacket breast pocket. A gold watch chain hangs on his waistcoat pocket where the solicitor frequently checks for the watch's presence. He offers Caitlin his arm.

'But before that inviting cup of tea, how about a whistle-stop tour of your garden?'

Caitlin beams and calls Colin over.

'This is as much Colin's as my project. I couldn't possibly show you it without him.' She leans into him in a daughterly manner.

With relish, she takes the two men into the herb garden, explaining how part of it has been planted using the same approach as the old monastic physic gardens, very regular and ordered with plants that heal and soothe, whereas other areas are a more haphazard mix of flowers, vegetables and herbs set out in a slightly wild and bohemian manner – much like Caitlin herself. Then she moves on to the main kitchen garden, talking through her planting plans for the coming year. As I watch them walk, the old familiarity of the garden brings on a surge of half-forgotten memories, faltering imagines that, like an old film, keep skipping frames: the aroma of earthy soil as I lay in my secret shelter, collecting slugs for my dad after rainy days, the smell of rosemary as my hand passed over it, wafting around the garden, harvesting my first carrot in my own tiny vegetable patch. These nostalgic memories hit me with a force that over-whelms me as I realise that I will no longer be here. The ties that have bound me to this place have finally broken. Despite my desire to fly, I know that taking off is going to be difficult after a forty-year grounding.

Finally, I can see that Robert senses an impatience to get to the tea table and that stiff drink. Taking Caitlin's arm again, he escorts her back to the house, leading our small party across the recently rebuilt wooden bridge and around to the front of the house.

Fittingly, it is a beautiful September day. As so often happens, early autumn clings on to the last vestiges of summer, making everyone thankful for the final remembrance of what has just been. The air is just that little bit fresher, the colours turning to bronze and orange, making the contrast with the spot-less blue sky just that little bit more thrilling, reminding us that this will not last, telling us to make the most of it. We all walk silently towards the house, each of us lost in our own thoughts.

On the lawn stands a picture-perfect set for tea: tables and chairs, white tablecloth, Ardbray's original rosebud tea set, scones, cake, butter and jam. Napkins flutter in the breeze and a bottle of whisky sits next to the teapot. With the image framed by the background of the loch and the hills behind, it all feels a little quaint, perhaps too picturesque and that feeling of nostalgia makes my eyes prick.

So no one can see my weakness, I turn to the front of the house and pretend to go and look at the newly planted roses at the front of the house. Something catches my eye and I go closer to see what it is.

Once the police had completed their investigations, Caitlin asked Colin to completely clean out the rose bed, put in new soil and plant it up with new roses. The original red rose had been an undisclosed gravestone, a secret held for over one hundred years, a blood-red reminder of Kitty's nemesis. The new roses are in their final bloom, all white with one dark red plant. Was it Colin or Caitlin that decided they'd keep that quirk, keep the reminder of what had once passed in this house? I bend down to look at the plastic identifier pushed into the ground by the base of the red rose bush. The words "Deep Secret" are written on it.

I look back and catch Colin's eye. He gives a flicker of a smile and a discreet wink.

I rejoin the party. Caitlin is handing around the scones, encouraging everyone to eat, the whisky is readily passed around and the teapot ignored. I sit back and let the chatter float over me, the alcohol is quickly loosening tongues, the cake bringing forth truths as it always has done.

My seat is facing the house and I look up to the façade. The red Sutherland sandstone still exudes its early evening warmth, but it now appears more defined, the eroded pointing along the whole of the front elevation has been replaced and it gives it the definition that had been lacking. The old gargoyles have been cleaned and mended with new, specially commissioned ones taking the place of any which were too ruined to restore. The new stone creatures are just as mischievous and cheeky as the originals, laughing, sticking their tongues out, pointing. Damaged roof tiles have been replaced and the moss growing on the sides of the walls has been scraped off. The windows are sparkling, and the climbing plants have been pruned and tied back. Altogether it feels like the house has finally had the long-awaited facelift, the tired and sagging face having been tightened and tweaked. The satisfaction of seeing this picture is making me feel unaccountably sentimental.

My runaway thoughts are interrupted by Caitlin hitting her teacup with a spoon several times and now standing up.

Clearing her throat in a theatrical manner, she starts to speak.

'Unaccustomed as I am to public speaking,' she jokes. We all roll our eyes and groan, 'I wanted to raise a teacup to you all.' She clasps her hands together, wringing them nervously. 'You've all brought me on a journey I never imagined I'd have been able to make. You've helped me realise a long-held dream and I'm forever in your debt. You know that this house is your home and you're welcome to stay here whenever you wish; I'll willingly throw out paying guests to accommodate you.'

She turns to her right. 'Robert. Your advice has been invaluable. Thank you for giving me so much background and family history. Thank you for being so invested in this house and making sure there was always the means available to keep it alive.'

Next, she turns to me. 'Greer and Colin. Ardbray has been your life's work and you should be proud of the important role you've played in keeping such a valuable house from crumbling away. I know it had become a burden and perhaps you feel that the life you led wasn't the life you intended.'

I shrink under the scrutiny, the truth she's speaking of.

'But there will be countless numbers of people who, unwittingly, will be thanking you for your part in bringing this house back to the public eye.' Caitlin puts her hand on her heart. 'Without you, I would never have been able to get this far in achieving a goal that's so close to my heart. I know that sometimes you've found it difficult and wondered whether I was the right person for the job. I hope that now you feel you can leave this house in good hands.'

I look at my hands, trying to get rid of the flush of red on my face.

'Eileen.' I can hear the smile in Caitlin's voice. 'You have brought us the energy and efficiency that I was lacking. You've brought us local knowledge that even Greer couldn't match, you've injected laughter and light-heartedness into our days that was much needed when we were in the thick of it, and I cannot fault your commitment to our retreat. Your belief in what I've been trying to achieve is truly heart-warming. And, please, never try to leave. I'm not sure I could do this without you.'

Eileen, for once not encased in her self-enforced work attire of dark trousers and white shirt, blushes the colour of her red top and intently studies the inside of her teacup whilst the rest of us murmur cheers and thanks.

'Ardbray,' Caitlin continues, looking up at the house, 'I have you to keep me on the straight and narrow. You welcomed me, accepted me and then when I was restoring and making changes, you guided me with your sighs of approval and creaks of disapproval. I can't fault your taste.'

We all turn to the house as if expecting a reply. The roses sway in the slight breeze, the gargoyles laugh, and the roof tiles shine under the sunlight.

'Kitty Maclean and her children.' We turn back to her, silent in anticipation, watching Caitlin closely. 'Flora and Callum for, almost daily, asking me to find their mother; their pleas pushed me to find what they were looking for and eventually bring her back to them. And Kitty, for approving of me. For not letting anyone else buy this house, for letting me find it. Someone once told me that houses are like dogs; they find you. It may have taken fifty years, but this house definitely found me, albeit by a very long and circuitous route.'

Caitlin picks up her teacup, the rosebud pattern still in perfect condition. 'I would like to propose a toast to you, my faithful and loyal friends. To Kitty, Flora and Callum for incentivising me to get my project off the ground.' She smiles at each of us around the table before letting her smile fade and lowering her voice. 'And finally, to Rosie, for giving me the best five years of my life.'

She looks down at the table, taking a deep breath, holding back the emotion. 'But, over the last few months, I've come to realise that good can come out of bad. If Rosie had not died, I probably wouldn't be here. I'd be in New York selling bagels and playing Mother. Instead, I'm here with all of you mothering me. Now, don't get me wrong, I'd take Rosie over Ardbray and you lot any day, but, in the unlikely event of that ever happening, I couldn't think of anywhere else I'd rather be.' She breathes out loudly. 'And I have Rosie to thank for that.'

Raising her teacup, she says, 'To you all. To Rosie.'

We all raise our glasses of whisky and drink in assent. An awkward silence follows, which Caitlin quickly cuts short.

'Please, eat, we need to gather our strength for this evening.'

Mention of the evening's festivities releases the tension, and the table is at ease again.

'So, Caitlin, tell me. What are the plans for this evening?' Robert asks.

'It's simply a ceilidh. Something to thank everyone who's been involved with the retreat from the beginning and an open house for the whole of Achfary who have been very accepting of this eccentric American and who' – she gives Robert a wicked grin – 'I am sure, are desperate to have a good nose around the place, having been deprived of any access for years.'

I try not to show my annoyance. Caitlin is right and I am wrong, I know that. This house needs to be opened up, I've said so myself. But, still, I can't help wanting to keep it hidden away. It's difficult to let it go, however much I need to. I don't want to be a witness to the glee on some people's faces, the thoughts they'll have on Kitty Maclean, the death of her family, the discussions about whether John Hardgrave was murdered, who was his murderer and what about those ghosts. It's all too personal and I'd rather not have to be a bystander to the gossip and the stories. But Caitlin has insisted we stay for tonight's celebration, the culmination of everyone's hard work.

She continues, 'We'll be having drinks on the lawn at seven, a buffet dinner in the dining room at eight thirty, followed by the ceilidh.' And then, with sudden ceremony, she says, 'Tonight will be the first annual Ardbray Ball.'

With a murmur of approval, she turns to me. 'Greer and Colin, you'll be pleased to hear that I've also agreed to open the gardens once a month throughout the summer, starting next May. Anyone can come, walk the grounds, inspect the walled garden and we'll turn the dining room into a café for the day. Finally, Ardbray can be enjoyed by others without the need for money or connections. Perhaps people will make this a destination, not just a place to pass through.'

'I'm sure you'll be in need of a hand. Perhaps you'd let us come back and help out.'

Colin looks at me with surprise. He's as astonished by my words as I am. Will we really want to come back so soon?

'I can't think of anything better.' Caitlin smiles.

Colin and I will be leaving tomorrow evening with no fixed plan. We are still on the lookout for a business to buy into. We're not ready to retire. But we've had little time to look into it. It feels as if we're about to jump, hand in hand, into a freezing cold loch, with no swimming costume on, and no life jacket. Up until now, I've always known what I'm going to do tomorrow, next week, next month and next year. Now I have no plans beyond a rented flat in Edinburgh. I know that the shock of the cold water on my skin will leave me breathless, but perhaps the jolt will push us out of our inertia, stop us from making excuses that we've been too busy to make any decisions.

'I hear some of your family are arriving tonight,' Robert says to Caitlin.

Caitlin looks at her watch. 'My brother Jim's flight has just landed at Inverness and my father should be there to pick him up. They'll be here in a couple of hours if all goes well.'

'And your sisters?' Robert asks carefully.

Caitlin shakes her head. 'No. I don't think this is quite their scene. Too far from a gym, their favourite take-out and a mani-cure. Perhaps if we'd invited the press to come and review our opening, they'd have turned up. They love a bit of press expo-sure. No. They aren't comfortable in my world of wellington boots, meditation and rain. Just like I don't suit their world of high heels, two-thousand-dollar dresses and sleek, straight hair.'

'How does your brother survive?' Eileen asks.

Caitlin raised her eyebrows. 'Good question. Why don't you ask him at the ball tonight? I can't wait to introduce you to him, I think you just might like my brother.' She says this with a note of mischief in her voice.

'Oh, no you don't.' Eileen wags her finger at Caitlin, a cynical smile on her face. 'You're not going to matchmake me.'

'Which reminds me...' Caitlin says, rummaging around in her skirt pocket. 'Tonight, we have dance cards. Everyone will get them when they arrive, but I'm giving you yours now.' She hands the cards around the table. 'Each card has your name on, so there's no swapping and some of your dances are pre-filled.'

I look at my card. First and last dances with Colin, Robert also has two booked in. I even have one with Jim. Dance cards seem so old-fashioned. I didn't think anyone used them anymore.

'But I've got three dances with your brother!' Eileen protests. 'Including the first and the last!' Her eyes are aflame.

'I do hope you have Duncan booked in on your card,' I say, unable to resist the cheap shot.

She shakes her head just that little bit too quickly. 'I'll be far too busy to dance.'

Twenty-four hours later, our bags are packed, we've filled a van with the few pieces of furniture we own, Colin's tools and my sewing machine and fabrics. We're ready to leave. We're both exhausted but know that if we don't leave now, we never will.

Last night we partied until the sun rose, neither of us could tear ourselves away. I didn't want to miss a moment, despite my longing to leave this burdensome house behind.

Ardbray House was teaming with people, everyone in their Highland dress: kilts, trews, and sashes, everyone beaming with wide smiles and happy laughter. The house shone, the gardens were lit up with streams of fairy lights, burning torches and large firepits. The band played until three a.m. when a breakfast of kedgeree was served on the lawn. My feet are so sore I could hardly put my shoes on earlier. Colin and I danced as if we would never dance again; we soaked it all up until we'd had our fill, knowing we'd never experience this again, knowing we were leaving.

Caitlin played the amiable host, giving guided tours of the house, doing her best to alleviate the insatiable curiosity about Kitty and herself, this strange, slightly dishevelled American heiress. Duncan followed her all night, like a loyal pet, occasionally managing to drag her onto the dance floor and then keep her there as long as possible. Those big cow eyes, unable to leave her face. She keeps him at arm's length, I suspect too scared to jump into anything with him. Maybe she's being sensible, maybe she's missing out. I expect they'll find out soon enough.

It's time to say goodbye. I've already walked through the house again, breathed the loch air, taken my last aromatic walk of the walled garden and listened to the running burn. The sights, smells and sounds of my life can all be experienced in just a few minutes. I've given Eileen a hug and I've said my last to the kitchen and front-of-house staff. I just need to find Caitlin.

Eventually, I find her pacing up and down the newly restored pier. Her hands are in her trouser pockets and she's concentrating hard on her moving feet. Every now and again she stops and takes a deep breath, before continuing. I approach her quietly, wary of intruding. Suddenly, she stops dead and looks straight at me.

'Greer!' She puts her hand to her heart. 'How long have you been there?'

'Only a moment,' I say, observing her flushed cheeks and her slight breathlessness. 'Are you okay?'

'No. Yes... No.' She looks around her and then back at her feet. 'The first guests will be here shortly. I feel sick. What if they don't like it? What if they hate my food, what if they want to leave? What if it all fails?' Her face is stricken.

I laugh. 'And what if they love it? What if they want to stay longer than they intended? What if they can't get enough of your food and tell all their friends to come and you're overbooked?'

She nods her head. 'Sorry. Overblown catastrophising. I'm told I'm quite good at that.'

'I came to say goodbye.'

She pulls herself together and becomes the person I know. 'It's going to be very strange without you around here. Ardbray without Greer Mackenzie won't seem quite right.' She turns to the loch and watches the breeze ruffle the still water.

'I'm sure she's found the right person. You're just what she needs,' I say this carefully as if I'm walking barefoot across a floor covered in broken glass.

'Who?' Caitlin frowns but continues to stare into the water. It's as if she's not really listening to what I'm saying.

'Kitty,' I say with a shard of ice.

She turns and looks back at me, her attention caught, her body suddenly taut. 'What makes you say that?'

'She's always needed someone to lean on. First my great-grandmother, then my grandmother, but even after her death she needed my mother and then me. I didn't want to put that burden on my own children. That was one of the reasons why I didn't have any.' It's a stark admission, something I've only ever voiced to Colin. But saying it feels final and these last few days have been full of finalities; this feels like the ultimate one. 'You remember when I first met you, I said that this house had some kind of hold on me, that I could never leave?'

'Something like that.' Caitlin's voice is quiet. 'But you did get out. You went to university in Edinburgh, and then didn't you stay on, find a job, find Colin?'

'Yes, I did. Originally, I didn't want to go. I felt impelled to stay here, but Kitty left me some money in her will which I was only allowed to receive if I left. So, reluctantly, I went to university, I studied interior design and, unexpectedly, I loved it. She was right, I needed to get away, but it was all much harder than it should have been. I kept being derailed. Some people have wings on their backs that hoist them above the bumps in the road. I had size fifteen boots that tripped me up on every path that I took, and I fell down every crevice that came my way.' I suddenly feel cold, even though the evening is holding on to the day's warmth. I pull my cardigan closer and fold my arms.

'In the end, I was too exhausted by everything that had gone wrong. It was simply easier to come back to Ardbray, to the life I was familiar with. I took the easy road; I came back to help my mother and took on the job she'd had all her life.'

'But if Kitty had wanted you to leave Ardbray, why would she make it difficult for you? Doesn't it seem a little preposterous? How could Kitty Maclean's ghost have been able to have had any influence over your life in Edinburgh?'

I can see the frustration on Caitlin's face. She's never had any belief in Kitty's impact on life at Ardbray following her death, she holds no truck with the theory that she changed people's lives to ensure her own happy ending.

'She needed someone to reunite her with her children. She thought I could do that for her.' My voice is rising, my own frustration mounting.

Caitlin takes a deep breath. 'Okay.' She waves away her irritation. 'But you said I was just the right kind of person for Kitty. What do you mean?'

I can't help but give out a snort before I turn to Caitlin and look at her squarely. 'I have no doubt that somehow Kitty was responsible for all that happened to me. She had to have had something to do with all those prospective buyers pulling out because they weren't good enough.

'When I was a little girl, just a few days before she died, she implored me to leave Ardbray, to make sure that when I grew up, I left and made my life elsewhere. She was vehement in her request. But I know she's the one who's kept me here, despite her words, despite the money. She used me to find you. But I think you've guessed that already.' There's a sour taste bubbling up, as if the very act of finally telling my story, the telling of my bitterness, is getting rid of it, is drawing it out. 'Somehow, she's had a hold on my life, on everything that I've done. I'm hoping that now she'll let me go, that perhaps the burden has gone.'

'By that, you mean you've passed the burden on to me.' There's a question creeping into Caitlin's statement.

I'm unsure of how to answer this. So, I keep it ambiguous. 'It's possible.'

'You mean this is some kind of "Tag, you're It" session?' Caitlin shakes her head vigorously. 'No, that's not true. We've done what she wanted us to do. We've brought her back to her family. Happy ever after. Kitty, Charles and their children have been reunited, and they can walk off into the sunset, go on up to heaven or wherever it is their souls are supposed to go.' She shrugs. 'And, if you say that she chose me to do what you couldn't, well, surely her battle is over. I've brought her family together and I've brought the house back to life. What more could she want?'

I blink at her fervour, not wanting to say what needs to be said. We both look over the loch silently; it's easier not to look at each other.

'I think they're still here,' Caitlin eventually says, her voice quiet, a note of resignation creeping in.

'I know,' I say, equally as quiet, relieved that she's saying what I should have.

She turns to me, a frown on her face. 'I thought you couldn't see them anymore. How do you know?'

'The toys.'

Caitlin's frown turns quizzical. 'What toys?'

'The children's toys. The old wooden toys that live in the wicker basket in the drawing room. You remember the ones I insisted stay in there, for your guests.'

She nods slowly. She'll be remembering the overheated discussion we had when we were planning what furniture and ornaments should be in the drawing room. I insisted the basket of children's toys be kept, maintaining that these old toys would add to the room's charm, even if they were unlikely to have any children as guests.

'Every night I have to put them out. If you don't, they cause havoc, overturning furniture, smashing the ornaments, pulling up the rugs...'

Caitlin watches me, her brow furrowed. 'Are you serious?'

'I know.' I put my hands up in surrender. 'It sounds unbelievable, but it's true. They've been doing that since the day Kitty first saw their ghosts. She'd put toys out for them every night before she went to bed. When she was dying, she told Eleanor to do it, just in case, and then when my grandmother got too ill, she told my mother to carry it on. And, you see, my mother needed me to carry it on after her; they were all too scared to tell anyone else.'

'Why didn't you tell me this before? You knew I could see them; you knew they trusted me. I could have helped. You could have passed that burden on to me before now.'

I shake my head. 'It's so ingrained in me that for ages it didn't occur to me to pass it on. I've been doing it for forty years; it's just part of my make-up, part of my every day. It's like brushing my teeth, I know I must do it or there will be consequences.'

Caitlin shoves her hands in her pockets. 'I've never seen toys out early in the morning.' Her words are harsh as if she doesn't believe me. 'Don't tell me that they are such well-behaved ghosts that they put their toys away after they've played with them?'

'No, I've always put them back,' I say as if I'm soothing an overtired child.

'What did you do when you went away? Who put them out and tidied them up?'

'Once my mother had died, once I was the only person left who they could rely on, I never went away, not for the night anyway. That's why Kitty never left Ardbray. They wouldn't let her.'

'No.' She shakes her head forcefully. 'No. You and Colin went away, you went on your little tour to find furniture, to find your fabrics and inspiration. What did you do then?'

'I asked Eileen to do it for me. We both knew it was only for a few days, that it would only be temporary. She understands this house, always has done. You see, her grandmother was a maid here. Eileen grew up understanding the quirks of working at Ardbray, she's known the truth about the ghost children since she was a little girl, she just chose to never let on.'

Caitlin stares, her mouth slightly open. 'Did you know this when she came for her interview?'

'Aye, that's why I recommended her. I needed to make sure the secret was kept. If we could make sure no one talked, kept the gossip at bay, until we were able to reunite Kitty with her children, then perhaps the reputation of this house could be kept intact.'

'But why didn't you trust me?' Panic, disappointment, suspicion, it's all running across her face. Her words are almost too quiet for me to hear.

'I had to make sure I really could leave. I was worried that if I told you too soon, you'd try to persuade me to stay.'

'So, just like Kitty, you used Eileen.'

I'm not going to answer, there's no point. We stand in silence overlooking the water as dusk begins to settle in.

But then she starts to pace up and down the pier. I can see her mind is spiralling. 'But surely now that Kitty has been reunited with her children, they will no longer look for her. Their whole reason for haunting this house is gone. Isn't that what happens? Ghosts have a reason for being around. That reason's gone.'

'Well, not last night.'

'Seriously?'

I nod my head slowly, finally meeting her gaze.

She looks back across to the other side of the loch. Hands back in her pockets, she begins to sway back and forth on the balls of her feet. I can see that she's working this through, the implications, the consequences.

'If the children are here, then Kitty must be here.' She looks around. 'Why? What kept her, what's made her stay?'

'Isn't it obvious?'

'No, it's not.' Her colour's increasing, her pupils have intensified.

'The garden. It's the walled garden,' I say carefully.

She looks at me sharply. 'What do you mean?'

'She's not going to let you get it wrong, she can't let it go. That garden, her life's work, her pride and joy; the main achievement of her life was destroyed on the night she died. She waited fifty-seven years to be reunited with her children and now that her garden has been restored to her as well, she's not going to let you mess it up.'

'But, like the house, it's been left in good hands. Do you think she doesn't trust me?'

'As much as she loved the house, it was built by Charles and his father. As you said yourself, they made it, she just lived in it. But she made that garden, she designed it, she let it grow, she enhanced it and made it into something that could heal people. It was an extension of herself. If you'd had your left leg amputated and, somehow fifty or more years later you were given it back, you wouldn't want to be parted from it again, would you?'

She snorts, shaking her head.

I laugh to break up the mood. 'Look, they won't do you or your business any harm. In fact, I bet it helps. Everyone loves a good ghost story. And we know they're friendly ghosts.'

'Well, they're friendly if they get their own way. And somehow, I feel that Kitty hasn't been as friendly as I thought she would be. She might hate what I've done to her garden.'

Suddenly, her energy returns and she's able to meet my gaze. 'Well, perhaps I can persuade Kitty to teach her children to put those toys away every morning.' There's a falseness to her voice. She clasps her hands together and faces me. 'I hate to seem like I'm trying to get rid of you, but isn't it time you left?' She begins to shoo me towards the house. 'Go, take your husband, get in your car and drive.'

'But...' I begin to protest.

'No, not another word. I'm sure I've got the measure of Kitty Maclean and her untidy children.' Hurriedly, she grabs me and gives me a quick hug before holding me out in front of her and looking me over. 'Go and have a life. Go and enjoy the real world.'

And now I'm here, I don't want to leave. It would be so much easier to stay. There would be no difficult decisions to make, I could stay in my cocoon, be safe and warm. But I can't find any words to say to Caitlin.

As we stand, in the twilight, the atmosphere changes and I feel a creeping sensation across my back. Goosebumps appear on my arms and the hairs on the back of my neck stand up.

'Do you feel that?' I ask. She nods.

We both turn towards the house. I'm expecting to see someone, I know we are being watched. But there's no one.

'The garden,' says Caitlin, and she starts to walk quickly across the drive, over the lawn. Then she begins to jog. I follow, my heart racing. We cross the patio at the back of the house and now we're running over the wooden bridge, crossing the burn and through the gate into the garden.

As we both stop to catch our breath, we see her, walking away, through the avenue of recently clipped lavender bushes, at the centre of the garden.

She has her hands behind her back and is carefully inspecting the planting around her. Every now and then she bends down and looks at a wooden marker at the end of a planting row or she rubs the foliage of a fennel plant and then crushes it in her fingers before bringing it up to her nose to smell. We watch her slowly walk around the garden, carefully examining every plant, occasionally nodding with a slight smile on her face, once frowning and shaking her head.

Finally, as Kitty Maclean reaches the far end of the walled garden, she turns and looks directly at us. This is the Kitty I've seen in the early photographs: young, proud, enquiring and full of energy. She has a transparent quality about her, her skin almost luminous. Her dark, wiry hair is slightly unruly, her cheeks delicately pink.

She tucks a wayward hair behind her right ear and smiles at us and then, picking up a stray leaf from the path, she strides out through the far gate.

AUTHOR'S NOTE

The cotton industry was built on shameful foundations. I cannot write a story about the cotton industry without acknowledging this. My characters were as ignorant of this as I was when I finished this book, but since completing this story I have read, and continue to read, widely around the subject, continuing to learn about our brushed-away history and supporting organisations that work towards reparations.

For more information here is a short list of further reading:

Empire of Cotton: A Global History by Sven Beckert (Knopf, 2014)
Blood Legacy: Reckoning with a Family's Story of Slavery by Alex Renton (Canongate, 2021)
Recovering Scotland's Slavery Past: The Caribbean Connection edited by T M Devine (Edinburgh University Press, 2015)
What White People Can Do Next: From Allyship to Coalition by Emma Dabiri (Penguin, 2021)

A LETTER FROM THE AUTHOR

Dear Reader,

Thank you so much for reading *The Herbalist's Secret*. I hope you enjoyed it.

If you'd like to find out about any of my further book releases, you can sign up to my newsletter here.

www.stormpublishing.co/annabelle-marx

I'd love it if you left a review and let other readers know about Kitty Maclean.

Loch More, Sutherland, where my fictional Ardbray House is located, is a place we used to drive past every summer holiday, with our kids, on our way to the Highland west coast. It's a five-mile-long ribbon loch with a single-track road running along one side and seriously remote. There's just one house on the other side of the loch, and from a distance it looked like an old house. I always used to wonder who chose to live there over 100 years ago when the roads were poor and the nearest train station was a four-hour slow and bumpy carriage ride away, the closest big town another hour's train ride? Even now it takes an hour and twenty minutes to drive to the nearest supermarket – can you imagine the effort it took to get glass, building materials and central heating parts delivered in the 1880s? Just thinking about the life that you would lead in such a place gave me the beginnings of a story idea.

Thank you again for reading my debut novel, I truly appreciate your readership. If you'd like to follow me on social media where I talk books, writing, Scotland and, occasionally, cake, I'd love to hear from you on Instagram or Facebook.

Annabelle

facebook.com/annabellemarxwrites

twitter.com/marx_annabelle

instagram.com/annabellemarx_writes

linkedin.com/in/annabelle-marx-284046200

GINGER CAKE

Like all good recipes, this has been handed down to me by my aunt, an inspirational cook and restaurant owner. And, like all good ginger cakes, this one improves with age.

Ingredients
5 balls stem ginger, chopped
45g fresh ginger, grated
5 pitted and chopped soft prunes
2 tsp dark marmalade
200g self-raising flour
1 tsp bicarbonate of soda
2 tbsp dried ginger
2 tsp cinnamon
2 tsp mace
½ tsp salt
115g butter or cooking margarine
115g dark brown sugar
115g black treacle
115g golden syrup
2 large eggs, lightly beaten

125ml milk

Butter a deep 20cm square cake tin and line with baking paper. Pre-heat the oven at 180°c (165°c fan oven).

Put the stem and fresh ginger in a small blender with the marmalade and prunes and blend until smooth. If it becomes too stiff, use a little of the milk to loosen.

Mix the flour, bicarbonate of soda, dried ginger, cinnamon, mace and salt in a large bowl.

Melt the butter, sugar, treacle and golden syrup in a small saucepan. When smooth, leave to cool.

Mix the ginger and marmalade mixture into the dried ingredients, add the cooled butter mixture, the beaten eggs and milk. Stir until smooth. Pour into the cake tin and cook on the middle shelf for 50 mins to 1 hour.

Leave in the tin to cool. Don't worry if it's sunken slightly in the middle, it's all the better for it. Best eaten 24 hours after cooking and will keep for at least a week in an airtight tin.

ACKNOWLEDGEMENTS

Writing maybe a solo task, but writing and getting a book published is a team effort, and I can't possibly go without thanking them for their help in bringing this book to life.

My love of Scotland was nurtured by Kassia Scott and her ever-welcoming parents, Caroline and the late, and much missed, Robert Mills. Without the multiple invitations to Sutherland and ultimate encouragement to move there, this story would probably still be lying somewhere beside the loch.

The late Willie Elliot for spending a long afternoon telling a complete stranger about life in Sutherland and on the Reay Estate and for giving me the all-important piece of information that pulled the story together.

The staff at the British Library and the librarians at Bath Spa University for finding obscure books about herbalism. If there are any errors in my interpretation of the world of herbalism, they are entirely mine.

Victoria Millard for giving me her opinion on the very first and, I'm sure, truly terrible draft.

My Faber Academy friends and extreme early readers, especially Anna Roins, Julie Ma, Louise Morrish and Lesley Quayle.

Those who gave me their invaluable opinion of later drafts: Amanda Wylie (forensic criticism), Ali Vellacott (sharp, insightful criticism), Kassia Scott (criticism only a friend you've known for over 40 years can give) and Rosemary Briggs (motherly criticism and invaluable insight into Highland life in the 'big hoose' in the early/mid 1900s).

Pepita Collins, my aunt and food hero, for letting me use her ginger cake recipe.

Philip Hensher for nudging me in the right direction.

My agent, Jenny Brown of Jenny Brown Associates, who has always believed in Kitty, sticking with her through thick and thin. Thank you for your cheerful support and valuable encouragement, and for loving the Highlands even more than I do.

To my editor, Claire Bord, for getting Kitty on first sight and for loving all things related to herbalism. This book has more focus and purpose because of you. To the rest of the team at Storm for their professionalism and friendly support.

To my greatest achievements – my sons, Harry and Harvey. For putting up with the piles of books and notebooks everywhere and always believing that this was a story that would get published.

To Andy whose quiet support has given me the opportunity to do what I love to do. None of this would have happened if it wasn't for you. I've always thought that you don't have to be extraordinary to be extraordinary. That's what this book is about and you're my extraordinary.

Printed in Great Britain
by Amazon

30097259R10209